WICKED BEDLAM

BEDLAM MOON TRILOGY
BOOK THREE

KATHY HAAN

ISBN 979-8-9855077-4-4 (eBook)

ISBN 979-8-9855077-5-1 (paperback)

ISBN 978-1-960256-11-9 (hardback)

First edition August 2022

Book cover design and map by Leo Burk and Kathy Haan

Edited by Fervent Ink

Published by Thousand Lives Press, LLC

To the dreamers, who were told they were too much, too big for this world.
On Wednesdays, we'll wear black.

NOTE FROM THE AUTHOR

This book contains sensitive topics and is not for those under eighteen (or the age of adult in your jurisdiction). Please see the website kathyhaan.com for a list of triggering topics.

ACADEMIA
BEDLAM PENITENTIARY
OCCASUS
DRACONU
REXUNA
CON
SEA OF TRIUNE
ACADEMIA

LUPORIA
SUNDAHLIA
TRISTIQUE ISLANDS
PARALLEL ABYSS
VECTUS
N
W
E
S
BEDLAM

RECAP

LANA

The sound of metal tearing earth cuts through the quiet. I shoot out of bed and cover my ears against the incessant blaring throughout the house. I can't think; my brain is on fire with the noise.

Our houselights flash in rhythm to the alarm. The buzz cuts off just as Pierce and his guards burst through the room, shouting, and find the kings and me stark naked.

"What's going on?" My groggy voice cuts through the cacophony of movement.

Pierce rushes to my armoire, grabs a dress, and tosses it at me. "My Lady, the portal's been breached. Get dressed and gather your belongings. We must get you to the bunker."

"What?" I say with a whisper, my voice lost in the frenzy.

Casimir crouches at my level and grabs my face. "It's the vampires, Lana. They've found us. We have to move you."

Terror surges through me. I nod robotically and he kisses my forehead.

"Pierce," Casimir says while releasing me. "I want you and the guards to make sure she's safe."

I shake my head and clutch onto Casimir's arm. "Don't leave me, please."

He kisses my cheek. "I'll be back, never far away." He turns to the guards and Pierce. "We can't let them take her. She's our last hope."

They all nod and my legs turn to jelly, and Grimm slips his arm around my waist and guides me to the bed.

"We have to put on shoes." He places a pair in front of each of us.

I barely register as I slip them on. My eyes dart to each of their faces and all I see is fear. I fumble with the shoes and whimper. "I thought the portal has never been breached before?"

Grimm tips my chin up to him. "It hasn't until now."

I can't keep up. "How did they find us?"

Grimm grabs the back of my head and kisses me while his other hand goes around my waist. "We don't know, but if they breach the bunker, you're to go straight into the portal. Make your way to the waterfall in Meloria and we'll collect you from there."

I break from his kiss. "I can fight, Grimm. Let me do this."

He shakes his head. "You're too important, Lana. We can't risk it."

"Don't you know how important you are to me?" I wipe my tears with the back of my hand.

Penn presses his lips to my forehead, and I breathe in his scent. I lean into him, letting his warmth embrace me. "We'll protect you to the end."

In a blink, we sift to the shelter. I've been here once before, during a tour of the castle my first few weeks here. It's less a bunker and more of an enormous one-room house made to house several thousand people for months.

Captain Zara pauses in front of me. "Pierce will keep you safe here. Do not open this door for anyone but myself or the kings, understood?"

I nod and she slips me some weapons from their holsters on the wall. "Just in case. Stay here until we come for you, or if they breach the bunker, sift to the falls."

I clutch the weapons, feeling their weight in my hands. "Okay."

The kings take turns hugging me and whispering sweet words about how they'll come back as soon as they can. They flash me smiles as they sift away.

The door closes with a snick and I'm alone, surrounded by concrete walls. A moment later, Pierce appears in front of me with a plate of food.

"The kings ordered this for you," he says with a small smile, his dimples falling into place.

I laugh. "I couldn't eat a thing even if I were starving. You go on and have it."

"Nah." He shakes his head. "We were just finishing breakfast when the alarm sounded. You doing okay, Lana?"

I glance at the plate and scowl. "Not really. My entire world is about to fight evil vampires who held me captive and have traveled literal realms to get me back."

"They're probably going to have a conversation first. Maybe get a little worked up, enough for the audience at least." He runs his hand through his blond hair.

My eyes narrow and I study his face. "You think?"

He nods as he pours a cup of coffee. "All will be fine."

"Sorry you have to babysit." I wince.

Before he can respond, Sarai and several other staff sift in with a handful of guards. Sarai throws her arms around me.

"I was so scared they got you!" she cries, and I return her hug.

"I'm alright." I pull away to look at her. "Everything will be fine. Speaking of, you should be with your family."

She shakes her head. "Mom is spreading Dad's ashes on Rexuna now, where they first met."

Pierce pulls her into his arms. "We're glad you're safe."

I turn to the guards. "Where are Rune and Titan?"

Lawson, a member of Zara's unit, answers me. "They've joined the fight. Not to worry, they can hold their own." He winks.

Sarai holds out a jar of tonic. "I brought you your chest medication."

"Actually, for the first time in Bedlam, my chest feels great." Every day and night, I've dealt with a terrible ache in my chest, but ever since I died, it's gone. Maybe I'm not tethered to Earth anymore?

Sarai smiles. "Glad you're feeling better."

We play card games for hours while waiting for news. It's almost suppertime when my kings sift in.

Grimm grabs my hand and pulls me into his arms. "We're getting you out of here."

I blink up at him. "What happened?"

"We know the vampires have an army with them on Convectus. There's a terrible thunderstorm preventing us from moving in to get them. The entire place is warded, so we can't sift to them," Casimir answers, and I turn around to face him. "I don't think we should wait for your coronation."

I lower myself to the couch. "When?"

"Now. We'll call in the army and a few of the members of court. This is strictly a precautionary measure." Penn offers me his hand. "Once we have the location of this brigade, we'll be able to plan an attack. As soon as you are High Queen, we as your mates, will have our powers increased. This way, we have a better chance of fighting the vampires."

I take his hand and we cross to the trunk Sarai brought full of our clothes. She hands me a purple floor-length gown and shoes with bows on the side. I strip and dress quickly while the other staff sift in and out of the shelter. Pure adrenaline fuels me, and I have little time to think about how much danger I'm in.

"Where will we do this?" I ask as I brush my hair.

"Right here. We have staff fetching banners and chairs, so it looks like the throne room." Grimm snakes his arms around my waist and kisses where my neck meets my shoulder. I lean back into him.

"I'm scared." It's the first time I've ever said it, and my voice cracks.

"We'll be at your side. I'm not planning on letting you out of my sight again." He squeezes me tight.

Penn turns me around and smooths my hair over my shoulders, then leans down and kisses the top of my head. "You're going to make a great High Queen."

Grimm and Casimir usher me to the front of the room where they've set up a makeshift throne. As hundreds of soldiers sift in, my nerves grow.

Pierce, Captain Zara, and several other soldiers move to the dais to brief me on what will take place. One in particular keeps his eyes pinned on me. Judging by his striking resemblance to Zara and Pierce, I'm going to bet this is Bellamy.

He makes to speak to me, but I raise my hand and lean in. "Whatever'll kill you for telling me, please, don't say a word. I've asked my mates to take my memory of you to prevent this. Please don't let it be in vain."

Bellamy flinches before turning his head towards my ear. "What we had was real, Lana. If the coming war means anything, someday you'll know the truth. I won't break the magic gag order if you don't want me to." He turns to look me in the eye. "I'm sorry."

I nod. "If it's any consolation, I'm sorry, too. I did what I had to do to keep you safe."

He presses a kiss to my cheek before returning to formation behind me. I swallow hard, but my emotions remain in check.

My kings join me on the dais, and the room falls silent. Casimir smiles at me, pushes my hair behind my shoulders, and plants a kiss to my temple before stepping to my side.

Penn takes my hand and kisses it. "Ready?"

I nod. "As I'll ever be."

Bellamy steps forward to take the crown from Sarai, meeting my gaze as he does. He hands it to Pierce, who passes it to Casimir.

Casimir nods and lifts his chin, commanding the room as he speaks. "Stand before us, soldiers of Bedlam. The time has come to crown our High Queen!"

My shout of "For Bedlam!" echoes through the room, and the soldiers all roar back. I'm touched by their willingness to fight for me.

Penn steps forward. "As your King, I vow to serve you with all that I have." He bends down and kisses my cheek, then returns to his place by my side.

Grimm takes a knee, kissing my hand. "I humbly bow before you, my High Queen, and I vow to protect you with all that I am."

Casimir bows next, taking both my hands in his and placing them on his chest. "As long as I live, my High Queen, you'll be safe. I vow to protect and serve you for all my days."

Pierce falls to both knees. "I pledge to be your right arm, High Queen Lana, and I vow to serve you with all that I am."

After swearing their fealty, the kings and my personal guard slice their palms open, swiping their blood across my face. I carve my hand, and the crowd gasps as glowing blue blood drips onto the floor.

I make my way around the crowded room, marking each forehead as the soldiers swear fealty to me, and I in return. When I finish with the soldiers, I vow my allegiance to my kings.

My mates kneel before me, each with a hand on the silver, jewel-encrusted crown. "I swear to serve you, my loves, and pledge to protect and provide for our people as High Queen of Bedlam."

I bow, allowing them to place the crown on my head. Magic sizzles in the air, marking the moment I officially become High Queen.

The sound of crunching metal bursts through the quiet. Bunker doors, believed impenetrable, blow open, spewing dirt and debris everywhere. Soldiers draw their weapons and turn towards the intrusion, but magic causes them to freeze mid-stride.

Like the parting of the Red Sea, the uniformed room of men and women split down the center, revealing the small retinue of infiltrators. They pause before stepping into the room, and I come face-to-face with who I presume to be my abductors.

I bare my teeth. The only inkling I have of something amiss is the surge of strength I feel coursing through my veins when my eyes land on the group, and an easing in my chest that startles me. Is it from the final culmination of something I feared for so long, or the relief of finally getting answers to why they stole something so vital to me: my memories?

I take in their faces, studying them, trying to discern whether I remember any. The most beautiful creature I've ever seen stands frozen at the front, eyes boring into me, as though I hung the moons. I immediately recognize him as fae, but that's as far as it goes. My gaze sweeps over the first row of vampires, their handsome features just as foreign to me as the first.

It's time to pay for your crimes, boys.

* * *

Finn

The ache eases in my chest at the sight of her. Lana wears royal blood on her face like war paint, giving a wild edge to her beauty. She bares her teeth at the sight of us before raising her hand to draw power from those around her.

A grin splits my face. *Remarkable.*

I siphon the magic from the room, leaving nothing for her to draw from before putting my hand in the air. With a slight pull, I snap the magic gag order in place over the realm preventing anyone from talking about what happened in the throne room all those moons ago. The king's eyes flare with fury, but they're in the same frozen immovable state as their army.

"Lana, I'm High King Finian Drake, but you call me Finn, or sometimes 'babe.' We're soul bonded mates, and you've been lied to." I motion towards the vampires. "Oz, Auguste, and Gideon are also your mates. They didn't take your memories." I gesture towards the kings. "*They did.*"

CHAPTER 1

LANA

There's something inherently cathartic about staring down the barrel of a proverbial loaded gun. I'm finally facing my captors after spending so many moons terrified of our inevitable encounter. All the tension, the fear, the anxiety of not knowing who I am, what the vampires want with me, and what the fae are planning to do about their infiltration, come rushing to the surface. It's terrifying, but it gives me a sense of clarity, like I'm outside looking in.

It's empowering, this moment, and I take a step forward. The makeshift throne room is large and dank, the air thick with the smell of dirt and machine oil. The distinct scent of urine wafts from where some of the soldiers stand frozen, their fear palpable even in their immovable state.

My gaze cuts to the procession of intruders. The obscenely gorgeous creature in front of me is a liar, his words laughable at best, because my kings would never do what he accuses them of. Kidnap me and steal my memories? They love me. I know it with the same certainty that I know the Earth's sun will rise in the east and set in the west.

But as I take in his features, there's a tugging in my chest. A ghost of a memory, just out of reach.

I open my mouth to refute his claims, but he continues speaking.

"I didn't tell you I was high king because I wanted to spare you the pain of having to make a decision between your vampire court and the fae court until I could figure out a way to give you both, but the time for secrets is over." His voice is laced with emotion and shock blasts through me before anger floods my veins.

So he already admits he's a liar. I take another step forward, despite my hesitation, because I'm drawn to him in a way I can't explain. My magic pulses in violent waves; my leash on it slipping, but not before I release Finn's hold on my kings. They stumble forward, shouting as they stand in front of me, protecting me from the trespassers.

"Don't listen to him, Lana." Grimm slides a possessive arm around my waist. His incubus power pours off him like sheets of molten lava, and my chest rises and falls in dramatic fashion, my breath coming quick.

Finn's honeyed words continue to spill from his lips, but their ruse is up when a tall vampire with sun-kissed skin, deep blue eyes, and dimples so pronounced they could cut glass steps out from the line, and in preternatural speed, surges towards the dais.

He's a blur of motion as he vaults over the twisted metal and the ruined entrance to our bunker, and I gasp as I realize he's coming for us. Instinctively, I step in front of my kings, shielding them as the vampire they call Gideon barrels towards us with ferocious intent in his eyes.

Fear like I've never known spikes through me, and without thinking, I raise my hand, pulling power towards me as I prepare to defend my kings; a surge of protective fury fueling me. I tap into a well of magic I didn't know existed. It's in the air, the ground, the very fabric of the realm, and it rushes to me eagerly as though greeting an old friend. A bolt of blue lightning laced with black flames flies from my fingertips. The heat emanating from the blaze is intense enough to singe the fine hair on my arms, but I don't falter.

It's too late for him to correct course, and he's barreled into by the sheer force of my magic. Gideon's fear-laced face cries out as he's struck by the magical bolt slamming into him. It throws him across the room where he falls to the ground with a thud; his body engulfed in flames.

Agony like I've never known lances through me at the sight of him lying there so still, and my chest expels all the air from my lungs as I crash to my knees. Deep, keening wails echo through the room as my kings rush to my side, but I can't tear my gaze away from Gideon's prone form.

Why is it so loud?

The shrieking shreds my eardrums, and it's only now I realize the sound is coming from me.

CHAPTER 2

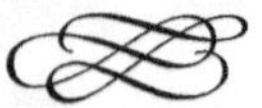

FINN

*M*oon fire.

She doesn't know what she's called upon. There's no way she could control it because I'm an experienced Luna fae and even I can barely control it.

Gideon's words echo across the space between us. *I've failed her.* His mind breaks in defeat.

His last thought surprises me. Misery etches his face, and I'd assumed it was from the pain, but no, it's his grief. Knowing his final moments were spent believing himself unworthy, my chest crushes as I witness the light snuff from his eyes.

Lana is doubled over; blood-curdling screams ripping from her throat as she gapes in confusion at the vampire she doesn't know she loves, who's lying unmoving on the ground. The wall of flames dies, and my heart shatters at the sight of his still form.

The room falls deathly silent as we all take in the scene before us. The popping and sizzling of fire against his skin is the only noise in the room. Horror scores the faces of the vampires next to me, and though a mere two seconds have passed since she struck him, I'm there to lift his body into my arms as I crash to my knees. Heat from the moon fire licks my skin, but it does nothing to me. I'm immune to her Luna magic, because hers and mine are the same.

The reality of what she's done hits me like a tsunami.

She killed her mate.

Anguished screams fill the room once more, and I can do nothing but cradle Gideon's lifeless body in my arms as I mourn the loss of my friend. Oz's words play on repeat in my head.

She didn't know, she doesn't remember.

What have we done?

The sound of Oz, Auguste, Maeve, and Pippa's pained cries fills the room, and I can feel their despair as if it were my own. It's a physical ache that has me clutching Gideon's body tighter as I try to absorb some of their pain.

Time stills, like trudging through sand, as my gaze swings from Gideon to Lana, whose watery eyes are wide and filled with panic. "I-I-I didn't mean to kill your friend ... I'm s-sorry." She starts for us, arm outstretched, but the kings place their hand on her trembling form and sift out, while we're left here reeling.

Oz, Auguste, Maeve, and Pippa reach my side and I shake my head to warn them away. "I need to douse the flames first."

Profound grief adheres to me like a second skin as I take in their devastated expressions. Auguste holds back a wailing Oz, who fights to reach Gideon; his best, and oldest friend. Maeve and Pippa cling to each other as they sob, despair drowning them.

I hold Gideon tight against my chest and use my power to put out the fire. The heat from his body dissipates, and the vampires sink to their knees, destroyed eyes seeking mine for clarity.

Few things can kill an immortal. How do I tell them—these people who've become family to me—that moon fire could even kill a god, and he didn't even stand a chance? The gravity of what's just happened evident in the stillness of the room.

I meet their grief-stricken faces, misery swamping me. "His aura is gone."

His aura was always red. A man who knows what he wants and

doesn't have a problem telling you so. He's seen a lot, and instead of letting it drag him under, he came out the other side fighting for the things he values. It's what I equate to someone full of passion—for life, for others, for belonging. This red, not like an Earthen tomato, but of mortal blood.

To see it extinguished so fast, leaving not even a shell of a man, shakes me to my core.

The sudden sound of bawling has me looking up to see Maeve collapsed in Pippa's arms, her body racked with sobs. With a heavy heart, I turn towards Oz, who's been best friends with Gideon for millennia.

The old me might've relished in Gideons' death—one less mate I must share with Lana. But the new me feels nothing but crippling pain and loss, perhaps not only because I know what this will do to Lana when she gains her memories, but because of how close I've grown to this vampire. This stubborn, competitive asshole who poked and prodded me day in and day out in our quest for Bedlam. Despite it all, I love him. Begrudgingly, but I do.

"He was a brother to me in all the ways that mattered," Oz chokes out, his voice thick with tears. His eyes meet mine. "You can bring him back like you did Bennett, right? Where's the dagger?" His head whips to the others, hand extended, desperation lacing his words. "Someone, go get the dagger, now!"

I give a slight shake of my head and watch as the light in Oz's eyes dims.

No one moves; they all just stare at me in equal parts disbelief and betrayal.

"What do you mean, no?" Oz steps closer, blue eyes flashing in unbridled rage. "You have to! Only you have the power to bring him back! You don't know what this will do to her when she realizes she killed him!" He hauls me to my feet, fingers biting into my arms. "You must bring him back!"

"There's no coming back from a death by moon fire." My voice rings hollow, even to my own ears.

The mournful wails of Pippa and Maeve permeate the room. Oz shoves me away from him with an agony-filled roar and I stumble, barely catching myself before I fall. Despair swamps me as I take in the devastation marring everyone's faces.

I swallow hard, bile rising in my throat. The desire to chase after my soul bonded mate is nearly overpowering, but I know if I leave now, I'll be outmatched facing the kings alone. And these people need me. They're my family, and I need to be strong for them, even if I'm barely holding it together myself.

* * *

"WAIT," I whisper. My words come out broken. "There might be a way."

Everyone turns to look at me, hope lighting up their features. I lower myself next to Gideon's body, my hands shaking as I brush what's left of his hair back from his forehead. There's hardly any skin, like a patchwork quilt held together by thin strips of flesh. My stomach churns and I fight the visceral reaction I have to such perfect skin being so damaged.

I grip the collar of my shirt and pull it over my head before meeting the eyes of my vampire army. "She didn't know."

Their eyes are glassy, and they nod, forming a circle around me as I rest on my heels. I place my tunic under Gideon's head. It won't do much, but it's better than nothing.

Before anyone can react, I release them, my wings unfurling behind me. Quiet murmurs cut through the silence in the crowd. Nearby, the vampires have stopped sobbing and watch with pained expressions. I hover for a moment before landing back in the middle of the circle, my wings folding around me. I fan one out and pluck several of the golden plumes tipped in blue.

Rivulets of cerulean blood pour from my wounds, but they barely register. I lean over Gideon's chest, placing the small bouquet of feathers on his charred skin. "For our mate, who is far better than any one of us."

I begin chanting in archaic fae, my voice low and melodic. The magic swirls around us, gaining power with each word. My army watches in rapt attention, their eyes gleaming with tears.

The power gathers, the sapphire light growing brighter and brighter until it's so blinding, I have to close my eyes. When I reopen them, Gideon's body is gone.

I suck in a breath and fight the tears that blur my vision. Around me, my militia is in various states of grief. Some are openly weeping; others have their heads bowed in mourning. Though they all understand I may be able to bring him back, they still grieve him. He's the right hand of the Vampire King. Mate to the Queen of Vampires.

The rot of fire and brimstone assaults my senses, and I gag, stumbling backward.

"What is this? Where is his body?! Who has taken him?!" Oz's voice rings through the air, his hands gripped in his hair. He's in the middle of the circle, his face a mask of ruin. Beside him, Auguste is pale, and his eyes reflect the smoke billowing in the room.

"It won't be long now." I rise to my feet. "Let's widen this circle."

They nod and move to the edges, making room for me. I take a step forward, my arms outstretched. A sliver of space opens, and I wedge my fingers in until I can put my hands inside to pull it apart.

A roar echoes through the room, and I stumble back but keep my hands on the portal, shielding my eyes from the bright flames licking up my wrists. This fire *burns*. From the gateway, inky smoke pours out and pools to the floor. It curls around the legs of the vampires, who kick it off them.

I shout, "Give him back, Aggonid. You can't have this one."

"If it isn't the golden child himself," a rich, poignant voice calls out from the ether. The sound alone makes the fine hair along my arms stand on end. "What will you give me for him?"

I curse under my breath. "I, Finian Drake, son of Luna, give thee Aggonid a boon. May you use it wisely."

An ominous gong vibrates through the room, into my chest, and into my very bones. It shudders so badly; I nearly lose my grip. Accompanying the noise is a bright flash. When the light fades, a charred, disheveled Gideon stands in the middle of the circle, his eyes wide and haunted.

I let go of the portal, and it blinks shut, but not before an evil chuckle escapes. Aggonid is what humans would view as the fae devil, and his realm is far worse than what earth-dwellers humans think of purgatory. I can't bear to imagine what being in his presence must have felt like for Gideon, but the anguish on his face gives me some idea.

Gideon's traumatized gaze inspects his naked body. He's undamaged, but his hair is a wild mess, standing on end.

"L-Lana." He furrows his brows and meets my eyes, his voice shaking. "Where is she? Is she hurt?"

I shake my head and fight the tears that are blurring my vision. "No, they sifted her somewhere after you died."

Gideon lets out a relieved breath and his shoulders sag. "Thank the gods." His troubled mien is so at odds with how I normally see this male. If the first words out of his mouth weren't about Lana's wellbeing, I'd have thought him possessed.

Oz crushes Gideon to his chest, and the vampire wraps his arms around him. "I thought I'd lost you, brother."

"Not likely." Gideon smirks, though the haunted look doesn't leave his eyes.

Auguste rushes in, clasping Gideon's shoulders and looking him over. Seeing him whole, he presses his forehead to Gideon's and takes a deep breath.

Their moment is interrupted when Maeve shrieks, yanking Gideon from Auguste's hold. "You big, stupid idiot! Don't you do that to me ever again!" Her hysterical sobs shake her entire body, puffy eyes shuttered.

Gideon enfolds her in his arms and presses her face into his chest. "Shhh, little hellcat, it's all right. I'm fine."

"You're not fine! You died!" she cries, her voice muffled.

"I know, and I'm sorry," Gideon murmurs. "But I'm here now."

I step back and allow them their moment, my heart heavy with the knowledge Lana will feel the weight of what she's done once I can restore her memories.

Gideon glances at me, and I see the understanding in the depths of his features. "You did this." Not a question, but a statement.

I give a shallow tilt of my head. He breaks from the group and claps a hand on my shoulder before pulling me in for a hug. "Thank you." He pulls back and looks at me, his cloudy eyes bright with unshed tears. A tremble in his limbs gives away the shock of this ordeal on his body. "For everything. Gods ... had you all not been standing here; I'd have thought I was gone for thousands of years. It felt like it in the underworld."

"Can you imagine how much trouble I'd be in with Lana if I let you stay dead?" I smirk.

He smiles, though it doesn't reach his eyes, and he shakes his head. "I told her I'd storm the gates of hell for her, and now I have."

We share a sad look, and I scoop my shirt off the ground and toss it to him. "Put this on, and we'll put together our new game plan."

We sit in silence for a moment before my attention catches on the frozen soldiers across the room. I pull the magic away from Bellamy, who runs over to us as soon as his limbs are free of their hold.

"Send word to your kings. I request a formal challenge for my role as High King."

He inclines his head. "I tried to tell her."

I blink, and a gnawing suspicion settles in my gut. "What do you mean?"

"Lana and I were ..." He pauses. "Close."

My eyes fall shut and I grit my teeth. "I was going to tell her about what the kings had done to her on the night of the ball, but they intercepted me, and I spent time at Bedlam Penitentiary for it."

Understanding dawns and I give a slow nod. "Thanks, Bellamy."

Compared to me, he's a relatively younger fae, but I always liked his confidence. I can see why Lana took a liking to him. Pierce, his older brother, was a favorite soldier of mine. Their sister, Captain Zara, fought alongside me in the last war, and always gave me a hard time about kicking her mate's ass the first time I met him. It was all a misunderstanding, and it didn't take us long to look past it all.

I take in the immobile fae around us. "Where's your brother?"

Bellamy casts a glance behind him and points to a fae with a large scar splitting his eyebrow, passing over the eyelid and down his cheek. I furrow my brows. I hardly recognize him.

Raising my hand, I unfreeze Pierce. "Take your brother and get the fuck out of here. I'll deal with the rest."

I mobilize the soldiers I recognize and give them orders to get everyone out.

CHAPTER 3

LANA

Where my kings take me, I don't know, nor do I seem to care. No sooner do we sift in do I crash to my knees, sucking in deep, uncontrollable sobs. Sand cushions my fall, and someone pulls me into their arms, but I'm too grief-stricken to know —or care—who it is. Under the crushing agony, it feels as though I'm buried alive, the only thing to keep me company is my grief.

I'm afraid of the darkness my soul has ventured into. It's a reluctant traveler, thrust into a black hole; a vacuum, dragging me under.

Pain lives here.

"Lana," Casimir's soft voice murmurs, and I cling to him, my nails like claw marks, seeking comfort before a torrent of misery claims me.

I killed a man.

It doesn't matter that he was about to attack my kings. I'm the reason someone grieves tonight. I did what I had to to protect the men I love, but the consequences of my actions leave me reeling.

"Why does it hurt so bad?" Tears slide down my cheeks, staining his chest. "Will I always feel this way?"

"Taking a life always comes with a price," Casimir soothes. "Often, the burden is what we carry on our conscience."

If this is what it'll feel like any time I kill someone, I'll never do it again. A gaping wound lives in my chest, spreading through my body and soul, an insidious manifestation of the darkest parts of me. I'm dying inside, and I know there's no coming back from this.

I.

Killed.

A.

Man.

Chatter behind me pulls me from my self-punishment. It's the first time I've noticed Grimm and Penn gathered next to us. Worry draws their features.

"Where is this place?" My bleary eyes dart around, taking in the surf lapping near me. It's too dark to see anything else.

"A small island just off Luporia. I maintain a private residence inside the lighthouse." Casimir gestures behind me and I glance at the towering, white-washed building. It'd be charming if it weren't so enormous.

"We can make you forget." Grimm steps into view, sinking to his knees. Dark hair hangs across his forehead, and his features pinch together.

I blink away. His Tahitian blue eyes remind me too much of the man I killed, though Grimm's are lighter. "No." I rock my head against Casimir. "This is a lesson I must take to heart. I can never forget what this feels like."

My mates cast concerned glances at each other. Casimir helps me up and scoops me into his arms before turning towards the lighthouse, sand falling like my own grip on reality. "Come, my love. Let's get you some rest."

I bury my head in his chest and let him carry me away from the pain.

By some miracle, I sleep. Despite being cocooned in warmth, I wake feeling out of sorts. Flopping Grimm's heavy arm off me, I take in my surroundings and frown. A cream-colored four-poster bed with filmy curtains dominates the room, while an assortment of furniture fills the remaining space. White, blue, and beige fabrics drape overstuffed pillows and couches; a scene I'd find cozy if I didn't feel dead.

Dread pools in my stomach. I killed a man last night, and while I know it was necessary, the act still weighs on me. Every breath I take, tainted, knowing I stole someone else's.

The door swings open, and Casimir strides in with a tray filled to the brim with comfort items. A smile brightens his face when he sees me awake. "Good morning, my love."

Doesn't he know I'm dying inside? That I snuffed the light from someone's eyes, and it's all my fault? Can't he feel this chasm wrenching me wide open? Or the darkness threatening to swallow me whole?

I'm drowning, Casimir, can't you see me?

His face falls when he takes in the tears gathering in my eyes. "Oh, Lana." He sets the tray down on the edge of the bed, liquid spilling over a cup, and pulls me into his arms.

"It hurts," I sob. "I can't stop thinking about it. Every time I close my eyes, I see his face."

Deep pools of blue, framed by thick lashes and a strong brow. The easy smile he wore when his eyes locked on mine in that throne room, as though I'd been both the question and the answer to life. Gideon's fearful mien is burned into my mind. I killed him, and the act feels like a betrayal. To him. To me. It plays on a loop in my head. Breathtaking beauty, cobalt flames, then ashes. I can still taste them on my tongue.

"It's natural for you to feel this way." Casimir rubs my back in slow, soothing circles, his thumbs pressing into my muscles. "In time, the pain will fade."

But the guilt never will. It festers and grows, a cankerous sore that poisons everything it touches. I don't know how to live with this.

I'm not certain I even want to.

"Drink this." Casimir hands me a cup of steaming tea, and I take it without protest.

The bitter drink burns going down, and I sputter a cough. "What is it?" I wipe the back of my hand across my mouth.

"A tea made from the sea grass grown along the shore. It will help ease your pain."

I take another sip, wincing as the liquid scalds my throat. "Thank you."

Easing into Casimir's touch, my body feels boneless as the sea magic buoys my limbs. Memories of tumbling through surf and sinking to the depths of the Parallel Abyss after a berserker slit my throat assails my senses. That memory leads to thoughts of oceans of cerulean eyes, a dimpled smile, and silky onyx hair from a man laid ruined at my feet.

I flip over onto my stomach, an iron grip on the King of Luporia. "Make me forget," I beg. "Not forever, but for now."

My mouth crushes to Casimir's, and he hesitates, as if he's reluctant to take advantage of his broken mate. *Please.* The word echoing in my head must convince him because soon enough, he's cupping my face and brushing the tears from my cheeks. He places a kiss to each, his lips lingering like a reverent prayer.

"Are you sure?" He tilts my chin until my eyes meet his. Concern swims in their depths.

Swinging my leg over his lap, I straddle him. "I need all of you right now," I whisper, afraid that if I speak louder, my fragile grip on reality will shatter.

He gives me a barely perceptible nod before sliding his arms under my thighs, lifting me so I can wrap my legs around his waist. I bury my head into his neck as he carries me out the door, past the living room, and up the stairs to our bedroom. Somewhere along the way, he must've communicated with Grimm and Penn to join us because as soon as I'm laid on the bed, they come into view and crawl onto the mattress.

Positioning himself behind me so I'm cradled in his arms and nestled between his legs, Casimir gathers my hair in his hand to have better access to my neck. I crane my head, giving him entrance to place his lips against my pulse. His canines scrape against my rapid heartbeat just below my ear.

"Do it," I beg.

Penn's heated gaze lands on mine just as Casimir sinks his teeth into my flesh. The pain gives way to pleasure immediately, the trading of blood between mates one of the most intimate things fae can do.

Desire pools low in my belly when Grimm uses his magic to occupy my mind. It pours over me like honey splashing a hot skillet, seeking, consuming, destroying all thought until it narrows to just one: an ache for my mates so fierce, I yank them towards me.

Their hands and their lips find me, and I sink into the feel of their skin against mine, forgetting for a moment just how ruined I am. Together, we chase our pleasure, our limbs tangled in sheets as a sea breeze blows the gauzy drapes in the window.

* * *

THE KINGS SPEND the rest of the weekend arranging defenses for the island so they can address the realm about impending war with the vampires. I sifted to court for a brief session, but came back just as fast, because it's hard to be around others when it feels as though my entire world has ended. How can everyone act as though nothing is wrong?

Can't they see that I'm a murderer? The stain on my soul?

While my mates busy themselves with our fortifications, I lazily stroll the rocky beach and try to come to terms with what I've done. I toe seashells out of their homes on the sand, stooping to pocket a couple of them to put in our bathroom for décor.

My mind wrestles with itself; on one side, it justifies protecting the men I love. On the other, the weight of the grief crushes me until I'm folding over myself, body wracking with sobs. The sliver of justification is but a speck of light in a sea of darkness, its mighty tempest demanding its due.

The sun beats on my neck by the time I make my way back to the lighthouse. I find Penn in the book-crowded study, poring over a map with a seriousness that makes my heart ache. Shadows mar his eyes, and his tousled hair makes me think he didn't sleep last night, though he held me 'til morning.

"Lana." He greets me with a tired smile. "Come, sit with me."

I take a seat on the powder-blue couch and watch as he returns his attention to the worn map, its edges frayed and curling. "What are you doing?"

"Trying to figure out the best way to protect the island." He sighs and rubs his eyes. "The vampires will be coming for you, and we need to make sure we're prepared."

"Have you given any thought to what you're going to say to the people?" I grab a navy throw pillow and tug it to my chest. "They're going to be scared."

"I know." He nods and looks up at me. "But we have to be strong. We have to show them that we're not afraid."

"And if we can't?" I whisper.

He takes my hand and squeezes it. "Then we fake it until we make it, darling."

CHAPTER 4

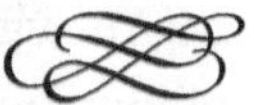

LANA

The men speak in hushed tones, but I can still hear their words clearly through the slotted vent in the floor. I'm supposed to be upstairs, sleeping, but their voices wake me. I flop over, pulling the fluffy eye mask off my head and readjust my bun to capture all my hair that escaped in the night.

The kings and I said goodbye last night because this morning, they're headed to Occasus, where they'll lead a battalion against the vampires. I'm to hunker down on this tiny Luporian island they've spent weeks reinforcing. To minimize attention to where I might be, I'm to remain here until my kings or Pierce come back for me. There are no communication devices to intercept, and if no one sifts to check on me, the vampires will have no clue as to where I'm hiding. In just a few weeks, we'll reunite.

"Do you think she believes Finn?" Grimm asks, his voice laced with something. Is that worry? Or is it guilt?

"I don't know." Penn sighs and something slams against the wall. The others swear at him before they quiet for a moment, determine I'm still sleeping, and continue. "What I do know is that this is eating her alive. She's not herself and hasn't been since that day. I've offered to take her flying, but she just shakes her head. Barely eats and doesn't even read anymore. Just stares across the water."

Blinking, I tear my eyes from the sea and train them on the vent.

"I can't imagine how she's feeling," Casimir clears his throat. "To doubt your mates. It's a lot to take in."

"She's bound to doubt us, especially after what she was told. She isn't stupid and she must be able to tell that we haven't been entirely honest with her." Penn's voice is tight. "But I don't think that's what's plaguing her. She has to deal with the fact that she killed Gideon. I don't know how she's going to get past that."

I don't hear the rest of their conversation on account of the roaring static in my mind and the wild gallop of my heart. There are few things I know for certain: my mates haven't been honest with me about something, the vampires busted through an unbreakable portal to get me back, and they have declared war on the fae. All because they believe me to be their mate. Now that I've killed Gideon, one of their own, do they want me dead? Is that why they've declared war?

The weight of it all presses down on my chest until I can't breathe. Resignation seeps into my bones; I need to get out of here, and I need answers. More than anything, I can't pretend to be okay when I'm not.

So, I do the only thing I can think of.

I run.

CHAPTER 5

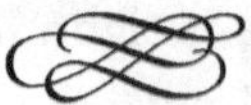

LANA

Heat assaults my skin the moment I step foot into the Wastelands. It's an unbearable, scorching sensation that feels like it's burning through my clothes and searing my flesh. There's no green vegetation in sight, and the ground is unnaturally dry and cracked, with giant bones littering the land. I'm not sure how anyone could survive in this place.

The air is thick and cloying, making it difficult to breathe. It tastes of ash on my tongue. A constant, blistering wind blows sand and bits of dried branches around, though it gives no reprieve from the merciless sun. It's as if the environment is working against me, trying to choke me to death.

This must be what Hell is like. Or, now that I'm fae—Aggonid's realm.

I'm here seeking the Crucey, a creature whose life I saved a few moons ago. Others fear her and call her evil, and she may be, but I think there's more to her story. She was forced into a life of darkness and pain, protecting the Tolden, or children of the woods.

The Wastelands make up the Northwest part of Convectus, on the other side of lush green mountains. Beyond it is the sea. If I traverse the barren lands, I should find the Crucey's home.

If I can survive the journey. There's no sifting here, and right now, the wind is so cutting, it'd shred my wings if I tried to take flight.

I know the kings will worry when they find me missing, but I need answers only one person is guaranteed to give me. I need to know if my mates are lying to me about the vampires. If they are, I'm uncertain what I'll do.

Trudging my way through the arid desert, I move with a conviction I haven't felt in ages. I must know the truth. Even if it hurts.

CHAPTER 6

FINN

I stalk into our encampment, my feet kicking up sand, past the line of vampires waiting for their human blood bags to feed them. We found a small group of witches here, on Sundahlia, sympathetic to our cause. This continent sits on the Eastern edge of Bedlam, and it took three weeks of sailing to reach it. The massive number of supplies and amount of non-sifting soldiers required the lengthy journey. There are only a handful of witches here, but they've been able to keep the blood suckers fed so they're strong enough to fight. These beasts only need to feed once a week, but at the rate we're fighting, they need to eat every other day.

I don't call them beasts or blood suckers as a slight. They fight valiantly for our cause, and I'm forever in their debt. Each evening, whispers of the Oriflamme Queen fill conversations around camp. A smile tugs at the corners of my mouth. With the way they speak about her, you'd think they love my mate almost as much as I do.

Stopping at the medical bay, I greet Pippa with a peck on her cool cheek. "How's he doing?" I ask, nodding toward where Wren lays. The shaggy-haired vampire is a pilot on Earth, and an integral part of their court. He took a bad hit a few days ago.

"He's healing, but slowly," she replies with a shake of her head. A blonde curl falls out of the bun she has piled high on her crown. "I'm worried about him."

"I'll heal him."

"You will? I—" Sebastian's earnest eyes meet mine and his muscles relax with relief at my words.

"Finn, you can't heal everyone. We need you to keep your strength." Pippa places her palm against my forearm.

"I'll be fine," I tell her with a wave of my hand. "Besides, if I can't heal him, who will?" I wince but can't take back the words. "Sorry, Pippa, I didn't mean it like that." I duck my head, feeling bad. She's a healer on Earth, using Earth medicine, and occasionally, magic, when Oz or another witch can help. Thankfully, vampires don't need sleep, but it also means she's worked around the clock to heal.

"I know." She sighs. "It's just that we can't keep relying on you, Alphie, and Rune to heal every injury. If I had some of the technology from Earth, I could make do, but I don't have magic to mend wounds like the fae."

Placing my hands on each of her slumped shoulders, I give her a reassuring squeeze. "The full moon is here. I'll be okay, and healing regenerates my magic. Rune, on the other hand, doesn't refuel his magic the same way I do. And Alphie's isn't near as strong as mine, especially as he's grieving Lana's memory loss. If someone needs healing, don't hesitate to come to me, okay?"

Rune, a fae made of shadow and storms, is one of my closest friends, and easily one of the strongest fae in Bedlam. His attention is divided between here and my old stomping grounds, so he operates at near-empty more often than not.

"Okay," she gives a resigned nod. "We just worry about you."

"I know, and I love you for it." I give her a wink. Both she and her mate, Elliot, have really helped me cope with everything that's happened with Lana. They're surprisingly easy to talk to without judgment and they keep our conversations between just us. Something about doctor-patient confidentiality.

Crouching beside Wren's still form on the cot, I place my hand over the festering injury just to the left of his heart. My skin glows as the magic stirs within me, and I let it flow into him. The ethereal blue mixes with the shadows in the room, and I get lost in the healing.

Wren's eyes fly open, and he gasps for breath. "What the—?" He sits up, looking around wildly.

I lean so I'm at his level. "You're safe, Wren. You're in the medical bay."

He looks at me, and I see the confusion in his eyes before he darts his attention to Sebastian over my shoulder.

"What happened?" Wren groans, his brow furrowed.

"You were hurt in battle." Sebastian blinks rapidly to keep the tears from spilling over.

"But I'm healed now," Wren beams, his eyes wide as he looks down at himself.

I shrug. "I healed you."

"But there were so many of us injured." He whips his head around as he sits up. "How did you—"

"It's okay, Wren," I try to calm him. "I was able to heal everyone. Healing refuels me."

He flips the blanket off his body and swings his legs over the side of the cot. "I need to go help, then."

"Wren, you need to rest," Pippa comes to stand beside me. "You've been through a lot."

"I'm fine," he insists as he stands. A little unsteady at first, but then he shakes out his legs. "Actually, I feel great."

Pippa glances at me, and I give her an imperceptible nod. "Should be fully healed."

I turn to leave the tent and hear Wren thank me.

"Of course," I reply with a smile, before exiting into the moonlight.

The fresh air hits me like a change in the tide, and I stop to take a deep breath. The scents of the forest overwhelm me—rotting leaves, fresh rain, and pine. It's a sharp contrast to the sterile smell of the medical bay.

Shaking my head to clear it, I start towards the far side of camp. Locating Rune's large, olive-green canvas tent, I duck inside. Oz,

Auguste, Rune, and Alphie are all gathered around a small wooden table, staring at a hand-drawn map.

"What's the plan?" I ask, coming to stand beside Oz. My eyes catalogue his mussed hair, shadowed bags under his eyes, and gaunt cheeks. His skin has taken on an ashy cast to it, far from its tawny color from his wedding pictures.

"We're going to launch a full-scale assault on Occasus tomorrow night," Rune says, his voice hard and unyielding. "That should distract them enough so we can locate Lana and extract her."

A smile tilts my lips. Grimm, the King of Occasus, and I always had a tenuous relationship because he couldn't respect my desire for saving myself for my soul bonded mate. As an incubus order, he couldn't understand, and often tried to get me to break my resolve. It didn't matter how much he tried to use his magic on me, or how many females he sent to my castle to attempt to warm my bed, nothing stirred me sexually. When that didn't work, he tried males. I couldn't be unfaithful to Lana, even if she wasn't mine yet, and I didn't know if I'd ever meet my soul bond.

Since puberty, I knew fate intended me to have one. The recognition hit me like a tsunami while I studied late one evening. All noise ceased, and the hairs on my arms stood up as a chill swept over me. A blinding white light materialized in the center of my towered room, and then my grandmother appeared before me. I'd never met her before that moment, but there was no mistaking the soft glow of her skin, or her uncanny resemblance to my mother.

Her beauty astounded me. With her long white hair pulled back in a loose braid, and her cerulean eyes sparkling with mischief, she looked like Earth's depiction of an angel. But looks could be deceiving, and my grandmother was the most powerful fae of her generation before she ascended as the next Luna goddess.

"Finn," she said, coming to stand before me. "I have come to speak with you about your destiny."

"My destiny?" I asked, confused.

"Yes," she replied. "You are destined for great things, my boy. But first, you must find your soul bond."

"My what?" I asked, still not understanding.

"Your soul bond is your other half, the person who was made just for you. And you, my boy, are destined to save realms. You can't do it without her."

Before I could ask any more questions, a spark of light flew from her hand and straight into my chest. Outside noise flooded my ears once again, and she was gone as quickly as she came. In her wake, a sense of knowing stirred in me. It was like she'd pried open my sternum and carved out a shelf meant only for my intended soul bond.

It was a defining moment in my life, and I carried that with me for thousands of years. The day I found out was easily one of the best days of my life; I was going to get the chance to love someone as deeply as my mother loved my father, though it wasn't reciprocated on his end. I just had to be patient and wait for him or her to come into my life.

Little did I know I'd spend millennia pining for my soul bond, though the wait was more than worth it.

Oz interrupts my reverie, and I'm pulled back to the present. "Where's Gideon?"

I glance around the tent. "What do you mean?"

"Weren't you two going to create blueprints of the rest of the castles today?" Auguste furrows his brows.

Rune sighs before I can answer Auguste. "He's probably off sulking somewhere."

The massive casualties during last week's siege have taken their toll on all of us, but especially Gideon. He's been withdrawn and quiet since we lost so many good men and women. I imagine his time in Aggonid's realm hasn't sat well with him, either.

No one likes to hear they're destined for Aggonid's realm.

Oz and I had a conversation about it because I had to know what kind of monster my soul bond was mated to.

Turns out, Gideon and Oz spent a lot of time in their early days as a vampire under uncontrollable blood lust. Before they'd learned how to properly train someone to control the feral urges, a lot of vampires were turned and let loose on the unsuspecting public. They both killed countless, innocent people before they could get reins on it.

Gideon compensates now by trying to be optimistic and laid back, though I see through it. Underneath, there's a lot of pain.

"He's not sulking," I grumble, my voice low. "He's grieving." I run my hands through Titan's silk obsidian fur, listening to the deep purr of the Phelvie's chest before I rise to my feet.

Rune nods, though I appreciate his loyalty to me. He and Titan both.

"He never showed, and I assumed he'd just gotten held up. When was the last time anyone saw him?" I keep my voice even though anxiety tightens my chest.

"I saw him two nights ago." Alphie takes a sip from his coffee mug. "He was heading into the jungle."

"Did he say where he was going?"

Alphie shakes his head. "No, but he looked like he was on a mission."

"Did anyone else see him?" Oz stands, his chair catching on the rug. Worry carves his features. He's been running himself ragged, barely eating, never sleeping, just surviving on pure determination to get Lana back. There's a small measure of comfort knowing I'm not the only one pining for her. That I'm not alone in my fight to get our mate back to safety.

Fae require sleep, refueling of magic, and nourishment to function. Not as much as humans, but enough to hamper progress. I couldn't do this without our combined efforts.

Auguste gestures South. "I saw him yesterday. He was headed towards the sand dunes, though that's not unusual for him."

I let out a frustrated breath and run a hand through my hair. "That's it then. I'll go find him." Maybe he got into the fae wine again. On Earth, he doesn't have to worry about getting drunk. Fae wine, though? He'd made the mistake of having a full bottle of it by himself. Oz and I had spent the entire night reassuring him that Lana still loves him, he's not a terrible mate for letting her go to Bedlam, and promising not to tell the others he'd gotten so drunk we found him trying to coax a spirit fish to fly into his net.

"We'll come with you." Oz grabs some swords and tosses them to Auguste and Alphie. They must fight with weapons, rather than their teeth, for fear of turning feral by biting into a fae. It's taken a lot of getting used to for them. What used to be their greatest weapon is now their biggest liability.

We head out into the night, calling Gideon's name as we go. I know he's grieving, but he needs to snap out of it. We can't afford to lose him, not now, not when we're so close to getting her back.

We search for hours, but there's no sign of him anywhere. It's like he's vanished into thin air. Rune had a storm surrounding our camp to keep it from prying eyes, so footsteps and scents have long washed away by now. There's no way to track him the traditional way.

Oz calls a halt to the search around dawn. "We'll find him," he says, but the worry in his voice is clear.

"He's out there somewhere," I say. "And we'll find him."

I've just got to locate something of his so I can do a locator spell. Only Luna fae can do this with their magic, but the spell requires something that belonged to the missing person for us to to focus on, so we'll need something that belonged to Gideon. I could also do a relocation spell with ingredients found in the far reaches of Bedlam, but we don't have that kind of time. That spell would drag Lana here, no matter where she is, or what she's doing.

I head back to the tent Gideon and Auguste share, hoping to find something that will help me find him. Both of their beds are impeccably made, which always surprises me. Auguste, I understand. He's got that tight-laced control about him. Gideon? Despite his laid back, but competitive personality, he's very methodical in his actions. The room is sparse, immaculate, and everything on his desk is at a perfect, right angle.

I slide open his drawer and rifle through it, but there's nothing that really stands out to me. I'm about to give up when I see a small, velvet box tucked into the back corner. I pull the purple container out and open it, revealing a delicate gold necklace with a shimmering crescent moon pendant.

Gideon's never been one for jewelry, so I know this must be special to him. Perhaps it's for Lana. Or Rose. I take the necklace and leave the tent, heading to find Oz.

"I found something of Gideon's," I hold up the necklace. "With this, I—"

"That's not his," Rose sidles up to me. Unshed tears make her eyes glassy, and I pull her into my arms. "Dad and Bennett traded for it when we passed through the Cerulean Isles because I loved it."

Her words hit me like a slap in the face. Of course, it wouldn't be that easy. "Do you know what he traded?"

The tears shining in her eyes break their dam and spill down her cheeks. "The dagger they made in Noble Wilds."

I take a deep breath and try to push down the wave of despair that's threatening to drown me. "Thanks, Rose. I'll keep looking." I'm careful with my words. I can't make a fae promise, especially one I don't know if I can keep. I'll do everything I can to find Gideon, but he's a vampire in a fae realm he knows nothing about. He could be anywhere.

I search the tent again, but there's nothing else that could possibly be of use to me. I feel like I'm meeting wall after wall, but I must find something. Stepping out of the tent, I nearly run into Oz.

"No luck?" he asks, and worry swims in his eyes.

I shake my head and hold up the velvet box. "I was hoping this would be something of Gideon's, but it's not."

"Thanks," Oz says, but I can tell he's losing hope.

"Rose said Bennet and Gideon traded this in the Cerulean Isles. I could sift there with them and try to track down which vendor they got it from? With any luck, I can find Gideon that way."

Oz claps me on the shoulder. "It's worth a try."

CHAPTER 7

LANA

My chapped lips crack and bleed as I press them together in a desperate bid to find some moisture. My throat is parched, and my eyes are gritty and dry from the constant wind and sand. I've been pushing against the wind for hours, and I'm so thirsty I can barely think straight. I don't want to open my canteen and contaminate it with the silt—I must wait for the gale to die down.

The sun rests high in the sky, a steady presence, and its relentless heat is a physical weight that drags me down. I can't see a thing through the sandstorm, though I feel the rays against my cheeks and reddened shoulders. The squall is so strong it's nearly impossible to keep my balance. I can't go on like this.

My legs crumble and I hit the hard dirt before positioning myself so I can rest my head against my aching knees. I'm so tired, and it's so hard to keep going. But I can't give up. I must find the Crucey.

I force myself to my feet and start walking again, one foot in front of the other. I rack my brain for a spell that might help me find my way, but I come up blank. It's too hot to fashion more clothes, no matter how much the harsh wind tears at my skin.

The Wastelands are my own personal hell. How does she keep the

Tolden in such an unforgiving climate? Is this how she keeps the werewolves away?

Eventually, I make my way to a small canyon. It offers a bit of shelter from the elements, and I gratefully tumble under its lip. The gorge is cooler, and I can finally rest. I lean against the rough wall, letting my eyes close. Sand grits between my teeth as I sleep, and my nose feels clogged with dirt.

I dream of the kings. They're in a dark place; the sound of wind pummels the field they're on, and they're each in different stages of panic. They're yelling, and though I can't make out what they're saying, their voices are full of tight-laced fear. I wake up with a start, my heart pounding.

Rising to my aching feet, I continue, the dream still haunting me. Guilt weighs on me. What if they're telling the truth, and I'm putting everyone at risk? But if they're lying to me, what then? Our blood bond ties me to them forever.

Unease stirs in my gut. If they've betrayed me ... *there's nothing I can do.*

After another hour, the sun hangs on the horizon, giving me respite from its sweltering rays. A gentle breeze stirs my hair, and the sand no longer beats on my skin. I deposit myself on a larger rock and eat some of my provisions. I take small sips from the canteen, careful not to indulge too much, though I want to gulp the entire bottle.

Inspecting my pack, I count my supplies. I have enough to last me at least a week if I'm careful. But I need to find the Crucey soon—I can't spend that much time in the Wastelands. Not with the war raging between the fae and vampires. Too many lives have been lost.

I pull myself to my feet and trudge on.

The moons rise in the sky, and I strip completely out of my clothes, eager for their beams. My skin glows, energy racing through every cell. My speed picks up, using the light from the moons to guide me. Not a creature stirs, nor do any bugs sing. It's entirely devoid of life. Even the wind seems to have given up.

My thoughts turn to the vampire I accidentally killed. The infiltrating army was grief-stricken when they saw what happened. If my kings are lying to me, it's possible I knew this creature. Does my subconscious know this? Is that why I had such a visceral reaction to his death? These musings keep my feet moving. One person—or creature—can provide me with the answers I seek.

I freeze when a shadow moves in my peripheral vision. My heart races as I try to see what's stalking me, but it's too dark, and the shadow is gone before I can catch a glimpse. I spin around in a circle, trying to spot it again while I throw my hands out to draw magic from whomever, or whatever, it is. But there's nothing. Only emptiness surrounds me.

Not a fae, then.

Paranoia sets in. I can't see what's tracking me, and I have no idea what it is. It could be anything. And if it's not fae, then it must be something worse. Little can survive in the Wastelands.

I pick up the pace, my heart galloping in my chest. The shadow seems to play with me, disappearing and reappearing just out of reach. Fear has me wanting to run the other way, but my fae magic calls to me, swirling under my skin like a physical need to leap out and connect with the pulse of the moons.

The shadow darts in front of me again, and I take chase. It's fast, but I'm faster. I catch a glimpse of obsidian fur before the ground falls out below me, and I tumble into the darkness.

I scream as I plummet down the hole, hitting my head on the way down. Then everything goes black.

CHAPTER 8

FINN

The putrid scent of rotted fish and seaweed fills my nose as I step out of the slip in space and into the Cerulean Isles. It's one of the vilest places in all the realms, but it's either this or Parallel Abyss when passing between Convectus and Sundahlia. The latter is just as treacherous as the Isles are disgusting.

Stopping along the rickety dock, I crouch until I'm at Rose and Bennett's eye level. I don't have to stoop far—they're tall already. "Do you remember their face?" I hold up the necklace.

They both nod, and Bennett speaks first. "Aye, we got it from a vendor near the edge of the market."

A smile tugs at my lips. He sounds a lot like Gideon.

Rose's smile is just as fond. "Was the witches' nephew who traded it to us."

I narrow my eyes at her and glance at Bennett, who sighs and chuffs a laugh.

"She's got a crush on him," he declares, and Rose's face turns red before she buries it behind her hands.

"I do not!" she cries, and I can't help but chuckle before I make a silent promise to ensure to keep an eye on the two of them.

"It's alright, Rose," I say, pulling her into a hug. "I won't tell anyone."
Except her other dads.

Releasing her, I stand and hold out my hand to her. She takes it, and I help her to her feet.

"Show me their stand," I say, and she tugs, leading the way through the market. Handmade goods, weapons, and trinkets line the rickety tables and booths. I've got the three of us glamoured in the same getup we had when we passed through here the first time, so we garner no more than a passing glance from the other patrons and shopkeepers.

The closer we get to the edge, the more rundown the stands become. There are fewer people milling about, and the stalls are selling nothing more than rubble. Anger stirs in my gut. We should have much better facilities for the fae, witches, and magical creatures who pass through here. They're only trying to make a living and shouldn't be partitioned to squalor. As soon as I take the throne again, I'll make this right. There needs to be safety and equity for everyone, not just those blessed with the most powerful forms of magic.

As we pass, I use my magic to discreetly repair some of the goods that have been damaged. I sweep through the place, pushing my power like a heavy fog through stall after stall, fixing a broken board here, a sagging awning there. I know it won't last, but maybe it will help them get by until they can afford to replace it themselves. Or, until I get back into power and can right all the missteps the kings took in my absence from the throne.

When we reach the last stall in the market, I know we've found the right one. The boy who mans it can't be more than eighteen Earth years, and he's got sun-ripened skin, a crooked smile, and a wicked scar on his breastbone. Most of the buttons are missing from his shirt, leaving his chest bare, though a necklace made of small, off-white shells circles his neck. He's also got a black eye, and his lip is split. I can feel the magic emanating from him, even from this distance. He's a witch, and considering he's so young, he must've only come into his power; Ebbswick keys rarely come this early. He wouldn't have been able to come here without one unless he was born in Bedlam.

"This is it," Rose says, and I step up to the table, scanning the goods. It's finer than some of the other wares on this side of the market, but the boy is selling it all for next to nothing.

I pick up a finely carved wooden box and examine it. It's inlaid with mother-of-pearl and silver and would fetch a high price in Convectus. "Did you make this?" I ask, and the boy's face lights up.

"Oh, that's my favorite," he says, and I can hear the pride in his voice. "Took me two weeks to make it, but I think it turned out rather well."

I inspect it closely. "It's beautiful," I say, and mean it.

His attention catches on Rose behind me, and his smile widens. A dimple forms in his right cheek, and something in my chest clenches. The need to destroy suddenly overcomes me. This boy is going to be trouble.

"*Rose.*"

I don't like the way he says her name, not at all. He wraps it around his tongue like he's tasting it, and his eyes darken as they rake over her body. I step in front of her, shielding her from his gaze. Bennett edges closer to me to help conceal her, too.

"Hi," Rose says shyly.

"What's your name?" I ask, and he finally rips his eyes away from Rose to meet mine.

"Mekhi," he says after clearing his throat, and holds out his hand. I shake it, doing my best to instill the fear of the gods in him with my grip alone.

"Well, Mekhi," I say, releasing his hand. "Look at my daughter like that again, and I'll rip your dick out through your throat."

Rose squeaks from behind me, Bennett gives a satisfied grunt, and Mekhi's eyes widen in fear. Good. He should be scared. No one gets to ogle Rose like that, no one.

"My apologies," Mekhi says, bowing his head, though the smirk on his stupid face belies his amends. "It won't happen again."

"See that it doesn't," I say, before turning to Bennett. "Got it?"

Bennett nods and pulls the dainty necklace from his pocket. Mekhi's brows furrow in confusion as he takes in the gold chain.

"Is there something wrong with the necklace?" Mekhi approaches, and I step in front of him again, forcing him back.

"No," I say. "But I need the dagger you traded this for. I'll give you gold instead."

Mekhi's eyes nearly bug out of his head at the mention of gold, and I can see the wheels turning in his mind. He's trying to figure out how much he can get for the dagger, and if it's worth more than the necklace. Muscles cord his fit frame, though he's just on this side of thin, as though he works hard but doesn't have enough food to fill his belly.

A man I hadn't noticed before steps out from the shadows of the stall, and I tense. His long dark hair hangs down his back in loose curls. His eyes are the same hazel as Mekhi's, and they narrow at the sight of us. He'd be handsome if he didn't look so … mean. His weathered face has deep craters from a scowl.

"What's going on here?" the man asks, and Mekhi immediately flinches.

"Nothing, Uncle Blain," Mekhi says quickly. "Just doing a bit of business."

The man's eyes land on me, and his lip curls. "You messin' with my boy here?" he hisses, and I raise a brow in question.

"Do I know you?" I ask, and the man steps forward.

He's not nearly as tall as I am, and his pot belly is at odds with his thin arms and legs. His fists are clenched at his sides, and hatred fuels his glare.

"You will," he says, and I have to resist the urge to roll my eyes.

Humans are so dramatic.

"I don't think so," I say, and the man's face turns red with anger.

"You will," he repeats, and magic swirls in his eyes. He's about to do something, and I don't want to create a scene.

"Bennett," I say, and he steps forward when I turn to him. "Take Rose to the bakery at the entrance to the market."

Bennett doesn't hesitate to take Rose's hand. I give her a reassuring smile before turning back to the man. Mekhi watches the two of them leave with an unreadable expression on his face. I could read his mind, though I haven't because I don't want to hear his thoughts about Rose. She might be an adult physiologically, but she's still a relatively young fae. We all dote on her, including Maeve, Annabelle, and Pippa, but there's something about not having Lana there to guide her that lends her a certain vulnerability.

"Mekhi and I were just discussing daggers. I'd like to buy one from him," I placate.

The man's eyes narrow, and he steps closer. I can feel the magic swirling around him, and I know I'm in for it. I don't think I'll be able to avoid a confrontation with this hothead.

"The boy ain't got no daggers for sale." He spits.

"I think he does," I say, and Mekhi flinches. "And I'm willing to pay a fair price for it."

The man whips his head to his nephew. "You trying to sell my dagger?!" He makes to strike Mekhi, but my hand on his wrist stops him.

"I'm not trying to sell your dagger," Mekhi says quickly, cowering away from his uncle. He turns towards me. "Sorry, sir, no daggers here."

When the shock of my hand stopping his blow wears off, the man whips around to face me. "How dare you touch me!" spittle flies out of his mouth as he roars, and I shrug.

"You were about to hit your nephew," I say, picking at a loose string on my shirt. "I couldn't let you do that."

"He's my business, not yours," the man says, as madness consumes him. His inky aura is insidious, like smoke curling and infecting everything it touches.

"I'm making it my business," I manage to say calmly, despite the rage simmering just under my skin. "You don't seem to be in your right mind. I think it would be best if you left."

"I ain't going nowhere," the witch says. He's preparing to do something, and I need to stop him before he hurts Mekhi or anyone else in the market.

"I'll leave," Mekhi says quickly, and he grabs his things before darting out from behind the stall. His uncle snatches onto his arm before yanking him back.

"You ain't going nowhere, boy," he growls, and Mekhi flinches.

"Let him go," I level him with my glare, and the man's face turns an angry shade of red.

"This ain't none of your concern," he snaps. "This is between me and my nephew."

"The boy is barely of age, and from the looks of it, you're not in your right mind," I say. "I think it would be best if you let him go."

"And what are you going to do if I don't?" the man challenges, malice in his voice.

I don't take my eyes off him as I pull on the elements around me. Faint moons hang on the horizon, getting ready to make their ascent in the sky. I call on their power, and the man's eyes widen when he feels the magic crackling around me and witnesses the glow of my skin.

"I suggest you let him go," I say, and the man's face pales. He quickly releases Mekhi, who darts away from him. "Now, I suggest you leave before I do something we'll both regret."

Blain doesn't need to be told twice. He grabs his things and quickly leaves the market. I watch him go before turning to Mekhi. He's standing there, ashen, and shaking like a leaf, his bright yellow aura mottled, poisoned with so much of his uncles', like ink trying to bleed into crisp, unmarred fabric.

"Are you alright?" I ask, and he just trembles.

"Yes, sir," he says, though fear darkens his features. "I'm afraid you only made it worse for me."

"What do you mean?"

"My uncle will be back, and he'll be angrier than ever." Mekhi sighs. "I appreciate what you did, but I think it would be best if you left."

"You're of age. Why do you let him treat you like this?"

"It's complicated," Mekhi says, pain etched on his face.

"Uncomplicate it. I can't help you if you don't tell me what's going on."

Mekhi takes a deep breath and starts to speak. "My uncle is the head of our coven on Earth. He's a powerful witch, one of the most powerful on Maui, and he doesn't take kindly to anyone challenging his authority. When my parents died, he became my guardian, and he's been abusing me ever since. He doesn't think I'm good enough to be a witch, so he uses me as his personal servant. I do everything for him, and he treats me like shit."

His story almost makes me regret the scolding I gave him for eyeing Rose. *Almost.*

"Were you born in Bedlam? Or Earth?" I ask.

"Earth," Mekhi says, and I bob my head in understanding. "My parents were killed on the road to Hana when I was five, and my uncle took me in. I got my Ebbswick key just before the last Bedlam Moon, and we came here so I can attend one of the universities, though I haven't received my invitation yet."

"Why don't you just leave?" I raise a brow. "You're of age. You don't need his permission."

"It's not that simple." Mekhi lets out a frustrated sigh. He casts a nervous glance behind me, eyes darting to each face in the crowd and his voice is just above a broken whisper. "My uncle has a hold over me. He's been using dark magic to control me. I can't leave him, no matter how much I want to."

"I see," I say, and I temper the anger bubbling under the surface of my skin, threatening to burst free. No one should have that much control over another person. "Do you want to leave?"

"More than anything," Mekhi says, desperation in his eyes. "But I can't."

"I'll see what I can do," I say, and hope blooms on his face. "But I can't make any promises."

"Thank you, sir," Mekhi bows his head.

"Don't thank me yet. I'm going to need that dagger back," I say, and Mekhi quickly retrieves it from a hidden comportment behind the table before handing it back to me. I pull more than a years' worth of gold from my pocket and press it into his hand.

Palming the blade, I turn and walk away, my mind racing with possibilities. I've got to help the kid, but I can't let the crowd know who I am. I'll have to come up with a plan, and fast, because his uncle isn't likely to stay away long.

CHAPTER 9

FINN

That night, we enter the merchant encampment along the outer banks of the larger island, my heart pounding in my chest. I'm not sure what I'm going to find, but I know I need to try. This might be our only chance to save Mekhi.

The first thing I notice is the smell. It's better than near the shops; it's an odd mix of sweat, dirt, and blood, and it makes my stomach churn. I hear the sound of metal against metal and see several men sparring in a makeshift arena. Others are gathered around a fire, eating and talking.

I scan the crowd for a sign of Mekhi, but I don't see him anywhere. We should've brought Teresa, and she could've sniffed him out with her werewolf's nose. My heart sinks as I realize that he might be in even more danger than I thought. I start to make my way through the crowd when someone grabs my arm from behind.

"Who are you? No customers allowed back here," the man demands, his amber eyes narrowed. "And what do you want?"

"I'm looking for Mekhi." I yank my arm out of his grip. "Keep your hands off me."

"Mekhi?" The man steps back. "What do you want with him?"

"I need to talk to him," I say. "It's important."

"He's not here," the man says, a protective gleam in his eye. "And even if he was, I wouldn't tell you where to find him."

"Please," I plead. "We're not going to hurt him. We just need to talk to him."

The man considers me for a moment, glancing at the twins before sighing and gesturing for us to follow him. We wind our way through the crowd until we reach a small tent on the edge of the camp. The man pushes back the flap and motions for me to enter.

I hesitantly step inside, and my heart stops when I see Mekhi lying on a cot in the corner, his face bruised and swollen. He's unconscious, and blood seeps from a gash on his forehead.

"What happened to him?" I demand, anger bubbling up inside of me.

"He tried to run away," the man says, hands curling into fists at his side. "His uncle wasn't too happy about it."

"I see," I say through gritted teeth. It takes all my self-control not to lash out at the burly man in front of me. "Does no one here have healing magic? And what about his uncle? Where is he?"

"He's gone to get some more supplies," the man says. "And we don't have any healers here. We're not that kind of camp."

Before I can make my way to the bed, Rose sinks to her knees beside Mekhi, her face pale. She places trembling hands on the wound above his brow and closes her eyes. A faint light glows from her palms, and his wounds begin to knit themselves back together.

"He'll be all right." Her voice shakes. "But he needs rest."

The man's eyes are round as saucers and his mouth gapes open. "You're—"

"You're not going to say a word," I growl, taking a step towards him. "Or else."

The man nods quickly, and I turn back to Mekhi. His color is starting to come back, and he's beginning to stir. I breathe a sigh of relief, glad that Rose could help him.

"Excuse me, sir," the man says hesitantly, and I cross my arms to face him. "But you can't leave him here for his uncle to beat on. He isn't safe."

"We're going to take him with us." It's not ideal, but I can't leave Mekhi here to be abused. I'll just have to find a way to keep him safe until we can find alternative arrangements for him. A place to live.

Far away from Rose.

"Thank you, sir," the man says, relief evident in his voice. "I can't tell you how much this means to me."

"What is he to you?" Bennett asks, curious.

"Just a boy I've looked out for since they arrived a few months back. His uncle is a cruel man, and he's not been kind to Mekhi."

The shopkeeper helps us load Mekhi into the wagon, and I give him a few gold coins to help cover the cost of Mekhi's escape.

"Thank you, sir," he says again, bowing his head. "I wish you luck on your journey."

"Thank you," I reply. "And thank you for keeping an eye on the kid."

We procured the wagon to divert any potential tailing, but it quickly proves to be a problem. It's not built for off-roading, and more than once we have to stop and adjust the wheels. Once we're out of the city proper, I'll be able to remove the dark magic binding him to his uncle, and then we can sift with no one seeing us.

We'll need to decide how trustworthy this kid is. That'll determine if he comes with us or if we'll need to get him set up somewhere safe; whether that's on Sundahlia, Rexuna, or one of the other continents.

I glance at Rose, who is sitting next to Mekhi in the back of the wagon. She's holding his hand and murmuring softly to him, and I can see the bond already forming between them.

"He's going to be all right." I meet her gaze. "I promise."

She nods, and determination hardens her eyes.

Here we go.

CHAPTER 10

FINN

Mekhi wakes soon after we reach a small crop of paduyi trees; their fragrance known to induce giggling and happiness if a gust of wind blows enough of its pollen your way. Tiny fae-flies help pollinate them, but they're mostly a coastal tree.

The young man is groggy and confused at first, but Rose is the first face he sees, which quickly puts him at ease.

"You've got healing magic?" he croaks out, disbelief evident in his voice.

"Yes." Rose shifts on her feet. "You probably have healing magic, too." She directs her attention towards me. "Right? I thought all witches could heal."

"Most can," I say. "But not all. And it's not as strong as what the fae have."

He makes to sit up, and pain lances his features. "My uncle—"

"He's not going to hurt you anymore," I say, my voice firm. "I promise."

Mekhi nods, and relief has his shoulders slumping. He's quiet for a moment before he speaks again. "Thank you for rescuing me."

"You're welcome," I glance at the sun. "We're short on time because we're looking for the twins' dad, and it won't be long before your uncle realizes you've left. We'll have to move fast."

I help him to his feet. For an Earth-dweller, he's tall. Maybe six foot two inches. The kids fit just under his armpit now, but it won't be long before they surpass his height.

"Wait—" Mekhi pauses. "Aren't you their dad?"

"One of them, yeah." I give him a half-smile.

He blinks, and then his face breaks into a dimpled grin. "That's cool."

I face him. "My soul bonded mate—"

Rose interrupts me. "My mom has lots of mates, just like I'm going to—"

"The hell you are!" Bennett, Mekhi, and I shout at the same time.

I whip my head towards the little witch. "You get no say in whom she mates!"

Who does this kid think he is? He doesn't even know Rose, and he's been in her orbit all but two seconds. Maybe I'd ought to sift him to monitor the Caspari, at least close enough to scare him, perhaps while they consume the garbage near Bedlam Penitentiary. They're more vicious there. Anywhere far, far away from her.

Scowling, I stop us in our tracks and pull him just off the path, ready to tell him exactly how I feel about his intentions with Rose. A light breeze picks up, rustling the trees and causing the paduyi pollen to drift our way. A giggle escapes my lips before I can stop it, and Mekhi's face breaks into a grin. No doubt he's had his fair share of run-ins with these trees during his stint in the Cerulean Isles.

"What's so funny?" Bennett frowns.

"You are," I say, still chuckling. "Let's get this enchantment removed from Mekhi and we'll sift back to camp."

After attempting to remove the dark magic several times, my laughter impeding our success, I sift our small group somewhere safe —and away from these damned trees. Mekhi startles when he realizes where we are, and I can't help but smirk.

"What is this place? I've never sifted before." he asks, his voice laced with wonder.

"The continent of Rexuna."

We manage to find a pocket of peace near my property on the mountain. Here, there are no other fae, no witches, and no pollen-bearing trees. At least none with the same reaction as the paduyi.

While we walk along a trail leading to the top of Rift Pass, Mekhi keeps migrating towards Rose, the two stealing glances at each other. I even caught him brushing a stray curl off her face and the little pecker looked like he was going to lean in and whisper in her ear, or maybe steal a kiss, before I inserted myself between them.

Mekhi settles on a large rock, looking out over the Sea of Triune. Far in the distance, a ship with three giant masts is visible, making its way towards the islands south of here. I wonder how many new adventures await those on board, and what kind of trouble they'll find themselves in.

"It's so beautiful," Mekhi says, interrupting my reverie.

"Yeah, it is." I sit down next to him, our shoulders brushing. "I come here sometimes when I need to think."

"What do you think about?" he asks.

I shrug. "Lots of things. Life, love, the future."

He's quiet for a moment, and then he speaks. "I used to think that my future was set in stone. That I would be a witch like my mom and my uncle, and that I would never amount to much more than that. But now..." He trails off, his eyes distant.

"Now what?" I prompt.

He looks at me, and there's a determination in his gaze that wasn't there before. "Now I know that anything is possible. That I can be more than just a witch."

"I think you're right," I say. And I mean it.

Even if I want to shove him in a hole full of vermini every time he glances at Rose. Violent, crimson creatures, they'll strip a man to his very bones in seconds. Seems a fitting punishment for thinking he has a chance with my daughter.

Sure, fae are overly protective of their young, but that's after hundreds of years of dwindling birth rates, kidnappings, and rumors of changelings popping up every so often. Fae royals have even more to worry about. Luna fae, in particular.

"So," he says, breaking the comfortable silence that has fallen between us. "What do we do now?"

"Now," I stand and offer him a hand. "We break the spell."

CHAPTER 11

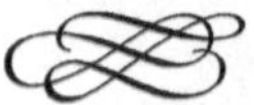

LANA

Coming to, I take a few minutes to remember what happened. My fae sight has a difficult time seeing in the dark, and the air has a metallic tang to it. I make to sit up, but can't control my limbs, and a fog clouds my mind. The back of my head and neck ache something fierce.

"Hello?" I demand of the darkness, my voice raspy and uncontrolled.

The sound of metal clanging against stone startles me, though I don't flinch. I can't seem to do anything. A light flickers to life in the distance, and a figure comes into view.

It's hazy, and as it gets closer, I make out a bare-chested man. Jeans rest low on his hips, and his smooth feet remind me of my kings'. My vision trails up his naked torso and across his strained arm to where he holds a thick metal chain. Attached to the end is a manacle of sorts. In it, my wrist dangles lifelessly. It catches me by surprise, though it takes a moment to register I'm locked up.

He stops in front of me, and I finally get a good look at his face. He's incredibly handsome, with high cheekbones, full lips, and bright green eyes. There's a rugged look to his face—crinkles line the corners of his eyes when he scrutinizes me, and stubble covers a square jaw.

His dark brown hair is shaggy and falls into his face in a way that makes my fingers itch to push it back if I could just move them. The color reminds me of French roast coffee, before I add tons of sugar and cream to it.

"Please," I croak. What am I asking for? I hardly recall.

He says nothing, only watches me with an unreadable expression.

My captivity comes back to me, and I urge my muscles to move. "Help me," I plead. "I won't hurt you."

He finally speaks, his voice like gravel. "I know."

Then he bends down and unlocks the manacle around my wrist. I fall forward, unable to catch myself. My cheek slams against the rough stone, and I cry out in pain. A snarl cuts through the air.

My eyes widen at the source of the noise. From my vantage point on the floor, I spy a giant vampire chained to the wall. He's huge for an Earth-dweller, maybe 6ft 5 inches, with muscles that bulge and ripple under his tanned skin. His eyes are black as night, not a single sliver of his irises show, and the light glints off deadly fangs. He looks feral, like an animal that's been caged and is ready to kill anything that comes near.

And he's looking at me like I'm his next meal.

I squint, trying to place where I know him from. My mind works to fit the pieces together, but fog clouds my thoughts, and I shutter my eyes for a moment before opening them again.

He pulls against his chains, desperate to reach me. The metal digs into his wrists, drawing blood, though he doesn't seem to notice the pain. All he cares about is getting to me.

The man in front of me steps between us, blocking my view. "You need to feed him again."

Again?

I try to summon my magic, but it's just out of reach. Something has a hold on me, paralyzing me completely. The only thing I can do is watch as the man unhooks the vampire's chain from the wall, using it as a leash as they both stalk forward.

Fear turns my blood to ice, and I can do nothing but scream as the vampire sinks his teeth into my neck…

CHAPTER 12

LANA

My eyes fly open as I wake gasping for air, my heart pounding hard in my chest. It feels like the vampire is still feeding from me, draining my blood. But I'm alone in the darkness. My mind swims, heavy with some kind of drug. It zaps my strength, clouds my thoughts, and gives me a strange sense of euphoria. Like maybe I could get used to this place if only I tried a little harder. Perhaps this place isn't as bad as I first thought.

The manacle around my wrist is gone, though I can still feel the weight of it. I'm not healing like I normally do. My head aches something fierce, and my neck feels wet. When I bring my hand up to check, it comes away slick with sticky blood. I try to summon my magic again, but it evades me. I'm still paralyzed and at the mercy of whoever holds me captive.

Light blinks to life in the distance, chasing the shadows, and the man from before comes into view. He carries a large, silver bucket, and the sound of sloshing liquid fills the air.

He stops in front of me and sets the bucket down with a thud. The noise carries in the large stone room. His hard eyes survey me before he stoops down and begins undressing me. I shriek and try to move away, but I can't move. He doesn't say a word as he strips me down to nothing.

Cool air hits my skin, and I start to shiver. The man reaches into the bucket and pulls out a cloth. Draping the damp fabric over my head, I attempt to scream, but it only comes out as a stifled whimper.

The man ties the cloth around my head, making it tighter and tighter. He retreats, and I relax against my restraints, relieved at his departure. I can't hear as well, nor can I use my magic to sense the presence of others in this building.

But then the water starts. It drips slowly at first, and then it comes faster and harder. The cloth soaks up the water and presses it against my face. It seeps through the fabric and into my nose and mouth. With clenched teeth, a scream claws its way out of my throat, but it's quickly muffled by the water.

I try to hold my breath, but it's impossible. My lungs burn for air, and eventually I give in and inhale. Water fills my lungs, and I gasp and choke. Panic consumes me, and I thrash against my restraints.

The water doesn't stop. It keeps coming, relentlessly flooding my lungs. I start to see spots in my vision, and my body goes limp. There's a ringing in my ears, and then everything goes black.

A crack of a whip awakens me, and I sputter, water purging from my lungs. I try to raise my hand to shield my eyes from the sudden light, but I can't move. My body is on fire. It feels like my skin is being peeled away. I scream, but it comes out as a sob, my flayed remains in scraps.

The man walks into my line of sight, and I spot the whip in his hand. Blood stains the leather, and I know it's mine. He lifts the whip again, and I flinch. But the blow never comes. Instead, he drops the flog and walks away.

I lay there, whimpering and in pain, until I finally drift off into oblivion.

Agony rips me from my sleep. It splits me in two while the man wrings out the bloody rag before dragging it against the bite marks on my neck, against the tattered remains of my skin. I hiss in pain, but he continues. Blinking his face into focus, I try to place my captor—again

—but I don't recognize this man. Why me? What did I do? He's methodical in his movements, as if he's done this before. Once he's finished cleaning my wounds, he reaches into the bucket and takes the rag to the rest of my skin.

"Who are you?" I croak. My throat aches, raw from screaming and from the water.

He pauses, smug satisfaction etched into the arch of his brow, a smirk framing his lips. For a moment, I think he's going to answer. But then he simply goes back to cleaning me.

"What do you want with me?" I cry when he moves over another bite mark on the inside of my thigh.

Again, he doesn't answer. For the first time, I notice the smell of something metallic, but not like blood. I shift my head to get a feel for it; a collar weighs heavy on my neckline. The sensation of it exhausts me; a sinister, slinking feeling emanating from it and working its way through my limbs. He finishes cleaning me off, dresses me, and steps back. He drinks me in for a long moment before turning and walking away.

I'm left alone in the darkness, shivering and confused. I have no idea what's going on, or why I've been taken captive. But I know one thing for sure.

I'm getting out of here alive.

CHAPTER 13

FINN

After breaking the dark magic infecting Mekhi, I sift us to camp. We stand just outside the wards where I work to remove our glamours. The witch startles at seeing our true forms, equal parts fear and awe.

He can't take his wretched eyes off Rose. Not until I release a feral growl, baring my teeth. That finally seems to snap him out of it, and he meets my gaze with fear.

"What the—?"

"You," I say, my voice low and deadly, "aren't to even consider courting her. She's not dating until she's at least five hundred, maybe six hundred years old."

He opens his mouth to protest, but I continue speaking over him.

"You will not speak to her, look at her, or even think about her. If you do, we're going to have a problem." My threat hangs in the air between us, and alarm etches his features.

"I'm telling Dad!" Rose pouts. "My other dads," she adds, and I whip towards her. I glamour her with the image of an old, decrepit witch.

"Oh, please, do!" I say, my voice dripping with sarcasm. "Please tell the King of Vampires, the Right Hand of the King of Vampires, and the scary, brooding vampire royal all about it. I'm sure they'll be thrilled to know that their precious daughter has caught the interest of a boy."

"What's wrong with that?" She stomps like a petulant child, proving my point entirely.

"What's wrong with that?" I echo, my voice rising. "What's wrong with that, you ask? I'll tell you what's wrong with that. He's a male, Rose!"

"Would you rather he be female?" she counters.

"No, I would rather he be nothing!" I roar. "I would rather he be a figment of your imagination!"

Satisfaction stirs in my chest when I glance at Bennett and see the same look of horror on his face that I'm sure is on mine.

"Finn, calm down," Roses says, her voice gentle. "You're scaring Mekhi."

"Good." I take a deep breath and count to ten before replying. I cross my arms over my chest, power radiating off me, when Oz and Auguste step into the clearing just on this side of the wards.

"What's going on?" Oz asks, doing a double-take at the glamour I have Rose in.

"This is the witch they traded the necklace with, and he'll be joining our camp. He has taken an interest in our daughter," I say, my voice tight.

"Oh?" Oz raises an eyebrow before a wicked, calculated gleam settles in his eyes. "Interesting."

He steps forward and smacks Mekhi upside the head. "You will not speak to her, look at her, or even think about her. If you do, we're going to have a problem."

Bennett cackles. "You guys practiced this, didn't you?"

"Shut up, Bennett," we both say in unison.

Fear paralyzes Mekhi for a moment before he nods his head frantically. He stands ramrod straight, eyes trained straight in front of him.

Auguste sighs but doesn't say anything as he steps forward and takes Mekhi by the arm. "Come on, I'll get you settled." He glances towards me. "On the opposite end of camp. Hundreds of tents away from Rose's."

As they walk away, I hear Mekhi mutter, "What did I do to deserve this?" The faint humor in his voice makes me suspect he might not heed our warning for long. The boy is already too far gone.

"You looked at Rose," Bennett and I say in unison once again.

We share a look before bursting into laughter. It feels good to laugh, even if it is at the expense of the poor boy who dares to think we'll let him court my daughter when she's barely out of maturity. Most of it is an idle threat, of course, but the kid doesn't need to know that.

"I think we might have gone a little too far," I say, once our laughter has died down.

"Nah." Bennett crosses his arms. "If anything, we didn't go far enough."

CHAPTER 14

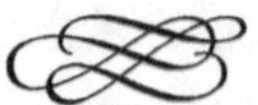

LANA

My captor stalks into the room, this time with a tray of food. He lowers himself to the bed and hooks his arms under my knees, lifting me up so I'm in his lap. I try to squirm away, but he holds me firm. Each movement against my raw wounds stains the dressings a deeper shade of crimson.

"You need to eat," he says gruffly.

I shake my head and turn my face away. I'm not going to make this easy for him, because it's probably poisoned.

He sighs and sets the tray down on the bed. He picks up a piece of bread and brings it to his mouth. "Fine, then you can go hungry." He takes a bite of the bread, and I watch in horror as he chews and swallows. If it's poisoned, he's going to die, and though I hate this man for what he's done to me, the thought of anyone dying unsettles me. My mind wars with itself, knowing how irrational it's being. Why would he poison himself?

But he doesn't. He simply sets the bread back down on the tray and looks at me. "Last chance."

First, he beats me, and now he's feeding me. It's a headfuck of epic proportions, and it loosens something feral in my chest. The need to eat, fight, and then maim.

When I don't show any outward signs of refusal, he brings it to my lips. I open, tentatively, and take a bite of the bread, chewing slowly. It's dry and tasteless, but I'm so hungry I don't care. I eat everything on the tray, including the water he gives me to drink, wincing at the ache the act causes to my sore throat.

When I'm finished, he sets the tray aside and looks at me. "Feel better?"

Trembles wrack my body from the agony, but I nod, and he slides me off his lap onto the bed. He stands and walks away, leaving me alone in the darkness once again.

If he were going to kill me, he wouldn't be feeding me. So why does he keep letting the vampire drink from me? And why is the vampire still feral, though he feeds from me morning and night? What does he want with me?

Since my captor moved me to this new room, I keep time by the sun out the window. He must know I'm Luna fae, though, because he places steel shutters over the glass, completely blocking me in at night. I tug on my mating bonds, but nothing responds. It's as though everything's been smothered; my magic, my bonds, my energy. The echoes of their presence are here, but I can't seem to make use of anything.

I've seen no sign of anyone else, other than the vampire, held here. My jailer isn't human—this much I know—but what he is? I can't place it. He doesn't seem to have any control over the vampire, other than the use of chains, which keeps me alive, I presume.

For now, I bide my time and wait for an opportunity to escape.

I know it will come.

And when it does, I'll be ready.

CHAPTER 15

LANA

"Where are your kings?" my torturer shouts, but I can barely hear him over the gurgling of the freezing water pouring over my face, into my mouth and nose, and into my lungs.

He wrenches me up by my hair, the sting of it ripping a liquid-filled scream from my throat. I reach for my magic, but it remains buried, forever evading my commands.

"I'll never—"

Crack.

A cry tears from my chest, the sting of his flog driving it out of me with force. Minutes, hours, or days, how much time passes, I don't know. My life revolves around his demands to know where my mates are, my refusal, and his subsequent torture. When waterboarding didn't work, he starts shoving my head into a bucket of water, trying to drown me. Still, I don't cave.

Fury lines his features today, but a crack behind his façade gives me a glimpse of the man underneath. He tires of brutalizing me. As time wears on, he's more open to my questions, though he doesn't answer them.

Until today.

Leaving me in my blood-soaked clothes, he stalks towards my door. I put as much bravado into my words I can muster. He terrifies me. "W-w-wait!" I panic. "If you won't tell me who you are, will you tell me who the vampire is?"

The cruel man meets my eyes and stills before a whisper of a smirk pulls at the corner of his lips. "They say he's the best tracker of any vampire in history. Powerful, too. He's an old one."

A memory prickles at the back of my mind. "I've seen him before," I breathe.

The recollection feels right, though I can't say why. I could've sworn this was the vampire I killed in the makeshift throne room when the vampires infiltrated the bunker just after my crowning.

Could this really be him?

The man quirks an eyebrow. "Yeah?"

I shake my head; the sensation dizzying me. "No. Maybe. I don't know. Do you ... do you know his name?"

"They call him Gideon." My captor's voice is void of emotion, but something in his eyes tells me he's not as indifferent to the vampire as he wants me to believe.

"It is him." I whisper, my voice a mixture of wonder and relief.

I didn't kill a man.

I.

Didn't.

Kill.

Anyone.

My respite is short-lived when the man moves closer, towering over me with a menacing look in his eyes. "Time for Gideon to feed," he growls.

I try to scoot away, but my sluggish limbs fail me. He grabs me by the ankles and drags me towards the door. My skin burns where it catches on the floor, and I scream and fight, but it does me no good. He's too strong.

He hoists me over his shoulder and carries me down the dark hallway to the derelict room where Gideon is kept. The vampire is chained to the wall, his head hung low. He lifts it when we enter, and his black eyes find mine.

A hunger like I've never seen before flickering to life in their depths.

The man dumps me unceremoniously on the freezing stone floor and steps back. Gideon lunges forward, his chains clinking with the movement. When he reaches me, he sinks his teeth into my neck.

I cry out in pain, acid burning in my veins, but he doesn't let go. He drinks and drinks, until I'm sure he's taken too much. My vision blurs and my head spins, before pleasure takes over. I fight to stay conscious, but it's no use.

The last thing I see before I pass out is the captor, leaning against the wall with his arms crossed, watching us with a satisfied smirk on his face.

CHAPTER 16

CASIMIR

My sword strikes the vampire in front of me, my fae speed far superior to his. I press my weapon down, feeling the vertebrae of the creature snap under the weight. Their life-force pools at my feet, soaking into the sodden ground of wildflowers and prairie grass.

A group of vampires across from me cast brief glances at each other before taking off towards where I stand on the battlefield. I shift into my wolf form as I leap towards them; a mess of snarls, claws, and teeth tearing into their flesh.

Their blood pours into my mouth as I rip out their throats, serving as adrenaline to my primal nature, the metallic scent blanketing my senses. A roar sounds from the skies, shaking the earth under my feet, and I don't have to look to know Penn has shifted into his dragon.

I shout a command into the minds of all the fae in the area. The vampires look around in confusion as the fae stop fighting and rush to other shifters. In a blink, the shifters sift every fae away from the area.

We watch from the outskirts as Penn banks before opening his giant maw and releases a plume of fire, the heat reaching where I stand, gaping. No matter how many times I see him in his order form,

I'm just as awe-struck as the first time I witnessed the power and beauty of his beast. He flies over the vampires, torching them all in one fell swoop. Screams punctuate the sound of sizzling skin.

None escape.

Pierce sifts onto the field just in front of me, eyes wide. "Your Highness," he says, breathless, "Lana is missing."

"What do you mean, missing?" Grimm barks, and my stomach plummets.

"She's gone," Pierce replies. "I went to bring her to Academia like you asked. I fortified a house nearby Bedlam Academy and when I sifted to the lighthouse to get her, she wasn't there."

Penn and I share a look, panic seizing the air from my lungs. We never should've left her.

"Did the vampires take her?" Grimm levels his eyes at Pierce, whose jaw clenches as though he's frustrated.

"We don't know." Pierce shifts on his feet. "She's just gone."

"You don't think she snuck off with Bellamy, do you?" The thought alone poisons my mind. We took her memories, but she's a smart woman, and knows Bellamy was keeping our secrets. It's not too far-fetched to think she might've gone to him for answers, especially after what Finn revealed in our bunker throne room.

Pierce averts his eyes. His little brother nearly sabotaged things for us. "I checked with Bellamy first. He's still stationed at the penitentiary."

Grimm curses and the thrum of magic swirls around him; a sure sign he's about to do something reckless. Penn's enormous presence descends on us, and just before he touches the ground, he shifts into his fae form.

"Penn," I grit out, "I'm going to try to find her. You stay here and help the troops line up the bodies."

He steps back, gripping his hair, even though I know he wants to go with me. He knows I'm better at tracking than anyone, thanks to my wolf's nose. I leave them with a battalion of fae and sift back to the lighthouse home where she's supposed to have been hiding out.

CHAPTER 17

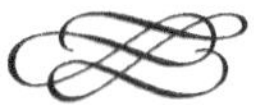

LANA

"**W**ill you tell me why you're keeping me? Why you need to keep feeding Gideon?"

I keep my eyes trained to the terrifying man as he makes his way across the room. Trying to talk to him is like trying to speak to a vicious dog, though I sense his resolve weakening. Bags darken his eyes, and his beard is scratchy, like he's spread too thin, choosing between whatever it is he does all day—when he's not torturing me— and sleep.

"Vampires." He glances my way. "When they feed from fae, it weakens them."

My stomach drops. "Why do you need me weak?"

I know the answer—it's obvious, but if I can keep him talking, get him to let down his guard a little ... maybe I can find a way out.

"So that you don't use your magic. I need both the collar and vampire saliva to keep you subdued. Who knew a high queen was so powerful?"

"What's your end game? What do you need from me? I'll help you, just let me go." *And stop torturing me.* My conscience tugs at me to think about the vampire, too, but I ignore it. If Finn is telling the truth, and Gideon is one of my mates, then why does he keep feeding on me? Granted, it doesn't hurt in the moment ... just at the beginning when lava floods my veins, and then pleasure and bliss take over. Sometimes, I pass out from it, and it hurts later. Likely because I can't use magic to heal my wounds.

Each time he's made to feed from me, I take some measure of comfort knowing I'm not alone. It's a fucked-up thought, especially considering he's taking from me, but when euphoria kicks in, my fear drifts away. It's just him and me, like a practiced dance meant to keep the monsters at bay.

"I was waiting for you to ask." He approaches the bed. "I need you to draw your kings here so I can steal their throne."

My mind wars with itself. This is what I need, right? For my kings to know where I am so they can rescue me. It's clearly a setup, though.

"I can't let you hurt them." I bite out. I'd rather face a thousand lashings, a million drownings before betraying their location or drawing them into a trap, even if it turns out they have betrayed me.

He shrugs. "Sooner or later," his eyes meet mine, "I will."

Drawing moisture from the back of my throat, I gather it with my tongue and launch a ball of spit at him. It lands on his cheek, though it isn't much on account of how weak I am.

He brings his hand to his five o'clock shadow, two fingers poised to wipe it off before he pauses. A shadow flickers behind his green eyes, and a decision is made in that moment. He slams me down on the bed with the full weight of his body before he slides an iron grip around my throat. Squeezing, he brings his face next to mine. So close, I feel the stirring of his warm breath on my ear, the pulse at the base of his neck.

"Lick it off." He squeezes tighter, my chin forced higher.

I desperately claw to get him to release me, but I can barely lift my limbs, let alone fight off a two-hundred-thirty-pound man made of muscle and sinew. My airway constricts, and I hold out as long as I can before my survival instinct kicks in.

Wincing, I draw my tongue up the side of his cheek, collecting my spit. If I could breathe, I'd gag.

He gives one final squeeze before releasing me. I draw air into my lungs, sputtering coughs in-between. I hurl insults at him and try to push him off me but he just chuckles.

His hand slides into the nape of my hair and he holds tight, forcing my head back so I look him in the eyes. Hate simmers in his steely gaze, belying the press of his erection against where he's settled between my thighs.

"I'll slit your throat and fuck your corpse in front of your whole kingdom if you ever disrespect me like that again." He punctuates his point by bucking his hips against me once. Twice. Three times for good measure, before pushing off me and stalking out of the room.

* * *

WHEN HE RETURNS in the morning, I can't meet his eyes. Instead, I keep them focused on a point across the room, a symbol I hadn't noticed before. Etched in the stone mantel above the fireplace is a wolf tearing into a round object I can't make out, its surface too worn.

Thoughts whirl in my head, spinning out of control. My breath catches when realization dawns on me. "You're a werewolf."

His spine stiffens, and I'm not sure what to think until he glances over his shoulder at me. A grin splits his face, and he winks. My heart thunders in my chest.

The sight is startling, dazzling, until he speaks. "Not as dumb as I thought you were, then."

"Why do you need the kings?" I attempt to summon my magic, but it alludes me still. "As high queen, I'm more powerful. I can give you whatever it is you need."

"When you're not being fed on from a vampire, that is." He approaches the bed with a stack of clothes.

I attempt to slide down the pajama bottoms so he doesn't have to, but I can't lift my arms. His heated gaze rakes over me as he undresses me, and shame invades my psyche, flaming my cheeks.

He's taken to putting me in clothes that are much easier to clean, seeing how I feed Gideon every morning and night, and he no longer whips me. He's moved onto hurting someone next door. I hear her screams at night, the crack of a whip, the gurgling of water.

It pains me, but not enough to give up my kings. This man knows this because he's stopped hurting me. Last night, he said I have twenty-four hours to tell him where they are before he begins to torture Gideon in front of me. Despite them both being monsters, only one of them hurts me consciously at the moment, and I can't have the vampire tortured for it. The person in the other room is just a random person whose face I can't name, but for weeks, Gideon and I have been locked in here together.

It's clear my captor is attracted to me from the way his greedy eyes take me in, despite his reservations about who, and what, I am. His lingering touch tells me as much.

Maybe I can use this to my advantage.

A plan formulates in my head, though the idea of it sends waves of nausea through me. Though attractive, his cruelty makes him hideous. "I want to help you." I still his calloused hand where he has my pants halfway up my thighs. *I won't let you hurt anyone else on my account.*

His suspicious eyes flick to mine for a moment, the look on his face melting to pure fire. I think of Casimir, and his need for touch. How it festers and has him nearly crawling out of his skin to be next to me. To feel the warmth of my hand on his bare chest. For my affection.

My voice drops an octave. "I want to feel you." I arch my back as much as I can, feigning hunger and desire. "Don't you want that, too?"

He swallows, his Adam's apple bobbing. So much passes behind his eyes. Desperation. Craving. Fury.

I fix my attention to where his erection strains against his jeans. "You want relief, don't you?" I wet my lips with my tongue, drawing his gaze. "I can give you that."

Come here, little wolfy, let me bite it off.

His chest heaves before he huffs a laugh. "Is that how you became high queen? Fucked your way through their castles?" Eyes narrowing, he continues. "You can't even move, and I'm not about to stop Gideon feeding on you. You're doing this to gain your powers back. I may be young compared to most of this realm, but I didn't get in my position by giving into a hot piece of ass, no matter how much you writhe and mewl."

Shit, I'm losing him. I roll my head side to side. "Tie me up if you have to. Your king doesn't have to know."

He arches a brow, chin drawing his features askew. "My king?"

"Your werewolf king."

He blinks, and a laugh barrels out of him. The room quiets, just the sound of our heaving chests filling the space between us. He's deep in thought before he speaks. "I'm going to fuck you." He shrugs. "Might even make it good for you, and in exchange, I won't torture your little pet." He glances at Gideon, now straining against his chains, the metal clattering against stone. "But in thirty days' time, you must tell me where they are."

My lips part; my mind whirring. *Thirty days* … and no one gets tortured. I can come up with a plan in that span of time to get us out of here unscathed. "Tell me your name?"

He positions himself next to me on the bed, entertaining my query. "Why?"

"So I know what I'm screaming when you fuck me."

The side of his mouth ticks up into a half-grin, and his eyes go hooded again. "Luka."

"Luka," I purr, rolling the name around on my tongue, trying it on for size. "Fetch Gideon to feed on me. It'll weaken me, and you can even tie me up when he's done so you know I won't hurt you while you use my body for your release."

The idea of letting this man have his way with me might've excited me in a very Stockholm syndrome way, in another time, another life, provided he hadn't spent the last however many weeks torturing me. But my mates have my heart, my soul. The idea of allowing someone who's inflicted so much pain and abuse on me to have his way with me makes me recoil inside. But I need to build trust, even if it means breaking the trust I have with my mates.

Our lives and the fate of the entire realm rely on it.

I sense the moment Luka resolves. He rises to his feet, not bothering to finish dressing me. A chill pebbles my skin, and I'm about to psyche myself out when he returns with Gideon in tow—in record time.

The vampire lunges for me, sinking his teeth into the first piece of flesh he can reach; my thigh tissue. He snarls and tears at my skin, a desperate need to pull the blood from my vein but it doesn't come fast enough. My face scrunches under the molten metal pouring into me, but my forehead softens when the pain gives way to pleasure.

Luka leans his shoulder against the stone wall, eyes intent on me, so much emotion passing on features, though I can't pluck any of them for inspection. Firelight from the hearth flickers across his face. As Gideon's feeding turns even more pleasurable, a soft moan parts my lips. Heat pools low in my belly. *There are worse places to be*, I decide.

I manage to bring my hand up to Gideon's head, my fingers threading through his silky hair. A low growl emits when I tighten my hold, and he snarls when I break the seal he had on my thigh. He lunges for my neck, a searing hot stab of pain causes tears to prick my eyes before ecstasy blankets me.

I meet Luka's heated gaze as my lips part on a sigh. Instead of drawing Gideon away, I pull him closer, pressing him flush to me. His hands tighten around my shoulders, claws digging into my skin, but he allows the contact. My gaze flicks to the vampire nestled between my thighs when his erection grows against my stomach. His pupils take up the entire space of his eyes, a feral predator with one—maybe two—goals in mind. He's been shredded to his baser instincts, and like many men, it's to eat and fuck. Go figure.

The pleasure he rings from my neck intensifies as the seam of his jeans rubs right where I need it most. I'm about to come apart beneath him when Luka rips Gideon off me, snarling, and hauls him from the room.

Luka storms back in the room minutes later with a length of chain I recognize from my first few days here. Each end has a manacle on it. He stalks towards the bed, impatience evident on his face.

"Do you still want this?" He grits out.

Why he's asking permission confounds me. He had no hesitation beating me, drowning me, dragging sobs from my body. "Yes," I breathe.

Lie, lie, lie.

His nostrils flare, and I avert my eyes. "I can smell your arousal from here," his voice rumbles.

Heat flames my cheeks. While Luka is a beautiful specimen of a man, though cruel, he doesn't do it for me. Gideon, though? I wince. I'll need to scrub my mind of the sight of his teeth sinking into my thigh once I'm out of here. Despite his feral nature, it's not easy to ignore his beauty. It's practically obscene.

Luka approaches the bed, positioning himself between my thighs. In two clicks, I'm tethered to the wall behind my head. He gives a small tug on the chain before settling back on his heels.

"This changes nothing." He narrows his eyes.

"I just need you to fuck me, Luka." I sigh. "I'm used to spending my days and nights spit roasted between my mates. It aches." I writhe under him.

Lie, lie, lie. Well, not about the part about being sandwiched between my mates at all hours. *That* part is true.

He flicks the button on his jeans before lowering his zipper. His cock springs free, full and thick. The end curves up, and shame rides parallel to revulsion swirling inside me. I pull my lips between my teeth in an attempt to keep a terrified whimper from escaping me.

Luka slides his jeans off before kicking them to the floor. His muscular thighs have a thick dusting of dark hair, and he keeps everything else neatly trimmed. I adjust my wrists to ease the ache where the metal touches my skin. A claw elongates on Luka's index finger, which he uses to slice through my shirt and bra. He makes quick work of the straps and sleeves, leaving both in scraps on the bed. They're not mine, so I don't protest.

His hands blaze a trail of heat up my chest, savoring the moment, and taking stock of the way my body reacts to his. He cups my breast, running his thumb across my pert nipple before leaning in to flick it with his tongue.

My eyelids flutter closed, and I turn my thoughts to Casimir. Their mannerisms are so closely related, he's the easiest to disassociate with in my head. So tactile. An exhale escapes me when his grip closes around my ankle. He tosses it over his shoulder, opening me up further.

"Look at me," he growls.

My eyes fly open, and I watch as he licks the full length of his fingers. His blown-out pupils bore into mine before my attention flits to where he uses that same hand to pump his cock.

I keep my eyes cast but look up when he just seems to keep stroking himself far longer than he needs to. The moment I meet his intent stare, he drives into me with the full force of a wrecking ball. Air rushes out of my lungs, and I screw my eyes shut.

Casimir.

Penn.

Grimm.

They're the ones fucking me. I sink deeper into my head until I'm able to open my eyes and see my mates in Luka's face. Relief meets pleasure with every piston of his hips.

When his lips crash to mine, I grant him entrance. Our tongues dual, as much as they can when I'm so weak, and he groans. He tugs my bottom lip between his teeth, sucking before pulling back.

He fucks me against the mattress with such force, I don't have the strength to keep us rooted into place. Luka takes notice of the strain on my wrists before wrenching me back into position and holding me there.

"Tell me you want this," he grits out as he flicks his hips up at the end of each thrust.

"I want this," I moan. I don't add my mate's names at the end of that sentence, although that's who I imagine above me right now.

He fucks like a man starved, and I'm his oasis and buffet in the middle of a desert. The pressure builds inside me, and when he presses his thumb against my clit, I pretend to fall apart beneath him. The act alone feels like a betrayal to the men I love, and I derive no pleasure from this.

My insides feel impossibly full the longer he remains between my thighs. I feel stuffed, just on this side of pain.

"Luka?" I furrow my brows, but he's lost and on the verge of finding his own relief.

He sits back on his heels and brings me into his lap before moving my other ankle over his shoulder. His arms wrap around the tops of my thighs as he drives into me.

Luka's breath comes in quick, short bursts. He grunts before spilling inside me, the warmth flooding every inch of my walls. Stilling, he releases my legs, causing them to fall open on either side of him.

He collapses against me, spent. We stay like this for what feels like minutes before I clear my throat.

"Luka?" How the hell is he still hard?

He grunts.

"Are you going to clean me up, or ..."

"Can't."

"What do you mean, you can't?" I force nervous laughter, though dread and shame nearly strangle me.

"Stuck."

"The fuck you mean, stuck?" I adjust my hips under him and feel a tug inside me. Alarm spreads through my body.

He gives me a low, warning growl. "Werewolves ... knot."

I shriek. "Get it out!"

An amused chuckle rumbles against my chest. "Give it time, it'll release."

"How fucking long?!"

He shrugs. "Don't ever know. A few minutes. An hour? My wolf will release you when he's ready, and you'll stay put until he does. Got it?"

Angry heat crawls up my neck and into my cheeks. "Why the hell didn't you say anything before?!"

"Women love it." He bucks his hips against me, making sure his pubic bone rubs my clit.

"That doesn't explain why you didn't say anything beforehand."

"I figured you knew, which is why I kept asking if you were sure about this."

"You asked once," I glower at him, and my face falls when he presses his thumb against my little bundle of nerves. For someone so hellbent on hurting me, he sure is spending a lot of time trying to pleasure me. His movements circle at my apex, and I shutter my eyes, pretending Casimir is with me.

"Come apart for me," he whispers. "Again."

His words yank me out of my fantasy, and I hide my grimace. I focus on faking it, doing Kegels to help my ruse, and this seems to satisfy him.

Inside, Luka deflates enough to slip out of me. I look between us and see a bulbous end on his penis. Curiosity keeps my attention on it far longer than is appropriate, so I wrench my stare to the wall. *I'm officially freaked the fuck out.*

He says nothing as he unlocks my wrists. Nor when he scoops his things up and leaves the room.

Okay then.

The moment he leaves, tears flood my cheeks. The weight of what I had to do, what I'll continue to have to do to gain his trust, is a burden riddled with guilt and shame.

Forgive me.

Luka doesn't come back to my room until nighttime. By then, I'm starving. I don't say anything to him about it, choosing instead to act as though I don't care. He doesn't bring me anything to eat, and I fight the urge to beg him for food.

I know he's doing this to weaken me, both physically and mentally. But I won't give him the satisfaction of breaking me.

If there's one thing I am, it's strong.

And I'll need to be if I'm going to escape.

CHAPTER 18

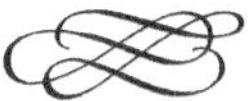

LANA

It's been two months since Gideon first fed from me. The cuts on my neck have long since healed, but the scars remain. A constant reminder of Luka's power over me, and my inability to heal, all because a vampire keeps feeding from me.

I've managed to glean a few bits of information from Luka, using lust to weaken the barrier he carefully erects between us after he spills his seed inside me every morning and night. He's waiting for the vampires to kill off a lot of the fae before making his next move.

The idea churns my insides. I must get out of here before that happens.

But first, I need to find a way to break through to Gideon. If I can keep him from feeding on me, I can get my strength back. And then, together, we can stop the werewolves.

When Luka leads Gideon into the room, I'm propped against the headboard with pillows, wearing nothing but a thin slip of silk. My hair is loose around my shoulders, and my skin is flushed with heat.

Luka's eyes darken when he sees me, but he doesn't say anything. He just stands there, staring at me like I'm a piece of meat.

"Come here," I purr, patting the bed beside me.

He hesitates for a moment before finally crossing the room with

Gideon in tow. He stops at the foot of the bed and looks at me questioningly.

"Tie him up," I say, motioning to Gideon.

Luka does as I ask, binding Gideon's wrists and ankles to the bedposts with thick ropes. The vampire growls low in his throat and tries to reach me but can't.

Once Gideon is securely restrained, Luka moves to stand next to me. I run my hand up his chest, feeling the hard muscles there. "Let me," I whisper, tugging on his shirt. I've spent the last several weeks slowly whittling down Gideon's feedings, so I have gained some strength back but no magic yet.

He doesn't resist as I pull it over his head and toss it aside. My hands explore his body, mapping out every smooth plane. Luka reaches for my manacles that hang near Gideon, but I shake my head.

"Please," I beg. "I want to feel you."

He shudders under my touch, and I can see him warring between giving in and sticking to what he's supposed to do. I won't attack today. It's too risky. Instead, I'll slowly build his trust while I work on getting Gideon on this side of humanity.

Luka steps back. Dammit.

Unhooking Gideon from the wall, he brings him within reach and Gideon pounces, knocking the air out of me. I stretch under him, the feel of his teeth in my neck like a drug I can't quit.

Through the haze, Luka speaks. "Let him feed, then you can feel me."

I sling my leg around the backside of Gideon, bringing him closer until we're flush together. My hand twines through his shorn hair. A low growl sounds against my throat, and when I use my heel to press him against me, he rumbles again.

"Gideon?" My voice is barely audible, a tiny whisper against his ear only he can hear. His breathing quickens.

Gripping his nape in my hand, I whisper his name again while pulling. I scream when he snarls. Luka hauls Gideon off me and drags him out of the room, and I school my features when he returns.

"Sorry, he was hurting me," I lie.

He comes to sit next to me and runs his fingers over the bitemarks. I wince and relax into his touch when he presses his lips to them. My hands roam over his shoulders, moaning as he buries his head against my neck.

"I like touching you," I lie again.

Luka pulls my slip over my head before peeling out of his sweatpants. He sinks into me on a sigh, and I cling to his shoulders while he shifts me into his lap. Sweat slicks our bodies, providing the perfect glide for skin against skin.

When he finishes and his knot releases me, he keeps me in his arms. I'm riddled with anxiety, desperate to get away from this monster, but I remain locked in his embrace. I want to claw his face, blast him with magic, and scrub my skin of him until I bleed. Instead, hours pass before he leaves the room. I'm left reeling from his extreme behavior. First, he tortures me. And now, he cuddles me? He's a mind fuck of epic proportions.

I've got to get out of here before I lose it, too.

CHAPTER 19

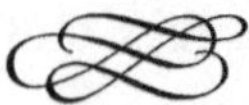

LANA

The first inclination I have of there being more than just Luka, Gideon, the women next door, and myself here is a shout in the distance. A shrill voice, high and panicked. Movement under the door startles me.

I tense, waiting for Luka to come into the room, but he doesn't. After a minute or so, I hear an eerie slide of metal on metal and then all is quiet again.

Light footsteps outside the room make me go still. Whoever it is, they're coming this way. The sound of a key in the lock and then the door swings open.

A petite woman with long, dark hair enters. She can't be more than nineteen, maybe twenty. Her eyes are wide and fearful as she looks around, taking in Gideon chained to the wall opposite me and me sitting against the headboard of my bed. This morning, Luka kept Gideon chained here because he had to hurry off somewhere.

"Who are you?" I demand.

"I'm Luka's sister, Katarina," she says, still looking around the room as if she expects someone to jump out at her.

"What are you doing here?" I ask. "Where's Luka?"

"He's gone to check on some things," she says, her eyes finally landing on me. "He left me here to keep watch."

Katarina looks scared and lost, and I can't help but feel bad for her.

"Why don't you come sit down?" I say, patting the bed beside me. "Was that you who screamed?"

She hesitates for a moment before finally crossing the room. She stops at the foot of the bed and looks at me questioningly.

"Yes, I saw something outside," she whispers, her eyes darting to the door as if she expects someone to come barging in at any moment.

"What did you see?" I ask, trying to keep my voice gentle. Paranoia and fear have my eyes pinned to an obscured corner of the room.

"I don't know," she says, shaking her head. "It was just a shadow."

I reach out and take her hand, giving it a reassuring squeeze. "It's okay," I say. "You're safe here with me." Although I have no magic yet, I have some of my strength back. Not enough to stand, but enough to adjust my pillows and flip through a book. She doesn't have to know otherwise.

Katarina nods and finally sits down on the bed. We sit in silence for a moment before she speaks again.

"Luka told me what you are," she says quietly. "Who you are."

"And what do you think?" I ask.

She shrugs. "I don't know," she says. "It's a lot to take in."

I nod, understanding how she feels. It's a lot to take in for me, too. High queen of the fae, and already failing miserably.

We sit in comfortable silence, lost in our own thoughts, until the door bursts open and Luka comes barging into the room.

"What the hell are you doing here?" he growls at Katarina.

She jumps to her feet, her eyes wide with fear. "I-I came to check on her," she stammers. "I was worried."

"I told you to stay put," Luka says, his voice low and dangerous. "You're not supposed to be here."

"Luka, it's okay," I say, trying to diffuse the situation. "She didn't do anything wrong."

"No, she didn't," he agrees, his eyes never leaving his sister. "But she's not supposed to be here."

"I'm sorry," Katarina whispers, her eyes downcast. "I won't come back."

"See that you don't," Luka says, his voice hard. He waits until she's left the room before turning to me. "What did she say to you?"

"Nothing much." I fidget with a thread on the blanket. "Just that she was worried about a shadow she saw outside."

"Did she say anything else?" he asks.

I shake my head. "No, nothing else."

Luka looks like he doesn't believe me, but he doesn't press the issue. "Get some rest," he says. "I'll—"

"Are you alright?" I interrupt him. He's been gone all day, and he's distracted.

He furrows his brows. "What do you mean?"

"You seem different," I say. "You're acting different."

"I'm fine," he says, the sound gruff. "Just get some rest."

He turns to leave the room, but I call out to him before he can go. "Luka," my voice is barely a whisper. "Come to me tonight?"

He doesn't say anything, but I see the muscle in his jaw tick before he gives a curt nod and leaves the room, locking the door behind him.

I sit in silence for a moment, contemplating what Katarina had said about a shadow she saw. It's possible she saw the same thing I see in the dark recesses of the room; a mottled figure, lurking in the shadows. I've seen her before, though she's more ethereal right now than the time I saw her in the woods after Aed killed himself.

She's here, but not. Watching and waiting.

But for what?

I'm not sure, but I have a feeling that whatever it is, it's not going to be good.

Relief floods my body when the form disappears. I shift my attention, fixating on Gideon, trying to see if I can spark recognition. Under his feral form, does he know who I am right now? Is this someone *I* recognize from an earlier life? Looks-wise, he's absolutely my type. I caught a whisper of dimples when he snarled at me earlier, and a strong jawline like his belongs on the cover of a magazine.

If he ever gains his humanity back, he'd at least make a formidable opponent in combat.

Gideon stops tugging on his chains, as though he can sense my thoughts, and I let out a relieved breath. I shouldn't feel bad for him—he's my enemy, after all—but it's hard not to. Especially when I know that it's my blood making him this way.

"I'm sorry," I say, even though I know he can't understand me. At least I don't think he can. "I'm sorry this is happening to you, Gideon."

For a moment, he just stares at me, his eyes dark with hunger. Something flickers in his gaze, softening his features momentarily, but then it's gone, replaced by the feral look once more.

He lunges at me, teeth bared, and I flinch back. His chains don't let him reach me from where he's tethered across the room, but it's still startling.

"I'm sorry," I say again, even though I know it won't do any good. "You don't deserve this ... and I'm glad you didn't die."

But Gideon doesn't hear me.

He's lost in the bloodlust, consumed by it. And I can only hope that someday, he'll be free of it. That we'll both be free.

I wait long past the time Luka typically has Gideon feed from me. Normally, he's in soon after he closes the steel shutters, but I've read a good ten chapters already. If this continues, maybe I can get through to Gideon, and I won't have to sleep with Luka to get him to soften his guard.

It's a double-edged sword; I need him to stop feeding on me so we can escape, but he needs blood to survive. Even if the blood makes him feral.

I'm not sure what to do.

Gideon's chains rattle as he paces back and forth, gaze pinned to me. He's hungry, I can see it in the wild look of his eyes, but he's also fighting it. He lets out a low growl, and I flinch, scooting back on the bed.

"It's okay," I say, even though I'm not sure if it is. "You're hungry, but I'm going to need you to hold off as much as you can because I have a plan to get us both out of here."

He gives little indication he understands or even hears me, though he stops pacing and sits on the floor, chains clanking as he does. He rests his head on his knees and closes his eyes, and I know he's fighting the hunger.

It must be so hard for him, always being on the edge of starvation, but he's holding on.

And for that, I'm grateful.

My voice is barely audible when I speak, knowing he can hear me with his vampire hearing. "Finn tells me you're my mate. If this is true, I'd love to hear how you and the others managed to send your mate to an entirely different realm, unprotected."

Gideon snarls at me, baring his teeth.

"Right," I say, scooting back further on the bed. "Guess that's a no, then."

I'm not sure what to do or say to him, so I just keep talking, hoping something will reach him.

"I know you're in there, Gideon. I can see it in your eyes, sometimes. Please, come back to me. We can figure this out together." But he just continues to sit there, silent and brooding. And I can only hope that someday he'll find his way back to me.

The lock on the door clicks, and I tense, heart racing.

Luka steps into the room, a satisfied smirk on his face. "I see you're still alive." He comes to stand next to the bed.

"For now," I mutter, throwing the blankets open. He watches my movements carefully, studying them. I tilt my head in expectation.

He quirks a brow at me. "It's time for Gideon to feed."

Before he can walk away, I loop a finger through his belt loop on his jeans. "One more thing."

He pauses, glancing down at my hand before meeting my gaze. "What is it?"

I tug him closer to me and pull his face to mine. "Trust me," I whisper, before kissing him.

He kisses me back eagerly, and I can taste mint on his tongue.

I pull away, heart pounding in my chest as I meet his gaze. "Please. I need you right now."

Luka nods, understanding what I'm asking, and I register the conflict in his eyes. He doesn't want to give in, but he will.

Plopping onto the bed next to me, I curl into his side, my head resting on his chest. His heart beats steadily under my ear, and I close my eyes, breathing in his woodsy scent.

He strokes my hair gently, and I fight the urge to cry. I need Casimir. Penn. Grimm. The line between what's real and what isn't blurs more and more every day, and I'm not sure how much longer I can hold on.

Please find me soon. Before it's too late.

Luka's fingers still in my hair, and I can feel the sting of tears on my lashes. I blink them away and take a deep breath, steeling myself for what's to come.

Gideon will feed, and I'll lose my magic. And a part of myself. The same parts of myself I lose when I take another man to bed who isn't one of my mates.

But it's worth it if it means we can escape.

And maybe, just maybe, I can find my way back to the people I love.

Luka makes to sit up, but I run my fingers over his stomach, stopping him. *Break down his walls.*

"What are you doing?" he asks, voice laced with confusion.

"I want to see your wolf," I say, before I can lose my nerve. "I want to see the part of you that's wild and free."

He hesitates for a moment before nodding. I sit up and scoot back, giving him space. How can he turn when it isn't a full moon ... or is it? I don't know how long I've been here.

Luka takes a deep breath and closes his eyes, his frame tense. I watch as his body contorts and morphs, dark fur sprouting from his skin as he grows larger and larger.

In a matter of seconds, a massive black wolf sits in front of me, silver eyes studying me intently. I reach out slowly, hand shaking, and stroke my fingers over his soft fur. He leans into my touch, and I can feel the rumble of a growl in his chest.

"You're beautiful," I whisper, before he shifts back into human form.

Luka looks at me, and I can see the surprise in his eyes. "Thank you," he says, voice rough, nostrils flaring, pupils widening.

I run my hands over his skin, exploring the planes and valleys of his muscles. *Build trust. Get him to let his guard down*, I coach myself in my head.

He hasn't said anything about my new strength, though he watches with careful eyes as I move.

"What are you thinking?" I ask when the silence between us stretches on for too long.

He glances at me, and conflict furrows his brows. "I'm thinking that I want to trust you," he says, finally. *Yes.* "But I'm not sure if I can." *No.*

"I understand," I say, though it pains me to hear the doubt in his voice. "We can take it one day at a time. I need you now, and you can have Gideon feed on me when we finish. Is that alright?"

He nods, and relief is clear in his features. "Thank you," he whispers, before kissing me.

I close my eyes and lean into him, letting myself get lost in the moment. If only for a little while. *Casimir. Casimir. Casimir.*

Luka braces himself over me, and I can feel his heartbeat against my chest. He pulls my sundress off over my head, and the cool air sends goosebumps across my skin.

A growl sounds from Gideon across the room, causing Luka to pause a moment, turn around to grin, and return to kissing me. He leans down, pressing a path from my jaw to my neck, and I arch into him, as if eagerly searching for his lips.

Gideon's low growl turns into a snarl, and I can feel his eyes on us.

"He's not happy," Luka says, amusement clear in his voice.

"I don't care," I whisper, running my fingers over his back. "I want this."

Lie, lie, lie.

"Are you sure?" He asks, pulling back to look at me.

I nod, and he kisses me again, deeper this time. My head swims as his tongue invades my mouth, tasting, teasing. He shimmies out of his jeans, never leaving contact with my lips. Luka slides his hand up my thigh, and I manage to force a hint of a smile against my lips.

"Yes," I moan, wrapping my legs around his waist.

He slides inside me in one smooth thrust, and I gasp, clinging to him. *Pretend it's Casimir.* My sweet, cuddly lupine mate is what I need. This is what will help me get through another day. He starts to move, each thrust harder and faster than the last, and I meet him stroke for stroke, pretending to be desperate for more.

Gideon's snarls turn into near-roars, and he throws himself against the stone wall, but we pay him no mind.

I pretend that Luka tips me over the edge first, that pleasure washes over me in waves as I scream out his name. He follows shortly after with a grunt, the feeling of his knot making it difficult for me to breathe—I'm stuffed.

We lie here together, Luka chuckling, and me wincing with every snarled protest from the vampire.

"I'm so tired," I whisper. "Bathe me right after he feeds, then come sleep with me?" I can't take another moment of this. I must break down any remaining barriers this man has against trusting me.

Luka stills. "You're a prisoner, Lana." It's the first I remember hearing him say my name. "I'm not sleeping with you."

"But you can fuck me." I don't mask the hurt in my voice. Instead, I weaponize it, hurtling it with the force at which his words struck me.

We both cry out when I shove him, his knot not quite small enough yet. I use the pain to fuel my anger. This will set us back weeks, but I just can't with him. Each day, I die a little more inside.

"Get. The. Fuck. Out." I punctuate each word, emphasizing my fury.

He's pissed, too. I imagine that hurt him just as much as it hurt me. He stalks across the room, naked as the day he was born, and yanks Gideon's chains off the wall where they're hooked. Tossing them so they're loose and the vampire can get to me without restriction, Luka stomps out of the room and throws the lock just as fast as the vampire tears after me.

I'm still completely nude, but that doesn't stop a feral monster. He pounces, and I bring my hands up just in time to stop him.

"Gideon!" I scold.

When he meets my eyes, stunned, I catch a small outline of the deepest of blue irises nearly swallowed whole by the pupil.

"Gideon," I gentle my voice. "It's me, Lana."

Holding my hands between us, his chest heaves under my trembling touch, tight-laced restraint evident in the way his muscles bunch.

"Am I your mate?" I ask.

His nostrils flare before he glances at my naked form under him. He snarls at Luka's seed seeping out of me. I flinch when he rips the comforter off the bed and places it between my thighs, as though he's trying to clean me up. Breath heaving, he sits on his haunches, palms face up on his thighs. He rests his chin on his chest and is quiet for several minutes. Blood drips on the duvet below him, a drop at a time.

"Where are you bleeding?" I reach out to him and my hand stills when he meets my gaze.

I stare into the prettiest set of blue eyes and tracking below them are bloody tears. He buries his head in his hands, sobs wracking his entire body.

Inexplicable grief opens a cavern in my chest, and I'm overcome with the urge to ease his pain, so I do. I wrap my arms around him, pulling his head into my lap. Leaning down, I whisper encouraging words into his ear. "We'll get out of here," and "I won't let you starve."

The faint stirring of magic under my skin startles me, but my mission to soothe this vampire overrides my excitement. Sliding my hand through his hair, I rest my fingers against his scalp, trickling the little bit of magic I have to ease his pain.

Gideon stiffens, whipping his head to the door. He tackles me onto my back and plasters his face against my neck, his lips resting against my pulse as soon as the door swings open. Luka strides in, freshly showered, looking all kinds of pissed off.

"The blood sucker stays in here to make room for new arrivals. You'll be his little blood bag for however long it takes. If you die, you die." He sets a pitcher of water on the end table and tosses an apple onto the bed next to me. Luka crosses to the bathroom and unlocks it, entering to clear it of anything sharp.

"You don't care if I die?" I make my voice breathy, knowing he expects Gideon's bite to bring me pleasure.

An unreadable expression crosses his face, but he schools it. "No," he grits out.

Fury courses through my veins, but I keep my expression pained. "Fine," I choke out.

He inclines his head towards the bathroom. "If he takes too much, you can always section yourself off in there. Provided you're strong enough to make it to the door."

"I'll miss you," I lie, earning me a snarl from Gideon.

Pain flashes on Luka's face before he turns on his heel and storms out. When the lock clicks, Gideon rolls off me and sits on the edge of the bed. My gaze drops to the crushing grip he has on the mattress.

I reach a tentative hand out before settling it on his shoulder. His rigid posture relaxes a touch.

"Are you ... okay?" I'm not sure what I expected him to do when Luka left, but this wasn't it.

He nods, still not looking at me, and rises to his feet. Pacing to the door, he presses his ear against it before returning to stand in front of me.

"He's gone," Gideon says gruffly. Pure malice reigns in his eyes. "I'll kill him. Then I'll move onto your kings next."

I pull the sheets over me, and it's my turn to snarl. "You touch my kings and I'll flay you where you stand!"

His face softens. "I'm sorry," he croaks. Gideon sinks to his knees, running his hands through his silky, knife-shorn hair. I fight the urge to reach out to him, to indulge in the feel of it between my fingers. When he raises his gaze to meet mine, heartache etches his perfect features. "You chose me, once."

A tear tracks down my cheek. Where it came from, I don't know. "W-what do you mean?"

His eyes glaze over, and his thoughts seem far away. He doesn't answer my question. "I spent so much time trying to prove my love for you. I still am." Gideon's voice breaks. He rises to his feet and closes the space between us, cupping my face in his hands. "I'm so sorry, Lana." He presses his forehead to mine and closes his eyes. "Please, forgive me."

"For kidnapping me?" I whisper. My voice barely registers, it's so quiet. I hold my breath for his response.

He shakes his head and chokes out a pained laugh. His eyes meet mine, and they temper. "You have a family. An entire army fighting to bring you back to Earth." He makes a wild gesture towards the shuttered window.

I search his gaze, looking for any sign that he's lying. There's none. "A family?" A stab of pain grips my chest, and the burn of tears presses behind my eyelids before spilling over their threshold.

Family.

He nods, his thumbs brushing over my cheeks where tears have left tracks.

"You're a mother, my Striga." Gideon's voice is gentle, his words a reverent whisper. "You have children. *Our* children."

I gasp, my hands fisting in the sheets. "What did you say?" Goosebumps line my skin.

"We have twins." He tilts my chin up. "And they're here, in Bedlam."

Gideon's words hit me like a tsunami. Like releasing the chord on a parachute, I'm yanked so far beyond anything I can comprehend, whiplash sending me into a state of shock. Children? Twins? *Our children?* I can't wrap my head around it.

A sob catches in my throat. He gathers me in his arms and rocks me gently.

"It's okay," he murmurs. "I'm here. I've got you."

And for the first time in what feels like forever, in this moment, I believe him.

I'm lost in my thoughts for several long minutes, running through every possible explanation as to why my kings might've lied to me—*if* what Gideon says is true. No one could be so cruel as to keep a mother from her children.

"The children ... are they safe?" I ask Gideon. We've yet to sleep tonight because I have so many questions and too few answers.

He nods, his expression solemn. "They are."

"And my ... family?" I can hardly bring myself to say the word out loud. It feels foreign on my tongue. Sure, my kings are my family, but I usually refer to them as my mates. They're such a huge part of me, it's exterritorial to label them outside of those carefully constructed confines. It's deep, whereas family is wide. They're so much more than that.

"As much as they can be." Gideon's lips press into a thin line. He pauses, the sound of the faucet dripping in the bathroom fills the space between us. "Most are fighting in the war."

A war.

Right. I'm the high queen of the fae, and there's a war going on between my people and the vampires. And allegedly, my children are here, in the middle of it. Unease stirs within me. I shutter my eyes and take a deep breath. When I open them again, Gideon is watching me intently.

"What?" I ask before turning my attention to a loose thread on the sheets.

"You're taking this far better than I expected," he admits. "I thought you would be ... out for blood, ready to exact revenge against the kings." He freezes with a preternatural stillness when comprehension dawns on him. "You don't believe me."

I meet his gaze, afraid of what I'll find. In it is the image of a man, broken. "I don't know what to believe," I say honestly. "A large part of me doesn't want what you're saying to be true, because those truths have implications far bigger than you or me. What I do know is we need to get out of here."

He nods, his expression grim. "I know."

"What are their names?" I ask, before I can lose my nerve.

"Rose and Bennett." Gideon's voice is filled with pride. "You named Rose after Auguste's first wife. Bennett, you named after Alphie Bennett, your dad."

A lump forms in my throat, the sting of tears threatening to spill again. I blink rapidly until they disappear. "My ... dad?" Gideon takes my hand and squeezes it gently.

"Your father is a good man, Lana. He loves you very much."

"And my mom?" I can barely get the words out. I've wanted to know about my life on Earth so bad, and now that it's here—allegedly—I don't know if I can believe it. I want to, and I don't.

"You've met her," Gideon says quietly. "We had a spy go to the castle, and that's how we found out the kings held her captive this entire time. She's the royal storyteller."

My stomach drops. No. It can't be.

"Anna?" I whisper.

Gideon gives me an imperceptible nod, and pity lines his eyes. "Her actual name is Annabelle Chapman, and that's one of the reasons the kings took your memory, and one of the reasons you ended up in Bedlam. You came to seek their help because she disappeared when you were eight years old."

The world tilts on its axis, and I grasp Gideon's arms to steady myself. This can't be true. My mom is *the royal storyteller*?

But even as I have the thought, memories surface. Memories of a kind woman with a haunted expression, always telling stories at the various banquets the kings put on. Stories of a woman who tried tricking the kings but didn't know they could read minds. *She was telling her own story.*

And now I know why she always looked so sad. Her soul knew what her mind couldn't comprehend or remember.

"It's okay," Gideon murmurs, pulling me into his embrace. "Finn, the twins, and Teresa rescued her as soon as we got to Bedlam. She's with your father now."

I take a shaky breath, trying to process everything Gideon has told me. If it's all true, then my entire life here has been a lie. But if it is all true, then I have a family who loves me and wants me back. I met Finn in the throne room, but the other name evades me.

"Who is Teresa?" I ask.

"She's a ..." Gideon grimaces. "Werewolf. The twins rescued her, and she's like a big sister to them now." He pauses, swallowing. "She's also related to your ex-fiancé."

"Fiancé?" I close my eyes and lean against Gideon. I can't deal with any more bombshells tonight. I need time to process all of this and figure out what our next move is.

"We'll talk about it in the morning," Gideon says, as though he can read my mind. "For now, try to get some sleep. I'll keep watch."

I nod and burrow into Gideon's side, trying to block out the sound of the werewolf howling in the distance. His arms tighten around me, and I feel safe for the first time in weeks.

Right now, I must believe Gideon. Whether or not he's telling me the truth, we're on the same side right now. I need all the allies I can get. I'll sort out what's true, and what isn't, later.

* * *

I WAKE to the weight of Gideon's body to my front and the press of his lips to my pulse just before the door swings open. My lids flutter, and I turn my gaze towards where Luka stands in the doorway with a tray of food, water, and a change of clothes for me. Jeans sit low on his hips, and his bare chest has remnants of moisture from a very recent shower. His wet hair hangs in his eyes before he does a very lupine-like shake of his head to get it out of his face.

I try to push away from the vampire, but he only tightens his grip, snarling. "Luka," I say, my voice coming out in a breathy whisper. "How kind of you to drop in."

The werewolf's eyes flick to Gideon, and he smirks. "I see you've been busy, pet."

Gideon growls but doesn't look towards the door. We've got to keep Luka from finding out he hasn't been drinking from me.

"He's been feeding most of the night." I scowl. "Thank you for the food, I'm starving."

My captor shrugs and sets the tray down on the table next to the bed. His spine stiffens when he's bent near me, and his nostrils flare.

His head whips to me, fear races through my body, and I hold my breath.

Shit, does he know Gideon isn't feral anymore?

I attempt to school my features. Luka's eyes dart between mine, and his breathing is heavy. I can nearly see the wheels spinning in his head.

"You need more food." He starts to turn away, but I call out to him.

"Luka?"

"Yeah?" He pauses, resting his shoulder against the frame. While it takes up a lot of space, he's not quite as big as my mates.

"You said there are new people next door. Who are they?"

Luka shrugs again. "Some fae who thought they could overthrow our kind. They'll be dealt with soon enough."

The door slams shut, and I look at the side of Gideon's face. "He's going to kill them."

Gideon nods, his expression grim. "I know. We need to get you out of here."

"We," I remind him. "We're in this together."

He hesitates for a moment before he nods. "Yes. We are."

CHAPTER 20

CASIMIR

"What do you mean, she's been kidnapped?" I jump to my feet. "Who took her?"

Anastasia, Penn's cousin, is a dragon shifter. They're larger than most orders of fae, but that's not why they're nearly impossible to capture. Dragons can melt any number of elements thanks to their obsession with treasure and their fire-breathing abilities. You can't handcuff them, nor can you keep them in a cell. They'll just melt the bars or cuffs.

The only way to keep a dragon captive is if they want to be.

Unless ...

"We're not sure," Pierce hesitates. "It's possible the vampires have figured out that biting a fae can incapacitate them."

I shake my head, but a startling sense of foreboding settles in my chest. If the vampires have found a way to subdue fae, then they're a lot more powerful than I realized.

"It will also turn a vampire feral," I argue, though I know it's a weak argument. The vampires have always been volatile, and they're not above using whatever means necessary to get what they want.

Pierce clears his throat before reaching into his pocket to pull out a folded-up cloth. He uncovers its contents, and I curse.

"Don't let that penetrate your skin!" I shout as I back away from the crushed vial and syringe.

If even a drop of vampire saliva, or its blood, hits your bloodstream, it will burn like acid before euphoria takes over. Then, your magic disappears, and you weaken to the point you can hardly lift your limbs. It can last days.

"There's another thing," Pierce says gravely. "The vampires have been seen with a fae. Someone other than Finn."

"What?" I growl. "A fae wouldn't align themselves with vampires!"

Pierce worries his lip. "I know. But we have a witness who saw them together. They couldn't get a good look at the fae, but they were able to describe the vampire. Oz and this fae were spotted sailing to Sundahlia."

"Oz?" I echo, staggered.

We severely underestimated the vampire's ability to adapt and strategize if they've not only found a way to subdue fae, but they've also managed to convince one of our own to join them. What does he want on Sundahlia when most of the fighting takes place on Convectus?

"What do you want me to do?" Pierce asks, his voice tight.

"Find out who the fae is," I say darkly. "And kill them. I need to tell Penn and Grimm."

Spying Lana's necklace on the dresser, I grasp it in my palm. *Where are you?* A whine escapes me.

"We're going to find her." Pierce places his hand on my shoulder. "We'll find them all, and then we'll kill these vampires."

Pierce sifts out of the room, and I brace myself against the wall, head in the crook of my elbow. My mind races as I try to come up with a plan, but it's difficult to think straight when all I can see is Lana's haunted face when she found out she killed the vampire. It's all I think about.

I pull out my cell and dial Grimm. He answers on the first ring.

"What is it?" he growls.

"It's Anastasia," I say, my grip tight on the phone. "She's been kidnapped."

"What?" he shouts. "How?"

I quickly fill him in on what Pierce told me, and his curse is loud in my ear.

"We're going to find her," he says gruffly. "I'll call Penn and meet you at Anastasia's place."

He hangs up, and I pocket my phone before sifting out. I arrive at Anastasia's house to find Grimm and Penn waiting for me in her front yard. Giant sculptures made of gold adorn the front lawn, their façades polished to a high shine.

"Any news?" Penn asks, his expression hopeful.

I shake my head. "Not yet. But we will find her."

Grimm cups the back of his neck. "We have to."

It goes without saying that dragons are one of the most resourceful orders of fae. While they don't have any more magic than most orders, their ability to pull elements from the land means unlimited financial resources. If the vampires have found a way to subdue them, then we're in a lot of trouble.

Penn places his hand on the magic sensor next to the silver door handle, granting him access to her house. He turns the knob, and we file in. Deep gouges mar the marble floor, and char marks scorch the obsidian walls. Piles of treasure sit on most surfaces, so it doesn't appear they came for her hoard.

"What the hell happened in here?" Grimm mutters as he looks around.

I shake my head, not entirely sure what's—

"Do you smell that?" Penn asks as he strides into the living room, nostrils flaring.

I follow close behind him, and breathe in the coppery scent of blood, and the acrid smell of something burnt. Buried beneath it is the unmistakable scent of werewolf. Like mine, but with a hint of sour pine needles.

"The vampires are working with the werewolves," I say grimly.

I spin around, my stomach churning. There's no doubt in my mind that they took Anastasia to use as leverage against the fae. But, why?

Lana is fae now. The vampires must know this won't end well for her. The only thing the werewolves want is to destroy the fae.

Our mate and high queen included.

CHAPTER 21

LANA

I watch as Luka places the steel over the window, the striations in his muscles rippling while Gideon buries his head in my neck. A soft sigh escapes me, and I don't have to pretend the press of his lips to my skin ignites something inside me. A very manly, satisfied growl rumbles in his chest as he continues to pretend to feed, and I clench my fists to keep from stroking my fingers through his hair.

One look at Gideon's eyes, and Luka will know the vampire isn't feral anymore. I need to stall him.

"You know," I say conversationally, though it comes out breathy. "The longer you keep us here, the angrier the fae will be. You're not going to be able to keep us here forever."

A satisfied smirk tilts Luka's lips as he places a large tray of food on the bed next to me. Two sandwiches, a giant salad with croutons, and pills. It's far more food than he's ever given me. Is he planning on sharing with me? And what are the pills for?

"I don't need to. Soon, the fae will do whatever I want."

"And what is it that you want?" I ask curiously, eyes still trained on the giant, tan tablets.

"Power," he says simply as he crosses to the bathroom across the room. "We want the curse broken, so we'll have magic. We'll be the creatures everyone fears."

"Why would you want them to fear you, Luka?"

It hardly makes sense. He can be tender, and obviously has a soft spot for his sister. If he rises to power, won't that make him a target, putting her at risk?

"It's simple, really," he calls while changing out my towels in the bathroom. "If they fear me, they'll do as I say, or at least level the playing field. No one will be able to challenge my authority. My people won't need the moon to turn at will, and we'll never again have to bow to the fae."

"And what about your sister?" I ask quietly. "What will happen to her?"

Luka is silent for several moments before he appears in the doorway. "Katarina will be safe. I'll make sure of it."

"You don't have to do this." I suck in a breath when Gideon shifts against my core; his hands gripping me tight. "We can find another way. Let me speak with my mates, and we'll come to a truce of some kind."

He doesn't say anything, but the resolve in his eyes tells me he's not going to change his mind.

Luka moves to us, and I flinch when he reaches out to touch my cheek. "Darling." The accent is heavy in his voice. "What do you think the realm will do when they know their high queen has been fucking the king of the werewolves?"

Luka is the king of the werewolves? The one I've been tasked to eliminate because he's been killing my kind?

Gideon snarls, and I tug on the nape of his hair to shut him up. We can't show our hand too soon.

"They'd never believe it," I spit.

A sultry laugh escapes him. He pulls a small silver device out of his pocket. Pushing a button on it, an image projects on the floor in front of us. It's a holographic video of Luka between my thighs.

"He's not happy," Luka says, amusement clear in his voice.

"I don't care," I whisper, before running my fingers over his back. "I want this."

Rage clouds my vision. When the fuck did he film this? Is there a camera in here now?!

"Are you sure?" He pulls back to look at me.

I nod, and he kisses me.

We look like two lovers. Co-conspirators.

He peels out of his jeans, never leaving contact with my lips.

The werewolf slides his hand up my thigh, smiling against my lips.

"Yes," I moan, wrapping my legs around his waist. He slides into me, and our satisfied grunts echo off the walls.

Luka clicks the projection off. Fury makes me see red. The werewolf king pockets the device before meeting my eyes, his own bright with victory.

"Shouldn't be more than a few days before we've hacked the airwaves and broadcasted this to all of Bedlam. If your mates don't come here to kill me, they'll come to kill you." He crouches so he's at my level. "But don't worry, love, I'll destroy them before they can do that. I won't let them hurt you." Glancing at Gideon with a sneer, he continues, "Not so sure I'll need this bloodsucker much longer, either."

He threads his fingers through my hair, grabbing at the scalp to hold me in place while he presses his mouth to mine. It takes everything in my power to keep my fangs in place, lest he know Gideon hasn't really been feeding on me this entire time and that I have full use of my magic back.

Luka's tongue invades my mouth before he breaks away. "I'll make you my queen." He grins. "Especially considering you carry my heir."

What. The. Fuck?!

Gideon stiffens on top of me, a snarl roaring out of him as he shoves back and hurtles himself at Luka. The werewolf's eyes widen, and he shifts at will, but not before getting tackled by a seriously pissed off—and starved—vampire.

He sinks his teeth into Luka's neck, the werewolf still stuck between man and beast. Shock over what he just said keeps me in place, and I watch in detached panic.

I didn't think fae and werewolves could procreate.

What does this mean? Not just as high queen of the fae, having the child of a sworn enemy ... and for my relationship with my mates? Both fear and shame churn in me.

I made a huge mistake.

I barely register Luka grabbing for the chair next to his head but use my magic to send it crashing into the wall before he can use it to strike Gideon. It splinters from the force, and I scramble to grab a sharp stake from its remnants.

A shout rings from down the hall.

My head whips to the door. "Gideon, we've got to go—now!"

His furious eyes meet mine before resolution settles in them. I place my hand on his shoulder and lean into his ear.

"Let go on the count of three and I'll sift us somewhere safe."

He gives me a tentative nod and I count out loud. On two, Katarina and a group of other werewolves file into the room.

"Don't hurt her!" Luka shouts. "She's with child!"

Since Gideon has stopped feeding on me for so long, I have some of my magic back, and I know what I have to do. I haven't felt strong enough up to this moment, but I now I can feel the certainty flowing through my veins. *We can do this.* They dart for us, but not before I've built the house on Tristique Islands in my head. As soon as I latch onto Gideon, I've pulled him through the slip in space and we land in the living room of the small cottage tucked away in the clouds.

The lights are off, and there's a startling sense of rightness bringing another male into my family's home. Not just any male, but Gideon. I don't voice this revelation out loud because even acknowledging it inside my head feels like a betrayal to my kings.

The vampire spins around, taking in our surroundings and checking for any threats. I don't mention I can tell no one else is here. He needs to do this for himself. There isn't another soul on this island, nor any of the others. When he sees we're alone, he pulls me into his arms and buries his face in my hair. Involuntarily, I inhale; his scent is one I've gotten used to over the time we've been locked away together. Even when he was feral, the aroma had a calming effect on me.

"I'm so sorry," he whispers. "I should have protected you better."

Shaking my head, I put space between us.

"I'm the one who agreed to it," I say, my voice breaking. "My mates ... gods." Crossing to the other side of the room, I slide against the cold wall until I sit on the floor. This high in the sky, the air is balmy, and chilly at night. It makes my hands cold, yet damp.

A single tear falls down my cheek, and then another, melting into the fabric of my top. I can't stop them. Gideon comes to sit next to me, but he doesn't touch me. He mirrors my position, knees bent, head buried in his hands.

"I did this to get him to trust me so we could get out of there," I say, my voice a weak whisper. "I didn't know ... I didn't know he would ..."

"It's not your fault," Gideon says, his voice tight. "You had no way of knowing."

The clock on the mantel next to me ticks a steady rhythm. We sit, not speaking, for a few minutes before his resolve snaps.

"Lana, I need to get you back to Earth," he says. "It's not safe for you here."

I shake my head. "This is my home. I am high queen of the fae, and I won't run from my consequences. If—*and I mean if*—my mates did lie to me and what you're saying is true, I can't ... I can't just let you take me away. They're my mates. Bound by blood."

He swears before bolting to his feet, his pacing across the floor indicative of his frustration.

"You're queen of the vampires. Mother to Rose and Bennett. Soul bonded to Finn. Mate to Oz, Auguste, and me." His voices breaks, and I catch a hint of an Australian accent in it. It's so at odds with the slight Italian one I detected earlier. "Best friend of Hannah Mae Yeung. Daughter of Annabelle and Alphie. You're a travel blogger and you spent your honeymoon with Oz in Patagonia before sailing to Antarctica. You were born a witch in Robbinsdale, Minnesota, and had a cabin an hour from the Canadian border. That's where your mother disappeared when you were eight. You were put in foster care until an Iowa couple adopted you. *That* is your life, Lana. Not … not this." He gestures wildly, his words catching in his throat.

"You don't understand. Even if everything you're saying is true." I bury my head in my hands, sobs wracking my body. "A blood bond between fae can't be undone … not unless I want to die, because that's exactly what will happen if I sever it."

Gideon pulls me into his lap and rocks me as I cry. "You're mine, too," he whispers against my hair. "And I won't let them take you from me. Never again."

My regenerative powers feel muted, and I don't glow when I dig my nails into his shoulders. Normally, inflicting physical pain on others will help refill my magic. I suspect the collar Luka placed around my neck is the culprit. My mind stirs with worry about how we'll have it removed—Gideon has already tried sheer force, and I tried magic.

We sit there until I finally fall asleep, exhausted from everything that's happened. When I wake, I'm still cradled in the vampire's arms, but now we're in the bed. I panic, thrashing, but Gideon presses a finger to my lips.

"Hush, now," he says. "You're safe. I promise."

Tentative relief washes over me and I let myself sink back into his arms. I'm not sure what the future holds, but if Gideon believes I'm his mate, then he'll protect me. I'm safe with him.

For now.

CHAPTER 22

CASIMIR

My eyes scan the ingredients in front of me, my fingers threading through the delicate Sundahlian sand. These are difficult to source, many of them taking us to the far corners of Bedlam, which is why it took so long to procure them. We'll use them for the spell to locate Lana's precise location and relocate her to us. We just need a few more.

We're seated at the long table in our dining hall, impatiently waiting for more of our guards to arrive with what we need. I don't know how long it's been since I've slept. Days? Weeks? I've lost track. The amber sconces adorning the wall flicker with fae light, just enough not to pitch us in dark. Coupled with the call of the pulsing, inky siren's heart on the table in front of me, it's nearly enough to have me nodding off.

A quiet beep comes from Pierce's phone, startling me out of my exhaustion-induced haze. He fishes it out of his pocket and shuts it off before setting it on the weathered table.

"The wards at Tristique Island have been breached." He stands. "It could be nothing, but we need to go now. It could be her."

Hope ratchets up my spine. I nod and stand as well, tucking my cell into my boot just as a chirp sounds from everyone's devices. This only happens when there's a realm or region-wide emergency, and not without our prior authorization. I glance at Grimm and Penn, and they shake their heads.

If we didn't do this, then who did?

After sending the link to the screen on the wall, we wait while the video clears.

The blood drains from my face as I take in the scene before me. Gideon, covered in blood with a feral look in his eye, is chained to a wall in a room I don't recognize. I follow his gaze to the bed across from him when a familiar moan sounds, and he snarls.

Our mate and queen fills our vision.

My fangs descend and I fight the urge to shift, my wolf clawing to break free. The need to protect my mate is overwhelming, but I know if I storm off half-cocked, I'll get us all killed.

There's a male standing next to her bed, but I can't see his face. Her hands roam over him, and he's pulling her dress off over her head. A sinister thought sinks into my chest, curling and swirling like poisoned ink through my limbs. That can't possibly be …

"Who the fuck is that?!" Penn shouts as he topples over his chair and stalks toward the screen.

Fury ripples through the room. Sweltering heat pours off Penn, and I stand frozen, unable to parse what's in front of me. Grimm has a preternatural stillness to him; his breath having ceased. Before anyone can give a voice to our fears, the male turns around to grin at Gideon and we see his face, confirming our suspicions.

Luka fucking Donović.

He's supposed to be dead because *we killed him*. We'd tossed his remains into the Triune Sea two years ago. There were rumors he'd been replaced by a new king, but that's not the case. We'd been unable to figure out who the new king was because there never was a replacement. It's been Luka this entire time. How did he evade us?

"No," I whisper as I shake my head. "This can't be happening."

"He's not happy," the werewolf muses.

"I don't care, I want this." Lana whispers.

I feel the heavy weight of Grimm's hand on my shoulder, but I shrug it off. Striding closer, I search for any semblance of coercion or trickery in the video, though I find none, because she appears willing.

"Why is she with Luka?" I demand. My voice comes out choked, as though I have a vice around my throat. Betrayal burns like acid in my chest. It travels along my nerves, ricocheting through my extremities.

My eyelids shutter when the beast beds Lana—my *mate*—but the sound invades my ears, and I can't block it out. Her cries, her whimpers, and finally her moans pummel my eardrums as Luka gives her release. My hands crush my ears when she screams his name. A desperate whine escapes me, and I know I'm not alone in my hurt.

It's bad enough she has another man between her legs, but to have our enemy—and another lupine species—over her? *In her?*

"This could be fake," Pierce stands in front of me and I pry open my eyes. "Now that we know who has her, we can find her."

My attention pauses on Grimm and then Penn. They're both crestfallen. I take in a shaky breath and nod. I need to be strong for them, for our people. We'll get her back, one way or another.

I push past Pierce and head for the door. "We're going to find her," I say over my shoulder. "And we're going to kill that bastard once and for all."

Just before we leave the room, Luka's voice stops us in our tracks. We turn towards the projection, and his face fills the screen.

"Your high queen carries my heir," he sneers. I crash to my knees. *"Together, her and I will raise the next generation of species. But first, the vampires and I will destroy any fae who oppose us. This is war."*

The video cuts to a clip of Lana burying her head against Luka's neck, the two moving in tandem. Agony sluices through me at the words that come next.

"As high queen, I'm more powerful. I can give you whatever it is you need. I want to help you," Lana's muffled voice cries.

"Is that how you became high queen? Fucked your way through the castle?"

"Yes," she breathes.

When did she start working with Luka? Was it before or after we made her high queen?

"She wouldn't do this—" Grimm interrupts my thoughts.

"That's her voice, and her image." All feeling drops out of my voice. It's cold, and it's hollow.

"You can't see her lips moving; we don't know that Luka didn't doctor this video and use words and phrases she's uttered in his presence to tell us this," Pierce argues.

"She's still fucking him." I spit. "And those are still her words." I don't want to believe what's right in front of me, but this proof leaves very little room for misinterpretation.

At least now we know where she's at—she isn't far from Bedlam Penitentiary.

CHAPTER 23

FINN

a hush falls over camp when Rose, Bennett, and I make our way through the wards. Magic prickles over my skin; a pleasant hum filling my ears. The sound of a thousand conversations dies down as all eyes turn to us.

Vampires sharpen weapons across their laps, cleaning them with fastidious care. Witches brew noxious concoctions in black cauldrons, their eyes narrowed in concentration. The sight quirks my lips. I'll need to show them how to accomplish offensive and defensive magic without the use of cauldrons. My gaze sweeps over the pockets of fae who polish gems and trinkets, pausing their work when quiet ripples through the camp.

I reach into my pocket and pull out Gideon's dagger, flipping it end over end before catching it by the blade. I offer it, hilt-first, to Mekhi.

"You're certain this is the blade?" It's not that I don't trust the kid, I just don't want to chase any dead ends.

He takes it from me with a nod of thanks before turning it over in his hand. A small smile graces his lips as his fingers trace over the intricate carving on the hilt.

"This is definitely the one," he says, his voice barely above a whisper. "It's the finest knife I've ever seen."

He passes it back to me, and I take my time inspecting it. Firelight gleams off the blade, reflecting in my eyes. I run my thumb over the edge, testing the sharpness. A satisfied grin spreads across my face when a bead of blood wells up on my skin.

"This will do nicely," I say before sheathing the knife and returning it to my pocket.

I tilt my head, indicating for the vampire royals to follow me towards Rune's tent. Oz, Auguste, Maeve, and Pippa trail behind us, their steps silent on the soft ground.

Rune looks up when we step inside, his eyes assessing us when he sees who I've brought with me. "Did you find something of his?"

The space is sparse, absent of any personal effects. But Rune has always been like that. He keeps a tight leash on things and doesn't show his hand unless necessary. He doesn't leave his enemies any reason to come for his loved ones. Never again.

My hand strays to the pocket containing the dagger. "We did."

I pull it out and hand it to him. He studies it for a moment before looking up at me. "Let's get started."

He clears off the table that'd been set for dinner, making room for the map of Bedlam. I step forward and unroll it, using rocks to keep the corners from curling up. My eyes catch on Rift Pass, and my heart lurches, the ache so fierce I have to steel my breath. The home I built for Lana, millennia before I met her, sits at the top. I blink away the moisture in my eyes and refocus.

By incorporating the map, I can pinpoint a more detailed location than if I simply viewed through Gideon's eyes where he's at, like I did when the twins were kidnapped by Dolphina.

We take seats around the tabletop; the space cramped from the amount of people in here. I try not to think about how this is just one more hiccup in our plans, or how frustrated I am about having to chase down Gideon when we could be spending this time getting Lana back.

Attention flitting to Oz, I take in his furrowed brows, his anxious pacing. I can tell he's torn. On one hand, he's worried about Gideon, and on the other, he's just as desperate as I am to get to Lana. Together, we've chased down lead after lead, but something must be blocking Lana's magic, otherwise I'd feel her and could have her with us in minutes. Vampires don't need sleep, but the exhaustion is evident on his face. He's not eating like he should. *'Everything tastes like ash,'* he'd said, and sometimes I catch him trying to conjure a spell as though it's muscle memory before he remembers he no longer has magic.

My phone buzzes in my pocket, and I fish it out. *Hmph*. A realm-wide push notification. I flip it over and I'm about to click the screen off when Lana's familiar moan cuts through the air, and my heart stops.

"He's not happy." A voice I haven't heard in years chuckles.

"I don't care, I want this." My soul bonded mate whispers.

Auguste and Oz shove their chairs back and scramble to stand over my shoulder. I'm frozen, unable to make sense of what we're seeing on the screen. In the corner, I catch a glimpse of Gideon, wild eyes trained on the couple in bed in front of him.

"Who is that?!" Oz bellows. Distress, devastation, and fury ripple across his face.

Blaring white noise fills my head, and I gain tunnel vision, unable to hear or see around me. I vaguely register dropping the phone as I stumble backwards, tripping over a chair and landing hard on my ass.

Gideon's howls tear through my mind, the pain and sorrow matching the scorching hot fire blazing through my chest and veins at seeing another man between her legs. Not just any man, but the one responsible for decimating a large portion of Luna fae.

"Finn, what the fuck is going on?" Auguste shakes my shoulder.

Luka Donović's voice breaks through my thoughts. "Your high queen carries my heir."

I don't hear what else he says because I'm roaring in agony, the ground shaking beneath me. It feels like my insides are being shred-ded, every inch of my body on fire. All I can think about is finding him and making him pay for what he's done.

CHAPTER 24

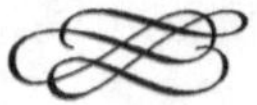

OZ

Grief clings to Finn like a second skin, the raw emotion pouring off him in waves. My own despair chokes me, a physical weight on my chest that makes it hard to move, despite my not needing to breathe. It's not just seeing Lana with another man, but witnessing Gideon so tortured, knowing he's been in agony this whole time.

The man says Lana is pregnant. With his child.

It takes a moment for the words to register, and when they do, I see red. All reason leaves me, replaced by a primal need to protect my mate. I lunge forward, gripping Finn's shoulders.

"Tell me where," I grit out. "And I'll destroy him."

His ethereal blue eyes meet mine, and I see my own pain reflected at me. "I already know where they are." Finn glances at Rune, and they share a haunted look.

He stands and moves to the table, body trembling with barely contained rage. His finger stabs at a spot on the map. It's a small island next to where they keep fae prisoners, on the Northernmost point of Bedlam.

"Right under our noses this entire time," Finn swears. "I'd recognize that room anywhere. It's where his ancestors murdered my mother."

Finn's hand clenches into a fist, and I know he's struggling to keep himself together. I pause beside him, offering what little comfort I can.

"We'll get her back," I vow. "And make them pay."

He nods, his body going rigid. "I'm going to kill him."

"I'll help you," I say. "We'll do it together."

He nods again, and I can feel his resolve hardening. There's nothing left but to go forward and do what needs to be done.

Early into the morning, we formulate plans to get Lana and Gideon out of Luka's reach—a snatch and grab operation. They're our priority, and the attack on Occasus can wait.

By nightfall, our people are in place, and we're just waiting for the signal from Rune. Our ships sway in the water, bought with Finn's hoard of treasure that rivals that found on Draconum. We're far enough back that we can't be spotted by anyone on Penn Island, but close enough that when the lightning strikes and the thunder cracks, we can move in quickly.

Finn paces the boat deck like a caged animal, tension drawing his features taut. I can feel his frustration and anger, a live wire under my skin. It's the closest thing to magic of my own I've felt in months. Sea spray dampens my hair, my eyelashes, and if I were mortal, I'd probably be freezing right now.

"It's almost time," I whisper, trying to offer some measure of comfort, though the rage boiling inside me is evident in my voice.

He nods, coming to a stop in front of me. "I can't lose her," he says, his voice breaking. "I can't."

"We won't," I say. "We won't let that happen."

My mind drifts to the first moment I laid eyes on Lana. It wasn't just tracks in her driveway that drove me to her cabin, but an inextricable pull that led me to her door. She'd been afraid at seeing a stranger in such remote woods, at least at first. I'd known the moment I caught sight of her that she was the one foretold to be my mate. It felt like coming home, a rightness buried deep within me that recognized her as the woman I'd spend the rest of eternity with. I hadn't known at the time that I'd be sharing her, but as I take in the small army of support on the boat, ready to battle any foe to get her back, I wouldn't have it any other way.

A flash of lightning illuminates the darkness, and seconds later, the boom of thunder echoes across the water. The scent of ozone fills my nostrils and I glance Finn's way.

"It's time," he says.

He gives me a final look, and then he's gone, leaping from the boat in full fae form, wings out, his glow the only lit thing in the sky before he dives into the water like a torpedo.

I follow, grabbing onto the railing before hoisting myself over and lowering myself into the ocean. The water is icy cold, but I push onward, driven by the need to get to Lana and Gideon.

Finn's golden head bobs in the water ahead of me, and I follow close behind. One by one, our team falls into place as we make our way to the island. Auguste. Pippa. Elliot. Rune. Annabelle. Wren. Alphie. Sebastian. Maeve. And a whole contingent of vampires right behind them. This is where Lana's supposed to be, but uncertainty gives me doubt. We've spent so much time chasing her, only for her to slip right through our hands.

As we reach the shore, sand sinking beneath our feet, the stench of blood infiltrates my nose. We spot the werewolf guards that are meant to be patrolling the beach, but they're all dead, throats ripped out. Who killed them? We inspect each one, ensuring they're truly dead and not just playing possum. When we're certain, we move into the trees, keeping to the shadows as much as possible.

Finn leads the way, silent and surefooted. I can feel his magic ahead of me, a bright light in the darkness, guiding us towards our goal. The place in my chest where mine used to stir is hollow. So hollow, it aches.

But there's no time to dwell on that now.

We move through the trees, careful to avoid any traps that might be set. It takes our small army twenty minutes before we make it to the outskirts of the skull-shaped castle. It's eerily quiet, not a soul in sight. The enormous stone structure is imposing; so large it towers over the woods decorating the island. No wonder the map made it look like it was just the castle, and the rest—barren sand.

"Where is everyone?" Maeve whispers what we're all thinking, but too unsettled to voice it.

"I don't know." Finn shutters his eyes, feeling into the landscape. I know, because I'd done it myself for millennia, the third sight like a snapshot of the land. "But we need to be careful."

He motions for us to split up, half of us going left and half going right. We'll circle the castle and then meet back up on the other side. It's slow going, and my skin prickles with unease. I can sense that something is off, but I can't put my finger on what it is.

Finn stops suddenly, and I nearly run into him. He holds up a hand, and I freeze. There's a sound coming from around the corner— a soft shuffle of foot against stone. He draws his sword, and I pull out my daggers. We move as one, silent and calculating, towards the sound. When we reach a small clearing amongst the copse of trees, his entire body tenses. I can feel his magic whip around us like a shield as he steps in front of me.

What is it? I think. Since losing my magic, I can no longer keep him out, nor can I speak into his mind, but he can hear my thoughts if he focuses on them, and he can speak into mine. He doesn't answer, and I peek around his shoulder to see what has him so on edge.

I've had to re-learn my entire approach to everyday life. From the mundane task of tidying a space, to big things like relying on my vampire senses instead of a field of awareness I had with my witches' eye. It's a sacrifice I'd make millions of times over to save Bennett's life, even though it's as though I'm working with my hands tied behind my back, whilst always blindfolded and facing unknown threats.

A group of five guards stand in front of a towering metal door set into the side of the castle. They're talking quietly amongst themselves, paying no attention to their surroundings. Amateurs. I sure hope these aren't the ones tasked with keeping Lana safe.

Rune's magic crackles like static electricity in the air, and I know he's debating whether to eviscerate them where they stand. Before we can decide what to do, the door swings open and the fae kings step out. Since seeing them in the throne room, I've committed their faces to memory, determined to never forget the monsters who took my mate. My wife.

Grimm, Penn, and Casimir pause, their eyes hard as they take in the guards. It's clear they're not happy with something.

"She's not here," Grimm grits out. "Lana nor Anastasia."

One lookout sheaths his sword, and the others follow. "What do you want us to do, Your Majesty?"

"Follow us," Penn stalks in our direction. "We'll do the damned locator spell."

Confrontation it is, considering there's so many of us huddled here, and not enough shifters to sift people to safety in time.

CHAPTER 25

FINN

Oz moves through the thick foliage surrounding the castle, but I put a hand on his arm to stop him. There's something else here—something I can't quite see. But it's there, lurking in the shadows.

Biding its time.

Waiting for the perfect moment to strike. I close my eyes and reach out with my senses, trying to get a feel for what's hiding. And then I see it—a faint outline of a body, almost invisible against the darkness.

A werewolf.

My eyes fly open and meet Oz's gaze. He nods, understanding what I'm trying to say. We need to be careful—there's at least one werewolf that we know of, and there could be more.

The swish of metal against gravel alerts us to the fact that the fae kings are on the move again. Grimm is in the lead, with Penn and Casimir following close behind. They're coming this way. It's now or never.

I take a step forward, magic popping around me as I prepare to fight. The fae kings and their guards startle when they see us, and I take advantage of their surprise. I shoot a bolt of magic at Grimm, but he dodges it effortlessly. He sneers at me as he raises his hand, prepared to retaliate.

But before he can so much as twitch his fingers, Oz is there. He slams into Grimm with the force of a freight train, taking him to the ground.

Grimm roars in anger as he tries to scramble away, but the vampire king is relentless. He pins Grimm down, his teeth bared in a snarl.

"Where is she?" Oz demands. "Where is Lana?"

"We don't know," Grimm spits out.

Movement in my peripheral vision catches my attention, and I turn just in time to see Penn and Casimir coming at me, their feet kicking up sand. I raise my hand, immobilizing them and their guards like I did in the throne room, although I let them talk. They struggle against my hold, but it's no use. The ground beneath us trembles from their power pressing against mine.

"What did you do with her?" I growl. "Where is she? And why are you working with the werewolves? Don't you know you can't trust any of them?!"

"We're not working with the gods damned werewolves," Penn snarls. "We thought he was dead!"

"But you are," I press. "You have to be. Why else would Lana be with Luka?"

"She disappeared a month ago, and until that broadcast, we didn't know where she was." Casimir's words end on a lupine whine.

Without Luna magic, the kings would've had to gather ingredients to do the locator spell, and those can take weeks to procure. I'm not sure which is worse, Lana in the king's clutches, or Luka's.

"What do you want with her?" I demand.

"We love her!" Casimir roars, his eyes flashing with anger. His wolf paces just under the surface of his skin, evident by the yellow cast to his irises. "All we ever wanted was for her to be happy."

"And you think she'd be happy with any of you?" I stalk towards them. "You're all monsters."

"At least we're not traitors," Penn spits out. "We did what we had to do to save Bedlam."

"She and I were saving it." I throw my hands up, spinning around. "We didn't need you to intervene because we would've handled it, but you ruined it all."

My hold falters for a moment, and Penn takes advantage of it. He breaks free and comes at me with a speed I didn't know was possible for a dragon shifter fae. I barely have time to react before he collides with me, sending us both tumbling to the ground.

I roll, trying to put some distance between us, but Penn is on me in an instant. His claws sink into my shoulder, and I cry out in pain. The rest of my hold on them breaks. I summon my magic, preparing to fight back, but before I can so much as lift a finger, there's a loud snarl and Penn is yanked off me. He hits the stone path with a thud, and I crane my neck to see Oz standing over him, his teeth bared.

"Don't touch him," Oz barks, his voice filled with menace.

Penn scrambles to his feet and backs away while I quickly heal myself. Before my wound can stitch together, I draw a dagger from its sheath and flick it at the guard closing in on Oz. He dodges, but not before the blade slices through his cheek. He hisses in pain and presses a hand to the wound. Out of the corner of my eye, my peripheral vision catches Grimm and Casimir getting to their feet, having been in a brawl with Maeve and Alphie. They're both bleeding, but they don't seem to be too worse for wear.

The kings are holding back. Is it because they know how upset Lana will be about them hurting her family once she gains her memories?

An ominous howl echoes through the trees, stopping everyone in their tracks. It sends a chill down my spine, and I feel the hairs on the back of my neck stand on end.

The werewolves are coming. *Gods damned full moons.*

Grimm whips his head, but not in the direction of the call. His eyes narrow over my shoulder.

"Rune," he spits out. "Should've known your allegiance only went so far."

I feel him before I see him; a mixture of static electricity and the scent of ozone. And then he's there, standing next to Auguste with a smirk on his face.

"What can I say?" Rune shrugs. "Finn's my best friend. Even then, his mother might have some words with me otherwise."

"You're going to regret this." Penn swipes at a streak of blood at his temple.

"No, I don't think I will," Rune counters. "In fact, I think this is going to be quite fun."

He cracks his knuckles and Titan, his Phelvie, materializes in a leap, a growl sounding as he lands and stalks towards the kings.

The ground trembles as the werewolves draw closer, and I know we're running out of time. There must be hundreds of them. We're out-manned, terribly. I can't freeze them all.

"We need to go," I say, my voice tight.

"What about the kings?" Maeve asks.

"We'll have to come back for them." I spin to face her. "But right now, we need to get out of here."

"Agreed." Oz moves to stand next to me, and although anger still simmers in his eyes, defeat and frustration live there too. "We'll deal with them later."

Without needing to tell them to, the weaker vampires crowd around me and I sift them to the boat before returning to the island in a blink for more. When I land, the kings have already disappeared with their guards. I whirl around, meeting the eyes of Rune, Auguste, Oz, Maeve, Pippa, and Alphie just as an enormous pack of werewolves reach us.

We're out of time.

They fall upon us with a bloodthirsty snarl, and I know we're in for the fight of our lives.

CHAPTER 26

CASIMIR

"No more dallying. We need to do the relocator spell, now." Penn grips the wooden chair, hands wringing the top rung of it.

Scorches mar the dais, victim to Penn's fury over Luka's hold on Lana. The throne room's drapes bear his claw marks where he involuntarily shifted into his dragon form. We have little control over our beasts right now, least of all him.

He shoves everything off the table, papers and books flying everywhere, and I wince as one of the vials shatters. We jump back, avoiding the noxious plume of purple smoke that rises from the broken glass.

"Penn!" I shout. "You could have hurt someone!"

"I don't care." He slams the bag of ingredients onto the surface. "We need to find them."

He paces the length of the room, his hands clenched into fists. As a dragon shifter fae, his temper is a natural result of his lineage, and until recently, he's always kept it in check. Lana and Anastasia going missing has everyone on edge.

"We'll find them," I say, trying to placate him. "Wherever Luka has taken Lana, we will find her and get her back. Same goes for Anastasia —she might be with them too."

His cousin is tough, though I know their last encounter didn't end well. That weighs heavy on him.

"I know." He sighs, running a hand through his hair. "I just hate feeling like I'm powerless."

"You're not powerless." I turn him to face me. "You're the gods damned king of Draconum."

He nods, and determination enters his eyes. He may feel powerless now, but he won't give up until we find Lana, nor Anastasia. None of us will.

The heat in the room dies down, signaling Penn's tempering anger. I usher him to a chair and take one next to him while Grimm calls Pierce and Captain Zara into the room.

We lean in around the table; everyone's faces tense as we empty the contents of the satchel onto the surface. The team we sent to gather these made sure to obtain more than we need for just one spell in case we need to do this again. Potent magic swirls around the ingredients, growing stronger and stronger as we mix them together.

"We need her hair." Grimm nods towards Pierce. "That will give the spell the best chance of finding her."

Pierce slips Lana's hairbrush out of his pocket and hands it to the king of Occasus. He pulls a delicate strand from the bristles and adds it to the concoction.

"Now, we need blood," Grimm says. "I'll add my own."

He nicks his finger with a small knife and squeezes a few drops of blood into the mix. The potion begins to boil and bubble, the ingredients swirling around in the cauldron.

"And finally," Grimm says. "We need power."

He glances at me, and I know what he wants. He wants me to use my magic to give the spell a boost. My heart clenches in agony, and I can't stop the whine from escaping my throat. It's a stark reminder of what's happened and why my magic is needed above the others. With my lupine magic, we'll have a better chance at locating her since she's carrying a werewolf child.

Werewolf. Child.

Not wolf, but *werewolf*.

I nod and place my hand on the edge of the cauldron. Magic pulses through me, and I watch as the colors in the potion swirl and change. It turns a deep red, almost black, and I know that it's done.

The spell is ready.

We all stand around the cauldron, waiting for the spell to show us where Lana is. For a moment, nothing happens. Just before I shove back to leave the room, the potion erupts in a column of smoke. Putrid decay fills the air, and I can taste blood in the back of my throat before it turns to ash.

"What the hell?" Penn mutters.

The plume of smoke twists and turns, coalescing into a vague shape. A location begins to take form, and I feel my blood run cold when I see where they have her.

The Wastelands? We can't relocate her to us with this spell if she's there. We'll have to go to her.

CHAPTER 27

LANA

*D*irt.

So. Much. Dirt.

It casts a thick film on my skin, and clouds of it fall off my shorts with every step I take. Courtesy of the dust storm that just swept through here an hour ago.

Gideon offers to carry me about every hundred yards, but I can't do that to him. As fae, I'm stronger, and have more stamina. He also hasn't eaten since he took a bite out of Luka a week ago, and that was after having starved for a while.

I recall going to the Atacama Desert in my mid-20s, but not anyone I interacted with while there. I thought that place was dry. A chuckle threatens to bubble up, but I quickly tamp it down, worried about my current mental state. If I start laughing, I might never stop.

The Wastelands are a place that even the fae avoid. It's a place of death, of decay. Nothing, save the Crucey and her Tolden, survive here.

I glance over at Gideon, catching him staring at me. "What?"

He simply smirks at me, like he's harboring a secret. I narrow my eyes at him.

He skips ahead and turns around to face me, walking backwards.

"You have no idea how ready I am for you to learn I'm telling you the truth. You don't remember it now, but you will soon, that I am honest to a fault."

I worry my lip. "Gideon, I—"

"No, Lana, it's alright. You've always tried to do the right thing. If I were in the kings' shoes, I'd expect you to trust me until you couldn't, and for you to verify what's real and what isn't. I take comfort knowing that it won't be long before you steal looks at me without guilt."

Heat flushes my cheeks, and before I can respond, he continues.

"It's alright, Lana, have your fill." He tucks his fist under his chin and angles it towards the sky. He peels off his shirt, leveling me with a hooded gaze. "It's hot out here, don't you think?"

I shake my head and check him playfully with my shoulder as I pass by him. The brief contact sends a rush of thrill through me, though I quickly tamp it down, dismissing it as the need for any semblance of affection.

The sun bakes my skin, and our steps begin to falter as the day wears on. Gideon casts me a worried look. He thinks I'm not paying attention, but I see the way his eyes dart around, always on the lookout for danger. The wind has died down, and I no longer have to squint to keep the sand out of my eyes.

"What are you thinking about?" I ask.

He startles, looking over at me. "Just... wondering how you're holding up. You can hop on my back? Or I could cradle you—you used to like that. Don't get me wrong, I like carrying you like that, too. Any way, really." He turns his puppy dog eyes on me and frowns. "I'm touch starved."

"If I'm being honest, I am too." My voice comes out as barely a whisper, but I know he hears me. I'm lonely; I don't know who I can trust, but I know someone is lying to me—whether that's Gideon or my mates, I'll know soon. I give him a weak smile. "Wishing I could sift us to the Crucey's hideout."

Everything is dead here, including the ability to teleport. Thankfully, I still have magic, though it won't do anything to speed up our journey. It'll be at least a few more days of trekking across this barren landscape before we reach where she's rumored to live.

Guilt rides parallel to the determination anchored deep in me. Gideon is sweet, even an insatiable flirt, but I can't trust him blindly. Not when it matters so much. The friend I saved in the woods all those moons ago promised she'd give me any answers I need, and I'm going to take her up on her offer.

"Are you okay?"

He and I both know I'm not asking about his physical condition. The past few days have been hard on him, with our constant sifting from continent to continent, searching for answers. But he's holding up better than I expected. No, what I really want to know is how he's holding up emotionally.

Gideon's been nothing but the picture of a devoted mate, willing to cross seas, barren landscapes, and starve just so I can find out the truth. Did my kings lie to me? What will I do if they did? I owe it to them to get answers before I react.

He plasters a grin on his face, his dimples coming out, despite the layer of dirt and grime that covers his face. "I'm good. Just worried about you."

"I'll be fine."

Chuckling, he shakes his head. It's a dark rumble of thunder on a quiet, cobbled street. I chastise myself for noticing. "It's nice to see you haven't changed ... much. You're still your stubborn self, always looking out for everyone else."

His words make my heart ache. I remember little of my life before Bedlam, but I've changed in my time here, though not in the ways he knows. And I never stopped looking out for others, even when I thought it would be better if I stopped.

"I haven't changed that much." I shrug. It's a half-truth, and we both know it.

We lapse into silence, and I let my mind wander as Gideon sets the pace. Adjusting the straps on his shoulders where he carries a backpack full of supplies I snagged from the lighthouse home, he winces.

"Gideon," I chide. "You need to feed."

He gives me a look, but I see the resignation in his eyes. He knows I'm right. He's been getting weaker as we travel, and though he won't admit it, I can tell he's barely hanging on.

His eyes dart to my abdomen, and my hands absently find their way there as well. He straightens his spine and looks away. "We should make camp soon."

A small breeze blows my way, and it's cool on my skin. My hand flies out to clutch onto Gideon's bare bicep.

"Gideon!" I cry out.

He whips his head around, looking for danger. I take off running in the opposite direction of the wind, my heart pounding, hope ratcheting up inside.

"What is it?" he shouts, running after me.

I don't answer, my only focus being on confirming my suspicions. The ground seems to ripple beneath my feet, and I know I'm not imagining it this time. I peel off my shirt as I run, and Gideon catches up to me, no change to his appearance despite chasing after me. A small part of me wanted to know if it activated his chase instincts.

"Lana!" he cries out, but I ignore him.

I barely stop enough to shuck off my shorts before I continue running. Gideon shouts as I leap off a ledge and into the air. The ground pushes up against me, and I let out a shriek as I'm engulfed.

The water is freezing compared to the sweltering heat of the Wastelands. Icy tendrils wrap around my body, a welcome reprieve from the scorching temperatures, and I fight to come to the surface. My head breaks through, and I gasp for air, only to be pulled under again. There's some sort of current dragging me down, and I shout for Gideon.

My body is tossed around like a rag doll, and I'm disoriented. Blinking, I swim towards the light. The sun. When I feel the air on my face, I gasp and shiver uncontrollably. Gideon is there in an instant, pulling me into his arms, desperately trying to lift me over his head to safety.

"What the hell happened?" he demands when he drags us onto the bank.

My lungs heave and I curl onto my side to cough out water. I can only tremble and shake my head. "It's like a riptide," I grit out. Which is weird, because this little oasis in the middle of the desert is maybe the size of a small pool, or a large hot tub.

There's no way there should be a current.

Gideon's brows furrow. "I didn't feel the riptide, only you felt like you weighed a thousand pounds."

I scowl at him. "Gee, thanks."

He grimaces. "You don't understand. I felt you getting dragged away, but I didn't feel the current at all. It's just like a swimming pool to me."

I still. "Is it because you're a vampire?" Sitting up, I tuck my knees against my chest to hide my nakedness. Though fae have no reservations about being naked, my mind is still very human, and knows modesty.

He shrugs before he cocks his head to the side. His hand comes up to cup my cheek, and I fight the urge to lean into his touch. "It's possible," he murmurs. "Or it's because you're a Luna fae. Think about it." He tilts his chin to look at the sky. "There are way more moons here than on Earth, and there, the moon affects the tides. I imagine it's even worse here."

"I've swum in plenty of bodies of water in Bedlam," I argue. "This is the first time anything like this has happened."

He nods thoughtfully. "It's possible that something about the water here is different. Maybe it's because we're so far from civilization."

I shake my head. "I think it has to do with the magic in this place."

Gideon's eyes narrow. "What do you mean?"

"The magic here is… different. I can feel it, right under the surface, like an enormous cavern of space holding it all." I gesture to the water. "It's like the water is magical, too, and I do think you're right; it's affecting me because I'm a Luna fae."

He is silent for a long moment. "It's possible," he agrees. "But we won't know for sure until we ask someone who knows more about the magic in the Wastelands than we do."

He stands and offers me a hand. I take it and let him pull me to my feet. He doesn't let go as he leads me back up the embankment, and I don't hate it. I'm glad for the support because my legs still tremble from the shock of almost drowning.

I follow in Gideon's sopping wet footprints, mud caking between my toes, my mind racing. If the magic here is affecting me, then what else can it do? And more importantly, how can I protect myself from it? It was like it was drowning me.

Taking in the sad state of my clothes littering the ground, I pick them up and attempt to shake out the dirt. Holes have ripped in the fabric, and I know they're beyond salvage.

I huff out a breath and turn to Gideon with a grin before setting to digging in the dirt with my bare hands.

He crouches next to me and arches a brow. "What are you doing?"

"You'll see."

I'm not certain it'll work, as it's relatively barren here. After I've dug a deep enough hole, I shove my torn clothes into the dirt and bury them before stepping back. My hands work quickly over the top of the soil, tamping it down.

When finished, I step back and brush my hands off on my thighs. "There," I announce with a grin.

Gideon watches the ground with suspicion, his eyes widening when he witnesses the dirt moving. Minutes later, movement ceases. I make quick work of uncovering my clothes and yank them out.

They're spotless, and no longer have holes.

"What the hell?"

"Do you have anything shiny? Coins?"

He nods and pulls a handful of gold fae coins from his sodden pocket. He hands them to me, and I drop them into the hole and brush dirt over it, listening for the jingle of metal and then chittering.

When it quiets, I rise to my feet and turn towards Gideon. "Ground gnomes." I beam. "They mend clothes."

He looks impressed as he inspects my now mended outfit. "That's… useful."

I shrug. "They're also very good at trading shiny objects. So if you want to gamble, you just have to bribe them with pretty things.

They don't speak, so you never know what you'll end up with in return."

He chuckles and shakes his head before his gaze turns heated. I hurry into my clothes, though I feel a flush crawl up my cheeks under his open perusal. After rummaging through our bag of supplies, I begin laying camp equipment on the ground. First, provisions, then tools for cooking and eating.

"What?" I ask when I catch him staring.

He steps closer, cupping my face in his hands. "You're amazing," he murmurs before lowering his head to kiss me.

I freeze, every measure of time narrowing to this very moment. My heart thrashes in my chest as his lips brush mine. Fireworks explode in my mind, neurons fire on all cylinders, and my body leans into his of its own accord. It's a thousand sighs on the wind, burning suns, and stars.

His mouth is soft, gentle, coaxing a response from me. His tongue sweeps into my mouth, tasting and teasing.

I moan and grip his wrists, my body molding to his. He slides his hands around my waist and lifts me onto my tiptoes as he deepens the kiss. My head spins, and I clench my thighs around his hips as he presses me against the sheer cliff wall we've stopped next to. He slides his hands up my back, over my shoulders, and cups my face again as he pulls away slightly, all too soon, and I'm left gasping for air.

"What was that for?" I whisper as I slide down his body and onto my own two, unsteady feet, swaying with the sudden loss of his support.

He gives me a dazzling, dimpled smirk and tucks a stray hair behind my ear. "You're amazing," he repeats before clearing his throat and stepping back. "Sorry," He shakes his head, his voice rough with emotion. "For a moment there, I'd forgotten we're in Bedlam, and not home, camping somewhere in the Andes."

"Chile?" My voice comes out ridiculous; small and pinched.

He nods and takes another step away from me. "We have a home there. It's where you married Oz. Where I turned your dad into a vampire, and where you gave birth to our twins."

"Oh." I swallow hard, my heart aching at the mention of my alleged family. " ... did my dad want to be turned?"

"I wouldn't have turned him if he didn't," Gideon says, his voice soft. "He'd only recently come into your life and was dying of cancer. It was the only way to save him."

Tears well in my eyes, and I blink them away. This is an intricate web of lies he's spinning if he isn't telling the truth. The pain is still there, nonetheless. "What's he like?"

"He's a good man," Gideon says with a sad smile. "And an even better father. He loves you very much and is so proud of the woman you've become. Loves your cooking too."

I return to the backpack of supplies and pull out the tent, and hand it to Gideon. "And Rose and Bennett?" I stumble over their names, their sounds foreign on my tongue.

"They're our children," Gideon says, his voice filled with emotion. "Rose is the spitting image of you. She's kind but has a wild streak. I caught her sneaking a koala in her backpack, and when I inspected her room, I found three more hiding in her closet with an entire ecosystem set up for them. Complete with water features, bamboo, and a skylight to let in the sun."

I snicker and raise a brow.

"And Bennett? He's protective but likes to play tricks on the family. After we returned the koalas to their rightful habitat, Bennett glamoured a couple so they appeared to be children. Claimed they were just shy, and it was Finn who saw through the ruse when Bennett tried to bring them to the grocery store." A smirk teases the corner of his mouth. "He's going to be the death of me one day."

"They sound … perfect," I whisper, my chest aching. I don't know why, but I feel like I'm losing something, even though I never had it to begin with.

Gideon and I set up the tent quietly, and I use my magic to heat the food I've placed in bowls. There isn't any firewood around, but this suffices. We devour it, sitting in comfortable silence on the ground before I catch him staring again.

"What?"

He shakes his head, a dismissive gesture.

"Gideon." I narrow my eyes.

He quirks a smile. "Your ears."

I reach up to cover them with my hair, embarrassment flooding through me. I don't get the opportunity because he grabs my hand in his to stop me. "They're adorable."

Dropping my gaze, I focus intently on scraping my bowl clean, despite there being no food left in it.

"Hey," he says, tilting my chin up to face him. "You might look different now that you're fae, but you don't need to hide from me. You could grow horns, wings, a tail, and it wouldn't ever change how I feel about you."

My heart stumbles, and his vampire hearing picks it up immediately. His face settles into a grin. If what he's saying is true, and he's really my mate, I know without a doubt what attracted me to him. It's not the deep-set dimples, the tease of his lips, or his just-fucked hair. No, this man is a charmer. If I'm not careful, I could find myself really falling for him, mate or not. The realization terrifies me, and I stiffen before mumbling something incoherent and rising to my feet.

I pause to take in his still-wet clothes. "Let me dry those for you," I say quietly.

His eyes meet mine, and so much passes between us, though we remain silent. He gets to his knees, devotion evident in the way he kneels before me. Like we've done this before. A thousand times. Fingers working at the buttons of the dress shirt I stole from my king's closet, he's methodical in his movements. I should look away, but don't, as he tugs one sleeve off, and the next, until he's bare chested in front of me.

My attention catches on a tattoo over his heart, and I reach out to trace the lines before I can stop myself. His body shudders under my touch. My lips part, and I suck in a breath.

"You have a tattoo of me?" I whisper. Human me. But me, nonetheless. The sting of tears presses against me, but I fight them back.

Fondness shines in his eyes, and a tiny smirk crosses his face until a dimple shows. "Yeah, I do." His hand comes up to capture mine over his broad chest, gaze never leaving mine. He entwines it with his before bringing it to his mouth and pressing his lips to my knuckles. "I got it to prove my love to you."

"What?" I chuckle and shove back.

"Did it work?" He stands.

I shake my head. "Gideon."

He steps towards me, fierce determination burning in his eyes. "Two-hundred-and-six."

"Two-hundred-and-six what?"

"Koalas. That's how many I could capture in thirty minutes at *Featherdale Sydney Wildlife Park.*"

"Why would you—"

"Fourteen crocodiles," he interrupts me.

"Gideon—"

"Okay, only twelve, but that's because the rangers kept shouting stuff like, 'get out of the water,' and 'we'll be forced to shoot if you don't comply,' at me and distracted me, so a couple got away." His voice turning mocking when he impersonates the rangers.

"Gideon!" I say, exasperated. "What are you talking about? Are you a zookeeper?"

His brows waggle. "Nah, I'm the beast. They couldn't contain me if they tried."

I playfully swat him with the button-up in my hand and set to using magic to dry it off before shoving it at him to get dressed. He shucks off his pants next, but I keep my attention above his waist. When he's fully clothed again, we crawl into the tent.

"Finn came to Earth when the kings stole your memories," he says quietly as he arranges the blanket, and I'm not sure where he's going with this. "To recruit your vampire mates to help get you back. You'd gone to Bedlam by yourself because you had to, and I was jealous when I heard you'd found yourself a soul bonded mate."

His eyes turn glassy, and my heart shatters at the emotion displayed on his handsome face. My fingers itch to sweep his onyx strands out of his vision, but before I can, he does it himself. Shame takes over his expression when he continues. "Even after I learned you had no control over your soul bond, I competed with Finn to see who's the better male."

"I ..." Thoughts run through my head so fast, I don't have the words to articulate them. "I don't know what to say."

There are so many things I should say, but they all hang on whether he's lying to me. If he is really my mate, I'd apologize, pull him into my arms, and show him just how much I regret that I hurt him. Even if it was out of my control. At this point, I fear both him telling me the truth, and him lying. Each conclusion seems impossible. Who is this vampire who's wiggled his way under my skin in such a short period of time?

We settle on top of the covers, not daring to go under them in these temperatures. It's cramped, and I'm acutely aware of his coolness and the spiced scent of his skin.

"It's going to be a long night," he murmurs, his voice low and husky.

I nod, my throat tight. I'm not sure how we're going to make it through the night.

But we must try.

CHAPTER 28

OZ

I narrow my eyes on the lupine creatures closing in on us. If I had my magic still, we might have had an advantage between Rune's, Finn's, and my power. But I gave it up to save Bennett —something I'd do a million times over.

Cataloguing our weapons quickly in my head, I know we're going to have to make every hit count. We're outnumbered and outmatched. Thankfully, they're not fae, and we can use our teeth if necessary.

The werewolves descend upon us, and I meet them with a growl of my own. My fangs extend and I slash out with my claws, tearing into the first wolf that gets close enough. Its blood stains my hands and a feral smile tugs at my lips. This is what I was born to do—to fight, to protect. And I will do whatever it takes to keep my family safe.

Even if it means giving up my own life.

The moons shine bright overhead, casting a milky glow on the tree leaves, and giving the werewolves and Finn an advantage. But I refuse to back down. I will not let them take us without a fight.

At my right, just out of the fray, stand two werewolves. One I immediately recognize as Luka, and the other, I imagine is his second in command. If my research is correct, his name is Tucker. I make to chase their way when a scream comes from my left.

I turn just in time to see one of the wolves slamming Pippa to the ground. Her claws are still in him when she lands, her head hitting a rock with a sickening crunch. She goes limp, her eyes glassy and vacant.

Fear and rage surge through me, and I launch myself at the wolf, sinking my teeth into his neck. I rip his throat out and toss him aside before falling to my knees beside Pippa.

"No," I whisper, my voice thick with emotion.

I gather her into my arms, and she makes a soft sound, her eyelids fluttering. "Oz," she whispers. "I can't see."

Tears blur my vision and I cradle her close. "It's okay," I tell her. "I'm here."

I can hear the fighting going on around us, but all I can focus on is Pippa. She's the doctor; the one always healing people with her gift of medicine, but I need healing magic. Shouting for Finn, I hope like hell he can get to us in time.

Glancing his way, I see he's used his magic to freeze at least a hundred of these werewolves but is fighting off one that jumped on his back.

I hold Pippa close as her body trembles. There's so much blood—everywhere. I apply pressure to the gaping gash on the back of her head, trying to staunch the flow, but it's no use. She's dying.

"Rune!" I bellow, rocking one of my oldest friends in my arms.

He's at my side in an instant, his eyes wide with fear when he sees Pippa. "Watch my back," he says, falling to his knees on the other side of her.

"Please," I beg, my voice breaking.

Rune doesn't say anything, he just pulls Pippa from my arms. His hands glow with a white light, and I bow my head, feeling helpless as I watch him try to save her.

I kill the wolf that gets too close, but my attention is divided. All I can think about is Pippa and the fact that she might not make it. I can't lose her—she's like a sister to me. Hope rekindles in my chest, remembering Finn or Rune can revive her.

And then she's gone; her light extinguished from this world. Rune falls back with a cry of pain, his hands shaking.

"No," I whisper, my heart shattering into pieces.

Rune doesn't say anything as he staggers to his feet. He looks around, his eyes hard and cold.

Blind fury fuels me as I tear into the pack of wolves. I fight with a ferocity I didn't know I was capable of, driven by the need to avenge Pippa's death.

A storm brews overhead, the wind howling in grief. The rain falls in a torrent, drenching us all. My gaze lands on Rune, and his eyes glow bright, startling some of the werewolves around him. The golden lines on his onyx skin burst with light.

He crashes to his knees and places his palms on either side of Pippa's head. Thunder cracks overhead and I shield my eyes from the bright flash of lightning striking in rapid succession from Rune's hand; from his lines, arcing around their bodies. When I can see again, Pippa is sitting up, her eyes wide and confused.

"What happened?" she asks, looking around.

No one has a chance to respond before the ground trembles and a deep rumbling noise echoes through the clearing. The trees around us begin to shake, their leaves rustling in a frantic dance.

"What's going on?" Maeve shouts, her brow furrowed. She wasn't witness to her sister's death, thank the gods, because she was blocked by a wall of werewolves.

A loud crack sounds and I whirl around just in time to see a massive tree falling towards us. I cry out and push Maeve out of the way, throwing myself on top of her to protect her.

The tree hits with a deafening crash, the ground shaking beneath us. I hear screams and cries, but they're quickly drowned out by the sound of splintering wood and rushing water.

I open my eyes to darkness and the sound of the werewolves moaning in pain. "Shit," I croak, my throat raw and scratchy.

Light from Rune blossoms around us, revealing the devastation that's been caused. The tree has fallen across the stream, damming it up. Water is quickly rising, flowing towards us in a raging flood.

"Move!" Finn shouts. "Now!"

We scramble to our feet and chase towards the only dry land left—a small island in the center of the lake that's forming. The water is up to our waists by the time we make it, and I help pull Pippa up onto the rocks.

The deluge sweeps the werewolves away, and I watch in satisfaction as they're pulled under, their screams silenced by the rushing water.

"What the hell was that?" Pippa asks, her eyes wide.

"I don't know," I reply, adrenaline still surging through my veins. "But I think we should get out of here before whatever it is comes back."

Rune trembles, his eyes having returned to normal. "It was me."

"What do you mean?"

"I used my magic to summon the storm," he replies. "I was trying to save Pippa."

"And you did," Pippa says, reaching out to touch his arm. "You saved all of us."

Rune nods, but he doesn't look relieved.

* * *

FINN and Rune sift us back to camp, each of us still sodden from the storm. Pippa is quiet, her eyes downcast. I know she's still shaken up.

"Are you alright?" I ask quietly as we sit by the fire.

She nods, but she doesn't say anything. I can tell she's trying to process everything that happened. Elliot holds her, cooing sweet words in her ear.

"I'm going to check on the others," Finn says, standing up. "Make sure they're all okay."

He leaves, and I'm left alone with Rune, Elliot, and Pippa. The silence is thick and heavy, weighing down on us like a physical thing.

Rose runs into the clearing, tears streaking down her cheeks. "Is it true, Aunt Pippa?! You died?" She crushes Pippa in a hug and sobs against her chest.

Pippa's arms wrap around Rose, cradling her. "I'm okay now, my sweet. It's nice to have the company of fae who can heal ... and revive." She smiles down at my daughter before glancing Rune's way.

"Thank you, Rune. I owe you my life."

"You don't owe me anything," he replies gruffly. "Just ... don't die again. It's really not fun to revive someone."

Pippa chuckles and nods. "I'll try my best."

Before we turn in for the night, Elliot surprises Rune by pulling him into a tight hug. "Thank you," Elliot whispers. "For saving my mate. I'll never forget it."

Rune hesitates for a moment before returning the embrace. "You're welcome."

CHAPTER 29

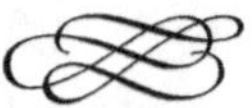

LANA

ormally, when you share a tent with someone in the sweltering heat, you do your best to avoid touching them. They often radiate so much warmth, you keep far away from each other.

But when you're sharing a tent with a vampire? It's the opposite problem.

Gideon is like an icebox, and he's more than happy to provide me with relief. He presses up against my back, his chest to my spine, and I can feel the chill of his body seeping into mine.

"Better?" he murmurs, his voice a low rumble in my ear. Echoes of our kiss invade my memory at the sound.

I nod and try not to shiver as his coolness spreads through me. "Yes, thank you."

He chuckles, as though he knows the sound sends a thrill straight between my thighs, and wraps his arms around me, pulling me tight against his chest. I should resist, I know I should. But it feels so good to be surrounded by his cool body; to have his arms around me.

I close my eyes and let myself enjoy the moment, pretending for just a little while that he is mine, and I am his, and we're just two lovers enjoying each other's company. That we're not in the middle of a war, fighting for our respective sides. That we're not potential enemies. Relaxing into his hold, the whisper of Gideon's lips brush against the pulse just below my ear. Nothing can stop the shiver that racks my body or the moan that spills from my mouth.

"Gideon," I gasp, clutching at his arms as he teases my neck with his teeth.

"Hmm?" he hums, his voice a low purr that vibrates through my body. His tongue flicks out, tasting the sensitive skin of my neck and sending a jolt of pleasure straight to my core.

"We shouldn't," I whimper, even as my body betrays me and presses back into his.

I'm met with the thick evidence of his arousal jutting against the apex of my thighs. I arch into him, my ass grinding against his stiff length.

"Oh, but we could." He drags my skin between his teeth.

I reach my hand to grip his scalp, his strands like silk between my fingers as I press his head against my neck in encouragement. My thighs squeeze together, desperate for friction, for relief.

Gideon's hand comes up to meet mine, intertwining with mine as he releases my hold on his head. He guides our conjoined hands down my neck and between the valley of my chest, an excruciatingly slow journey. Pausing to flick his thumb across the tight bud of my breast, I release a weak mewl when he travels further south, earning a chuckle in my ear. My breath hitches when he presses the tops of my fingers under the band at my waist.

A hungry growl stirs in his throat when our fingers dip into the entrance to my channel. "You're soaked." His voice comes out thick, laced with desire. "For me."

I can't deny it, excuse it away, or utter a single word; my breathing rapid as he slowly gathers the slickness between my thighs and drags our fingers to my aching bundle of nerves. He pins the blade of our hands there, teasing me with leisurely circles until I'm nearly begging him for more.

I take over, increasing the speed and pressure, desperate for release. His cock ruts against my underwear, the two pieces of fabric separating us, denying what we truly crave. Gideon loosens his hold on my fingers, leaving me to my clit as his spear into my channel. A deep, keening moan escapes me, spurring him on to slip another finger inside me.

"Please," I beg. What for? I don't know.

His lips latch onto my neck just as I spasm around him, pulsating as pleasure rockets through me. I barely register having released his cock from his shorts where he's gone commando, but I have enough conscience to keep my underwear on as I guide his erection between my sticky thighs. It glides with ease, jutting against my clit with each piston of his hips.

"Tell me what you need," he grunts in my ear. "Anything."

My head swivels from side to side, unable to put words to what my body demands. Unwilling to give a voice to the ache left unsated. Three little words sit on the edge of my tongue, and it takes an act of the gods to keep me from shouting it out loud just as we climax together. Hot ropes of Gideon's seed coat my thighs, my underwear, my stomach.

He rolls me onto my back, his hands coming to cup my face. Our mouths meet in a reverent prayer. My heart thunders in my chest, as though it could chisel space right inside my rib cage, etching Gideon's name through sheer will alone.

Our kiss breaks too soon, and deep pools of blue drink me in. Gideon drags his thumb across my bottom lip, sight transfixed on my tongue that meets it. He blinks away, lost in thought before tucking me into the crook of his arm. Neither of us makes a move to clean me up, as though we both enjoy the idea of him having left his mark on me, no matter how crude it might seem.

It's not long before I've stopped sweating, and my skin no longer feels sticky. I relax into Gideon's embrace, eyes trained on the canvas walls, watching the faint flicker of the moons through the clouds.

"Lana?" he whispers, his lips brushing against my ear.

"Hmm?"

"I know you're not ready to believe me, but I want you to know that I am telling the truth. About everything." He pauses and I wait for him to continue. "I know it's not what you want to hear, that the males you love have done something so heinous, and I promise I will give you all the time you need. But please, believe me when I say that I am one hundred percent committed to you. I will do whatever it takes to help you remember who you are, and to keep you safe. Even if you decide not to believe me in the end."

"Gideon..." I sigh, my heart aching. I want to believe him, and I don't. What does it mean if he's telling me the truth?

"I know, love," he says, his voice full of understanding. "Just know that I am here for you, and I will never give up on you. No matter what."

Closing my eyes, I let out a shaky breath. I believe him. I don't know why, but I do. And that scares me more than anything else.

CHAPTER 30

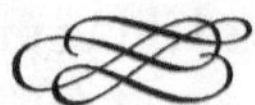

LANA

Sometime late in the night, Gideon shoots out of bed, plastering himself to the opposite end of the tent. The only noise is the sound of my labored breathing and the whip of the wind against the canvas.

My supernatural sight immediately narrows on him once I've realized we're not in danger. He bares his fangs. His pupils take up most of his eyes, and a low growl emits from his chest. My heart thunders, drawing his attention as I freeze, my breath held, listening for the rapid heartbeat that's a telltale sign he's feral, or about to be. My hand comes to my neck, feeling for any wounds, but I find none.

Something is wrong.

Realization sinks in a moment later, and my features soften.

"Gideon, you need to feed." The message comes out even, a skill I've practiced at court, despite the fear paralyzing me. I feel like I'm trying to reason with a velociraptor.

"No," he snarls. "Can't. Weaken. You." He punctuates each word through clenched teeth.

"If you don't, you're going to hurt me," I say, keeping my voice steady, though my shoulders have already relaxed. "Please, Gideon. You need to do this."

He shakes his head and presses even further against the wall, taking the tent with him. "No, I can't. I'll be feral. Uncontrollable. Never again."

Pausing, I consider our options for a moment, all while having to crane my head because the roof presses against it with the pressure put on the wall. Gideon needs to feed, or he'll starve. When he eats, he'll turn feral, and I'll lose my magic temporarily, no matter what. Unless ...

A thought niggles at the back of my mind, and I take a deep breath.

"What if I let you feed from me?" I say slowly. He's shaking his head before I even finish speaking, and I put my hands out in a placating gesture when he attempts to interrupt. "Enough for you to get your fill, whether you take a few seconds, minutes? However long it takes. As soon as my powers come back, I'll make you a fae, and you'll never want for blood again. I'm high queen, so I can do it without help."

A preternatural stillness comes over Gideon, and he stares at me in shock. Blue bleeds back into his eyes; his pupils taking a temporary respite, and his fangs slide back into their recesses. "You'd do that for me?"

I draw the blanket further up my lap. "Yes, I would. I know how much self-control it takes for you to not ... do what you need to do. I can't imagine how hard it must be. So, let me help you. Please."

He doesn't say anything for a long moment, and I wonder if he's going to refuse. But then, finally, he nods, a look for all the world as though I hold it in my hands.

"Alright," he says softly before sinking to his knees, though he keeps his distance. "Promise me something. I can't stop feeding once I'm feral. I can't hurt you, Lana. It'll kill me. Knock me out, lop off my head, distract me, whatever you must do to get me to stop feeding. I give you permission to do it."

I hesitate for a moment before I nod. "All right. We'll work something out." The thought of killing him, though, sends a raw jolt of fear through me. Now that I don't have Gideon's cool skin plastered to mine, it's hot, so I throw off the covers.

He nods and crawls towards me with caution. I blink away the wild, this-isn't-the-time-to-imagine-him-naked thoughts running rampant in my head. When he's close enough, he reaches out and strokes my cheek with the back of his hand.

"Thank you, Lana," he whispers as he moves in. My breath hitches because I think he's going to kiss me, and I don't know if I want to tell him to stop. A dimpled smirk crosses his face, and I know in that moment he knows exactly what I'm thinking. He pauses so his mouth is right against my ear, the sound of his next words sending a delicious thrill through my core when his lips brush against my pulse. "For everything."

Before I can respond, Gideon sinks his teeth into my flesh and I gasp, the bite having caught me by surprise. Pain blossoms in my neck, quickly overshadowed by pleasure as his tongue laves the wound. My head falls back, and my eyelids flutter shut as he sucks, a fevered, ferocious pull at my vein. Arousal courses through me, pooling low in my stomach and to the crevice between my legs. I moan softly as his mouth works its magic, my hand threading through his hair to keep him close.

I sigh as he sucks harder, the vibration sending a bolt of desire through me. My fingers tighten, and my other hand moves to his chest, feeling the steady thump of his heartbeat beneath my palm as I arch into him. Normally his heart beats so softly, I can barely hear it, even with supernatural hearing. But when he's feral, it's like thunder, detonating against his ribcage in hurried claps. It's meant to serve as a warning; that he is a beast, and I am but his meal to devour. For a moment, with him between my thighs like this, I allow myself to give into it.

It's not so bad being his prey.

I barely registered my magic drain, though now I miss the thrum of it in my veins and the current of it along my neural pathways. I'm so lost in pleasure, it's not until my fingers and toes begin to numb do I remember he's feeding from me.

Fear strikes me when I remember something else we'd forgotten to factor into all of this. *I'm pregnant.* Panic grips me, and I cry out, using the adrenaline to fuel me. It takes everything I have to pull him off my neck. Not just because he's strong, but because I'm weak.

How much blood can he take without killing us both? I have serious reservations about having a child with a man that's not one of my mates, but it's still my child, and I will protect him or her with vicious ferocity. Gideon snarls, trying to get to any part of my flesh he can reach. His pupils swallow his irises and blood smears his mouth and chin. Even rabid, he's beautiful.

The thought and my momentary hesitation leave him an opening, and he tackles me, pinning me beneath him. When he pierces my neck, I shout, but I'm too feeble to get him off me. Longing rockets through my body, and I arch into him. He drives his erection against my core; a steady pressure that doesn't let up. I find my hips undulating against his, seeking friction, anything to relieve the constant edging I get from his bite.

"Gideon," I call out weakly. My vision grows hazy, darkness creeping in.

From his position over me, I have access to his shoulder. I clomp down on his flesh like my life depends on it—because it does—and don't stop until the metal tang of his blood fills my mouth. He growls, adjusting his position, and giving me enough room to grip his erection. I wince, hesitant to do what I need to do to get him to stop feeding.

I brace myself to injure him but change my mind at the last second. Though it might work to get him off me, I can't permanently injure his goods. Instead, I bring my knee up with all the strength I can muster, straight into his junk.

Nothing happens.

Instead, I feel my magic begin to swirl and build inside me as Gideon feeds. It tingles my extremities, giving me feeling once again in my limbs. I focus on it, letting the power build until I can sense it just at the surface of my skin. Then, I let it go.

Gideon's mouth instantly disengages from my neck, and he rears back, his onyx eyes wild. I take the opportunity to scramble away from him, putting what little distance I can in the tent. He attacks me, and I scream, my power surging until it feels like it's boiling inside me.

His weight presses into me, and before he can sink his teeth into me, I freeze him. Not in the literal sense, but in the way that he can't move.

Why I have my magic right now, I don't know, and I wasn't sure I could use the trick Finn used in the throne room the day the vampires stormed into my coronation ceremony. They say he's also a Luna fae, so he and I should have similar powers. I didn't know how to use this skill, but my body seemed to know exactly what to do when it mattered the most.

The cool of his body does nothing to temper the heat I felt moments ago. He snarls in my ear, but at least he can't bite me. With him hovering just above me, I only need to wait him out until he's coherent again.

* * *

"Lana," Gideon croaks, his voice tight. "Are you okay? Why can't I move?"

"I used my magic," I say, breathless, because I've been crossing my legs for at least a day and a half. My bladder has grown so big, it pushes against my other organs, making it difficult to take deep breaths. I've tried to scoot out from under him, but couldn't, and I would've hurt him if I used magic.

I release Gideon, and he shifts to the side so I can get out.

"How did you have magic?" he calls out to me, but I'm too busy running from the tent to relieve myself.

After finishing my business and washing up, I return to the campsite and plop down next to the tent opening, exhausted. With my bladder having been so full for so long, I didn't get to sleep, and I'm ravenous.

I tear into the food we brought, not caring that it's cold. I wolf it down, and only then do I realize I devoured Gideon's portion for the day, too. He doesn't need real food as a vampire but enjoys eating just the same.

"Lana." Gideon's voice pulls me from my thoughts, and I look up to see him watching me with a bemused expression. "Are you going to tell me how the hell you had magic to stop me?"

I shrug. "No idea. I didn't at first, not for a long time. But then, I felt it surge in me."

"What do you mean, you felt it surge?"

"It was like ... empty. Nothing, not even a stirring. And the next moment, there was this well of magic inside me, and I didn't know how to access it. But then, it just ... overflowed. I don't know how else to explain it."

He studies me for a moment before nodding. "Do you think it was the baby?"

"Maybe." I whisper.

He falls silent after that, and we both just keep our gazes on the horizon. After a while, Gideon speaks up again.

"Lana, about what happened earlier ... "

I wave my hand dismissively. "There's nothing to apologize for. I know you couldn't help it. In a few hours I should be strong enough to make you fae, and you'll never have to worry about that again."

He plops down beside me. "When you were just a witch, you loved me feeding from you. Did I..." his voice is thick. "Did I hurt you?"

A giggle bursts out of me. "No, Gideon, not really."

"What do you mean?"

I brush his hair back so I can get a good look at his face. Concern scores his features. "It felt ... good," I hesitate. "Really good."

Dropping my hand, I avert my gaze from his heated eyes.

He stretches out next to me, languid and comfortable. "Good to know," he says, his deep voice sending vibrations through me. His shirt rides up, giving me an eyeful of his abs, and he smirks, a knowing glint in his scrutiny. "I've missed it. I'd feed while we made love, and it enhanced the feeling for both of us. You sure you don't want to give that a try before turning me fae?" His dimpled grin nearly undoes me.

After he pats the ground, I take his cue to lie next to him. My body curls against his, relishing the coolness, and the contact. My thumb traces his chiseled jaw before he tilts his chin and captures it playfully between his teeth. His mouth closes around it, his tongue sending a delicious thrill straight to my core. A whimper escapes me as he pulls me to straddle him.

Before I can say a word, he sits up so quickly, I squeak and nearly topple over.

"Lana!"

"What?" I shrill, hand coming to my chest to settle my racing heart.

His eyes are wide as he grabs my shoulders. "I know how to get your memories back!"

"What? How?"

He's so excited, he hauls me to my feet and swings me around in a circle. "When we secured our mating bond, I could sense everything that's inside you. All your memories, they're still in me. I can give them back!"

He sets me down, and I stare at him in amazement. "How do you do that?"

Stilling, he winces.

"What?"

"I feed from your thoracic vein, acknowledging the mating bond."

Pausing, I try to think back to my anatomy textbooks from high school. "The one in my chest?"

He nods.

"No." I take a step back from him. "No way."

"Lana, it's the only way."

I shake my head. "We'll see the Crucey first. If she tells me you're being honest, then you can. I've already dishonored my mates enough. I won't have you feeding from my gods damned breast." Nor will I give him the opportunity to secure a mating bond. Not until I know for certain.

He watches me for a moment before nodding. "All right, Lana. We'll do it your way. But you won't be able to change me into a fae, not before I give you your memories, so we need to hurry to find your friend."

CHAPTER 31

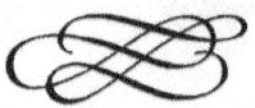

OZ

Waves break against the shore, the sound a gentle serenade as I stand on the sand, gazing out at the water. It's been days since we arrived in Occasus. With me is a small contingent of fae, a dozen witches, and thirty or so vampires. The twins are with their grandparents on Sundahlia, Auguste has Mekhi and a group on Luporia, Rune is with a small battalion on Draconum, and Finn is at his home on Rexuna so he can pinpoint Lana's location. He's got a few pieces of her clothes there, and as soon as he gets her whereabouts, he'll sift back to Occasus to let me know.

After Pippa's death, we decided it's best we don't have the entire family fighting on the same front to help minimize targeted attacks like the one we had with the werewolves. We've launched small, coordinated operations on different continents to keep the enemy guessing while we work to locate Lana, and so we don't draw too much attention before we strike. It's a good strategy, and so far, it's been working.

This makes communicating a lot slower while in the fields, especially since we have to use covert methods of contact so it isn't intercepted by those loyal to the kings. We fear that's how the werewolves were able to know the exact time we planned to arrive at the skull-shaped castle where Luka kept Lana and Gideon.

They won't catch us unaware again.

It shouldn't be long before we've freed Lana and given her back her memories. To have her in my arms again, breathing in her scent, watching her eyes shine brightly as she gazes at me with such love and adoration? She's so deeply embedded into every fiber of my being; I'm a shell of a man without her.

The sound of tandem footfalls captures my attention. I turn to see the grief-stricken faces of Rose and Bennett. My heart sinks, and my brain conjures up every possible reason for their sadness.

"What's wrong?" I ask, my voice laced with concern. It's times like this when I wish I still had the ability to read minds.

Rose sniffles and takes a step towards me before she collapses into my arms, her body trembling as she cries. Bennett is right behind her, and I wrap an arm around him, too.

"It's Teresa," Bennett says, his voice breaking. "She left us."

"What do you mean, left us?" I ask, confused.

Bennett reaches into his pocket and pulls out a crumpled note. He hands it to me, and I smooth it out so I can read it.

Dear Bennett and Rose,

I'm so sorry. I can't do this anymore. By the time you've read this, I'll have gone to join a pack. Please don't try to find me.

Teresa

"I don't understand," I say, handing the note back to Bennett. "Did something happen? I thought she was happy with us." I admit, we've all been so preoccupied with the war and finding Lana that we might've put Teresa's werewolf origins on the back burner. Guilt settles in my stomach like a rock.

"She was," Rose says, wiping at her tears. "But I think she started to feel like she didn't belong."

"I tried to tell her that she did," Bennett says, his voice laced with pain. "But she wouldn't listen to me."

"Did you tell her how you feel about her?" I ask.

Bennett nods, and Rose sniffles. "I did, but she just said we couldn't be together because she's a werewolf and I'm fae."

I run a hand through my hair, frustration coursing through me. "Do you know where she went?"

Bennett shakes his head, and Rose shrugs. "She didn't say."

I pull them both into a hug, wishing I could take away their pain. "I'm sorry. We'll figure this out, okay? I promise."

But even as I say the words, I know it might not be that easy. Teresa is a werewolf, and Bennett is fae. If they want to be together, it's going to take more than just a little effort. It's going to take a miracle with all the history between the two species.

* * *

COME NIGHTFALL, I plan to venture into the city to see if I can get any information on Lana's whereabouts. By morning, we'll have captured the fae army hidden in makeshift barracks along the South end of Occasus. After seeing Gideon feral on the video feed, Bennett had the idea of taking our vampire blood and injecting it into the fae armies to temporarily neutralize their powers and strength. That was before we learned that Teresa ghosted us all. Just up and left, leaving Bennett and Rose heartbroken.

Our goal in Bedlam isn't to kill—although I have no problem protecting our family—it's to immobilize their troops, win the war, and place Finn back as High King. There's no sense in killing off armies that'll soon be under his command.

With that, I head back to the compound we've set up just outside the city. Pippa and Elliot have a station set up to draw blood from the vampires. Once a vampire finishes, the witches give the vampires some blood to help restore what they gave away. It's a process that takes most of the day, but it's worth it to have everyone fully functioning when we move in.

I find Wren amid it all, his arm outstretched as Pippa draws blood from him. He's speaking with her in low tones, and she nods in understanding before he moves to the next station.

"How's it going?" I ask him as I fall into step beside him.

"As well as can be expected." He gives a weary sigh. He's a younger vampire, and he hasn't let go of the muscle memory of breathing. "No word from Finn yet?"

I shake my head. "Not yet. He's working on it, though."

He can see right through my apprehension. I survey the forest obscuring our location, eyes tracking a sustai bird making an awful mess in the trees. When the twins were kidnapped, he was able to get a read on where they were in mere minutes. Finn left two days ago. We haven't heard from him since.

"If he isn't back by morning, I'll try to reach the twins." I hesitate. "As Luna fae, they are likely strong enough to do the spell themselves. They'll need to sneak into the castle again to get something of Lana's, but I think they can do it."

"I agree." Wren takes the witch's proffered wrist in front of him. He sinks his fangs into her skin, just as Sebastian sidles up to me.

"All set?" Sebastian asks as he looks over the crowd.

A flicker of jealousy passes over his face as he glances at Wren feeding from the witch's wrist, but he's quick to dismiss it. The two aren't mated yet, but given how much time they spend together, it's only a matter of time until the bond is sealed. Wren notices the fleeting look and stops feeding.

"Yes," I say as my ears prick at the sound of someone calling my name.

I turn to see Killian, our hired spy, running towards us, a panicked look on his face. The electronic spy glass he carries is clenched in his fist, and I can see the fear in his eyes.

"What is it?" I ask as he comes to a stop in front of us. His chest heaves, his skin sunburnt.

"All the kings have mobilized back to Rexuna," he says, his voice shaking.

Wren's attention snaps to him at the words, and he moves to my side. "Why would they do that?"

"I don't know, but they're leaving their posts unguarded." Killian shoves the device into his pocket. "If we move now, we can take the barracks. Occasus only has its low-level unit in place."

A plan starts to formulate in my mind, and I can see the same thing happening with Wren. "We need to move now," I say. "If they're all in Rexuna, maybe they have a lead on where Lana and Gideon are."

He nods, and we start issuing orders to the vampires and witches. We must move fast if we want to take Occasus by surprise.

In less than an hour, we're on the move. Wren and I lead the charge with our inner circle of vampires at our back. The rest of our forces are close behind, but they'll hang back until we give the signal.

We reach the outskirts of the fort and take cover in the trees. The sun hangs on the horizon, casting an orange glow on the leaves, and Occasus will be expecting their night shift soon. That's when we'll move in. I send a group of vampires to scope out the entrance and report back. In the meantime, Wren and I go over the plan one last time.

"Remember, our goal is to immobilize and capture," I remind him. "Avoid killing anyone."

While the fae have no qualms about eliminating us, we're playing towards a different goal. Even if I want to take revenge on them for lighting an entire field of vampires on fire, the bigger picture matters most.

He nods. Wren was a fighter pilot in WWII, and he's killed more than his fair share of people. He reminds me a lot of Auguste, with his polished exterior and calm demeanor. But where Auguste is all hard edges, Wren is more like a blade of grass in the wind. He's adaptable and can change course on a dime.

The group returns, and we finalize our plan. Then we wait for nightfall.

As the sun dips below the skyline, we make our move. Our witches head in first, using their magic to mask our approach. Wren and I split up, each of us leading a group towards one of the entrances. The main guardhouse has twenty-five soldiers, all asleep, and four on patrol. The vampires with us are silent as we move through the trees, and when we attack, they take the guards down without making a sound.

We move through the fort, securing each building and taking out the sentinels. It's easier than we thought it would be, and soon the entire fort is under our control.

Now we just have to wait for the shifter fae to sift each soldier to the prison cells at Finn's castle on Rexuna. They're warded from magic, so not even a dragon shifter can get out. It's in the Northern region of the continent, and despite his five-hundred-year absence, the staff remained faithful to their king.

We bind the soldiers, just in case they burn through the small bit of blood we gave them to sift them, and then we make our way back to the main guardhouse. That's where we'll hack their security system and find out what communications have gone out about the kings' return to Convectus.

"Oz," Wren says, his voice low as we step into the comms room. "You should see this video."

I join him at the bank of monitors, my heart sinking as I take in the scene. The entire court is assembled in the throne room, and they appear eager, happy even.

"What is this?" I ask, my voice tight as I glance at the bottom right corner of the screen to check the date. It's from several days ago.

"I'm not sure," Wren says, his fingers flying over the keyboard as he tries to access the audio. "Look at the sack they're focused on."

I lean closer, my blood running cold when I see the black bag on the stairs. "What do you think is in it?" A nagging feeling tells me I already know.

"Let's find out," Wren says, finally getting the audio to work.

"And it's all here?" Grimm asks the assembled team of guards in front of him.

"Yes, your majesty." A guard kneels on the dais, emptying the rucksack of its contents. One by one, he places the items back into the bag, identifying them. "Heart of a siren, fang of a basilisk, Occasus ruby, Sundahlian sand, bones of a traitor, moon fire ashes, Sea of Triune salt, ground gnome treasure, wood from a shipwreck, a compass, muscle of a berserker, sustai bird excrement, eye of a cyclops, and petal from a moon flower."

"*Excellent,*" *Penn says, his voice pleased.* "*Now all we need is the blood of a mate.*"

"They can't have gathered all the ingredients for the relocation spell already, could they?" I whisper.

"Looks that way," Wren says, his brow furrowed. "We need to find Lana and Gideon before they do."

CHAPTER 32

LANA

For two more days, we search for entrance to the Crucey's alleged habitat, but we find nothing. Gideon grows impatient, and I can sense his excitement to try and give me my memories back. But I hold firm, telling him over and over that we need to find her first.

He doesn't argue with me anymore, but I can tell he's not happy about it, though he tries to compensate by dialing up his charm. He's a smooth talker, but now he's laying it on so thick, even I'm starting to believe his words.

"Lana, love," he croons as we sit around the fire one night. "Would you believe me if I told you I spent months trying to get you to reveal your feelings for me?"

I raise a brow. "Actually, that's about the least far-fetched thing you've said to me yet. You are persistent."

He gives me a lopsided grin. "I wanted you from the first moment I saw you. You were so different than anyone else. When you greeted me at the door, I just knew."

"Knew what?"

His eyes intensify as he gazes at me. "That you were destined to be my mate."

I swallow hard. "Gideon ... "

"I know you don't remember, but we have a bond. A connection that goes deeper than just physical attraction. I can feel it, and I know you can too. My first actions towards you weren't kind." His voice is thick with emotion. "I've spent the entire time you've been in Bedlam, in their clutches, wondering if this was the price I had to pay for my slight against you."

Swallowing, I attempt to slow my breathing. "I don't understand?"

"It was Thanksgiving, and when you opened that door to welcome me into your home, I brushed right past you, blatantly disrespecting you."

"Why would you do that?"

"Because I knew the moment I acknowledged the way you made me feel, with only a single glance your way, I was done for. Oz helped me see reason, and after that?" He's so close to me now, I can sense the faint beating of his heart. "You're mine, Lana. And I'm never going to let you go."

He kisses me then, and I can taste the truth of his words on his lips. It's soft, but there's an urgency to it. A need that seems to be coming from deep inside. As his tongue slips past my teeth and into my mouth, I whimper. Brick by brick, the wall I've been holding between us begins to crumble, and I let myself fall into the kiss.

Gideon pulls me onto his lap, and I can feel the hard length of him pressing against my core. Arousal spikes through me, and I eagerly grind myself against him. He growls deep in his throat, and his hands tighten on my hips.

"Are you sure?" he rasps out. "Because once I start, it'd take Aggonid himself to stop me."

The mention of Aggonid seems to startle him, and I meet his haunted gaze. The same one I've caught on his face when he gets quiet, as though reliving the torture of his time in fae hell. It shakes me out of my lust-filled haze.

I pull back from him.

"Fuck," I whisper. "I'm sorry, Gideon, but I can't."

Standing, I walk away from him, trying to distance myself from the feelings his words evoke in me. They're so strong, so intense. And they scare me.

* * *

"WHAT IF THE reason we can't find the entrance is because it's hidden?" Gideon props himself on his elbow next to me in the tent. A sandstorm rages outside, and we've been cooped up for hours.

"What do you mean?"

"I mean, what if the entrance is hidden by magic? We wouldn't be able to see it unless we knew where to look."

I sit up, considering his words. "The pond?"

He shrugs. "It's possible. The entrance could be underwater."

"But how would we get in?"

He shrugs. "I don't know. Maybe we could use magic. The current recognized you for a reason."

"Alright." I fiddle with the zipper on the backpack I took from the lighthouse. "You'll need to hold onto me, and I'll create a barrier, so I won't drown when I'm dragged under."

I'm in as little clothing as I can muster without being indecent, on account of the heat, my tiny shorts and tank top hiding nothing. Gideon strips down to his boxers, and I can't help but stare. He's so well-built, all hard muscle and smooth skin. When I questioned him about dressing down, since the heat doesn't bother him, he said it was only fair because I'm teasing him by being practically naked.

My gaze lingers on his tapered torso, dipping to the sharp V and envisioning what I might find below. Our brief encounters in the tent and quick glimpses only leave me hungering for more time to memorize every detail.

Gideon hooks his thumbs in his waistband, shimmying them down, down—

"Striga, if you keep undressing me with your eyes, we're both going to end up naked." His honey-laced voice interrupts my blatant thirst for him.

I imagine guilt riddles my features when I swallow thickly and avert my eyes. My hands reach for a blanket, anything to busy them so I don't find them tracing the taut curve of his pecs, or the narrowed dip of his hip.

I wish I'd thought to bring a book or a deck of cards to keep us busy. Instead, we've been lying around in the tent, talking, stealing glances at each other. Gideon has told me stories of his life before he was turned. He grew up in the Dolomites thousands of years ago, and his family were farmers. He had a happy childhood, even if it was a bit boring.

"You've been there, you know." Gideon's voice breaks into my thoughts.

"What?"

"To the Dolomites. You went there with me."

I shake my head. "Sorry, I don't remember it."

He nods. "It was before ... well, it doesn't matter now. Just know that I'll take you there again one day, and you'll see how beautiful it is."

The wind dies down, and Gideon stands. "I think the storm has passed. We should go."

He holds out his hand to me, and I take it. We pack everything quickly, and Gideon wears the backpack. Stalking towards the direction of the pond, it's eerily quiet, and the air is still.

"Let's fly there," I say.

Fae don't normally take their wings out for anyone but their mates, but I think I can make an exception for him. He's immortal and has little use for my life-reviving feathers.

I peel out of my shirt and shorts, leaving me in just my underwear. Gideon's eyes darken as he watches me, and I can feel the desire emanating from him.

Shaking it off, I focus on my magic. My wings appear, their weight bearing down on my back. Gideon's mouth drops open, and he reaches out to run his hands over them. A shudder runs through me at his touch, but I ignore it, doing what I can to resist the urge to ask him to stroke them again. My body glows under the arousal, and his nostrils flare.

"They're so soft," he whispers. "I didn't think you could get any more beautiful ..." His words are revenant, and they wash over me like a caress.

Heat creeps up my cheeks and I clear my throat. "Thank you. Are you ready?"

He bows, gesturing to me in a way that says, 'after you,' and I open my arms to him. He steps into my embrace, and I wrap them around his waist. Taking a deep breath, I jump into the air, flapping my wings to gain altitude. It's difficult carrying his substantial weight, but not as difficult as it is to ignore the way his body feels against mine or the electric pulse that seems to run between us every time our skin touches.

Somehow, I keep my focus. We soar over the desert, the wind whipping through our hair. Gideon whoops with delight, and I can't help but laugh.

It feels good to be flying again. It's been too long.

For hours, we fly. It's somewhat cooler the higher we are in the sky. The sun sinks, and color splashes the barren landscape, turning it into burnished gold. The moons loom large on the horizon, standing like sentinels over its charges.

"This is amazing," Gideon says, his voice full of awe. "I've never seen anything like it."

"I know," I whisper. "It's one of the reasons I love it here."

When my arms tire of holding him, Gideon holds me. But every time his hands are free, he's taken to caressing my wings when I soar. I tried to hide the pleasure it gives me at first, but eventually, I give up. My breath hitches with each stroke, and my body is on fire by the time we land near the pond.

I set Gideon down gently, and I reluctantly release him. "I'll set up the tent," he says, his voice thick with desire.

Nodding, I walk to the pond, determined to put some space between us. It's still and calm, reflecting the stars that are shining overhead. It's so peaceful here.

I lower myself to the edge of the pond and dip my toes in the cool water. Out of the corner of my eye, I spot a very naked Gideon running towards me. He jumps over my head, and cannon balls into the pond with a loud splash.

I shriek and flinch back as cold water drenches me. "Gideon!"

He surfaces, laughing. "It's called skinny-dipping, Lana. You should try it sometime."

I don't have it in me to scowl at him because I'm too busy laughing at his ridiculousness. "I'll have you know, I've skinny dipped. Quite regularly."

Something flashes across his face, and I grimace. "Sorry, that was really insensitive of me."

He shakes his head. "It's okay. I know you didn't mean it that way."

I undress, blatantly ignoring the heated look in his eyes. Scooping water by the handful, I make quick work of washing myself using the soapberries I'd shoved in my pocket before we set out on our journey. I don't fully submerge myself for fear of drowning. Once I'm dressed again, my attention turns to Gideon.

He swims to the edge of the pond and stretches his arms across the ledge. I can't help but admire his body. He's a beautiful sight, all tanned skin and muscles rippling with each stroke. My heart races as I watch him, and I have to fight the urge to strip down again and join him.

It would be so easy to just give in, to let myself be consumed by him, like a match to oil. But I know that if I do, there will be no going back. And I'm not sure if I'm ready for that.

Just as I've had the thought, Gideon swims towards me, capturing my ankles. His hooded gaze is full of intent as his hands move up my calves before settling on my inner thighs. He kneads my legs, sending heat right to my center. He presses cool lips to each knee, dragging against my skin, leaving fire in its wake.

My head falls back and my eyelids shutter when his mouth lands at the small triangle between my thighs. Through the fabric, I feel the cool breath he forces out of his lungs straight against my core. My eyes fly open, and his nostrils flare as he drags in more air.

"Fuck, you smell good," he croons.

His teeth capture my flesh through my linen shorts, and he tugs my clit between his lips, rolling the bud between them.

I gasp, hands flying out to grip onto his hair. Meaning to push him away, my body involuntarily tugs him closer. I couldn't stop myself if I tried. "Gideon—"

A deep moan escapes me when he sucks, eviscerating any half-formed objection on my tongue. Before I know what I'm doing, I've hooked a thumb to where the fabric is bunched and tug it to the side, giving him complete access to my soaking sex.

Pools of desire swims in his gaze when it meets mine just as he swipes his tongue from the bottom to the top.

"You taste even better than I remember." His groan rumbles against me. "I just needed a taste."

His pinched features share his barely contained desire, and for once, he's the one with enough sense to stop before we go any further. Gideon settles next to me on the ledge, and I'm left reeling from the all-too-brief encounter. He gazes up at the stars, brushing my shoulder with his. "When you were gone, I wrote to you every day. Each of us has a journal filled with letters, waiting for the day you come back to us," he says, his voice melancholy.

"Oh, Gideon," I whisper, my heart aching for them, despite my heaving breath and lust-raddled brain. "I'm so sorry."

Even if he's being dishonest, and all of this is an elaborate scheme to turn me against my mates, he appears not wistful, but crestfallen.

"It's not your fault, Lana. We knew the risks when we agreed to this," he says. "Not that any of us had much choice."

We sit in companionable silence before he nudged me. "Let's eat, then go to bed. We'll jump in the pool at first light."

CHAPTER 33

LANA

We wake early, eager to see if our hunch is right. After devouring our food, Gideon bounds over to the pond, and I follow close behind. In just his boxers, he dives in, whipping his head around a lot like Casimir does when he breaches the surface.

A grin splits his face, and it's a beautiful sight. His blue eyes are alight with happiness, and his white teeth glint off the reflection of the sun on the water. "Do your little magic thing and get in here with me."

I laugh and conjure a protective barrier around my head so I can breathe under water. I strip down to my underwear before joining him. It's colder than it was last night, on account of not having time to bake in the sun yet, and it feels good after the long flight yesterday. Gideon swims over to me, and his eyes darken when they settle on my body.

His arms wrap around my waist just as the current starts pulling us towards the center of the pond. "Atta girl," he breathes, "I think it's time."

The flow strengthens, but Gideon doesn't fight it this time, and keeps an iron grip on me. It's not long before we're pulled under, and everything goes dark. We spin rapidly, tossed around like seashells in the surf. The next thing I know, I'm gasping for air, and light shines all around me. I blink rapidly, trying to adjust to the sudden change. It takes a moment for me to realize that Gideon and I are no longer in the pond. We're now in some sort of cave, surrounded by a waist-high pool of water.

"What the hell?" I mutter, turning in a slow circle.

Gideon pops up next to me, eyes wide with wonder. "I don't know, Lana, but I think we just found the Crucey."

I whip my head behind me just as she croons, "Lana, welcome to my home." Gone is her shaggy fur, grotesque maw, and long claws. If it weren't for her wise eyes and her creaky voice, I wouldn't have known this was her.

Standing on the bank is an elderly woman, her back hunched with age, which is so at odds with everything I know about fae. Is that what she even is? How old must she be to show wrinkled skin? She wears a long dress made of leaves and twigs, and her gray hair is streaked with green.

"Come, child," she croaks, beckoning me forward.

I hesitate for only a moment before I wade through the water towards her. Gideon follows close behind me, his hand on my lower back.

"Who are you?" I ask when I reach her. Just to be sure.

"I am the Crucey, but you can just call me Crucey. And you, my child … it's so good to see you again," She taps her chest with her palm.

"That's well and all, but could you just tell her I'm really her mate?" Gideon interrupts. I elbow him because he's being rude. Instead of shying away from my touch, he captures it, looping his arm through mine.

Crucey raises an eyebrow as she glances his way before returning her attention to me with a bemused smirk. "Come, dear."

She takes my hand and leads me deeper into the cave. It's damp and cool, with a loamy smell that makes my nose crinkle. The walls are rough and mossy, and stalactites bedecked in auburn, crimson, and cerulean blooms hang from the ceiling. There's a narrow passage leading deeper into the dark, and though Crucey is my friend, I think,

I keep on high alert as we step around towering columns. Gideon stays tucked to my side, looking around with fascination.

Crucey stops in front of a large stone door covered in lichen. "Through this gate lies your destiny, Lana," she says, before pushing it open, the pressure changing in the small corridor as she does.

I step through the doorway and into a brightly lit cavern. Hundreds of little faces peer up at me, and a gasp escapes my lips. So many *children*.

I've never seen a fae child before.

"Who are they?" I whirl around to face Crucey. "What is this place?"

"They, my dear, are the Tolden," Crucey says as she comes to stand beside me. "And you are *their* high queen, too. This is their refuge."

I blink in surprise before crouching down so I'm at the Tolden's level. A familiar face pushes through the crowd, causing a tear to roll down my cheek. I'd recognize those eyes anywhere. Instead of the little bundle of fur I'm used to, though, a beautiful child with amber wings stands before me.

"Hi," I whisper, opening my arms for him.

This is the baby I saved from the werewolves all those months ago when I first met Crucey. He wraps her arms around me and squeezes. "Thank you."

"Always," I say, tears streaming down my face. I pull back and look at another, older face moving to the front. I recognize her, too, and not just because of the mischievous grin she sports.

"You're the one who told me to unite the realms," I breathe. In the forest when Aed had taken his life. A shadow version of her had spied on me in Luka's room, too.

"And you will," she says with a satisfied nod. "Just like the prophecy says you will."

I gape at her in shock before looking back at Crucey. "What prophecy?"

"You are the child of both light and dark worlds, Lana. Born in both realms, and you will unite them as one." She peers up at me. "Wicked Bedlam and Broken Earth need each other."

I shake my head. "I was born in Minnesota."

She smiles. "Yes, you were. And then, you were made fae in Bedlam."

My knees weaken, and Gideon catches me before I can fall. "You okay?" he whispers, worry carved into his features.

I nod, even though I'm far from okay. Months ago, I agreed to be high queen, but didn't agree to anything about solving the world's problems. I'm in way over my head.

Crucey takes my hand and squeezes. "You are strong enough, child. I have faith in you."

She dismisses the Tolden, who scurry to tunnels jutting off from the room, until it's just the three of us again. An older Tolden bounds in, heaving our gear we left along the bank and sets it in front of us before running out before I can thank him.

"What now?" I ask, feeling lost.

"Now," she smirks. "The truth." She inclines her head for us to follow.

CHAPTER 34

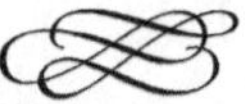

CASIMIR

"She's going to see the Crucey," I hiss, slamming my fist into the wall. A portion of it crumbles, tumbling to the floor.

"What?" Grimm asks, coming to stand beside me in Lana's room. I've taken to spending most my days and nights here, looking for some semblance of comfort amongst her things.

"Lana told us the Crucey owes her a boon and would tell her whatever she wanted to know." I pace, tugging on my hair. "She's going to know we lied to her. That we stole her from her mates."

"What are we going to do?" Penn growls, worry stamped into his features.

I pause to look at him. "We're going to tell her the truth. We need to hurry," I whine, using my magic to nurture the plants lining the window. "If the Crucey tells her, there's no chance we'll ever get her back."

We sift to the throne room. Gathering the leftover ingredients from our last finder spell, I shove them in a bag with provisions and camping gear, just in case. The others gather their things and meet me back on the dais.

Pierce, Captain Zara, and Sarai sift in moments later with their own gear. "We're coming with."

I nod, knowing we'll need their backup, and Lana's maid will be a neutral voice of reason. In minutes, we sift to the entrance to the Wastelands. Knowing time is of the essence, each of us don our wings and take flight, using the tug of our mating bond to help us locate where she's at in the region. It's not very accurate, but together, it's a stronger compass.

We're immediately hit with a wall of heat, and the air shimmers with magic. We fly as fast as our wings will take us, stopping only long enough to rest a few hours, eat, and drink. As we get further into the Wastelands, it becomes impossible to fly, so we trudge along on foot.

Three agonizing days tick by, but we're finally close. We circle a pond several times, unable to find where the trail leads, though the pull is strongest here. She has to be here, somewhere. Landing, we make camp along its bank. I shuck off my shirt so I'm just in shorts and dive in, swimming laps to help me think.

When I break the surface, I see the others gathered on the shore, looking at something. "What is it?" I ask, swimming over.

"Your mate," Zara says with a grin, holding up a piece of torn, red fabric.

I take it from her, my heart pounding as realization sets in. "This is Lana's."

The current pulls me under so suddenly, I'm slow to react from the shock. I hear muffled shouting before the deafening roar of the water drowns them out. It's pitch black, and I don't know which way is up, on account of getting tossed around like I'm in a whirlpool.

Blinding light causes me to shut my eyes reflexively. When I blink them open them again, I'm standing in waist-deep water in the middle of a fae light-drenched cavern. Seconds later, splashes let me know the others have followed.

"What the actual fuck?" Penn gasps, looking around.

The cave is enormous with a ceiling so high, it's lost in the shadows. Glimmering light dances on the water and along the walls from what must be thousands of fae-flies.

We all just stand there for a minute, taking in the surreal beauty. It feels like we're in another world.

"Did the Crucey do this?" I ask while wading to shore. My voice echoes off the walls, and the fae-flies scatter, taking a lot of the light with them.

We pull ourselves out of the water, each inspecting the place for any signs of Lana. A tinkling sound of laughter has us all on edge and we whip around, searching for the source. It's then we see a tunnel on the far end of the room, light spilling out from it.

"That way," I say, already moving towards it.

The others follow, and we find ourselves winding through narrow passageways, the light growing brighter the further we go. Moisture clings to the walls, dripping onto the path at our feet. The laughter becomes more distinct, and I know without a doubt that it's Lana. We spill into another chamber and stop dead in our tracks.

Lana. My heart bursts with equal parts relief that she's safe, and sheer panic at our impending doom.

She sits atop a large, moss-covered boulder in the center of the cave with an old woman who looks to be made entirely of light. At their feet is a sizable, black crystal ball on a rough-hewn stand. The woman's hands rest on the glassy surface, not bothering to glance our way.

Lana turns as we approach, and surprise brightens her face. "Oh, my gods. H-h-how did you get here?" Her eyes dart between our soaking wet band of mates and supporting crew. She's like a skittish animal, caught in a hunter's sights. My heart clenches at the trepid look on her face.

"We came for you." I approach her. "We've been so worried, and we saw Luka's video, and had to know if you were okay." I want to pull her into my arms and never let her go, but I know we need to explain first. Guilt crosses her features, sending my stomach bottoming out.

The old woman cackles, and the sound reverberates off the walls like nails on slate. It's then I spot the vampire standing in the far entrance to the cavern, fury in his eyes.

His fangs lengthen as he steps forward, and I know he's about to attack.

"No!" Lana jumps up, running to meet me.

She throws her arms around me first, and I melt into her touch. My mate.

"Please, Gideon, don't hurt them," she begs before reaching out for Grimm and Penn to join in the hug.

She pulls back when she sees Sarai and rushes to meet her best friend, though she can't quite meet her eyes, and she stops short, as though coming to her senses. Guilt riddles her maids' expression before turning to hurt at the dejection.

"I'm so sorry," Lana says, her voice shaking as she faces her mates. "Everything got way out of hand with the werewolf king. I have so much explaining to do."

Gideon lets out a snarl, and I rise to meet it with my own. The old woman interrupts us with a chiding remark and calls Lana to her.

"My child, you may want to sit down for this," she whispers, and dread surges through every inch of me.

Lana trembles and takes a seat on the giant rock, looking a little pale. Gideon joins her, wrapping a possessive arm around her shoulders, and I let out a whine. I want to be the one comforting her. I don't know if I'll ever get that chance again.

The woman levels Lana with a sad look. "Gideon speaks the truth."

Lana lets out a keening wail, and Gideon pulls her into his lap, rocking her back and forth. Her hands fist in his bathrobe, and she buries her face against his chest as the sounds of her sobs break me.

I sink to my knees, feeling both her heartbreak and my own through the mating bond. I can't lose her. I won't.

"Lana—" Grimm cries out to her.

"How could you?!" She shrieks, her head snapping up to glare at us. It's a sound I've never heard come from her before. "How could you take away my memories? My friends? My mates? My life? *I'm a mother*!"

She quakes in both fury and grief, and magic swirls around her. It's wild and uncontrolled, and I know she's seconds away from lashing out.

"Lana, please," I beg, crawling towards her. My wolf paces under my skin, urging me to be near her. "We're sorry, so sorry."

"You will be," she snarls, her voice dripping with venom. "I'll make sure of it."

And with that, dozens of enormous fae, of a species I don't recognize, file in. They wear chain metal armor, laced with greenery, and their long, black hair is pulled back in low ponytails. Their eyes gleam red with malice, and I know we're in trouble, but right now, I don't even care.

I've let her down. Told her she could trust me, and I failed. I will make this right. I must make this right.

The guards seize us with little effort because we don't put up a fight. Our only concern is for Lana, and the agony of grief she's feeling as we're hauled away.

CHAPTER 35

LANA

Betrayal is like a cold wind, numbing the soul. I can't feel anything as I watch them take my friend and mates away. I'm frozen in place, my mind a blank slate, before the gale knocks down the walls I'm desperately constructing in my mind and the pain comes rushing back in.

It feels as though someone has reached into my chest and ripped out my heart. I can't breathe, can't think, can't do anything but feel the agony of loss. They were my everything, and they took it all away.

Twice.

First, when they ripped me from my life. And now, when they ripped me from my second. I stand between two worlds, tethered to each side with a broken heart.

I'm completely and utterly alone.

It takes me a while to register the cool body embracing mine. I blink, my vision clearing as I peer into deep blue eyes framed with thick lashes and a strong brow, and the deafening roar in my head fades enough for me to hear the sweet words Gideon coos to me.

"I'm so sorry, my little striga. So very sorry."

My face crumples again, and I sag against him, my body trembling. I can't do this. I can't be strong anymore.

"Make it stop," I wail, my hands fisting in the soft terry of his robe as I try to crawl inside of him. "Please, Gideon. Make it stop."

He lifts me as he stands, carrying me out of the cavern and into the corridor leading to the bedroom Crucey set up for us. I don't know how long he walks for, but eventually, we arrive at our destination. The bedroom is luxurious, with a great bed covered in sumptuous linens, a roaring fire, and a sitting area. Deep purples, greens, and golds dominate the space, and a faint shimmer of magic dances in the air. White Fae-light shifts to a muted blue, meant to soothe, and heal. Flickers of orange dance in the fire, and I can feel the heat begin to seep into my bones, chasing away the chill.

He gently lays me on the bed and tucks me against himself, stroking my hair and murmuring words of comfort. I cry until I have no tears left, until I'm a wrung-out shell of a person. And still, Gideon doesn't leave my side.

He holds me through the night, and I eventually drift off to sleep, feeling a little bit safer in his strong embrace.

It's not enough, though. I know it won't be enough to stop the hurt, but at least for now, I have Gideon. And I'll take whatever comfort I can get.

Sometime hours later, I wake to an empty bed. I sit up, panicking for a moment before I spot Gideon in the corner of the room, his back to me as he types into a cellphone. I can see the stiffness of his shoulders, the way his hands are clenched into fists, and I know he's upset. How many nights have my hands catalogued this man? Felt every plane. Sought his embrace?

I swing my legs out of bed and go to him, wrapping my arms around his waist and burying my face in his back. He stiffens for a moment before he relaxes and leans back into me.

"I'm sorry," I whisper, my voice hoarse from crying. "I'm so sorry."

"It's not your fault, love," he says, turning around so he's facing me. He cups my face in his hands and kisses me gently. "None of this is your fault."

"I know," I say, tears welling up in my eyes again. "But I can't help but feel like it is."

"You may feel that way, but it's far from the truth," he says, his voice soft and gentle. "But I promise, we'll find a way forward."

I gesture to the phone on the table. "Do you get reception down here?"

He smiles at me. "No. I thought I'd try getting in touch with Oz or Auguste, but I'd have to go to the surface for that. I didn't want to leave you by yourself."

"I appreciate that," I say, my stomach growling. "But I'm starving."

He chuckles and kisses me again. And gods, does it feel right. "We'll get you something to eat, and then how about I eat?" He raises his brows, innuendo thick in his tone. "Or, I could eat first, then we'll feed you."

He hoists me into his arms and my legs wrap around his waist. He doesn't stop there, though. Maneuvering me so my thighs straddle his head, he buries his face against my core, tickling me and earning him a giggle.

I wriggle out of his hold and slide down until my feet reach the cave floor. "It's hardly fair you know just how to tickle me, but I don't know where to tickle you yet."

"After I eat, you will."

"My memories," I whisper, realization dawning. "You want to give my memories back."

He nods. "I'd say it's about time, wouldn't you?"

I smile at him and search his eyes. "Yes, I think it is."

CHAPTER 36

LANA

We emerge from our room, dressed for the day, and immediately find a pair of guards outside our door.

"Hi," I say, a little startled.

"Your Majesty," they say in tandem and drop to their knees.

I glance at Gideon, and he inclines his head. I clear my throat. "You may rise. Please, can you show us where we might find some food?"

"Of course, Your Majesty," one of the guards says and stands, leading us down the hallway.

The other guard falls into step behind us, and I can't help but feel a little self-conscious with everyone bowing and scraping.

Lush vegetation lines the walls, and I lean in close to inspect a crimson flower, only to have Gideon's hand close around my arm, stopping me.

"What is it?" I ask, confused.

"That one bites." He grimaces. "It got me yesterday while I stood in the cavern entrance, waiting for you to finish your shower. I had the guards show me which ones were safe after that."

"Ah. Are you okay?"

He smirks at me. "This one," he points to a different flower, green, and oozing, "spits acid."

I raise my brows. "Really?"

He responds by ushering me further away from it. "It's amazing the things you find down here. And this one," he cups my cheek, "is an aphrodisiac."

I blush and look away, but not before I see the heat in his eyes.

"What about this one?" I ask, gesturing to a blueish red flower with long, thin petals.

"That one," he drawls, his voice going low and husky. "Is for later." He plucks it and stuffs it into his pocket.

"What is it?" I whisper.

"Another aphrodisiac," he murmurs conspiratorially, a wicked grin on his face.

My stomach chooses that moment to growl again, and Gideon chuckles. We pick up our pace, following the guard, who leads us down a corridor lined with fuchsia flowers leaking some sort of sap, catching fae-flies in their traps.

"You're paying attention, right?" I nudge him. "I've been too busy staring at all the vegetation to really take note of where we're going."

"Of course, love," he says easily. "I've got a good memory for these things. Best tracker on Earth."

"Is that so?" I raise a brow.

He nods, a smug grin on his face. "You'll see."

We break into a boisterous cavern, filled with Tolden children running and playing. Their laughter echoes off the walls, and I can't help but smile at the sound.

A moment later, a beautiful woman approaches us, a smile on her face. The greenery around her face bleeds into her hair, and I can see why the children were playing here. It's like a scene from a storybook.

"Your Majesty," she bows. "I'm Madison, one of the Tolden chefs. Do you know what you would like?"

"Hello, Madison," I say warmly. "That's a very Earthen name for a fae," I point out.

She smiles. "When we come of age, we get to choose our own name," she explains. "One of the older Tolden snuck in an Earthen movie or two, and I fell in love with the name. But I assure you, my cooking is one hundred percent fae."

"I'm sure it is," I grin before glancing at Gideon and turning back to her. Keeping my voice low, I ask if she has any non-fae blood.

"As a matter of fact," she says, her voice filled with excitement. "I do have some non-fae blood. Will you drink Caspari?"

I choke on my own spit when I squeak. "Caspari!" I exclaim a little too loudly.

Gideon narrows his eyes. "Aren't those the creatures that eat trash?" His nose wrinkling.

Madison's face flushes. "They don't just eat trash," she says indignantly. "They're gentle creatures that happen to enjoy a good garbage meal every now and then. The hordes that roam near the cities are violent because they only have garbage to eat. They're ravenous, and if you keep them fed well, I assure you, their blood is perfectly fine to consume."

Gideon's face softens. "I'm sorry," he says contritely. "I didn't mean to offend you."

"It's quite alright," she says, waving away his apology. "I know they don't look like much, but they're good creatures."

"I've never actually seen one." I shrug.

"I appreciate your hospitality, Madison. Caspari blood and regular food is fine." Gideon pulls me into his side. "I'll have whatever you're feeding my mate."

She glances towards me. "I'll eat anything," I say with hesitation. *Almost* anything.

A pleased smile graces her face. "Excellent. Please, follow me."

We follow Madison through the bustling kitchen where wide-eyed Tolden sink to their knees when they see me. I give them a nod of acknowledgement before turning my attention back to our chef.

She leads us to a small, secluded room where a table is already set for two. There's a bountiful spread of fruits, vegetables, meats, and breads. My stomach growls again, and I hastily sit down, grabbing a piece of bread and tearing into it.

Gideon chuckles and sits down next to me, piling his plate high with food. I watch in amazement as he devours everything on his plate and then some.

"Aren't you going to eat?" he asks, gesturing towards my still full plate.

I pull a piece of bread apart. "Yeah." I try to keep the melancholy out of my voice. "I'm starving, but it's hard to eat with a broken heart."

His smile falls. "I understand," he says quietly. "Do you want to see if we can bring this back to our room?"

"I don't want to seem ungrateful," I hesitate. "But yeah. I would like that."

He rises, holding his hand out for me. I take it, and he helps me to my feet before leading me out of the small dining area. Madison gives me a small smile as Gideon asks for the food to be brought to our chambers.

We make our way back in silence, both of us lost in our own thoughts. When we enter, Gideon immediately goes to the tiny table and pulls out a chair for me. The guards place the food down, and retreat.

"Have you given any more thought to what we talked about?" he asks, his voice low. Fae-light flickers from the lantern on the wall, accentuating the sweep of his lashes.

Sitting down, I sigh while picking at the bread on my plate. "I want to do it tonight," I whisper. "My life was stolen from me. I can't keep living like this; feeling fractured all the time. I want to know who I am, Gideon. I have to. And then, I need to get back to our family."

His face is solemn. "I agree." He places his hand on mine. "We should have Crucey on standby just in case your magic doesn't come back like it did last time."

He moves to sit next to me, and we eat in silence. When we're both done, he takes my plate and sets it on the table before turning to me.

"Are you sure you're ready for this?" he asks, cupping my face in his hands. "I won't be coherent to comfort you when you need it most."

I nod. "I have to be." My voice trembles. "I can't keep living like this, Gideon. I need to know who I am."

"Very well." He places a kiss to my forehead. "I'll go get Crucey."

He stands, and I watch him leave the room. When he returns, he's carrying a small black box, hope lighting up his face. He sets it in front of me before opening it. Inside is a glass vial filled with a thick, red liquid.

"What's this?" I ask, picking up the ampoule.

"She gave me some of her blood; says it'll make me immune to the effects of yours."

"Oh," I say, setting the bottle down. "That's good."

He nods, his face serious. "Yes," he shifts to face me. "It is, but it's only a temporary fix, and her blood suppresses the nourishment I'll get from yours. I'll need to feed again in a couple of days."

Palming the vial, he tilts his chin to the ceiling and downs it in one smooth movement before turning back to me. Cupping my cheek, he places a tender kiss to my lips.

"I love you, Lana," he whispers. "No matter what happens, know that I will always love you."

"I love you too, Gideon," I whisper back. Though this version of me has only known him a couple of months, my soul knows, and saying the words doesn't feel like a lie.

The widest grin adorns his face, and I know in this moment, I'll do anything to be the reason for more of these. It lights up his entire demeanor, as though nothing can shake him.

Gideon lifts me, cradling me against his chest. For the first time today, a surge of happiness and safety fills me. He carries me over to the bed and lays me down, settling his weight next to me. His fingers trace my delicate curves, pebbling them with goosebumps. The press of his lips against my skin is like a prayer, a confessional, a devotion, and a sermon. He takes his time acquainting himself with my new body, like a luthier carefully tuning and listening to how it responds to his ministrations.

My hands come to his face, my thumb stroking the deep grooves of his dimples. I lift my head to kiss each of them. "I love these."

He captures my chin, bringing me to his mouth, where I feel him smile against mine. His palms come around the back of my head, sliding until they cup my pointed ears. "I love these." Pulling back, his thumb presses against my lips, forcing my smile. He drags it until it rests against my dainty fangs. "But these are my favorite."

His tongue darts out, smoothing across the front of them. It's an odd, erotic thing. I drag his bottom lip between my teeth, applying just enough pressure not to break the skin, earning me a deep rumble from his chest. Nipping at it again, I fall back into the cushions.

Love and adoration fill his eyes when he helps me remove my clothes, stopping to praise me with his lips. "You're so beautiful. I missed this, so fucking much."

He kisses me, his mouth urgent and demanding. His hands roam my body, igniting a fire within me that only he can satiate. He rolls so I'm on top of him, my legs spread out on each side of his, and he sits up, his abs contracting into the stuff of a romance novel cover. Showering my neck with his lips, a moan escapes me, heat licking up my spine like a flame.

A predatory growl rolls in his throat before he pulls back. "Are you one-hundred-percent certain? Because once you do this, Lana, I am never, ever letting you out of my sight again."

I swallow hard, my heart pounding in my chest. Helping him out of his clothes, I nod, in case I'm not clear on my intentions. "I'm sure," I whisper. I don't think I've ever been so sure about anything in my life.

He captures my mouth with his once again. His kiss is filled with so much emotion, so much love, that tears fill my eyes. Breaking the kiss, he studies me, his eyes crowded with concern.

"What's wrong?" he asks, wiping away the tears that have tracked down my cheeks.

I shake my head. "It's just ... I don't think I've ever felt so loved before," I whisper. "Don't get me wrong, I love my kings, and they love me. With them ... it started as tinder, and slowly stoked to a lit torch I will carry always." I shrug. "Magic decrees it. But I didn't *burn* for them, and I didn't crave them the way I do you. You're a brush fire; seeking, consuming, destroying everything in its path in the best of ways. If you aren't in my life ..." I worry my lip. "it'll ruin me."

With anyone else, my confession might've been scary, or too

forward. Too intense. Not with him. My gut clenches at how close I came to losing this vampire. Losing *them*. I don't remember the others —not yet—but if they're half as good as he is, the rest of my days will never look the same.

Gideon cups my cheeks in his large palms before kissing me again. This time, it's soft and gentle, filled with reverence. When he pulls away, he takes my hand and brings it to his chest, placing it over his heart.

"Feel that?" he asks, his voice low and thick with emotion. His heart races against my palm, screaming to make itself known. "That's how much I love you, Lana. You own me, body and soul."

I nod, my throat constricting. Gideon loves me, truly loves me, and that knowledge fills me with a warmth that spreads through my entire body.

His mouth claims mine, his tongue delving deep, and I moan. He flips me onto my back and settles between my legs. When he pushes inside me, I cry out, my body stretching to accommodate him, like a ship finally coming home.

He starts moving then, each thrust harder and faster than the last. I meet him stroke for stroke, our bodies moving in perfect synchronization, as though we were always meant to be.

As though we've done this a thousand times.

His hand comes between us, and he places his thumb right against the apex of my thighs, rubbing me in the same practiced way I get myself off when my mates are away, and it's just me with a good book. If there was any doubt about how well he knows me, this erases all doubt. My breath comes in shallow pants, and my nails score down Gideon's back as he pushes me over the edge.

He gives me a lopsided grin when his eyes meet mine. I press my lips to each dimple and run my palm against his scratchy stubble. When he cups my breast, my nipples darker than they used to be pre-pregnancy, he places a kiss at the swell. I give him a nod, and he sinks his teeth into my flesh. The pleasure is immediate, and increases a hundred-fold, eliciting a moan from deep within me, accessing a place hidden away. Gideon's release spills into me, and he stills his hips.

A moment later, a deluge of memories pummels me. Gideon as a child, carnage from when he was first turned, the immediate recognition of who I'm meant to be to him one Thanksgiving afternoon, my wedding to Oz, him turning my dad into a vampire, accepting the mating bond, the fear and worry at the birth of our children, and the heartache of saying goodbye as I step into the portal.

Then there's memories after I left, of nearly losing the twins to a mysterious illness, finding out I died, learning I have a soul bonded mate, and finding out I died again.

A sob breaks loose at the memory when my moon fire engulfs him in flames, and he crumples to the ground. The horror of realizing all the good he did in his life didn't recuse him from the damage he caused when he first became a vampire. Aggonid's torture. Getting yanked from hell by Finn, purposely getting captured by the werewolves after tracking me in the Wastelands, just so he could keep me safe. The agony of watching me sleep with Luka, though he was feral, and couldn't control his actions or words to stop it.

I'm wailing by the time my own memories surface. Losing my mother at such a young age, moving from home to home until the Sawyers adopted me, excelling in college despite my abusive and controlling fiancé, getting cheated on. Meeting my best friend, Hannah Mae. Losing the Sawyers, traveling the world, and coming home for answers. Meeting Oz, falling in love, resisting the attraction to Gideon and Auguste, giving in, nearly dying several times, and the despair of having no choice but to step through the portal to save my children.

When it's over, Gideon holds me close, his heart thrashing against my chest. My tears mingle with his, and my entire body racks with sobs. He rocks us, praising me, and whispers sweet words in my ear.

I fall asleep in his arms but wake off-and-on throughout the night, deep, keening sounds wrenching from my broken soul.

CHAPTER 37

CASIMIR

I can't stop my wolf from howling along with each of Lana's wails as they continue to echo throughout our cell. I'm certain the Crucey had us placed in this chamber so we could hear what we've done. How much we've shattered our mate.

I lay on my back, staring up at the stone ceiling as I try to silence my mind and block out the sounds of her pain. But it's impossible. And I deserve every second of this torture. I've never felt so low, so helpless.

Penn, Zara, and Pierce could easily dissolve the steel bars of this cell and get us out of here because of their dragon order. But they won't. Because they know we all need to atone for what we've done.

Sarai was not as privy to everything that happened, but she's complicit, too, though I'd never lay the blame at her feet. The gag order kept her quiet in the beginning, but when Finn broke it, she could've said something then. They all could've. Their loyalty to us was their undoing.

We chose to lie. Our pursuits started out noble—we were trying to save our realm—but the morality of it quickly became skewed. And we lost sight of what was truly important.

Our mate.

If I could go back and change things, I would. In a heartbeat. The raw pain radiating down our mating bond doesn't even temper when she passes out from exhaustion. It just continues to beat at us relentlessly, a physical ache that makes my beast want to tear through the bars and go to her.

But we can't.

We must stay here and wallow in our misery until she's ready to see us again. We don't deserve forgiveness, but I'll take whatever she's willing to give. And I'll spend the rest of eternity making it up to her.

Sometime in the late morning, judging by the commotion in the hallway outside our cell, a guard comes for Sarai.

"Your presence is requested," he says gruffly, before leading her away.

I sit up, eyes darting to where Pierce shouts for them not to harm her, desperately trying to pry Zara off his arm so he can get to Sarai.

"Lana won't let anything happen to her," she spits, and he relaxes marginally.

Hours later, they bring in food, but no one eats. We haven't the appetite. By nightfall, judging by how the underground has quieted down, the door to the room opens, and this time, Gideon is escorted in past our cell door. My wolf growls at the sight of the vampire.

"If Lana were okay with it, I'd rip each of you from limb to limb for what you did to her," he seethes, his fangs bared. "But she's not, so I'll have to settle for this."

He punches me in the face, and I topple to the ground. But I don't fight back. I let him have his anger. I deserve it.

Penn gets to his feet, but Gideon doesn't spare him a second glance before tackling him. They hit the ground with a thud, and I hear the unmistakable sound of bone crunching as the vampire pummels him.

Pierce roars, and Zara holds him back again. "Let him have this. Luna knows we earned it."

Gideon stands, wiping the blood spattered on his face with the back of his hand. He wheels around to face Grimm, whose moniker matches his expression. "And as for you ..." Gideon doesn't finish his sentence before roundhouse kicking him, sending him flying into the bars.

"That is for daring to touch my mate," he says, before spitting at his feet.

He swings his head to stare down Pierce, and glances once at Zara. "Unhand your brother. I won't lay a hand on a woman."

She steps back, hands raised.

"You were her personal guard, tasked with protecting her. Did you think stealing her memories, robbing our children of their mother, and lying to her was protection?" Gideon shoves Pierce. "In my court, we'd rip the throat out of your treasonous ass before burning your corpse."

He lands his last line with a punch to Pierce's crestfallen face.

"You took the most precious, loving woman and denied her of any chance of having peace in her heart. Lana will carry this with her for the rest of eternity, knowing the males she loved more than herself didn't love her enough to spare her this pain. You don't deserve her mercy."

Gideon stalks out, leaving us shellshocked.

CHAPTER 38

LANA

Gideon helps me out of the bathtub where I've spent the last three hours soaking. Floral aroma wafts off my skin, thanks to the oils and scrubs supplied by Crucey. A gift for an ailing heart, she called it. She and I both know my ticker is fine, physiologically speaking, and the rest goes unsaid. It's suffered mortal wounds, millennia of trauma in the span of a few days.

He wraps me in a bathrobe before pressing a kiss to my temple. "Are you sure about this?" He asks.

I nod. "Positive."

I have a gap in my memories from the time I stepped through the portal to the day they hauled Finn out of the throne room, claiming he was a zealot. Who are my allies?

Dressing quickly in a hooded sweatshirt and sweatpants, I emerge from the bathroom to find a guard standing at my doorway next to Sarai. Her long, tangled hair spills over her shoulder, and her reptile eyes are wide, unblinking, as though she's in shock. Inclining my head towards the chair, he ushers her to it while I cross the room to sit on the bed. Gideon joins me, a comforting arm wrapped around my back.

"Did you know they took my memories in the beginning?" I keep the venom out of my tone. Not until I know details.

"Yes, but—"

I interrupt her. "Were you prevented from speaking about it by the magical gag order the others were subjected to?"

"Yes." She looks like she wants to say more, but she keeps her mouth shut.

She looks near to tears, but I keep going. "When Finn broke the order, were you aware you could then tell me?"

Her face shutters, and fat droplets pour down her cheeks. "Yes."

I nod at the guard. "She's free to leave. Please take her to the surface."

"But—"

"Sarai, you were supposed to be my friend, maybe even my best friend." My voice breaks, and after taking a deep breath, I continue. "And if you weren't my friend, then you were just my maid. You're fired."

Her reptilian features flicker under her skin when she breaks down in sobs as the guard hauls her out of our room.

* * *

SOMETIME LATER, Crucey hovers in my doorway, her wise eyes cataloging every emotion flitting across my face. "You did what you had to do," she says softly.

I raise my chin in fear of spilling tears, not trusting myself to speak. Gideon shifts next to me, and I lean into him. "I know." My whisper is barely audible. Though the justification of it doesn't make it hurt any less.

"Do you want to talk about what happened?" she asks, and I can tell she already knows.

"We need to stop the war." I stand, cradling my belly. A warmth radiates from it, magic-filled love spilling into every nook and cranny inside me, bathing me with peace. "I can't have any more of my people slaughtered."

On either side. A war that should've never been.

Crucey nods, and I know she'll do everything in her power to help. "Before you go to the surface, we need to discuss this." She places a hand on my abdomen, and I know she can feel the child growing inside of me, just as sure as the moons rise each night. My child's father is our sworn enemy.

"I'm not sure what you want me to say." I adjust uncomfortably, stilling when my baby nudges Crucey's hand in acknowledgement. A proverbial fist bump.

"You need to be prepared for what's to come," she says softly. "This will not be easy, and what if he comes for your child?"

"I will protect my child with my life," I say fiercely. "No one is taking my baby from me." My womb stirs with urgency, as though the very idea sends him or her into panic, too.

She knows all about that. It's who she is; the Crucey, protector of the Tolden.

"Why are they called child of the woods?" I tilt my head to study her. "What does it mean?"

"It is an old, old term." She smiles sadly. "It's also why the father of the child in your womb is our enemy."

A low growl erupts from Gideon, and I touch his arm to soothe him.

"It's a long story." She sighs. "The short version is that a royal wolf fae had an affair millennia ago. His mate was a Luna fae. Because fae mate for life, she cursed him and all the offspring he had with his wood order mistress. Their offspring were the first werewolves."

She takes my hand and tilts my head to follow her. "Come with me, and I'll show you why they're children of the woods."

The tunnels wind through the bedrock, and I can feel the magic swirling around us the further we go. It pulses, growing in strength the closer we get to our destination. This is what I felt at my feet when we were on the surface. After a few minutes, we come to a stop in front of a door. It resembles a tree, and a carving of a moon takes up the center.

"Brace yourself, dear," she whispers before whisking the door open.

My hand flies out to grip Gideon's forearm as a gust of wind rushes past us into the darkness. Damp earth and the scent of pine fill my nose as we step out onto a small ledge. A gasp escapes me as I take in the sight before me.

It's like a speakeasy, hidden from the world. Instead of debauchery and spirits, flora and fauna flourish in a giant, underground ecosystem. The delicate tinkling of a stream can be heard in the distance, and all manner of birds speckle the trees.

The forest is vast and seemingly endless. The trees are old, their trunks massive, and leaves of all colors adorn them. Stretching from tree to tree are interconnected rope bridges, and small lights flicker in the distance. Upon closer inspection, there are tree houses built into the branches, some high and some low. They remind me of the stories my mother used to tell me about orphans stolen from London, who grew up in a fantasyland with no parents, no rules, pixie dust, and an evil pirate with a hook and a dislike of clocks.

A flock of fiery red birds takes flight above the canopy, swooping and diving in an intricate dance before soaring to the top of the cavern. The sight takes my breath away, and through our mating bond, I can feel Gideon's wonder as well.

I cry out when one of the birds miscalculates and tumbles straight into a rocky outcropping. It bursts into flames and is immediately consumed by the inferno. The other birds scatter in all directions, and their distressed cries echo through the trees.

My breathing stalls, and I grip Gideon's arm tighter as I try to make sense of what I'm seeing. From the ashes, a new bird is born. Its plumage is damp, but it's already drying and fluffing out. It looks at me with wise eyes before taking flight, joining the others in their dance.

"Is that..." I choke the words. Tears stream down my face as I stare in awe at the rebirth happening before my eyes.

"Yes," she nods, her own eyes shining with unshed tears. "That's a phoenix. They're Tolden."

The flock lands on a ledge, shifting into fae as they do. They're all women, with flame red hair, and they watch me with curious eyes. Some have reddish pink hair, like soft sheets of magenta that shouldn't exist in nature, but they do. Recognition registers on their faces and they sink to their knees, heads bowed.

"Your Majesty," they say in unison. Their voices carry to me on the wind.

I take a step back, shaking my head. "No, no, no. You don't need to call me that. Lana is fine. Please rise."

"But you are the high queen," one of them says, rising to her feet. Her crimson tresses seem to flow of their own accord, like billowing sails in wind. "I am Morte, and you are our leader."

Crucey nudges me. "And we are your subjects, my dear."

Gideon's eyes twinkle with amusement, and I can feel his pleasure through our bond as well. "I think you're going to have to get used to this," he says, wrapping an arm around my waist and pressing his lips to my temple.

Shifting my attention to the phoenixes, I offer them a hesitant smile. "It's nice to meet you all."

"And you as well, your majesty," they say before taking flight once again.

The panorama spreads out before us, and I spot other Tolden milling about on the bridges and in the tree houses. There must be thousands of them. In the distance, a waterfall spills from a cliff into a river below, its banks lined with luminous flowers in every shape and color. A breeze passes through, and the flowers bend towards us in greeting.

"What is this place?" I breathe.

"Castanea," Crucey coos.

"What does this place have to do with Luka?" I ask.

She inclines her head. "All will be explained in time, my dear. For now, let us enjoy the beauty of Castanea. Come."

Taking Gideon's hand, we follow Crucey as she ambles across a rope bridge. It sways dangerously with every step, though she doesn't appear phased. The Tolden watch us as we pass, their eyes filled with reverence.

We reach the other side, and Crucey leads us to a large tree house, willow-like purple branches make up the roof, spilling over the side. It looks like it was built for a giant, with a doorway big enough to fit a combine. Inside, the ceilings are vaulted, and there's a fire roaring in the hearth.

Pillows and blankets are strewn about, and it looks like the perfect place to curl up with a good book.

"This is where you'll be staying tonight while our network attempts to get in touch with your vampire family. It's our understanding they're spread throughout Bedlam now, heading up multiple fronts as to not concentrate the entire family in one place in case of an attack. We'll try to get them here as soon as possible," Crucey says. "Make yourselves comfortable. I'll have someone bring you some food."

Gideon and I trade looks. "Thank you, Crucey," he says. "We appreciate your hospitality."

"Of course, my dear." She bows before turning to leave.

"Wait," I say, stopping her. "What about Luka?"

She smiles gently. "That's why we're bringing your family here for the time being. This way, we can figure out how to stop the werewolves from slaughtering our Tolden for their hearts, and from the destruction they're wreaking on the rest of the fae. We can't do it without them."

"Why do they want their hearts?" Gideon frowns.

"It cures their werewolf curse." Crucey's face is a mask of pain. "And it kills the Tolden." She gestures to the woods. "The Wastelands weren't always barren. The Luna fae who cursed the werewolves took the forest with her and sought shelter underground. It's why we have Castanea."

This used to be at the surface? She must've had incredible power to transport all of this.

Crucey turns, and I can see the grief in her eyes before she disappears out the door.

Gideon takes my hand, and we sink down onto a pile of blankets and pillows. "I'm sorry, Lana," he says, his voice full of remorse.

I place my hand on his cheek. "Whatever for?"

"For not being able to keep you safe," he says, his eyes haunted. "If I had just been stronger, faster, better, you wouldn't have been taken from me."

I cup his face in my hands. "It's not your fault. You did everything you could. I know that. And we're going to get through this. Together."

My fingers lace through his silky hair as I pull him down for a kiss. He tastes of sorrow and anger, but underneath it all, he's still my Gideon. And I know that so long as we're together, we can face anything.

Even an army of werewolves.

CHAPTER 39

LANA

The forest quiets; the only sounds are the tinkling of the river and the roar of the waterfall at the far end of the cavern. Gideon traces lazy patterns on my stomach, and I let out a contented sigh.

"Do fae ever feed from their mates?" His whisper is a gentle caress against my skin. "It's my favorite past time, and something I'll miss about being a vampire."

Heat flushes my cheeks. "Yeah."

He furrows his brows for a moment, before understanding dawns on his face. "I don't want to know, do I?"

I shake my head. "No."

I don't mention how my kings and I regularly feed from each other. How it became a consistent part of our intimate moments after we sealed our mating with a blood bond. I know Gideon would be jealous, and I don't want to upset him.

"I'm sorry." I reach for his hand, pulling it in mine. "I'd still like for you to feed from me when I turn you into fae."

With anyone else, I'd ask. But not Gideon—I need to reassure him that he has the same privileges my other mates have. That his desires matter, and I desire them, too.

He flips me onto my back and hovers over me, his eyes filled with love and lust. "Thank you," he says before burying his head against my neck, placing the tenderest of kisses to my pulse.

I moan as his fangs scrape against my skin, and then he retreats. I sit up on my elbows, confused, until I take in his blown-out pupils and the sheen of sweat on his brow.

"What's wrong?" I ask, my heart thudding in my chest.

"It's getting harder to control. Crucey was right—I've already burned right through the blood I took from you."

He runs a hand through his hair, frustration evident in every line of his body.

"It's okay." I scoot closer and wrap my arms around him. "When you're ready, I'll turn you."

He nods, his face buried in my chest. "I'm ready now." His voice comes out hoarse, restraint twisting against the words.

I pull away and take his face in mine. He trembles under my touch, giving me one of his signature smirks. I run my hands over every inch of him, memorizing the feel of his skin, pressing my lips to his furrowed brow. While he won't change a ton going from vampire to fae, this is the face I fell in love with. Every imperfection, every line, every scar.

"I love you," I whisper, my voice shaking with emotion while I trace his bottom lip with my thumb.

"I love you, too." He kisses me then, and I can feel the hunger in it. The need for my blood.

I pull away and take a deep breath. "If you're sure, I need to add a silencing barrier to the room. It was excruciating when I turned, though it was over in minutes. Yours may be a little more difficult because you're a vampire, I'm not sure, but I'll do what I can to ease the pain with my Luna magic."

He shrugs, and I cast the barrier. I have him lay so his back faces my chest, and he's nestled between my thighs. I wrap my arms around him, holding him close as I begin the transformation. Closing my eyes, I pull from the energy in the tree, its bark rough when I rest my cheek against it.

My magic reaches for its ancient roots, tangling with them, and the tree creaks in protest. I soothe it with a stream of magic, asking for its permission before taking what I need. When it acquiesces, I funnel the power into the well inside me.

Below the roots is a place of vitality, and I pull from it, too. It takes me a moment to recognize it's the water table, its surface rippling, providing life to the tree. I coax more magic, and the roots of the tree begin to glow, just as my skin does.

The light spreads up the trunk, and I continue to feed the reservoir inside me. When I'm sure I have enough, I begin to funnel it into Gideon. His body thrashes as the magic fills him, gritting out his groans through clenched teeth before he can't take it anymore. I keep a steady stream going, even as his body turns rigid, and he screams.

His cries are like a blade slicing through my soul, but I don't falter. I continue to give him the magic he needs to complete the transformation. When his body finally goes limp, I reluctantly release the power and collapse against him.

The room is eerily silent, and I'm afraid to look at him. I take several deep breaths before finally turning him over. His eyes are shut, and his face is pale, but he's breathing. *Breathing.* Color floods into his cheeks, and his eyelashes flutter before his gaze meets mine.

He stares at me for a moment before a grin spread across his face. "It worked." He sits up, inspecting his body, turning his hands over. "I can feel it, surging under my skin." Hooking a thumb under his waistband, he pulls it taut to peek before snapping it shut and whipping his head up to look at me.

"Seriously? This is what I was competing with?!" The look he gives me is an odd mixture of crestfallen and disbelief, chased by an unhealthy dose of self-pride when he realizes he's got it now, too.

I shrug, my lips quirking up in a half-smile. "Well, you're still all mine." I settle into his lap. "If it's any consolation, I loved it before, too."

He chuckles, wrapping his arms around me. "Oh, I haven't forgotten that." He kisses me, and I can feel the magic in it. It's different from before, but no less potent. When he finally breaks the kiss, he rests his forehead against mine. "Thank you, Lana. For everything."

"You're welcome, Gideon. I love you."

"I love you, too."

Leaning back, I place my hand on his pec, where my tattoo used to reside. "It's gone," I whisper.

He nods, his eyes sad. "You can enchant me another one, can't you?"

"I don't see why not," I say, cupping his cheek.

He smiles, and I can feel the love in it. "I want one of these." His fingers trace the marks swirling my arms.

"I think these are the mating bond tattoos from Finn and my kings," I whisper, my heart in my throat. "You, Auguste, and Oz deserve to be here, too."

We still have our mating bond—nothing has happened to it, even though he's no longer a vampire. These tattoos are magical and give an outward statement of the love between us.

He nods, his eyes shining with unshed tears. "I would be honored."

"First, I have other things in mind."

His darkening eyes tell me he and I share the same thought. Breathless, I meet his lips as he flips me onto my back. He kisses me deeply as his hand travels up my thigh. An inferno sizzles along its path.

I moan as his fingers find my core, teasing me with feather light strokes to prime me for his new girth. He takes hold of his cock, sliding it through my slick folds, its blunt head nudging against my clit with each pass. I angle my hips in an attempt to take him in, tortured by the slow, drawn-out teasing of his length against me.

"Please," I beg. "I need you."

He chuckles, finally easing inside.

"So fucking tight," he hisses, his words nearly drowned out by my moan.

Pushing up on my elbows, I watch him drive into me, our bodies slapping together in a wet, blissful rhythm.

He leans down to capture my nipple between his teeth and sucks hard, eliciting a cry from me. We rock against each other, stroke after stroke. Faster and harder he goes, his new strength giving him unparalleled stamina. His hips tilt, rubbing right against my clit with each pounding of his body against mine.

"Gideon." I gasp as he brings me to the edge of reason.

Reaching behind me, I wrap my hand around his balls; a gentle, yet firm hold on him. They draw tight and he curses just as I feel my orgasm grow nearer and nearer until it explodes within me.

He gives one final thrust and stills as he lets out a deep guttural moan. I cling to him, my nails digging into his back as he follows me over, our bodies joined as one.

Gideon's head falls forward to rest against mine, and we both lay there, trying to catch our breath. Magic sizzles between us, an electric pulse sliding under our skin, mingling in content.

CHAPTER 40

LANA

*U*nderneath my cheek, I listen to the steady thump of Gideon's heartbeat, feeling the rise and fall of his chest with each breath. His arms wrap around me, a cocoon of warmth I've only felt from him in a freak dreamscape when he was human in the Dolomites.

His voice is thick with sleep when he finally speaks. "Gods, I forgot how amazing it is to actually need sleep, and to wake up feeling rested."

I smile, nuzzling into him. "Just wait until you get wings," I tease.

He laughs, the rich, baritone vibration rumbling through his chest. "You're going to let me take you in the sky, right?"

"...take me?"

He chuckles again, and the sound is like music to my ears. "It's all I've thought about since you offered to turn—"

A knock at the door interrupts whatever he was going to say, and he lets out a groan. "I don't want to share you yet. I still need to test out the goods."

"I'll get it," I say, untangling myself from his arms.

I pull on a robe and cinch it tight before making my way to the door. Opening it, Crucey greets me.

Her glassy eyes reflect deep emotion I can't quite decipher, but she gives me a watery smile. "Your parents and children are here."

I let out a cry, gripping the door handle to keep from crashing to my knees. "Where?! Are Oz and Auguste with them?!"

"They're in the main cavern; they just came through—"

I don't wait for her to say anything else; I take off like a shot down the rope bridge, its wooden slats creaking under my pounding feet. Curious Tolden whip their heads my way as I race past them in a blur.

Through the winding tunnels, I bump into a guard or two caught unaware as I careen around a corner, my apologies a mangled cry as I vault through entrance after entrance. Gideon catches up with me by the time I reach the cavern, and he takes my hand as we make our way to where my family is waiting.

Nothing could've prepared me for the sight before me—my parents and my twins, all here in Bedlam with me. My babies; two stunning, full-grown fae; a perfect mixture of their fathers and me. And then there's my dad, his arm around Mom's shoulders, his eyes twinkling and her beautiful, fawn-like features taking up her face.

Tears stream down my face as we meet in the middle, crushing each other in a hug. I have no words to articulate the enormous relief I feel to have them here after all this time. Neither do they. We hold each other, basking in the warmth of finally being together again.

"I'm so sorry," I whisper when we finally pull apart, my voice a ragged mess.

Rose has my mother's doe eyes, Gideon's dark silky hair, a dainty nose and skin like glass. Her expression is pinched in a way that makes my heart ache. Tear tracks mar her cheeks, and she opens her mouth to speak but no words come out.

"It's okay," I say quickly, pulling her into a hug. "I'm here now."

"You're so beautiful," a surprisingly deep voice calls out, and I turn to face Bennett.

He has Oz's dark complexion, strong jaw, and a mop of waves on top of his head that make him look like he just stepped out of a Grecian urn. His eyes are my own, though thick eyebrows frame his face, and he's got his daddy's lashes.

"How'd you get so handsome?!" I cry, throwing my arms around him.

He squeezes me tight, far tighter than I thought possible. "I missed you, Mom." Though I last saw them when they were just newborns, the soul knows. Just as the tide knows to come in, and the moons to wane. They were a part of me, now they are a part of my world.

"I missed you too, sweetheart. So much. Where are your dads?" I glance behind them, my heart sinking at the empty space in the cavern. Tears drown my cheeks.

I pull away to look at Bennett, really look at him. "Have—"

"Dad?!" Rose shrieks. "What happened to you?!"

I whip around to face Gideon. He stands with his arms crossed, a smirk on his face. "I don't have to drink blood anymore," he says with a wink. "I'm fae now."

A delighted laugh spills from her lips, and she runs to him, throwing her arms around his neck. "That's amazing! You're freakishly tall now."

"I know," he laughs, ruffling her wavy hair. He looks over at me then, and his eyes soften. "I'm sorry, Lana."

"For what?" I ask, stepping closer to him.

He takes my hands in his, and I'm surprised at the strength in his grip. It matches my own now. "I don't want to steal your thunder."

My heart constricts. "You could never. They're not here, are they?" I try, and fail, to keep my voice steady. Worry settles in my stomach.

Gideon crushes me to his chest as I hear him inquire about Oz and Auguste.

"Still trying to get in touch with them." A sound like a melody speaks from behind me and gives my shoulder a squeeze.

Like stepping into old roles, Gideon prods for more. "When's the last time you heard from anyone?"

"A couple of days," the familiar voice assures him. "I'm sure they're fine; just hard to reach now that we've spread out."

But I can tell by the way her voice wavers that she's not as confident as she's trying to sound. I release Gideon and face the woman whose words sang so many lullabies, infused me with so much love, and spoke with so much conviction about my worth I believed her until she was taken from me, and the world made me think otherwise.

"Mom." Emotion clogs my throat. On trembling legs, I stumble her way.

She opens her arms as I fall into them and hold me tight as I sob into her shoulder. It feels like coming home; the scent of her just as I remember it. She pats my back, her touch warm and secure. She smells of wildflowers and sunshine, and I close my eyes, taking a deep breath. After nearly three decades without the feel of her warmth, her love, I'd given up hope of ever knowing that feeling again, save for the brief moments I bargained with time to see her again.

"I thought I'd lost you," I whisper when I finally pull away.

Her eyes shimmer with unshed tears as she cups my face in her hands. "Never, baby. I promise. I fought like hell to make my way back to you again. We all did."

"I'm so sorry," I cry, tears streaming down my cheeks. "This is all my fault."

"No, no, no," she shakes her head, and I'm enveloped in another hug. "It's not your fault, baby. You didn't know. We should have been more careful. I'm just so glad you're safe." She pulls back, attention coming to my swollen belly. "I made a lot of mistakes, too, but none more so than not being here for you when you needed me the most. I promise to make it up to you every day for the rest of my life."

"I love you," I choke out.

"I love you, too, baby." She kisses my damp cheeks. "There's someone else who's been dying to see you again."

She takes my hand and leads me not towards Gideon, Rose, or Bennett, but to the back of the cavern where someone else stands in the shadows, waiting for his turn.

Dad.

He gives me a sad, tear-filled smile as I approach him, and I pull him into a crushing hug. "Dad," I choke.

"I'm so proud of you," he whispers into my hair. "You've become everything I ever wanted you to be, and more."

"I missed you." I cry, tears soaking his shirt.

"I missed you, too." He kisses the top of my head and holds me tight. "Nothing will ever separate our family again."

His words are a vow, and I know he'll keep it, even if it's not bound by a magical decree. We're finally together again, and nothing will tear us apart.

"I'm sorry, Dad," I whisper. "For everything." Sorry for causing Mom to leave him. For giving Dolphina Darling a reason to poison him, thus giving him terminal cancer, and having to become a vampire. For denying him the chance to raise me.

"I know," he says, voice gruff with emotion. "But there's nothing to forgive you for," Dad assures me. His calming magic pours into me. "I blame those terrible kings."

My heart clenches, the memory of their betrayal still a fresh, soul-deep wound. "I do too," I whisper, my voice trembling.

It's humiliating how easily I believed them. I pant, feeling the rage so fierce, it nearly matches the agony splicing through my chest at their betrayal. The mate in me wars with the broken parts of me, wanting to protect them and excuse away their behavior, but I can't. What they did was about the worst thing you can do to someone you love, and I'm not sure I can ever forgive them.

But that doesn't mean I can't try to understand why they did it.

"Do you think we can ever forgive them?" I ask, looking up at Gideon. His expression is pensive, and he rubs his chin.

"I don't know," he says finally. "A part of me understands doing terrible things to keep you in my life—who wouldn't—but I love you enough to want you to be happy first and foremost. They did the unthinkable before they knew you, but you have to consider all they made you endure after they fell in love with you and made you theirs."

His voice waivers, and I see the raw hurt in his eyes. It reflects my own, and I go to him, wrapping my arms around his waist.

"If anyone can forgive them, it's you," he continues, his voice soft as he cradles my head against his chest. "But no one will blame you if you don't—least of all me."

"I think," Dad pipes up, drawing our attention. "That we need to give her some time and let her make that decision when she's ready.

What they did was wrong, there's no denying that, but they are her mates, no matter how much we don't like that they're bonded."

"And she loves them," Mom adds. It's a statement, not a question. She's always been so perceptive.

I swallow hard and nod. "I do," I whisper, and it comes out choked. "But that doesn't mean I'm going to just forget what they did."

"Of course not, my little Striga," Gideon says, his hand coming up to cup my cheek. "But they are a part of you, just as you are a part of them. You have to find a way to make peace with that, or it will eat you alive. Just let me know if you want me to get rid of them, and it's done, alright?"

His eyes dance with mirth, and I can't help but laugh. "Gideon, you're terrible."

"And you love me for it." He winks.

I shake my head and roll my eyes, but I can't help the smile that comes to my lips. "Yes, I do."

I turn back to my parents and children. "Follow me. I have some people I'd like you to meet."

CHAPTER 41

CASIMIR

ommotion on the other side of the door draws our attention. My arm flies out, trying to get the others to hush so we can listen to the muffled conversation.

"Do your parents know you're here?" a deep, but hesitant, voice calls out.

A female laughs. "Of course, they do, they've sent us to check on the kings."

There's a moment of pause, and I can't hear anything but the sound of heavy footsteps.

"They what?" the male exclaims, and I hear something hit the floor with a thud.

The door swings open, and a fae peeks her head in, eyes darting to each of us. She inclines her head, and a male drags the body of a guard into the room. He deposits him against the wall before turning around to face us.

As soon as I get a good look at their faces, my blood runs cold.

While we've never met, there's no mistaking it; these are Lana's children. And they're here for revenge.

A smirk crosses Rose's face when she sees our reaction. "It seems you know who we are," she purrs. "Good."

"Get on with it," Penn growls, stepping forward.

Zara steps in front of me, holding a hand out to stop me from intervening.

"Though you deserve it, we're not here to kill you," she says calmly. "We just want to talk."

"Talk?" Bennett scoffs, side-eyeing his sister. "What could we possibly have to talk about with the people who enslaved our mother and stole her memories?"

She gives her brother an exasperated look. "Have you any idea what it'd do to Mom if we killed her mates?" She turns her scowl to me, before pausing her attention on each one of us. "No matter how satisfying it would be to see the life drain from their eyes."

A muscle ticks in Bennett's jaw, but he doesn't say anything.

"Now," Rose continues, "I think we should all have a chat, don't you?"

The twins settle on the stone floor outside the cell, and we pull chairs closer to the bars. For a moment, no one says anything. The only sound in the room is the sound of Bennett's restless tapping foot.

Finally, Rose clears her throat and begins. "We know what you did," she says coldly. "What we want to know is why."

"And what you're going to do to make it right," Bennett adds.

I exchange a look with the others before turning back to the twins. "I can't speak for the others, but I can tell you why I did it."

"Please do," Rose says, hurt seeping into her voice.

Bennett glances at her and takes her hand in his.

Taking a deep breath, I begin. "It's my bloodline that's to blame." I avert my eyes. "Millennia ago, a king in my family had an affair on his mate, who was a Luna fae." Never mind it's virtually unheard of. This is the only recorded affair in history of mates in Bedlam. They weren't soul bonded, but they still took a blood mating bond. "His mate cursed the king and his mistress; any offspring they produced became werewolves. Magic-less, and only able to turn when the moons are full."

"What happened to the Luna fae?" Bennett asks, sadness lacing his voice.

"She was banished," I say quietly. "In return, she cursed the land where they'd made their blood vows to each other. The forest disappeared, and in its place: you've got the Wastelands. Magic began to die, especially when the werewolves retaliated and started killing Luna fae in droves."

Rose's voice is barely audible when she asks, "Where is she now?"

"She's the Luna goddess." I give her a sad smile, and the twins gasp before whipping their heads to each other, silently communicating between themselves.

"That doesn't explain why you stole our mom." Bennett finally speaks up.

"I was getting to that," I whisper. "In the beginning, it was a means to saving the realm. We needed to make a high queen to restore balance. Luna fae are the only fae with magic, who supply it to the rest of Bedlam, and without them, we fade. We've been dependent on magic for so long, that without it, we start to wither and die." I take a deep breath before continuing. "But the more I got to know your mom, the more I realized that she was so much more than just a vessel for magic."

"And then you fell in love with her," Rose supplies. It's not a question.

"Yes."

"So, you just decided to kidnap her and make her your mate?" Bennett asks, his voice tight.

I shake my head. "No, it's not that simple. I was going to tell her, I swear. We all were. But then your family showed up, and things got out of hand."

"You still could have let her go," Bennett growls. "But you didn't. You took her away from us, and you stole her memories."

"I know," I say quietly. "And I'm sorry. Truly, I am. But I love her." Glancing towards the others, I hang my head. "We all love her. And we would do anything to keep her safe."

"Anything except let her go," Rose says bitterly while chucking a pebble across the floor. It skids to a stop at my feet.

"It's not that simple," I plead with them. "Your mom is in danger.

The werewolves will stop at nothing to eradicate the fae, especially Luna fae."

"You robbed Finn of making her high queen. Together, they would've saved the realm," Bennett grits through clenched teeth. "They are soul bonded."

Grimm clears his throat. "You're right." All eyes turn to him in shock. "Finn should have been the one to crown Lana as high queen. It was his birthright, and we took that from him."

"So, what are you going to do about it?" Rose asks, her voice trembling.

Grimm looks at each of us before turning back to the twins. "We're going to make things right."

"And how do you expect us to just forgive you?" Bennett growls. "You've ruined our lives."

Penn approaches the bars, wrapping a hand around one. "We did," he says quietly. "But we're going to make it up to you. We promise."

"How?" Rose's voice warbles.

The door flies open, and in walks a furious Lana, flanked by Gideon and her guards. The sight of her takes my breath away as always. Her long, dark hair cascades down her back, and her blue eyes are flashing.

She takes in the scene, eyes softening when she spots her children. "What's going on here?" she asks, her voice tight.

"We were just talking," I say quickly. "Trying to explain some things."

"I see," she says, her eyes flicking to Grimm. "And what exactly were you trying to explain?"

"The truth," Grimm says quietly. "About why we did what we did."

Hurt flickers in her eyes, but she quickly schools her features. "I see," she says again. She looks at her children, who are both staring at her in disbelief. "Is this true?" she asks them, her voice shaking.

They both nod, and she takes a step back, her hand going to her stomach.

"Lana," I say, taking a step towards her. "Please, let us explain."

"Explain what?" she asks, her voice breaking. "How you took me away from my children? How you stole my memories?" Tears stream down her face, and my heart shatters. "Humiliated me in front of the entire realm? Or was it how you tied yourselves to me forever?"

Gideon wraps his arm around her waist when she staggers. "Come on, Lana," he says softly. "Let's go."

"No," she says, shaking her head. She steps away from Gideon and approaches the bars. "I want to know how they could take my love and use it against me." The pain in her voice is palpable, and I can't take it anymore.

"We love you, too," I whine, my wolf pacing just under my skin, desperate to soothe our mate's pain. "All of us. Please, just give us a chance to explain."

"And why should I?" she asks, her voice trembling. "What could you possibly say that would make any of this better?"

I take a deep breath, knowing there's only one thing I can say that will convince her to hear us out. "Because we're going to tell you everything. No more secrets."

Lana stands there for a moment, her blue eyes searching my face. Finally, she nods and takes a step back. "Okay," she says, her voice barely above a whisper. "I'm listening."

We take turns telling Lana everything that happened, starting with the moment we met her. We tell her about our decision to share her, make her high queen, and save the realm. But we ended up falling in love with her, and we couldn't let her go.

"So, you see," I say, concluding our story. "We love you, Lana. More than anything. And we're sorry for what we did."

She's quiet for a moment, her eyes flicking over each of us. Finally, she nods and takes a step forward. "Okay." Through the bond, agony lances through me. Tears stain her cheeks as she rests her head against the bars. Chest heaving, she pushes away from the cell and turns on her heel before quietly leaving the holding area. The door shuts and swings back open right away as Gideon chases after her.

Rose and Bennett don't say a word, and climb to their feet before leaving, too.

"Fuck."

CHAPTER 42

LANA

The sight of my grown children talking animatedly with the phoenix fae loosens something in my chest. I missed out on so much, not getting to see them grow, but having them here now, it's like a piece of my heart has been mended.

"They're beautiful," my mom whispers, coming up to stand beside me.

I smile, my throat tight. "They are."

"You must be so proud," she says, and I can hear the unshed tears in her voice.

"I am," I reply, my own voice wavering. "But I'm also sad. I missed out on so much."

"But you're with them now." She gives my hand a squeeze. "And that's all that matters."

I nod and lean into her side, letting her comfort me. We stand there like that for a while, just watching our family interact and get to know each other.

It's a start, I think to myself. A good start. But there's still so much to do. I have mates to find, and a realm to save. But with my family by my side, I know anything is possible.

Two days tick by, and there's still no sign of Oz, Auguste, or Finn.

I'm starting to get worried.

"Gideon," I say, coming up to him where he's leaning against a tree, watching the twins play with Tolden in the river. "I think we need to go out and look for them."

"You're right," he replies, his voice tight. "But we need to be careful." He sinks to his knees, cupping my abdomen. "We don't want to leave our children unprotected."

My stomach flutters. "We can't just sit here and do nothing."

"I know," he stands, his forehead coming to rest against mine. "But we need to be smart about this. We'll have to leave the twins with your parents." He kisses me, tucking a curl behind my pointed ear. "We will find them, Lana."

"I need to call the fae off, too. No more war." If I can't remove the stupid rule about Finn needing to earn his throne back, then what good am I as high queen? Archaic rules have no place in the twenty-first century.

It isn't easy convincing Rose and Bennett that they need to stay behind. Yes, they're full-grown fae, but they're also untrained, and we can't worry about their safety while we're trying to find the guys. In the end, they see reason, and begrudgingly agree to stay put.

It's nighttime when Gideon and I go the surface. He holds onto me while I fly, since his wings haven't come in yet. As soon as we reach the vegetation-covered mountain range marking the exit out of the Wastelands, we land. Flying three days straight has my back screaming at me, and I know Gideon's has to be, too, from holding onto me.

Crashing to my knees, I wince as I maneuver my wings back into place. Gideon rushes to my side, his hands hovering over me as if he's not sure whether to touch me or not.

"Are you alright?" He asks, his voice full of concern.

I nod, wincing as I try to stand. "Just a little sore."

Taking my hand, Gideon helps me to my feet. "We should find a place to rest for the night. It's been a long day, and we both need to recharge."

My stomach growls. "I could use something to eat, too." I rub it. "I'm starving."

Gideon chuckles and gathers me into his arms. "I'll take care of you, my mate," he says, placing a kiss to my forehead.

"You can help with something, actually." I smile coyly at him.

He smirks. "I'm listening." His heated gaze drinks me in.

"Kiss me," I say, my voice low and husky.

Gideon's eyes darken, and he doesn't hesitate to claim my mouth with his.

He kisses me deep, his tongue sliding against mine in a sensual dance. My body ignites with desire, and I moan into his mouth.

Breaking away, Gideon rests his forehead against mine, his chest heaving with labored breath before pulling back and marveling at my glowing skin. I explained to him how I recharge my magic, but it still amazes him to witness it.

"More."

A satisfied smirk crosses his face as he looks into my eyes. "As you wish, my queen." He presses his lips to mine, his hands coming to rest on my lower back.

I melt into him as our kiss grows more passionate.

My stomach growls again, and I reluctantly pull away from him. "I really am starving," I say, my cheeks flushing with embarrassment.

Gideon chuckles before setting me down.

"I think I'm charged enough to sift us somewhere safe for the night." I pull him to me for one more kiss. "Someplace with food."

Hesitating a moment, I attempt to reason where I should take us. Cerulean Isles is an obvious choice because no one can interrupt us there, but that's where I mated my kings, and I don't want to think about their betrayal right now. It might complicate things if I take him to any of the castles. The lighthouse feels like the safest choice— located on a Luporian island just North of the mainland. Casimir built the house, and the memories of killing Gideon played in my mind on repeat while there, but I can rewire those memories this way.

Closing my eyes and looping my arms around Gideon's trim waist, I sift us to the seaside home.

He gasps as we land in the soft sand of the private beach. "What is this place?" He looks around, his eyes wide as he takes in the lapping shoreline and the thatched-roof cottage a few yards from the water. Attached to it is the giant, working lighthouse, the light currently sweeping across the water.

I smile and release him from my hold before making my way to the chalet. "This is one of my favorite places," I say over my shoulder. "When court life got to be too much after my coronation, we sifted here for the quiet."

Gideon follows me inside, his eyes sweeping over the homey furnishings. With my magic, a fire crackles in the hearth, and the lamps flicker to life.

"It's beautiful," Gideon says, coming up behind me and wrapping his arms around my waist.

I turn so I'm facing him. "It was here that I decided to go to the Wastelands," I whisper.

"Did something happen?" He takes my face in his palms, eyes darting over my features as if looking for something.

"You died," I choke out, the memories of that day rushing back. I push them away and take a deep breath. "You died, and it was all my fault."

My heart aches as I say the words, pain lancing through me. Gideon watches me, his expression softening as he realizes what I'm saying.

He pulls me into a hug, and I cling to him, burying my face in his chest as the tears fall. "It wasn't your fault," he whispers, stroking my hair. "It wasn't your fault, my little striga."

Gideon holds me as I cry, his words of comfort washing over me like a balm. As the tears subside, I pull away and give him a watery smile.

"Let's get you something to eat," I say, wiping the moisture from my cheeks. Gideon nods, and I lead him into the kitchen.

I rummage through the cupboards, pulling out a pan and some ingredients to make a simple stew. Gideon leans against the counter, watching me as I cook. We take the food up the lighthouse stairs, out the patio door, and onto the deck. The breeze is salty and cool, and the stars are out in full force. Gideon sets the food down on the small table before pulling me into his lap.

We eat in silence, both of us content to just be in each other's company. As we finish our meal, Gideon takes my hand and presses a kiss to my palm.

"Thank you for bringing me here," he says, his voice soft.

I lean against him. "Thank you for coming with me."

With a full stomach, I snuggle closer to Gideon, my head resting on his chest as we watch the stars. His heartbeat is slow and steady under my ear, and his arms are warm and strong around me.

A tingling sensation in my chest has me sitting up straighter. I place my hand over my heart, and Gideon stills. "What is it?" he asks, his voice tense.

I shake my head, not sure how to explain the feeling. "I don't know," I say slowly. "I just feel like something is happening."

Gideon sits up, his expression serious. "What can I do?"

Rising to my feet, I peer across the inky shallows, trying to make sense of my sudden urge to cross it. "We need to go," I say, my voice decisive.

"Where?" he asks, but he doesn't argue. He knows better than to try and stop me when I've made up my mind.

"The other side," I say, pointing to the dark horizon. "Something is waiting for us there."

With a nod, Gideon takes my hand, and we sift across the water. As we land on the other side, I get a feeling of déjà vu, and dizziness washes over me. He catches me as I stumble, and he looks around with a frown.

"What is this place?" he asks.

Trees as dark as the Black Forest of Germany make up the woods before us, their branches reaching like skeletal fingers towards the sky. There's an eerie feeling to the place, and I can sense the power that hums in the air, a weighted, murky presence so at odds with what I know about magic.

I shake my head. "I don't know," I whisper, shivering. "But we need to find out." Something pulls me to keep moving, to press onwards.

We start forward, both of us on edge. The further we walk, the more the feeling of unease grows, until I'm practically vibrating with it.

Something's wrong, very wrong. And whatever it is, it's coming for us.

Gideon's steps falter, and he comes to a stop, his body going rigid. "What is it?" I ask, my voice tight.

"Do you feel that?" he says, his voice low.

I nod, my heart pounding in my chest. "What is it?" I ask again.

"I don't know," Gideon grabs my hand. "But we need to get out of here. *Now.*"

He doesn't have to tell me twice. Facing him, I attempt to sift, but can't. It's like something is holding me back. Conjuring a ball of flames in my hand, I toss it in the air, just to test if my magic works.

"You can't sift?" Gideon asks, his brow furrowed.

I shake my head and try again, but still nothing happens. "No," I say with a frown.

He curses under his breath and looks around. "Whatever this place is, it's blocking it."

A rustling in the bushes, and trembling under our feet has us both on alert, and Gideon pushes me behind him as he steps forward. The bushes part, and a creature I've only ever seen in children's stories steps out.

It's small, no taller than my waist, with large eyes and giant, pointy ears. Layered upon its green, sallow skin, are patches of brown fur, and its hands and feet end in sharp claws.

But the most disturbing thing about it is the fact that it's wearing clothes. A pair of brown overalls, to be exact, and a red plaid shirt. As we stare at it, the creature blinks, its long lashes fluttering. It opens its mouth, full of bone-tearing teeth, and lets out a high-pitched, rattling shriek.

Before I can even process what's happening, more of the creatures come out from the trees, swarming around. There must be at least twenty of them, all armed with spears and knives. And they're coming straight for us.

Gideon grabs my hand, and we start running, the goblins following close behind us. It doesn't take long for one of them to dart from the woods in front of me. He grabs my foot, and I go sprawling, Gideon's hand ripped from mine.

I cry out as I hit the ground, and Gideon skids to a stop, turning to fight them off. I try to get up, but the goblin that tripped me is holding onto my ankle, its piercing grip surprisingly strong.

Gideon kills two of them before they manage to drag him down, and I pull from the elements around me, using it to freeze the goblin that's holding me.

With a curse, Gideon fights his way free and yanks me to my feet. The goblins are frozen in place, but I know it won't last long. I haven't figured out how to keep a hold of the freeze while distracted.

"Let's go," Gideon says, and we start running again.

Each hobble on my injured ankle spurts rivulets of blood into the sand, but I don't dare stop. The further we get from the goblins, the better.

We make it to the water, and I'm relieved to see the moons shining down on us, helping fuel my magic. They cast a milky glow on the water, and I can see the other side.

"Can we swim?" Gideon asks, and I tilt my head.

"You know we can swim."

"I wasn't sure how well we could swim as fae," he says, and without warning, he grabs me and jumps in. No doubt he's remembering having to save me from almost drowning in the little pond in the Wastelands.

The cold water takes my breath away, and I cling to Gideon as he starts swimming. Sometime between our run along the shore and us jumping into the water, the hold on my magic slips, and the goblins are no longer frozen.

I can see them on the shore, their tiny figures running along the sand, following us. They pause in the surf, watching as we swim further and further away. If we weren't tracking their movements, I wouldn't have believed it when they disappear right in front of us.

Gideon pulls me into his side, eyes darting across the water as he tries to find where they went. "Do you think they can swim?"

"I don't know," I say, equally as confused. "But whatever they are, I don't think we should stick around to find out."

His lips set into a thin line, and he continues for the shore. We make it to the other side, and I drag my leg out of the water, gritting my teeth at the pain. Gideon reaches down and snags my foot, lifting my leg up to get a better look.

"Teach me how to heal this." His eyes meet mine, and they hold a steadiness that I know means he's serious.

"Okay," I say, and he sets my leg down before scooping me into his arms and carrying me out of the water.

He sets me down on the ground before lying down beside me, and I rest my head on his chest, listening to the steady thump of his heart. I close my eyes and reach for my magic, letting it flow through me. I instruct him on how to use it to heal the wound, to feel the individual cells and coax them back together.

He's a quick learner, and soon the pain in my ankle fades away, though an echo of something dark remains. It coils just under my skin, though the pain disappears. I let out a tentative sigh and snuggle closer to him, ignoring the niggling thought at the back of my mind that something isn't quite right about the injury the goblin gave me.

"I thought only shifter fae can sift?" Gideon asks, and I shrug.

"Yeah, that's what I've been told."

"So how did they just disappear like that? And what did they want?"

I shake my head, just as confused as he is. "I don't know."

We sit in silence for a while, the scent of salt on the wind. I close my eyes and let out a deep breath, trying to clear my head. When I open them again, I sit up with a start.

"What is it?" Gideon asks, and I point to the water.

"There's someone in the water."

Someone is swimming towards us, and I can't tell if they're friend or foe. Gideon sits up, his hand going to the dagger at his side. We haven't had the time for any magic lessons yet. He stands and moves to the water's edge, and I follow.

The figure is close enough now that I can see it's a man, not a fae.

"Don't come any closer—"

I don't register what's in his hand, or what he's doing, until I feel the sharp prick in my neck. I reach up and touch the spot, my fingers coming away red. Grasping the thing tugging at my skin, it sticks, but gives way with more effort. I palm the small, feathered dart and stare at it for a moment before my vision blurs.

The last thing I see is Gideon lunging for the man as everything goes black.

* * *

I come to slowly, my head pounding, tongue thick in my mouth. The incessant beeping of a machine is the first thing I register, followed by the smell of antiseptic. I try to open my eyes, but they feel like they're glued shut.

"Lana."

Someone says my name, the sound garbled, and I try to turn my head towards the voice, but my body feels like it's weighed down by bricks.

"Lana, can you hear me?"

Flashes of tangled limbs, the scent of cinnamon, tattoos on a chiseled chest, the press of a firm hand against my throat, and brooding eyes fill my memory at the voice, but I can't quite lasso it closer for inspection. I try to open my mouth to speak, but nothing comes out.

"You're finished if you've hurt her in any way," someone growls.

My mind flares, trying to put the pieces together. It feels like I'm stuck in molasses, and everything is moving too slowly.

Gideon. He's here, too.

Who does the other voice belong to? It sits right on the edge of the fog, just out of reach. Someone sweeps a finger over my cheek, and I try to lean into the touch, but my head lolls to the side.

"Lana, can you open your eyes for me?" Gideon's voice is closer now, and I force my eyelids upward.

The light is blinding, and I let out a slow blink. Gideon's face comes into focus, and I let out a sigh of relief. He looks tired, dark circles under his eyes, but he's here.

"What happened?" I ask, my voice sounding rough even to my own ears.

"You were shot with a dart containing vampire blood."

Panic fills me at his words, and I try to sit up, but Gideon pushes me back down.

"The werewolves?" I croak.

"No," Gideon says, angry eyes glancing over to the other side of the room. "A witch who didn't know you had your memories back."

I follow his gaze, sweeping my eyes over the timid young man standing there. *The one from the water*. He can't be more than eighteen, and he looks like he's about to piss himself under my mate's harsh stare.

My attention swings to the other side of me and I startle when I see Auguste's piercing eyes, finally registering the palm he has on my cheek. I let out an anguished cry and fling myself at him, wrapping my arms around his neck.

"I'm so sorry," I whisper into his ear. "I'm so sorry."

We hold each other, neither of us speaking, and I try to block out the sound of Gideon and the other man arguing. Breaking apart, Auguste presses his forehead to mine and closes his eyes.

"Not as sorry as I am," he says quietly. "Never again, Lana. I won't let anyone take you from us again."

I learn that the young man's name is Mekhi, and he'd shot me to immobilize me so he could bring me to my mates, thinking I was still under my kings' thralls. Gideon was about to rip the poor kid's throat out when Auguste came around the island in a boat.

"How long have I been here?" I take in the clinic-like setting I'm in and try to sit up.

"A few hours," Gideon says, coming to stand by the bed. "We

flushed your system of the vampire blood, so you should start to feel close to normal soon."

"Who is we?" I ask, looking between Auguste and Mekhi.

"Fae we trust," Auguste says. "They're friends of Finn's."

"Is he here?" my voice is quiet, and nerves flutter in my stomach. I don't have any memories of him, other than the guards dragging him out of the throne room. Knowing he's important to me, but not having the memories of why, is a special kind of torture.

"No," Auguste squeezes my hand. "We're trying to get in touch with him. He's on Rexuna, attempting to use a locator spell to find you."

"I see," I say, my voice laced with both relief and disappointment. How would I even act around him? "And Oz?"

"He's on the Southern end of Occasus, last I heard." Auguste climbs onto the bed and pulls me into his lap. I rest my head on his chest and let out a deep breath.

"I'm so sorry," I say again, tears slipping down my cheeks.

"It's not your fault, love," Auguste presses his lips to the top of my head. "You couldn't help it."

"I'll leave you two to catch up," Gideon hops up, and I hear the door close a few moments later.

Anxiety churns inside me, dread a crushing weight on my chest. I have so much to make up for, and I don't know if I can ever forgive myself.

"Did he tell you what happened?" I ask, not wanting to, but needing to know. Me, carrying another man's baby—again—and the risk it poses to everyone.

"Yes," Auguste nods. "I know everything."

"And you're still here?" I ask, lifting my head to meet his gaze.

"Of course," he says, cupping my face in his hand. "Where else would I be?"

"I thought you might hate me," I admit, tears welling up in my eyes again.

"I could never hate you," Auguste says, his voice full of emotion. "I love you too much."

He kisses me then, deep and probing, and I try to convey all the love and remorse I'm feeling into that one kiss. The devotion he pours back rewires my brain, firing on all cylinders that Auguste will never give up on me. In that moment, every doubt I've had, he erases. Every fear, he bulldozes with a steady hold at the base of my neck, the faint pressure eliciting both heat and control. When we finally break apart, I'm breathless, and he nips at my bottom lip, taking care not to break skin.

"I love you, too," I whisper, my voice thick like honey. "All of you."

"We're going to get through this." Auguste grins, and my heart soars, knowing I'm the cause of his joy. "Together."

CHAPTER 43

FINN

Our home is just as Lana and I left it before she had her memories stolen. The glass of water on her bedside table, the book she was reading face down on the mattress, and though it's been many moons, her scent lingers in the air.

How can I feel her in every fiber of my being, yet feel so hollow at the same time? It's as if a part of me is missing, and no matter how many times I tell myself that she's coming back; that we'll find her, I can't shake this sense of unease. I've spent millennia waiting for Lana, only to have her and lose her. If I were a better male, I'd walk away, let her go, and save her the pain of having an inadequate soul bonded mate. But I can't.

I'm not whole without her.

I pace the length of our room, my restlessness growing with each passing moment. My magic has been on fumes because I've barely slept, hardly eaten, and have sifted from place to place, trying to hunt her down. Stepping out onto the balcony, I undress, bathing in the moons' beams to refuel. The crash of the waterfall drowns out the racing of my heart, just barely—it's as though it could gallop right out of my chest and chase her down itself.

As the light washes over me, I close my eyes, palming Lana's hairbrush. The stiff bristles press into my skin as I begin sorting through time and space to locate her. I've done this countless times since she was taken, but each time I come up empty. Until now. Now that I've got something of hers to amplify the spell.

The brush grows warm in my hand before the scene around me begins to swirl and change. I'm surrounded by darkness, but there's a light in the distance, and I zero in on it. When the scene solidifies, I'm in a sterile room, with a bed in the center. On that bed is Lana.

But she's not alone.

Three other males are with her, two of which touch her. The haze clears, and I recognize Gideon and Auguste. Something loosens in my chest at the sight; this likely means she knows they're her mates. My gaze slides over Lana's prone form, an unsettling feeling muddying my relief. Pulsing from her ankle and wrapping around her calf is a black tendril of magic I've only ever seen on one realm, and it isn't Bedlam.

"What the fuck?" I mutter, taking a step closer to the bed. My skin prickles, the hair on the back of my neck standing on end. There's something off about this situation.

Lana's eyes flutter open, and I see the fear in their depths before she slams them shut again.

"Lana," I call out, but she can't hear me. I try to move closer, but it feels like I'm wading through syrup. The wisp of black magic thickens, and I swear it moves closer to Lana's heart.

"No," I say, my voice breaking. "No, no, no."

The scene zooms out, and I recognize the scenery; they're in Luporia. I fight against the invisible force holding me back, trying to move closer, but it's no use. I'm stuck here, watching as the black magic consumes Lana. I rip the vision away, focusing instead on building the scene again in my head so I can sift there. I need to get to her.

Now.

My feet skid to a stop on the tile floor of the clinic, the sounds of shouting ringing in my ears. Gideon and Auguste whip around at my appearance, their eyes wild and full of fear.

"Where is she?" Gideon's broken voice begs.

Mekhi races into the room then, his gaze bouncing between the three of us. "She's not in the lobby, either."

"She has to be here somewhere," Auguste says desperately. "She was right here ... she was just right here! And then she vanished!"

I storm over to the bed, yanking the blankets off. At the foot of the bed is a black, sticky substance that reeks of dark magic. I touch it, and my hand comes away stained with blood.

"What the hell is this?" Auguste hisses, his fangs descending.

A coil of fear snakes through me. "I think I know where she is."

CHAPTER 44

LANA

One moment, I'm snuggled in bed with Auguste and Gideon, and the next, I wake in a forest full of dark trees. Their branches scrape against the sky, blotting out the moons and stars. I'm lying on my back on a bed of leaves, my head resting on something soft.

I sit up, and my gaze collides with a large, black furry creature. At first, I think it's a wolf, but then it opens its mouth, and I see a long, pink tongue lolling out. Its familiar eyes twinkle with mischief.

"Who are you?" I ask, scooting away from it.

The werewolf makes a disbelieving chuffing noise and sits down, its attention never leaving me. I look around, trying to get my bearings. The last thing I remember is going to bed with Gideon and Auguste. I try to stand, but my ankle throbs painfully, and I stumble. The creature is there in a flash, catching me before I hit the ground.

"Easy," it says, its voice gruff.

That's when I realize it's no longer in beast form, and instead, the heat of Luka's body sears into mine. I scramble out of his hold and put some distance between us.

"What the fuck are you doing here?" I demand.

Luka shrugs, looking far too comfortable for someone who's

supposed to be my enemy. "I could ask you the same thing. I assumed you missed me, and somehow had me sifted here." He puts on an unaffected air, but I see through it. He was hoping I missed him.

Recoiling, I glare at the king of the werewolves. "Never in your wildest dreams."

Luka's gaze sharpens. "What do you remember?"

"I remember going to bed with Gideon and Auguste." I scowl. "And then I end up here, in your lap."

"Do you remember anything else?" Luka asks, his voice tight.

I shake my head, and a wisp of fear winds its way through me. "What did you do, Luka? Where the fuck are we?" Hobbling on my still-injured leg, I try to escape through the forest, but meet a barrier of some sort.

"I don't know," Luka says. "I've tried to go through the trees, but there's some magical wall blocking it." He looks around, his regard landing on something in the distance. "But I think we should go that way."

"Why?" I ask, my hackles rising. I just want to get out of here.

"Because that's where the path is," Luka says, already moving in that direction. "It was the last place I was going to attempt before you showed up, and I didn't want to leave you here by yourself."

I follow him, my heart thrashing in my chest. In the few minutes I've been in his presence, I've tried to sift away, blast him with my magic, and maim him with my claws. But nothing stirs under my skin. Not my power, nor my feral form. When he raises a brow at me, I know that he knows. Wherever this place is, I don't have access to my power.

The path leads us to a clearing, and in the center of the clearing is a large tree. Its trunk is as wide as I am tall, and its branches twist and turn, reaching for the sky. Luka stops in front of the tree, his eyes searching the ground. It's littered with leaves and debris.

"What are you looking for?" I ask, moving to stand next to him.

"Footprints," Luka says. "But there are none. No scent, either. All I smell are the trees, the damp ground, and your arousal." He swings his gaze towards me.

"I was in bed with my mates," I spit, more to myself than to him.

Luka nods, his eyes still scanning the clearing. "Uh huh."

"Why is every king so full of himself?" I mutter.

Luka chuckles, and I fight the urge to roll my eyes. "It comes with the territory, love."

"Don't call me that."

"You are the mother of my child," Luka shrugs. "But fine, what would you like me to call you?"

"How about Lana?" I say through gritted teeth.

"Lana," Luka repeats, and I shiver at the way my name sounds on his lips. "I admit, it's a beautiful name. Though, I think love suits you better, don't you?"

I ignore the compliment and move away from him. "You and I are never going to happen."

"And yet, here we are," Luka leans against the tree, his arms crossed over his chest. "In this place, wherever it is, with no magic and no way to escape. It seems like the universe is conspiring to make us be together."

"The universe can go fuck itself," I mutter.

"Careful, love," Luka says, his voice low and dangerous as he prowls towards me. "You're starting to sound like someone I'd like to make my queen."

"What the hell is wrong with you?" I demand, shoving him. "I have more than enough mates, thank you very much. Besides, you're my enemy. I'd rather scour my veins with acid than ever be yours."

"I am your enemy." Luka wraps his arm around my waist, tugging me close to him, and nuzzling into my neck as I try to push him away. "But that doesn't mean I have to be. You're beautiful, and I reminisce about the feel of your breath on my heated skin, the quiver of your thighs wrapped around me, and the face you make when you—"

I snort and finally break away. "You're full of shit."

Luka gives me a pointed look, an unguarded openness to his eyes. "Maybe, but that doesn't change the fact that I want you. You carry my heir. And I think, in this place, we're going to have to find a way to work together."

"No," I say, planting my hands on my hips. "I'd rather die."

Something passes over his expression. "I won't let that happen." Luka stills, then shrugs. "But suit yourself. I'm going to find a way out of here, with or without you."

And with that, he turns and walks away, leaving me standing in the clearing by myself. He's going to make a liar out of me.

I hobble there for a moment, considering my options. I could follow Luka and try to find a way out with him, or I could stay here by myself and hope that someone comes to find me, because I won't get far on my own with my injury. Neither option is particularly appealing, but Luka is my best bet for finding a way out of here. With a sigh, I start to follow him. Hopefully, we can find a way out of here before he gets any more crazy ideas.

* * *

LUKA and I systematically target every single section of the perimeter, looking for any weakness, any way out. But it's like the place is one big puzzle, and no matter how many pieces we put together, we can't seem to find the exit. We're confined to a section of woods, approximately fifteen acres in total, but it's not perfectly square, nor is it symmetrical. The trees are the only constant, their trunks knobby and thick, their branches spindly and reaching.

The undergrowth is dense in some places, and in others it's almost nonexistent. The ground is uneven, with roots and rocks poking up at odd angles. And the pervasive feeling of being watched never goes away, no matter how often we check over our shoulders.

"This is pointless," I mutter, throwing my hands up in frustration. "There's no way out of here."

After a few hours of searching, we take a break. We sit in silence, our backs against the giant tree near the center of the clearing. I close my eyes and tilt my head back, doing my best not to think about my injury.

"Are you going to tell me what happened to your leg?" Luka asks, breaking the silence.

"No," I say, opening my eyes and looking at him. "It's none of your business."

"I think it is," Luka says. "Since we're stuck here together, we should at least try to be civil."

"Civil?! You kidnapped me, captured my mate, used me as bait, recorded our conversations—"

"Is that what they call it on Earth? I must admit," he croons. "I love the way your body sings for mine. Less of a conversation, and more of a sonnet."

I glare at him, my hands clenched into fists. "You're a monster."

"Yes," he agrees. "Your monster."

"No," I say through gritted teeth. "Never. I'd have killed you fifty times over by now if I had my magic."

"It's the Nordic-looking vampire, isn't it?"

I freeze. There's only one vampire he could be talking about. How does he know who Auguste is? I think he looks more like Tom Cruise from the original Top Gun with way more height and bulk, but some liken him more to a dark-haired Norse god because of his tattoos and brooding.

"What about him?" I finally say, trying to keep my voice even.

"He's your dom."

"What the *hell* are you talking about?"

Luka shrugs. "I can see it in the way you interact with him. The way you defer to him, the way your body responds to his. He's the one in control, and you like it."

"You're insane." I feel my cheeks flush. He's just trying to get me flustered. It's nothing like that between Auguste and I, and I'm certain he's never seen the two of us interact, unless he spied on us on Earth. Sure, he's dominant in the bedroom, but it's hardly a dom/sub relationship. Not sure the others would be okay with that. "You don't know anything about me."

"I know enough." He looks at me, his eyes boring into mine. "But I want to know more."

"Why?" I ask, genuinely curious. "What difference does it make to you?"

"It doesn't," he says with a shrug. "I'm just curious about you, that's all."

I study him for a moment, trying to decide if I believe him. Deciding I don't, I close my eyes and lean my head back against the tree, effectively ending the conversation.

But Luka is nothing if not persistent. "I can help you," he says after a few moments.

"Help me with what?"

"Your leg."

I open my eyes and glare at him. "You can't help me."

"Let me see it." He scoots closer to me.

"No." I try to scoot away from him, but my injury and the angle I'm at on the ground prevents me from moving too far.

"I'm not going to hurt you," he says, his voice gentle. "I just want to see."

Against my better judgment, I slowly roll my pants up to my thigh, gritting my teeth against the pain. Luka sucks in a sharp breath when he sees the wound. Blood so dark it looks black seeps from the punctures, and the marks around it, mottled blue streaks running up my calves. Gideon healed me, but for some reason, it was only temporary.

"What happened?" he asks, his voice laced with disbelief.

"I was attacked by a wild animal," I lie. I'm not about to tell him I had the urge to cross the water where some entity called for me, only to get attacked by some goblin-like creature.

"What kind of animal?" he asks, his brow furrowed.

He's almost convincing. Like he actually cares, though I know his cruel streak. I've been at the mercy of it more times than I can count, and I'd be a fool to ever think otherwise. "I don't know," I shrug. "It was dark, and I couldn't see it."

Luka is silent for a moment before he speaks. "I can help you," he says again.

"No," I say, shaking my head. "I don't need your help."

"You don't have your magic, you're injured, and you're in the middle of enemy territory. You need all the help you can get."

I freeze, suspicion gnawing at something deep within me. "How do you know where we're at?" I ask slowly.

Luka shrugs again. "I just do."

"No," I say, my voice firm. "You tell me how you know, or I'm not telling you anything."

He studies me for a long moment before he speaks. "I have my ways," he says evasively.

"That's not good enough," I growl. "I want to know how you know."

"Fine." He sighs. "I have spies everywhere, including other realms."

"Everywhere?" I echo, my stomach sinking. Afraid to voice my question, but needing to know, I grit out, "We aren't in Bedlam anymore, are we?"

He shakes his head. "No, you're not."

"Where are we?" I whisper.

"Romarie," he says. "The Dark Fae realm."

I vaguely recall learning about the various realms during my training on Convectus. There are five I remember, not including Earth. But Romarie… I know next to nothing about it, other than it's ruled by a band of evil, rogue fae. And we're right in the middle of it.

My legs give out from under me, and I sink to the ground. Luka catches me before I fall all the way and eases me down gently. The world around me swirls, and I fight to keep conscious. If I give in to the darkness, I'll be at Luka's mercy. And I can't let that happen.

"Let me heal you," he purrs, his fingers tracing the frown on my face.

I jerk away from him and scramble to my feet. "No," I say, shaking my head. "I don't need your help."

Auguste taught me to know my enemies, so I know how best to defeat them, and there's one trait werewolves possess that's the closest thing to magic there is. And that's their ability to heal with their saliva.

Luka's cruel hands have caused me enough pain, and I won't let him inflict any more, even if it is in the guise of helping me. "I can take care of myself," I say, my voice breaking, sweat beading on my forehead from the effort of staying upright.

"You're weak," he sneers, and vindication floods my body. *This* is the Luka I know. Sure as I knew the sun will rise tomorrow, I knew he'd show me his true colors again. "You can't even stand without help."

He's right, I can't. But I won't let him know that. "I'm not weak," I say, my voice a hiss. "I'm stronger than you'll ever be."

He steps closer to me, and I take a step back. My back hits a tree, and I have nowhere to go. "We'll see about that," he says, his voice a low growl.

He reaches for me, and I flinch, preparing for the pain I know him to inflict without mercy. But it never comes. Instead, I'm surrounded by a warm, comforting presence, and I sag against the tree in relief before my brain remembers the sting of his whip, the pure terror of drowning by his hand, and the smarting of his grip against my scalp as he dragged me to where he had Gideon chained.

"Get away!" I round the tree, placing it between us.

This is a trick.

He draws up short. "You're afraid of me." Hurt flashes across Luka's face. His brows draw together, concern etched into the lines marring his forehead.

The ghosts of his torture haunt me, and I can't let him anywhere near me. He may be able to fool anyone else with his act, but I know better. Every instinct tells me to run. "You kidnapped me. Brutalized my body." My voice cracks, hysteria wobbling it. "Held me captive so you could kill my mates, and now, your heir grows in my womb. I'm not afraid of you. I'm *terrified* of you!"

I won't give into his promise of comfort.

Never from him.

He takes a step towards me, and I take one back. "Lana, please," he says, his voice imploring. "I never wanted to hurt you."

Lies. All lies.

"You're a monster," I say, my voice shaking with anger and fear. "And I'll never forgive you for what you've done."

He flinches as if I've physically struck him, and I take some small measure of satisfaction in seeing the pain I've caused. It doesn't make up for all the hurt he's inflicted on me, but it's a start.

"I'm sorry, Lana," he says, his voice breaking. "I never meant to hurt you."

And with that, he turns and walks away, disappearing into the darkness through the trees.

I sink to the ground, my body trembling with exhaustion and relief. I thought for sure he was going to kill me. But he didn't. He walked away.

Why?

Why does he keep fucking with my head? I'm not going to stick around to find out. I need to find a way to Bedlam from here before he comes back, to the arms of my mates. They're the only ones who can protect me from Luka now. Dragging my injured leg behind me, I pave my way through the forest, reaching high and low around the perimeter for some give in the barrier imprisoning us. There's no way out.

A startled shout escapes my lips when something brushes against my arm, and I whirl around, ready to fight. But there's no one there. I'm surrounded by trees, their leaves rustling in the breeze, but otherwise, there's nothing. No one. Shaking my head to clear it, I start to walk again, my body on high alert.

A hysterical cry barrels out of me when something yanks on my hair from behind, and I reach up to grab whatever it is. My fingers close around a handful of leaves, and I tug, but they don't come loose. I'm being dragged, my feet scrabbling for purchase on the ground as I'm pulled backwards towards whatever is behind me.

The leaves tighten their grip on my hair, yanking harder, and I cry out in pain. I try to grab onto something, anything to anchor myself, but there's nothing to hold onto. My nails crack and bleed as I drag them through the dirt, tearing up the soil.

My nails scrape against the bark of a tree as I'm pulled past it, and I grasp at the rough surface, trying to hold on. A sob catches in my throat, but it doesn't escape.

I'm being pulled further and further into the forest, away from where Luka went.

And I have no idea who, or what, is taking me.

* * *

I AWAKE WITH A START, my heart pounding in my chest. It takes me a moment to remember where I am and what happened. Dragged through the forest, not a sound escaping me, and then darkness.

I'm still in the woods. But I'm not alone.

A girl, no more than nineteen, hovers a few feet away from me, her long white cardigan billowing around her in the breeze. Black leather pants hug her legs and strapped to them are tiny daggers. Black hair flows around her like a silken curtain, and her green eyes have a yellow cast to them, searching mine as though she's trying to recognize something in me.

She's beautiful.

And she's not human.

"Who are you?" I ask, my voice shaking.

"Teresa," she says, her voice gentle, shame causing her to hide her face. "I'm sorry about what happened. Luka made me send the Crownsees to bring you back to our compound for healing, but they're giant, tree-like creatures and aren't always gentle. You must've bonked your head." A whine escapes her throat, and I instantly recognize her for what she is. She isn't fae.

Werewolf.

"Why?" I ask, confusion warring with the fear inside me. I *knew* there was more to our situation than he let on. He's behind this. "Why would he make you kidnap me?"

"He's my alpha. I can't disobey his command." Her voice breaks. "He bartered with some goblins to get you here, but I don't know what he wants with you. No one in the pack does, and it's causing a lot of unrest amongst the ranks." A tear escapes her eye, and she quickly wipes it away. "Please," she pleads. "You have to help me. He's going to kill me if I don't do what he says."

I hesitate for a moment, torn between my own need to escape and the girl's plea for help. But I can't just leave her here.

"Okay," I say, getting to my feet, wincing at putting my weight on my leg. "I'll help you. But we have to find a way out of here first."

"I know a way," she says, her face lighting up with hope. "Follow me."

She takes off into the woods without a backward glance, and I follow close behind her, hobbling on my injury. We walk for what feels like hours, the silence between us thick and oppressive. I'm on edge, my senses stretched to their limit, but there's no sign of Luka or anyone else from the pack.

Eventually, we reach a small glade, and Teresa stops, turning to me with a smile.

"This is it," she says, gesturing around her. "This is the way out."

I follow her gaze, and my heart sinks. There's nothing here but trees.

"It doesn't look like anything," I say, my voice flat.

"I know," she says, her smile faltering. "But it's the only way."

"How do you know?" I ask, desperation creeping into my voice. "Are you sure?"

"Yes," she says, her eyes pleading with me to believe her. "Please, you have to trust me."

I take a deep breath and nod. "Okay ..."

She takes a step towards me, her hand outstretched. "Close your eyes," she says, and I do as she asks.

I feel her cool fingers brush against my forehead, and then I'm falling. Tumbling through darkness, the only sound is my own screams.

And then, suddenly, I'm freefalling through the sky, the wind rushing past me. I scream again, my stomach lurching as I plummet towards the ground. I hit sand with a bone-jarring thud, the air knocked out of my lungs. Laying there for a moment, dazed, I attempt to sit up, cradling my stomach. I prod it, relaxing when I feel a reassuring kick.

"Shit, are you okay?"

I turn to see Teresa crouched next to me; her face filled with worry.

"I think so," I gasp out, my voice rough. "You could've warned me."

She laughs, relief flooding her features. "Yeah, sorry about that. I wasn't sure how else to get you out of there."

"What did you do?" I ask, still trying to catch my breath.

"I opened a portal," she says, shrugging. "It was the only way I could think of to get you out of there without them knowing I was behind it."

"A portal?" I repeat, my brow furrowed. "To where?" And how can a werewolf open a portal? They have no magic.

Her eyes shine with unshed tears. "I wanted to take you someplace safe, but it had to be somewhere Luka can't reach us easily. This is as safe a place as any."

"Where are we?" My eyes catalogue the miles of beach stretched out before us, crystalline water lapping at the sand. It looks like paradise.

"This is Australia," she says, a small smile touching her lips.

My legs weaken beneath me, a memory tugging on my mind. A memory of another beach. Of another time.

"You're Rose and Bennett's friend," I whisper, seeing her in a new light. The dusting of freckles across the bridge of her nose, her bright green eyes.

"Yes," she says, her smile widening. "I'm Teresa McKenna."

Ross Van'Astor's cousin. My ex-fiancé who was cruel and who I caught cheating on me just two days after our engagement. I can't hold it against her, though I'd be lying if I said it didn't give me pause.

Glancing behind her, I take in the sprawling villa perched atop the cliff. "This is my place, isn't it?" I ask, and she nods.

I'll address how she managed to open a portal to Earth later, because it's not a Bedlam Moon, and she has no power. I limp towards the steps leading up to Gideon's house, my heart pounding in my chest. I don't know what I'll find when I get there, but I have to see for myself.

Pushing open the door, I step into the entryway, my heart in my throat. The scents of my children, my dad, and my mates permeate the air, the memories of them hitting me like a ton of bricks.

"We have to go back to them." I start to shake, my knees giving out on me. I would've hit the floor if Teresa hadn't been there to catch me.

"I know," she says, her voice gentle as she helps me to the couch.

"But we can't right now. Luka is still looking for us, and he won't stop until he finds us. We have to lay low for a few hours, until it's safe to go back."

.

* * *

STRETCHING out my leg on the couch, I turn towards where Teresa angles her body near me in the armchair. "So," I say, clearing my throat. "How did you get mixed up with Luka?"

Last I heard, she was with a contingent of vampires, fighting the fae.

"It's a long story." She sighs, leaning her head back against the cushions. "But the short version is that he captured me when he saw me with the vampires, he forced me into his pack, and he's been using me to try and get to you. He threatened people I love; said he'd kill them if I didn't join him."

"Why?" I frown, not understanding. "I thought he wanted the throne."

"He does." She nods. "But he also wants you. He's obsessed with you, and it's beginning to piss off a lot of the pack, ambling for any reason to challenge him. It's going to get him killed."

A cold chill runs down my spine, and I fight the urge to shiver. "Why me?" I whisper. "He spent weeks torturing me, bleeding me out, only to impregnate me."

"I don't know." She picks at a string on the couch cushion, twirling it around her finger. "But I think it has something to do with imprinting on you."

"Imprinting?" I echo, my brow furrowed.

"It's a werewolf thing." She sighs again. "When we find our mates, we imprint on them. It's like we're drawn to them; can't stay away from them, no matter how hard we try."

"So, he's imprinted on me?" My voice coming out strained, stomach twisting into panic.

"It would appear so." She worries her lip between her teeth.

"Though I'm not entirely sure how that's possible, considering you're not a werewolf."

I swallow hard, trying to push down the bile rising in my throat. "Why? Why would he imprint on me?" There's an edge of hysteria to my voice.

"It's nothing he can control." She softens her words. "It just happens."

"Great," I mutter, scrubbing a hand over my face. "Just great."

There's a knock on the door then, and Teresa jumps to her feet, tensing. "Who is it?" she calls out.

How would someone know we were here?

"It's Hannah," a familiar voice replies, and she visibly relaxes, going to open the door.

My best friend steps into the house, her gaze going straight to me. "Lana!" she cries, tackling me.

"Hannah," I breathe, shock robbing me of words, pure joy filling my chest until I can scarcely draw air into my lungs.

"I can't believe it's really you." She pulls back to look at me. "Jesus." She gazes up at me. "You're so freaking tall!"

I chuckle, the sound strange to my own ears. "Yeah," I say, glancing down at myself. "Fae tend to be."

"Yeah," she echoes, her brow furrowed. "Does this mean you can hear better?" She stands on her tiptoes to run a hand over the tips of my pointed ears.

I nod, fighting the urge to cringe away from her touch. "Yeah," I say, my voice coming out a little strained.

Her eyes narrow on mine. "Don't you dare shy away from me." She smacks my arm, and I wince. "I'm your best friend, and I've been worried sick about you! Where are the guys? Maeve?" Her attention drops to my stomach, hand flying to her mouth. "Omigod. Are you …? Is it …" She's rarely at a loss for words, but they seem to evade her now. Her pitch drops as she whispers, "It's Finn's, isn't it?" Her grin and the waggling of her eyebrows undoes me.

"They're still in Bedlam." My voice comes out thick. "I had to escape a werewolf who has imprinted on me. Impregnated me."

She visibly recoils as though I've struck her. "What?" she utters, her eyes wide. "That's not possible."

"It is." Teresa speaks up then, her voice solemn. "Apparently, werewolves can imprint on anyone, regardless of species. And it seems Luka has imprinted on Lana."

"No." Hannah shakes her head. "Back up a minute. It's not Finn's?" Her eyes dart to where I cradle my rounded stomach.

"No." I shake my head, not trusting myself to say more.

"By a werewolf you're trying to escape from?" she clarifies, and I pull my lips between my teeth. "That's…oh my god." She sits down hard on the couch, her face pale. "This is a nightmare."

"I know," I agree, sinking down onto the couch next to her. "I don't know what to do."

"We'll figure it out," she says, her voice firm. "We always do."

But I can't shake the feeling that this time, we won't. That this time, we're in over our heads. Hannah and I sit on the couch, our eyes wide as we stare at each other. This isn't how I wanted our reunion to go, but I suppose it's better than her never knowing what happened to me.

"So." She finally speaks up, breaking the heavy silence that had fallen between us. "What now?"

I shrug, not trusting myself to say more. I'm so tired, and my head is swimming with all that's happened. All I want to do is curl up in a ball and sleep for a week.

"I think," Teresa speaks up then, her voice hesitant, "that it might be best if we head back to Bedlam, but we need to get you healed first."

Hannah's eyes scan my body like heat-seeking missiles. "What's wrong with her?" she demands, her voice sharp.

"She was poisoned," Teresa tells her. "It's still in her system, and it's slowly killing her."

"Poisoned?" Hannah and I both speak at the same time.

"With Vallani goblin venom," she whines. "Luka meant to win you over by pretending to rescue you in the dark fae realm, but he didn't know it would be like this. That you wouldn't just fall in love with him. Not after everything he did to you."

"How do we fix it?" I ask, my voice trembling. Fear ratchets up my spine, and I have to fight to keep from shaking. "My baby—"

"There's only one way," Teresa tells me, her voice gentle. "But it's risky."

"I don't care," I say, my voice firm. "I'll do whatever it takes to save my baby."

"And your mates," she adds.

I stiffen, my hand going to my stomach protectively. "What about them?" I demand. "Are they in danger too?"

She nods. "Luka won't stop until he has all of you," she tells me. "And he needs them out of the way. He's obsessed and wants you for himself."

"So we have to go back," I say, my voice trembling. "We have to stop him."

"Yes." She shifts in her seat. "But it won't be easy. He's got an army of werewolves at his disposal, and he won't hesitate to use them. I only escaped because I stole his portal stone. There are only a few left in existence … created when the most recent Luna goddess ascended."

"How?" I ask, worry lancing through me about what she'd risked to get me to safety. "I thought only fae royalty could use those."

"Luka is the king of the werewolves," she tells me. "It works for him because his line stems from the original, cursed wolf fae. He's got royal blood. And because you were with me, we could use the stone."

Yes, I suppose I am high queen of the fae. My eyes sink to where I absently rub my abdomen. Royal blood … *and* I'm carrying his child. He had me poisoned so he could save me, win my heart, and what? Kill my mates? Turn me into a werewolf like him?

No. I won't let that happen.

"What do we have to do?" I steel my voice. "Tell me what to do, and I'll do it."

Teresa nods, her expression determined. "I can heal you." She averts her eyes. "But you won't like it."

"How?"

"You have to force me to turn into a werewolf, and then I'll need to use my saliva to close the wound on your leg."

"No." I shake my head. "I won't make you hurt yourself to heal me."

"It's the only way," she tells me. "It'll be fine. It's getting easier and easier each time I turn."

I startle when Hannah's hand lands on my arm. "Lana," she implores. "She's right. It's the only way."

My eyes dart to hers, and I see the truth in her words, and I sit with them for a moment. "Okay," I whisper. "I'll do it."

Teresa inclines her head before she stands up and moves to sit on the marbled coffee table in front of me.

"Ready?"

I take a deep breath and straighten my spine. "Yes."

My hands rest on her sternum, pushing as much power as I can into her. I watch as her green eyes start to bleed yellow, and her canines lengthen into sharp fangs. Her body contorts painfully, her bones snapping and crunching as they stretch and reform.

She cries out, her voice a mixture of pain and a snarl as her transformation completes. Her putrid breath washes over me, and I fight the urge to gag.

Instinctively, my hand goes to my stomach to protect my unborn child as Teresa looms over me, her eyes wild and feral.

"Do it," I whisper, rolling my pant leg up. The wound is still seeping blood; black veins spiderweb up my calves, reaching my thighs, and I know it won't be long before I'm too weak to even stand.

Teresa leans down and sinks her teeth into my leg. Pain explodes through me, white-hot and blinding. I scream, my body going rigid as I fight to stay conscious.

I feel her tongue lap at the wound at my ankle, and the fire in my blood begins its retreat. The blackness fades from my vision, and I take a shaky breath as I fall back against the couch. Hannah grips my hand tightly, her eyes wide and full of worry.

"It's okay," I tell her weakly. "I'm okay."

But am I really? I've been imprinted by the werewolf king who wants to kill my other mates, I carry his heir, and I've yet to get in touch with my other mates.

How am I supposed to save us all when I can't even save myself?

* * *

NIGHT FALLS, and my heart aches, because I've got to say goodbye to my best friend. Though I'd love to take her with me to Bedlam, it isn't safe for her. Never for a mortal.

"I'll find a way for us to see each other again." I crush Hannah to my front, her head barely reaching my chest now that I'm fae.

"I know you will." She nods, her eyes glossy with unshed tears. "Be careful."

"You too," I whisper before turning towards Teresa.

She palms the portal stone, and I take one last look at the home I'm meant to share with my mates in the human realm before the swirling mist pulls me under. It's not like sifting, nor is it like the portal I traveled through when I first came to Bedlam. This time, it feels like I'm being dragged through a tunnel of barbed wire, every inch of my body on fire.

I scream until my throat is raw, and just when I think I can't take it anymore, I'm spit out onto the hard ground.

I lay there for a moment, trying to catch my breath as the pain fades away. When I finally sit up, I see that I'm in some kind of dungeon. There's a small window high up on the wall that lets in a sliver of moonlight, and I can just make out the iron bars that block it.

The door to my cell slams open, and I scramble to my feet as Luka stalks in. When Teresa and Hannah first formulated this plan, I was skeptical, but soon realized it was the only way.

His eyes immediately find mine, checking for injury, before darting to Teresa and narrowing. "You little bitch," he seethes. "You took her from me!"

"No, it wasn't her fault," I interject before Teresa can say anything. "I tricked her by stealing your portal stone and threatened her life to heal me."

Betrayal flashes in his eyes, and he pauses, weighing my words, measuring whether my story is true.

"Fine," he grits out. He moves aside for Teresa to scramble out of the cell before shutting himself in with me. "But that doesn't change the fact that you're mine."

"I'm not yours," I snarl, my lip curling in disgust. "You tried to kill me."

He takes a step towards me, and I back up until my shoulders hit the stone wall. "You're mine," he growls, trapping me between his body and the wall. "You carry a part of me inside you."

I try to push him away, but it's like trying to move a mountain. Testosterone pours off him, his hulking frame seeming to grow with his possessiveness. "Get off of me!"

"Not until you admit that you're mine." His hand comes up to grip the hair at my scalp, yanking my head back. "You are mine, Lana."

"No, I'm not!" I cry, my vision blurring with tears. "I'm Gideon's, Oz's, Auguste's, Grimm's, Penn's, Casimir's, and Finn's! You have no claim on me!"

A dangerous chuckle rumbles in his chest, and he brings his face close to mine. "What's one more?" he whispers before claiming my lips in a brutal kiss.

It takes everything in me to keep my magic at a bay. It swirls inside me, desperate to attack this man, put him in his place, under my heel. But I can't. If I use my magic, he'll put another collar on my neck. This means I can't injure him, or I'll glow. I can't let him bed me, or I'll glow, no matter how repulsed I am by him—there's no denying baser, carnal desires. I can't do anything that would give myself away.

The only thing I can do is stick to the plan, which is why I soften under his touch and return his kiss with equal fervor. A satisfied groan rumbles in his chest, and he presses me harder against the wall. His hand drops from my hair to snake around my waist, pulling me flush against him. I fight the urge to gag as his tongue invades my mouth, and instead allow my magic to coil around him. It won't hurt him—not yet—but it will make it easier for me to control him right when I need to.

He pulls away with a satisfied smirk, and lust hangs in his eyes. "That's my girl," he murmurs, before turning to walk out of the cell.

The door slams shut behind him, and I sink to the ground with a sigh. This is going to be a long, long night.

Sitting alone in my cell, I turn my thoughts to my mates. Most of them can read minds when in close proximity, but what if I found a way to amplify my thoughts? Could they hear them from far away? Maybe I can carry them on the wind, guiding them to wherever they're at. I've tried to sift out of here, but he's got it warded, which means he's got a powerful fae on his side.

I settle myself in a meditative state, clearing my mind of all distractions. I focus on the image of Oz, his handsome face, and penetrating eyes. To Auguste. To Oz. Finn, even, though I don't remember him yet. And though they don't deserve it, I try for Grimm, Casimir, and Penn, too. I send all my love and hope to them, willing them to hear me. To let them know I'm safe, and even if it's the last thing I do, I'll find my way back to them.

Not a single stirring of wind reaches me, wherever I'm at. Burrowing down, I allow my magic to seep into the stone below me, into the bedrock, reaching, feeling for the elements that helped me once before. My power spills into the water table far below, and I use it to nudge the molecules of water, willing them to obey me.

At first, nothing happens. And then, ever so slowly, the water changes direction, swirling around me in a gentle eddy. I direct it up, through the rock, towards the surface, but it doesn't budge any further.

Okay, I reason with it. *No going up. How about sideways?*

This time, the water listens, and a small trickle starts to make its way through the cracks in the rock. It spills into chamber after chamber, across thousands of miles, the echoes of my words resounding in its wake.

Keep going, I urge it. *Find my mates. Tell them Luka has me in a cell somewhere, but I have a plan to get Teresa and I out of his clutches.*

The damp, cold cell fades away as I become lost in my mates, and for a moment, it's almost as though I can feel them with me. Their shock, their anger, their worry. And then it's gone, and I'm left with nothing but the sound of my own heartbeat, echoing in the emptiness of the cell.

But it's a start.

CHAPTER 45

FINN

"Do you feel that?" I ask, turning to Gideon.

He stands, frozen, next to a shocked Auguste, both training their ears to listen for any sound in the silent night. "What was it?"

I shake my head, not trusting myself to say anything. It felt like ... like Lana. But that's impossible.

Faint words ripple through my mind, and I still. Not a breath escapes me as my eyes dart around the barren landscape of the Wastelands. Crouching low to the ground, I strain to make out the words, but they're just beyond my reach.

Gideon and Auguste join me in pressing our heads to the cracked dirt, and finally, the words come through loud and clear. My heart clenches at the melodic sway of them.

Tell them Luka has me in a cell somewhere, but I have a plan to get Teresa and I out of his clutches.

The stir of her magic wraps around me like a caress, leaving goosebumps in its wake, despite the fear threatening to take me under. She's alive. And Teresa is with her?

"Lana's alive," I whisper, not daring to speak any louder.

Gideon nods, his face tight with resolve. "We have to find her."

CHAPTER 46

CASIMIR

Hunger claws at my empty stomach, but I haven't the appetite to eat the rations guards bring to our cell. We no longer hear Lana's cries, and it's been a long time since she listened to our reasons for destroying her life.

I can take her wrath, if only she would acknowledge me.

A stirring below my feet has me lifting my head, eyes darting to the others, wondering if they feel it, too. It's as though water laps at a pool cover, trapped.

I'm on my feet in an instant, pressing my ear to the stonework. And then I feel the comforting presence of Lana's magic, along with reassurance. Words, faint and barely there, but they're there, nonetheless.

Tell them Luka has me in a cell somewhere, but I have a plan to get Teresa and I out of his clutches.

I scramble to my feet, eyes wild. "Luka has her," I breathe. "She's not even here."

The others are on their feet in an instant, and we all stare at each other in dawning realization.

"We have to find her," I say, already moving to the door of our cell. "Now."

There's no hesitation for Pierce, Zara, and Penn. Their hands wrap around the bars, and they pull with all their might. The metal screeches in protest, but it starts to give before turning into molten slag, and we spill out into the hallway beyond with barely a thought.

We take off at a run, not caring who sees us. We must get our mate. Nothing else matters.

Shouts fill the air as we burst through the tunnel, dropping guard after guard who try to stand in our way. The layout of the underground is a blur as we run, but Lana's magic pulses in my veins, leading us ever closer to her.

"Stop!" a woman shouts, and I recognize her voice instantly.

Annabelle.

I skid to a halt, and the others follow suit, attention turned to Lana's parents and children, who appear to have just been swimming.

"What are you doing?" Annabelle demands, her gaze flicking to the neutralized fae and the unconscious guards at our feet. "Have you lost your minds?"

"Luka has Lana," I say, not caring if they hate me for it. "We have to find her."

Annabelle's face pales. "What do you mean?"

"He has her locked in a cell," I grit out, desperate to go to the surface to find her. "She used her magic, carried it through the water table to reach us. Said someone named Teresa is with her, too."

At this, Bennett shoves forward. "Take us to her," he demands.

I start to shake my head, but then Annabelle steps in front of her grandson.

"We'll let you go," she says, her voice firm. "But you have to promise to bring my daughter back safely."

"We promise," I say, already moving to the tunnel, ignoring the tingle of magic stirring in the air at the vow.

The others fall into step behind me, and we take off at a run until we reach the pool of water we first entered the Crucey's chamber through. We don't hesitate to jump in, and the water closes over our heads as we start the long journey back to the surface.

Clambering out of the pond, I take a look around, trying to get my bearings. We take to the skies, flying as fast as we can towards the mountains.

We're coming, Lana.

CHAPTER 47

LANA

The ground is unforgiving and cold beneath me, and the air smells dank. I shift, trying to get comfortable, but it's impossible. My belly is swollen with Luka's child, and I can't seem to find a position that doesn't make my back ache.

I've been here for weeks, imprisoned in this cell. It's worse than the room he had me in when he first kidnapped me. At least that place had a bed. I know he's angry at me for trying to run away. But I can't give up because we have a plan.

A sudden noise sounds outside the door of my cell, and I sit up straight, heart pounding. It swings open, and Luka steps through, followed by Teresa.

"Hello, love," he says, a cruel smile on his face. "Had enough of your imprisonment?"

I get to my feet, holding onto the bars of the cell for support. "Please," I beg.

His gaze drops to where I cradle my stomach. "You're going to give me a daughter," he says, pleased. "A strong heir."

"I'll be with you." A tear tracks down my cheek. I don't have to fake it. "You don't have to keep me in the cell."

He studies me for a moment before nodding. "You're right," he says, coming closer and unlocking the door. "Because you'll do what I say now, won't you, love?"

I inwardly cringe at his term of endearment. There'll never be love between us. "Of course."

"Good." He takes hold of my arm and leads me out into the hallway. "It's been too long since you've warmed my bed."

My stomach churns, and I fight the urge to vomit. This is the part of the plan that I dread the most. But I know I must do it.

For my mates. For our child.

I will do whatever it takes to keep them safe.

On our way through the halls, we pass a dining hall full of werewolves, and my attention catches on Katarina, Luka's sister. The look she gives me is one of sorrow, and I mentally shelve that tidbit for later. Maybe I can make an ally of her, too.

Luka drags me up the stairs to his bedroom, and I try not to let my revulsion show. Underneath his beauty, he's a monster, and I will make sure he pays for what he's done—in due time.

He leads me to his bed and pushes me down onto the mattress. I fight the urge to cringe away from his touch as he starts to undress me, his mouth hungry as it presses to my exposed skin. Stilling his hand on the button of his jeans, I meet his gaze.

"Allow me," I whisper.

He shakes his head. "No, I'm going to savor this." His hand strokes my curls out of my face. "You're so beautiful, Lana. I'm so happy you've realized nothing will keep me from you. Not now. Not ever."

He doesn't give me a chance to respond as he starts to lower his jeans. I force myself to remain still and keep my gaze on his. This is the most difficult part of the plan. I have to let him think he's won, that I'm completely under his thumb. Otherwise, he'll kill me. This much I know.

Teresa said it's not uncommon for rejected mates to kill those they've imprinted on.

Lowering himself to my side, his arm wraps around my swollen belly. "My heir," he whispers reverently before kissing me. "My love."

As his mouth moves over mine, I close my eyes, turning my

thoughts to my mates. I imagine it's Casimir's hands, cupping the back of my neck. That it's Oz's heavy weight pressing into me. It's Gideon, playfully tugging on my bottom lip. And Auguste, who controls every kiss.

Though I'm only projecting the scene playing out before Luka, making him think this is all really happening, it still feels like a betrayal to my mates. Hannah and Teresa spent hours with me, working to perfect this bit of magic before we left Australia.

With Teresa, I'd made her think she'd just won the lottery. Then, I'd made her think she could fly, which turned out to be a terrible idea as I'd caught her leaping off the couch.

I'd made Hannah think she was back in high school, her and I flirting with the foreign exchange student from Switzerland in the back of Spanish class. Then, I made her see the thing she wished for most. I wasn't sure it'd work, but as Luna magic is the source of all magic, I only needed to mold it and shape it into whatever I wanted, coaxing it to bend to my will. When I had dropped the façade, tears streamed down Hannah's face, and I clutched her to my chest, horrified as she sucked in big, ugly sobs.

When I'd asked her what she saw, she'd said it was me, her, my mates, and *her mate*. She was terrified to tell me the rest, and I wheedled it out of her. My gut still churns, knowing she thought she couldn't trust me with her deepest desire.

She wants to be a vampire so she can live forever with CJ and Maeve. Mated to Maeve. Her love for her child, CJ, keeps that desire at bay—for now. He has autism and sensory processing disorder, and she doesn't want to change him, or his gifts, which we're afraid turning him into a vampire would do. My heart breaks for her impossible predicament.

When I make Luka think he's come inside me, and he's dressed and snuggling against my side, I drop the façade. Luka presses his lips to where my tears track down my cheeks. My eyes fly open, and his features sharpen when he takes in the glow of my skin.

"I knew you felt this too." He leans in to take my mouth. Relief softens my spine. He's not angry I have my magic and isn't going to tamp it.

Just like that, the tables have turned. Now it's my turn to play the game. And I will make him regret ever underestimating me.

"I love you," I whisper against his lips, embellishing my words with just a touch of magic.

He freezes, his eyes softening as they dart between mine. "I love you, too," he whispers back before pulling me into his lap, a possessive hold around my waist.

I allow myself to sink into him, relief and a touch of triumph welling up inside.

It's all part of the plan.

CHAPTER 48

FINN

*D*irt grits my teeth, the arid landscape offering little reprieve from the heat. It's been weeks since Lana vanished, and we're traversing the Wastelands.

"What the fuck are they doing here?!" Gideon's snarl stops me in my tracks where we've made camp. I fix my attention to the sky where his is trained and see the group of flying creatures circling overhead.

My eyes narrow, blood pressure rising as the fae in our group hiss and take a step back. They land, and I tackle Grimm first, knocking him to the ground. Beside me, Gideon has Penn in a headlock.

Pierce moves to pull me off where I have Grimm pinned to the ground, my teeth poised to tear into his neck. "She'll never forgive you if you do that." His calm voice filters through the red haze.

I blink, realization dawning as I take in Grimm's panicked expression. Snarling, I shove off him and stand.

"What the fuck are you doing out of your cell?" I demand.

The fae in question scrambles to his feet and dusts himself off. "We escaped," he says matter-of-factly.

"And you just happened to find us?" I raise a brow.

He shrugs, face smug. "Luck, I guess."

I don't buy it for a second, but before I can say anything, Casimir cuts in. "We're on our way to rescue Lana."

Stilling, I turn to face him. Did she talk to them, too? I ignore the green, ugly rage that wants to take root and blossom. Instead, I focus on my mate and the fact that she's in danger. Again.

"What do you know?" Auguste, ever a voice of reason, steps up beside me.

Casimir's gaze meets mine, and I see the same determination that I know is reflected in my own eyes. "I imagine only what you do: Luka has her and someone named Teresa." He says it like he wants me to tell him who Teresa is, but I won't.

Captain Zara steps into my line of sight, her blonde ponytail swaying before settling across her shoulder. "I'm sorry, Finn."

My gaze snaps to hers. "What for?"

"For following my orders. That my orders hurt you." Her voice is soft, and I see the sincerity in her lilac eyes.

I give her a tilt of my head in acknowledgement. "Seems like only one of you was willing to do the right thing," I growl. "Though the thought of Bellamy's hands on my mate wants me to punt him to the next realm, he at least had the balls to do what you and Pierce never could."

Once upon a time, Zara and I fought side-by-side, and I was good friends with her mate. I understand her need to follow orders, even if they hurt those she cares for.

"If we want Lana back safely, where she belongs," she makes a point to take in each of us, "then we need to work together." Always one to cut to the chase, this one.

Everything in me wants to tear into the kings, rip them limb from limb, cursing them for taking Lana from me. But Zara is right. Hoarding our knowledge can only hurt our mate. I step forward and thrust my hand out, like we had so many times before, back when things were different. "I'm in."

Captain Zara takes it with a tight smile, the relief in her posture evident.

"As am I." Gideon steps up beside me and takes her hand in his.

"And I," Auguste says.

One by one, the rest of our group agrees.

It's time to take down the king of the werewolves and get our mate back.

CHAPTER 49

LANA

My hair spills over Luka's pillow as he sleeps soundly beside me. Fury wars with duty inside my head, and I know I need to leave before I do something I'll regret, like murdering him where he lies.

I ease out of bed, being as quiet as possible so I don't wake him. I throw on some clothes and sneak out the door, careful not to let it slam. My feet pad softly down the hall until a whimper reaches my ears. Following the sound, I end up in front of a closed door.

I hesitate for only a moment before I open it and slip inside. The first thing I see is a fae, huddled in the corner with her arms wrapped around her knees. Her eyes are wide and frightened, and she flinches when I take a step closer.

"It's okay," I say softly, holding my hands up in a non-threatening gesture. "I won't hurt you."

The woman doesn't say anything, but I see the way her eyes dart around the room, taking in the chains that are bolted to the wall. On account of the way blood spills from her forehead and into her vision, I'm not sure how much she can even see right now.

"What's your name?" I ask, taking another step closer.

"Anastasia," she finally responds, her voice shaking.

"Okay, Anastasia," I say in a soothing tone before the name registers. "Wait—you're Penn's cousin, aren't you?" I remember her now—I'd overheard her complain to Penn about my being in Bedlam when he took me to the dragon's castle on Convectus. I'd thought he was cheating on some woman with me and foolishly ran away before hearing the entire conversation.

Her eyes widen, and she nods. "H-How do you know that?"

"It's me, Lana," I whisper. Drawing moisture from the air, I gently direct water so the blood marring her vision washes away.

Recognition dawns in her expression, and she takes a step forward before she seems to remember the chains and stops. "Lana?"

I nod and take her hands in mine. "It's going to be okay, I promise." Taking in the collar around her neck, rage boils inside me. I know who did this to her, and I will make him pay.

"What are you doing here?" she asks, but I'm busy reaching to the magical clasp on the back of her neck. It'd taken forever for Gideon and me to figure out how to get the damned thing off my neck. It operates similar to those Chinese finger traps I always got at carnivals as a kid. You must push it together until it's so tight, you can hardly breathe until the clasp reveals itself.

"I'm here to get you out of here," I say as I tighten the necklace, earning me a small whimper from her, then I release the catch and carefully remove the collar.

Anastasia rubs her neck where the collar was and looks at me with gratitude. "Thank you."

"Don't thank me yet," I say as I start working on the chains. "We have to get out of here before Luka wakes up."

"I don't understand," she says, but I shake my head.

"I'll explain later," I say as the last of the chains fall away. "Let's go."

I take her hand, and we slip out of the room. I lead her towards the back door, but a noise has me stopping in my tracks.

"Luka's awake," I whisper to Anastasia before leading her in the opposite direction. "Turn left, then the second right. You'll come to a room with a barred window."

I don't need to tell her she can use her dragon magic to melt the bars and escape.

"What about you?".

"I'll find my own way out," I say, giving her a push in the right direction. "Now go!"

I don't wait to see if she does as I say before turning and running in the opposite direction. Using my fae speed, I skate into the empty dining hall just as Luka rounds the corner.

"There you are," he says, relief clear in his voice. "I was worried when I woke up and found you gone."

Wrapping my arms around myself, I shrug. "I just needed some fresh air."

"You should have woken me up." He cups my cheek, and it takes everything I have not to flinch away. "I would have gone with you."

"I'm sorry," I say, untucking my arms and sliding them around his waist. "You were sleeping so soundly; I didn't want to disturb you."

I rest my head on his chest and breathe in his scent, fighting the urge to gag. I may be *his* mate, but that doesn't mean I have to like him. For once, I'm thankful I don't have to reciprocate the bond, because I'm not a werewolf. I feel nothing, other than revulsion.

"I missed you." He nudges me with his chin, and I bite the inside of my cheek to keep from saying something I'll regret.

"I missed you too," I say instead, hoping he doesn't hear the lie in my voice.

"Come on," he says, taking my hand and leading me back upstairs. "Let's go back to bed."

I don't say anything as I follow him, my mind racing. Now that Anastasia has escaped, it won't be long before Luka puts two and two together. This moves up my timeline, and I need to be prepared.

Slipping into bed next to him, he wraps his arms around me, pulling me close. "I love you." His breath stirs against my ear, and I stiffen in his arms.

"I love you too," I say, my voice a strangled whisper.

I close my eyes and try to block out his touch, but it's impossible.

All I can think about is how I need to get away from him before it's too late.

* * *

MY HEART ALMOST SOFTENS, watching Luka press his lips to my belly, whispering sweet words to our baby. But then, I remember who he is. What he's done. What he plans to do.

I can't let myself forget.

"You've even more beautiful, swollen with my child," he purrs in my ear. "Though, you probably have a whole litter in there if we're being realistic."

I freeze, my blood running cold. "What did you just say?" I manage to choke out.

He chuckles, and it sends a shiver down my spine. "You're not the only one who's been hiding things, love," he says, and I can hear the amusement in his voice. "Did you really think I didn't know? That I didn't have eyes on Anastasia's room when you helped her escape?"

I try to pull away from him, but he tightens his grip on me. "Let me go," I hiss, struggling against him.

"And why would I do that?" he asks. "You're my mate, and you're carrying my child. Children. Should we find out?"

Reaching up, I claw at his face, trying to do as much damage as possible. He releases me with a curse, and I scramble out of bed, putting as much distance between us as possible.

"You're a monster," I spit, and he laughs, prowling towards me like a predator.

"No, love," he says, his voice soft, with an undercurrent of danger. "I'm just a man who knows what he wants. And I want you."

I back up until I'm pressed against the wall, and he steps into my personal space, caging me in with his body. "I'm going to have you, Lana," he whispers, and I can see the madness in his eyes. "One way or another."

Pushing him away, I roll out of his reach, but not before he grabs hold of me. He leans down, his teeth scraping against my neck. "Mine," he growls, and I recoil.

This is it. I have to get away from him before he kills me. Or worse.

"Don't hurt her, she carries your child."

Luka freezes, his hand cupping my throat until my chin juts towards the ceiling. I take advantage of the momentary distraction and shove him away from me. He stumbles backwards, and I make my escape behind his sister.

"Katarina," Luka growls, his voice full of menace.

"She's right." I step out from behind her, putting myself between them. "I am carrying your child." Or children, I think, but I don't say it out loud. "I'm sorry, Luka, I'm a little emotional right now. Forgive me?"

Conflict swims in his eyes, and I know I've won this round. But it's only a temporary reprieve.

"Of course, you're right," he says, his voice softening as he approaches me. "I'm sorry for upsetting you."

He kisses me gently, and I bite back a retort. I must tread carefully, especially as he knows I let Anastasia go and hasn't yet punished me for it.

"I'm just tired." I pout, yawning for emphasis. "I should probably lie down."

"Alright." He tugs me towards the bed, and I go willingly. Fae pregnancies, while rare, are short and draining. I need all the rest I can get.

Luka settles me into bed, and I close my eyes, feigning sleep. I can feel him watching me, but I don't open my eyes. After a few minutes, I hear him leave the room, and I let out a sigh of relief.

The next morning, Luka gets called away for a meeting with his pack, and I take the opportunity to explore the compound. It's a maze of corridors and rooms, and I quickly get lost. Not that I mind; it gives me a chance to snoop.

I raid the kitchen and am in the process of making myself a snack when I hear footsteps approaching. Quickly shoving the food into my mouth, I turn around, putting on an innocent expression.

"Luka said you might be hungry." The guard assigned to keep an eye on me says. He's a big dude, mildly attractive, and has nice teeth. He's been civil to me the entire time I've been here, so I decide I don't hate him.

"Tucker, right?" I ask, and he nods. "Don't tell him I'm stuffing my face with pie, and I'll let you have some, too."

He hesitates for a moment, before breaking into a grin. "Deal."

There's something so disarming about sharing a meal with your enemy. I just have to chip away, a little at a time. We settle into wooden, high-backed chairs in the den, and I push a plate towards him. "So, tell me," I say, taking a bite of molten fruit filling, "How'd you earn the precious role of keeping an eye on Luka's mate?"

He shrugs, shoveling a forkful of crust into his mouth. "Luka and I go way back," he says. "He's like a brother to me."

"Lucky you," I mutter, and he snorts.

He stills the fork just in front of his face. "You'll never want for anything." He glances at me, shoveling the pie into his mouth, and continues to talk around it. "Luka will take care of you."

"Except for my actual family," I bite out. "He stole me away from them."

"Luka is your family now," Tucker says. But he says it in a way that's both probing and laced with what I suspect is anger. *Odd.* "You're his mate. That's all that matters."

I shake my head, but I don't argue with him. There's no point. Tucker is loyal to Luka, and there's nothing I can say that will change his mind.

"Finish your pie," I say, standing up. "I'm going to my room."

"I'll walk you," he says, following me out of the kitchen.

I don't say anything as we walk, and neither does he. There's a tension in the air between us, and I can tell he's not happy with me. Did he expect me to just give up everything and everyone I love for his friend? I'd never.

When we reach my room, I slip inside, and Tucker doesn't follow me. Perching myself on the windowsill, I watch storm clouds gather on the horizon; their sudden onset much like my brooding. Lightning flashes in quick succession, followed by raucous thunder, and it gives me pause.

A tingle of magic stirs in the air. Hope ratchets up my spine. The wind whips around the compound, and steps pound down the hallway, headed straight for my room.

The door bursts open, and Luka stalks in, his expression thunderous. "What the hell are you doing?" he barks, coming to stand in front of me.

I shrug, trying to look nonchalant. "Just enjoying the storm." I glance at him.

He narrows his eyes at me, and I can see the wheels turning in his head. "You're up to something," he growls. "I can feel it."

"I have no idea what you're talking about." I wrap my arms around his neck, pulling his face to mine. "Kiss me."

He hesitates for a moment, before giving in and claiming my mouth with his. Thunder cracks, and the ground trembles, but we ignore it.

When he finally pulls away, his eyes are dark with desire. "I have to go." His voice is rough. "I'll be back later."

"I'll be here," I say, and he gives me one last lingering look before he leaves.

As soon as the door clicks shut, I jump off the windowsill and begin to pace. My eyes train on a shadowed form moving across the sand. It's too far away to make out who it is, but I have a feeling.

Heart pounding, I open the window and climb out onto the ledge. The wind whips my hair around my face, and I cling to the windowsill to keep from being blown away. The figure draws closer, and now I know without a doubt.

It's Oz.

He's come for me.

CHAPTER 50

CASIMIR

"Aggonid's bowels, Ana, where have you been? We thought you'd been kidnapped!" Penn crushes his cousin to his chest. Her arms flail under his grasp as she tries to breathe.

The sound of water lapping against the hull is so at odds with the tension in the air. We're in the aft cabin of a tall ship, our path charted to skirt around Luporia when we stumbled across her on the beach.

"I was," she squeaks out. "But I escaped. Your mate helped me."

"Lana? Where is she?!" Finn, Auguste, and Gideon jump from where they were seated at the table. They hadn't cared about Anastasia's return until just now.

"She's with Luka." Anastasia winces, and Gideon pales. "But she's safe. For now. I think they've killed all the other fae they had at the compound—I didn't hear any more of their wails. Haven't heard them for weeks now." The haunted look in her eyes says more than her words ever could.

"Will you show us where they have her?" I grip onto the hair at my scalp, willing my body not to whine in worry. I must be strong for my mate.

"I can take you to her." Anastasia pauses on each of us. "But we have to hurry. I'm not sure how long werewolf-fae pregnancies last, but Lana looks pretty far along. He'll never let her go, especially not once the baby arrives."

The room quiets as her words wash over us like a dam breaking. A baby. With Luka. The sledgehammer those words carry is almost too much for any of us to bear. I want her to have *my* baby—to have all our babies. Not that feral dog's.

"We're coming with you." Auguste steps forward, his features set in a grim mask. "All of us."

Anastasia nods her head, and we all follow her out of the room.

The compound sits atop a small mountain range off the Tristique Islands. It isn't even on the map, so it must be a recent build. Nestled on a bed of sand in the center of a lake, the only way to get there is by boat or helicopter, unless you can sift. My wolf paces just under my skin, desperate to teleport to her right away. But we need to be smart about this. We have the element of surprise on our side, and we want to make sure we use it to the fullest extent.

Anastasia leads us by boat to the outskirts of the compound, where there's a small opening in the fence. Finn cloaks us so we remain undetected. "This is as far as I go," she says. "I told you mating her would bring us nothing but trouble." She scowls at Penn and then glances at Finn when he lets out a low growl. "Hey, don't get mad at me about it. I told this lovesick lunk of junk he needed to leave her alone because of your soul bond. I was on *your* side."

This placates him, but barely. "For once, we agree," is all he says before turning away from her and towards the compound. A line of windows on the upper-level wink back at us in the darkness, and a shimmer in the air next to the entrance draws our attention.

How did he get a portal here? He's a werewolf.

"He must've coerced the portal from one of the fae he took captive," Finn mutters. "It's got to be a portal stone."

"You don't think he took her to another realm, do you?" Grimm asks, his voice tight with worry.

"I wouldn't put it past him." Finn's muscles bunch up, like he's ready to level the whole building.

Pain twists my gut; each inhale a battle. The irony that we did this very thing to Finn—stole his mate from him—doesn't escape me. And now we're on the other side of it. My beast howls inside my head, demanding I take action.

I close my eyes and let out a shaky breath, trying to calm the storm inside me; its clawed grip on my brain begging me to rip and tear into everything to get her back. Power rolls off Finn in waves, and I can tell it's taking everything he has to keep himself in check. We all feel the same way.

A shout pierces the night, and a woman's cry follows it.

Lana.

Without another thought, we all take off towards the entrance of the compound at a dead sprint. Grimm and Penn materialize next to me, their eyes glowing brightly in the darkness. I can hear Anastasia's boat puttering away as we leave her behind.

The entrance is unguarded, and the doors are unlocked. We don't bother to be quiet as we make our way through the building, calling out her name. There's no sign of her anywhere. A few of the doors we try are locked, but a quick burst of fae strength takes care of that.

We split up, each of us searching a different section of the building. Every room is empty, until I come across a set of stairs leading down to what looks like a basement.

I make my way down, holding my breath as I try to listen for any sign of her. A muffled cry echoes through the hallway, and I take off towards the sound. The closer I get, the more certain I am it's her.

I find her in a small room, curled up in a ball on the floor, the metallic scent covering up her natural aroma. My beast's whine ends on a snarl. She wears a thin nightgown, and her feet are bare. Her hair is matted and tangled, and there are bruises all over her body. Sitting on her neck is a collar emitting a sinister, coiling black magic.

I'm not sure what it does, but I know it's meant to hurt her. Her eyes are wide and wild as she looks at me, and fear haunts her face. She opens her mouth to speak, but no words come out.

Instead, a stream of blood runs down her leg, pooling at her feet. I kneel next to her and gently brush the hair out of her face. "It's okay,

Lana," I murmur, keeping my voice steady, even as fury fuels me. "We're here to take you home."

She shakes her head, a strangled cry coming from her throat. Her body trembles so hard, I'm afraid she's going to shatter. Hysteria coats her next words. "My baby," she whispers. "He took my baby. They have Rune and Oz, too." Tears slide down her face, and she starts to cough, causing a rush of blood and liquid to splash on the floor.

I gather her into my arms and stand, agony sluicing through me at every whimper she makes as I cradle her close to my chest. *My mate.* I can feel the magic emanating from the collar, and I know we need to get it off her as soon as possible.

"We'll find them, Lana," I promise. "I swear it."

Then I turn and carry her out of the room; her body shaking with sobs the entire way.

CHAPTER 51

FINN

Casimir rounds the corner; my entire world in his arms.

Lana.

Rage boils my blood, and I see red. All I want to do is tear him apart for having taken her from me. I stop short when I take in her state.

She's hurt. Badly.

Bruises mar her skin; blood stains her nightgown crimson. And the black magic collar around her neck. My heart clenches in my chest, and I fight the urge to howl in pain. Rushing to them, I flinch when she recoils from me.

Then I remember: I'm still a stranger to her.

The realization steals the breath from my lungs.

I want to tell her that I'm one of her mates, that she knows me, but I don't want to scare her any more than she already has been. In no time at all, I can burn through the spell keeping her memories of me at bay, but it would be too much for her to take all at once. Whatever has happened to her since she's been in the werewolves' hold has been traumatic enough.

My body burns with the desire to yank her out of the wolf's arms, but I know I need to be patient. For now, I'll content myself with following them as they make their way back to the boat.

When she registers that we're leaving, she starts clawing out of Casimir's hold. "No!" she screams. "We can't leave! They have my baby. And Oz—"

I try to calm her down, but it's like she's not even hearing me. She's completely lost in her panic, and I can see the terror in her eyes. I know exactly how she feels.

When she was first taken, I thought I was going to go insane. The only thing that kept me going was the hope that I would find her again. And now that we have, I'm not going to let anything happen to her.

Auguste swoops in, taking Lana from Casimir, a steady presence to ground her. The others search the entire compound, but there's no sign of Lana's baby, or her other mates. It's like they just disappeared into thin air.

Luka had been planning this for weeks, maybe even months. He was patient and methodical, waiting for the perfect opportunity to strike. And he did it without any of us seeing it coming.

Now, we're left with nothing but the aftermath of his treachery. Lana is injured and bleeding, her baby is missing, and Rune and Oz are too.

We regroup at the boat, and I can see the defeat that has slackened everyone's face. It feels like we've lost before we even had a chance to fight. Lana's wails split me open, and I ache for her pain.

Gideon pulls Lana into his arms and sinks to his knees, rocking her back and forth as she cries. Torment haunts his eyes; the way his hands shake as he holds her.

He whispers soothing words where he rests his head against her hair, but it does nothing to stop her sobs. I want to comfort her, too, but I know it's not my place. Not yet. Not until she has her memory of us back.

"Can you tell us what happened?" He cups her cheek. "You know I was the best tracker as a vampire, and now that I'm fae, my tracking skills are even better. I can find them, Lana. But I need to know where to start."

Lana's face crumples, and she nods. "They came for me—"

"Who did?" Auguste asks gently.

"Oz and Rune. I saw them crossing the sand, and I climbed out my window to jump down." Her lips disappear between her teeth.

I glance at the compound, noting the row of windows high above the ground. She could easily fly out of them, but that might've drawn attention, so it makes sense that she would've jumped. Pregnant or not—and she was probably doing what she thought was the safest option for her baby, rather than risking staying and having them exposed to that monster.

She draws air into her lungs before continuing. "The werewolves descended on them before I had a chance to, and Tucker caught me trying to go to them." She holds up her hands, deep gouges marring the tops of them. "He pulled me in, slapped this thing on my neck, and started beating me. I d-don't know if my b-baby is even alive."

"You said they took your baby?" Casimir plops down next to them in the sand.

"I went into labor, right there in my room. I was so scared, and in so much pain, but I tried to push through it. Tucker took my baby, and everyone left. I don't know where they went." She clutches onto Gideon's tear-dampened shirt. "Luka imprinted on me. He ... he thinks I'm his mate."

Mate?

"You took another mate?" Penn growls.

The audacity of this mutinous lizard. He's one to talk. I'd boil him alive if it wouldn't hurt Lana, and I'd rejoice in dancing on his ashes after I tossed him in a volcano.

She shakes her head. "No, I feel nothing for him." Lana can barely keep her head up, her body trembling with exhaustion.

I approach them with my hands out. "Lana, I need to heal you." She can heal herself, but she's been through so much, the thought probably never crossed her mind. I can bear this burden for her, give her physical peace until I can help ease the emotional toll.

Her pupils blow out when her attention lands on me, and she turns into Gideon's chest as though shy. A flush creeps into her cheeks, and I tug my lips between my teeth to keep the smirk off them. Despite her not remembering who I am, her reaction to my appearance remains unchanged.

We were made for each other.

Gideon whispers something into her ear, something so low even I can't hear, and she shifts in his lap before giving me a small, "okay."

I settle behind her and pull her back against my chest, so she's leaning into me. My wings flare out on either side of us, cocooning us in our own little world. This isn't necessary for healing, but this is my first time touching her since that day in the throne room so many moons ago, and I want a modicum of privacy just to revel in it. I rest my chin on top of her head and close my eyes, sinking into the familiar feeling of being joined with her.

Her scent fills my senses, and I can feel her magic swirling around us, mixing with mine until it's indistinguishable where one begins and the other ends. My palms run over her wounds. I let my magic flow into her, seeking out the injuries that need to be healed.

Bruises cover her arms and legs, some of them old and yellowing, others still a deep purple. I heal the ones that are still fresh before moving on to the rest.

I can feel her body relax into mine as the pain fades away and her wounds heal. When I'm done, I tuck a stray hair behind her ear and press a kiss to the top of her head.

"Thank you," she whispers, her voice laced with sleep. I can heal her physical injuries, but the emotional toll of having your mate and child taken from you is something that will take time.

"Rest now, my soul," I murmur. "We'll find them."

CHAPTER 52

OZ

I snarl at the werewolf drawing blood from my neck. She startles and takes a step back, her hand going to the hilt of her knife. I'm shackled to a wall, thick chains weighing my limbs. The room we're in is long and narrow; the stench of werewolf permeates the air, and I taste it on my tongue. Blood pools at my feet from a wound on my abdomen; the carpet so saturated a small puddle of it sits on top.

"Lana." My voice comes out rough. "Where. Is. Lana?" I breathe, wincing from my injury.

The memory of spotting her hanging from that window as a werewolf hauled her up by his claws assails me. My shout came too late.

"I'm sorry," she says, swallowing hard. "He's making me do this."

Her eyes dart to the burly werewolf pacing across the threadbare room and back to me. Her entire body is tense, like she's ready to bolt at any moment.

I strain against my binds, desperate to find my mate. I catalogue the room, looking for anything or anyone that can help me get out of here. No tables, no chairs, and just a few guards mill about. It looks like a rec room that's been stripped of any recreation.

My attention catches on Rune, chained next to me, slumped like he's been drugged. I'm betting they used vampire blood on him, just like they did Lana. Next to him, also chained, is *Luka*.

Keeping my voice low enough so only the woman at my neck can hear me, I ask why he's chained.

She whispers, "He's not alpha anymore. Tucker is." She tilts her head towards the angry-looking man behind, wearing a hole through the carpet with his back-and-forth.

An infant's cries fill the air, and all the blood in my body turns to ice. "Is that ..."

The woman gives me a barely imperceptible nod.

Lana's baby. My useless vampire heart thrashes against its prison of bone, convinced that love alone could rescue her, that it could carve itself right out of my chest and lay itself at her feet in exchange for her safety.

The werewolf draws the needle out of my neck, capping it before setting it down on the table next to me. *I'm sorry*, she mouths.

I strain my neck to look around for Lana, fear for her racing through my veins. "Where is she?" If her baby is here, she must be, too. She has to be.

I grunt when I strain against my binds. I pull air into my lungs; the feeling so foreign. I keep pulling, breathing in deeper and deeper to expand my chest, trying to break free, but all the strength in the world doesn't matter against power. If I still had magic, I could bust out of here. Like an old friend, I feel the caress of it, gossamer dancing around my wrists and ankles where I'm tied. They've got to have a fae or witch on their side.

Not here, she mouths to me, backing away until she's standing next to Tucker.

Tucker steps forward, his hand fisted in the woman's hair as he drags her against him. "Katarina, what did I tell you about talking to the prisoners?"

"I'm sorry, Tucker," she says, her voice shaking. Her face is in a grimace, flinching back from him before he drags her to his face, leaning in and biting her lip. She cries out before gritting, "I won't do it again."

"Keep your hands off her!" Luka roars, yanking against his chains.

Tucker releases Katarina and stalks towards Luka with a feral grin on his face. "You're in no position to give me orders, pup." He clocks Luka in the face, and the crunch of bone cuts through the silence. Luka's head snaps back, but he doesn't make a sound. Tucker turns his attention to me. "As for you, vampire ... I have plans for you." His gaze shifts to Rune, lip tucked against his cheek in a smirk. "All of you."

He stalks out of the room, and Katarina sinks to the floor, her face in her hands.

Luka spits out a mouthful of blood. "Mutt."

I meet his gaze. "What did he do to you?"

"Nothing I didn't deserve," Luka says, his voice rough. "Though I couldn't tell my wolf otherwise, I betrayed them by imprinting on Lana."

Rage boils in my veins, under my skin. I've got to get back to her. But first, I need to know what's planned, so I can figure out how I'm going to rescue Lana's baby and get Rune out of here. "And what about us?" I ask. "What does he want with us?"

Luka glances at Katarina before answering, grief shattering the façade he'd been keeping on his face. "He wants to use you as bargaining chips. He thinks he can trade you, Rune, and my baby for something he wants."

"And what is that?" I growl.

"A cure." Luka's scrutiny meets mine, and he's schooled his indifferent face back into place. "He wants a cure for the werewolf curse."

Realization sinks in, weighing heavy in my gut. Finn's mother, the Luna goddess, is the one who cursed an entire line of wolf fae. *He's going to try to trade us for a way to lift the curse.* But with whom?

CHAPTER 53

OZ

That night, the werewolves drag us to a rocky valley surrounded by towering mountains. Wind whistles through the peaks, their gusts causing Rune's hair to whip across his face, and the full moons cast an eerie glow over the scene. A bonfire blazes in the center of the valley and gathered around it are dozens of werewolves, perched on stumps and felled trees that have left a trail in the mud from where they were dragged by the tree line. Nestled against the woods are rows of colorful tents.

Us prisoners remain chained. Instead of walls, we're tethered to enormous trees spaced apart as though magic were used to put them here. Likely using the same spell I taught Lana back in our home in Dubuque that caused her to break the ceiling when the seed grew too big.

Tucker stands in front of the fire, his arms crossed over his chest as he surveys the crowd.

"Tonight, we make a stand," he says, his voice carrying over the hushed crowd, the pop and crackle of the fire seeming to emphasize his point. "We've been pushed around for too long, treated like second-class citizens. No more. It's time we took our rightful place in the world."

A growl rises from the pack, and Tucker lifts his hand for silence.

"I know many of you are skeptical," he continues. "But I have a plan that will change everything. We will be free of the curse, and we will no longer be under the heel of the fae."

My attention snags on Teresa, who's standing near the back of the crowd. Her gaze meets mine, and I see the fear in her eyes, and I imagine it matches my own. *Fuck*. What is she doing here? She's supposed to be with Auguste. If she's not ... then where is Auguste? Did something happen to him? Dread settles in my stomach like a stone.

"To make this happen, I need your loyalty," Tucker says. "I need you to stand with me, no matter what. Can I count on you?"

The pack breaks into cheers, and Tucker smiles, pumping his fist to the sky.

"Good. Because tonight, we strike a blow against our enemies. We take what they hold dear, and we use it to get what we want." He pauses for effect before continuing. "Tonight, we sacrifice a fallen alpha, a wicked fae, a vampire king, and the high king of the fae's daughter."

Ice floods my veins. Pandemonium breaks out. Werewolves howl, their eyes glowing with excitement, while I try to figure out what Tucker is getting at. Fae king's daughter? He can't mean ...

"That's right," Tucker says, his calculated gaze landing on Luka. "Don't think we didn't know how *soul bonds* work," he sneers. "It doesn't matter if it's your seed or not, any product of a soul bonded fae will always have a large percentage of her partner's DNA. Isn't that right, blood sucker?" He turns his attention towards me, and my gut coils with fear. "You've got a set of twins."

"You don't fucking touch them!" I roar, battering against my binds.

He tuts. "Don't you worry your pretty little head, beast. They're not here." He takes a step towards Luka, who's growling low in his throat. "And what do you think the Luna goddess will give me in exchange for the child of a high queen?"

Luka lashes out, hoisting his legs to kick, but Tucker dodges easily. "Don't bother," he laughs. "I know you're not stupid enough to think you can take me on by yourself. Lana weakened you the moment your wolf claimed her."

Luka's growl turns into a snarl. "I'll kill you for this."

Tucker chuckles. "You're welcome to try, but I wouldn't recommend it." He looks out at the pack. "Who wants to be the one to bring me the high queen's daughter?"

The pack erupts into chaos as werewolves fight to be the one chosen. Tucker finally points to a large male near the front. "You," he says. "Gather her from the witches' tent."

It takes me a moment to recognize the sound of fury-driven keening is coming from me. Red clouds my vision, and I rage against the injustice of this, and being unable to stop them. My fangs cut through my bottom lip; the feel of my blood dribbling down my chin unlocks something inside my memory. I still, then begin sawing my teeth until the cold liquid fills my mouth so full, I have to keep them pressed together to keep from spilling any more.

Breaking from the circle, the massive werewolf makes his way towards a group of tents along the edge of the valley. Teresa tears from the pack, tackling him. The moons rise from behind the mountain peaks, allowing the full Bedlam Moon to shine down on the valley. In their light, I watch as Teresa shifts into her wolf form, remembering they can shift at will only during the Bedlam Moon. Otherwise, they can only shift during a full moon. She sinks her teeth into the werewolf's neck, ripping into his jugular.

The werewolf howls in pain, shaking his body to get the much smaller werewolf off of him. Teresa hangs on, growling and snarling as she tears chunks of flesh from the werewolf's neck. He brings a hand up to stem the flow of blood, but Teresa latches onto his wrist, her teeth sinking deep.

"Stop!" Tucker shouts, throwing all his alpha power behind the word.

Teresa falters, her body going limp as she releases the werewolf's wrist from her teeth. He stumbles back, clutching his neck as he tries to stem the flow of blood.

"What is the meaning of this?" Tucker shouts, gesturing to the still shape in the grass.

She shifts back to her human form, chin held high as she meets Tucker's gaze. "Proving to you I'm the better werewolf," she says defiantly. Spitting out a wad of blood from her mouth, she turns to the injured werewolf. "With your permission, I'd like to finish him off, alpha."

Tucker grins and raises a brow. "Vying for Queen, are you?"

She shrugs. "I figure it's about time a woman took her rightful place next to her alpha." Her false bravado is evident when I catch a hand gesture I know is meant just for me. It's the same one Finn used when she shifted so many months ago in Gideon's basement, helping her understand she's safe. "Lana had no business being Luka's queen. She isn't even a werewolf, but a disgusting fae."

The werewolf on the ground struggles to get away from Teresa, but she's relentless. She sinks her teeth into his neck and rips out his throat. He attempts to howl in pain, but it comes out gurgled, his body going limp as he bleeds out onto the ground.

Teresa stands over him, her chest heaving as she pants. Wiping the gore from her mouth with the back of her hand, she turns to Tucker. "Satisfied, alpha?"

He nods. "Very," he says. "Please bring the princess and witch to me."

A cold feeling settles in my gut, wondering how she's going to get us out without being seen. I keep my lips pressed together, silently begging her to look my way, but she's already gone, melting into the darkness.

Loping out of the night, a large werewolf comes to stand next to Tucker. "What would you have me do, alpha?"

Tucker glances down at the body of the werewolf Teresa killed. "Get rid of him," he says. "And make sure the princess and her witch are delivered to me unharmed."

The werewolf nods and drags the body away while Tucker walks back to join the rest of the pack. Teresa comes back a few minutes later, an infant in her arms, and ice floods my veins when I see the witch behind her.

Though I never met him, there's no mistaking the resemblance between the witch and Mekhi. He has the same onyx hair, dimpled cheeks, and hazel eyes, though his features are harder, colder. There's no doubt in my mind this is Mekhi's uncle.

In his hand is a blade, and I know what they intend to do.

"Please," I beg, my blood flying from my mouth, soaking into the grass as I try to reason with Tucker. My words come out garbled, my lips too mangled to articulate well. "Lana will remove the curse, and no one has to get hurt."

"That's where you're wrong," he spits. "I asked her to remove it already, and she said no. This is all on her."

I crane my neck to the sky, my voice distorted and barely above a whisper; agony wrenching from my very soul as I recite the words I know will stop this all. I speak them with such conviction, knowing the blood I've spilled at my feet will be enough. "I, Osgood Finlandian Ankida, King of Vampires, Mate of Lana, Father of Rose and Bennett, give my life in exchange for Lana's baby." I don't even know her name, but the sentiment is the same.

Tucker nods at Mekhi's uncle. "Do it."

The witch steps forward, and I see the blade in his hand gleaming in the moonlight. He raises it high, and Luka and I scream as he brings it down, meaning to plunge it into the infant's heart. At the last second, Teresa swings out of the way, and the blade sinks into her chest instead. She staggers back, clutching at the wound as she falls to her knees.

Angry storm clouds appear, the roll of thunder drowning out my roar, lightning flashing so fast and bright we all shield our eyes. A loud BOOM echoes through the clearing, and when the light fades, Mekhi's uncle is gone. In his place is a pile of ash.

Crouched next to Teresa's limp form, infant tucked in her arm, a hand on the pommel of the dagger stuck into the werewolf is the Luna goddess. Malice glows in her eyes and she swings them towards Tucker. Fury rolls off her in waves.

"You," she says, her voice like ice, lassoing everyone's attention. "You dare to harm my grandchild? Any child of Lana's is a child of my son's."

He steps back, shaking his head. "I-I didn't know," he stammers. Though we all heard him. *He knew.*

Her lip curls in a sneer. "You will pay for your insolence," she says. She holds out her hand, and a bolt of lightning hits him square in the chest. His body ignites, and he burns to ash just like Mekhi's uncle.

Something clicks in my head, a puzzle piece slotting into place. My eyes flick to where Rune slumps against his binds, the webs of gold splintering across his skin. Flitting back and forth between the goddess and Rune, I start assembling more pieces together. He has a Phelvie, which is only created during the ultimate sacrifice. He said it happened during the war … that he did it to save Finn.

The goddess turns to me, and I see the sadness in her eyes. Though I no longer have magic, I can feel her attention on my thoughts, and a forlorn smile curves her lips. "You are very perceptive," she says.

I swallow hard, watching as she heals Teresa, and crosses over to where Rune dangles. With a press of a hand to his temples, the manacles disintegrate, and he collapses to the ground. She rests a palm over his heart, and his eyes flutter open, as though he were only sleeping.

He blinks at the goddess in confusion for a long moment before his vision clears and he sits up, pulling her to him, forehead to forehead. "You came," he whispers.

"Of course, my love," she replies. "I would never leave you alone." Gold tears spill from his eyes, and she presses a kiss to his lips.

Titan, his Phelvie, materializes, running its tongue up the side of her face. The goddess smiles and pets the large cat before it fades away again.

"I'm sorry," she says, "You know how much I wish I could stay."

Rune clears his throat, but it does no good. His voice is thick when he talks. "I know." His words break. "I love you."

"And I you." She glances at the sky. "Always. I'm never far away."

With one last look at Rune, the goddess turns to me. A simple touch to my binds breaks them, and I stumble forward before catching myself. She places the baby in my arms, and I cuddle the sleeping infant close.

Her hand comes to my face, rubbing her thumb across my lips and they no longer ache, the touch of her magic but a blip against my skin. "Brave Osgood, it's not your time. You will take care of her," she says. It's not a request. She knows any of Lana's offspring will be treated as my own, whether or not they're my blood.

A gasp echoes from the crowd, and Luna whips around, her power flaring, before tucking away. Finn, Auguste, Grimm, Penn, Casimir, and Gideon sift in, all six of them rushing our way.

"Mother," Finn breathes, dropping to his knees in front of her.

"Oh, my sweet boy," she whispers, tucking a stray hair behind his ear. "I've missed you."

He buries his face in her skirts, and she cups his cheek. "I know, love, I know. But I'm always with you." Her gaze drifts to me and the bundle in my arms. "All of you."

"Where is she?" I call out, my voice edged in panic.

A moment later, Lana sifts in on a run. My chest squeezes, relief a palpable thing. I'm moving towards her, but my limbs feel like I'm trudging through mud, I can't move fast enough. She crashes into me, her arms thrown around my neck, the baby in between us. Her fae body still molds perfectly to mine. I pull air into my lungs, a foreign practice for me, but one I need in this moment. To smell her, to see her, to know she's really here. Months and months of worry, heartache, despair, and determination all fade away in this moment.

"Oz," Lana chokes. Her trembling hands skirt over me, immediately seeking out my injuries and healing them. They rove over her baby, and she pulls her into her arms, tears raining down her cheeks.

Her shoulders slump in relief, a mother's desperate wish to see her baby returned to her having come to fruition. Lana's legs give out, and we end up on the forest floor. My hands cup her face, her breathtaking fae features equal parts foreign and familiar to me. Dramatic lashes frame her blue eyes, and soft curls plaster to her damp skin. It's still her face, but some of the angles have sharpened, and areas have smoothed out. My fingers brush against the pointed tips of her ears, and my thumbs sweep the moisture tracking under her eyes.

My forehead presses to hers, and I just hold her trembling body, silent tears mingling with those splashing down my face. How long we sit here on the loamy soil, wrapped in each other, I don't know. It could've been seconds, hours, days. None of it matters. Not now that we're together again.

Soft murmurs reach my ears, and I raise my head to see Luna placing a kiss to Finn's cheek. He gives her one last look over his shoulder before she ascends into the sky.

I open my mouth to tell Lana, "Let's go home," but I pause. Where is home to her now? She's mated to two different sets of men; those Earthside, and those in Bedlam. As much as I want her back with us, that's not something I can force on her.

Clutching the baby to her chest, tears welling in her eyes, I can't read her mind anymore, but I know she's having the same war in her head. She's trying to decide who she wants to be with, and it rips my heart out.

"Can we go to Convectus Castle?" she asks. "I think we have some things to sort out."

My stomach drops, but I swallow hard and give her a nod. It's time to face the music.

CHAPTER 54

LANA

Gideon, Auguste, and Oz stand at the foot of my bed, nervousness flitting across their faces. I'm not sure what to say, or where to even start. So much has happened in such a short amount of time. The kings had rounded up the werewolves, holding them in cells in the dungeon until we can figure out what to do with them. Rose and Bennett, along with my parents, are on a walk with Novaleigh in the courtyard, each taking turns carrying her in the baby sling.

"Sahira," Oz starts, but I shake my head. Before the hurt look can settle on his face, I speak.

"Can you guys just hold me?" I plead. "I need to feel you close."

They don't hesitate, all three of them crawling into bed with me, just like we used to. Oz positions himself behind me, wrapping an arm around my waist and tucking me back against his chest. Gideon takes my hand, our fingers lacing together, while Auguste cuddles up to my other side. I close my eyes and take a deep breath, the scent of my mates filling my senses, soothing the ache in my soul.

"I'm sorry," I whisper. "For everything."

"You don't have anything to be sorry for, Sahira," Oz says, his voice gruff.

"That's not true." Sure, I might not have been at fault for a lot of it; I was lied to, tricked, and taken advantage of. But I also know that a lot of decisions I made hurt the people I love. Guilt washes over me as I think about Luka. "I have a confession, and I'm not sure how you guys are going to take it."

They stiffen around me, and I swallow hard before continuing. I can hear Gideon's pulse pick up in his neck and feel Oz's grip on my waist tighten.

"I had to do some things you won't like. I slept with Luka."

Auguste lets out a low growl, while Gideon's hand tightens around mine. Oz is silent behind me, his body rigid.

"We know, my little Striga," Gideon says, his voice low. "That's how babies are made, yeah?"

I tense at his words, not sure if he's being serious or not. When I don't say anything, he lets out a sigh and presses a kiss to my temple.

"You don't understand. I slept with him repeatedly," I clarify, my heart pounding in my chest. Shame consumes me, and their silence isn't helping.

"Did you have a choice?" Auguste's brooding voice cuts through the darkness, and I know he's not going to like my answer.

"Yes? No? Maybe. I don't know," I whisper, tears welling in my eyes. "He was trying to get the kings' locations, and he'd beat me every time I refused to give them up. He saw I wouldn't cave, so he moved onto hurting others instead. The only way I could keep him from hurting them was by ... warming his bed." I suck in deep, gasping breaths. "I don't ... I don't want to take Nova's biological father from her. Not until she's old enough to make a decision herself about his role in her life."

My mind wars with itself. Unpacking it all, digging into the muddy, ugly truth of it, I start to realize how selfish I was being. Luka is a monster, and I let him touch me, let him have a part of me, because I was weak. Fear made me do it. It was because I remembered the crack of the whip, and the feel of drowning by his hand.

On the other side of it, if his attention was on me, it wasn't on anyone else. That was something I could live with.

The quiet in the room is deafening, and I can feel the tension emanating from my mates. I'm not sure what to say, or how to make them understand.

"Sahira," Oz starts, emotion thick in his tone. "We can't even begin to understand what you went through. But you have to know, we can never fault you for doing what you had to do to survive." His palm presses against the tears on my cheek. "Gods. You don't have to tell us anything. If you never want us to bring it up again, we won't breathe a word of it. If you want to share everything, anything, we'll be here, ready to help you dissect it, or just listen. Whatever you need."

"And we will always be here for you," Gideon adds.

"Thank you," I whisper, afraid to speak. I'm not sure what else to say, so I just lay there in their embrace, soaking in their warmth and love.

CHAPTER 55

LANA

My feet pad across the cool tile, and I turn the corner to find just who I've been looking for. He hasn't noticed me yet, and I take this opportunity to appreciate this perfect specimen of a man. Bare feet propped on the coffee table at the center of our bedroom, he has a book in one hand, and his other strokes the spindly fingers of a yalsome root. He's reading about the magical properties of fae flora and fauna because he sacrificed his magic to save our son, and now relies on more natural methods of going through life.

Inky black hair obstructs his view, and he blows air out of his mouth to put it back in its place. He looks so focused, so studious, that I hesitate to interrupt him, but I need him.

"Hey," I call out, and Oz glances up. His features soften and he plasters a smile to his face as he closes the book and sets the root on the coffee table. He rises, crossing to where I lean against the wall.

"Sahira." his accent burrows into my bones just as sure as the kiss he places on my forehead. His eyes meet mine when he pulls back, and I can see the wheels turning in his head, the inability to read my mind so foreign to him he's taken to carefully inspecting my expressions to determine my intent. His brows pinch when he takes in the way I blink back tears. "What is it?" his hand cups my cheek.

I shake my head. "I'm okay." I give him a sad smile. "Just thinking about how difficult it must be for you to navigate life without magic to guide you."

"Hey now." He pulls me into his arms. "Exchanging my magic to save Bennett was a tiny price to pay. A choice I'd make a million times. I don't need magic to guide me because my heart led me back to you."

His thumbs sweep the tears that have spilled down my cheeks, and I lean into his touch. My arms come around his neck, fingers lacing behind his head.

"Sing to me?" My chin quivers.

His mouth tips up in a whisper of a smirk. "Anything for you."

I rest my head on his chest, listening to the deep timber of his voice as it soothes me. For hours, he holds me, our steps swaying all over our room in a slow dance. Safe in his embrace, he serenades me like so many times before.

THAT EVENING, Gideon, Oz, and Auguste take the family to the stables to check out the horses. I sent them there without telling them about the hostlers—one is a pegasus, the other is a unicorn. I can't wait to hear their reactions.

While it'd be best to see it in person, I have other pressing issues to address. Namely, Finn. He's to meet me in my room in a few minutes. I wanted to do it somewhere private, and while the other kings have conjoining rooms, we'll be using a spell to seal my room for our meeting. I'm not sure what to expect with Finn. What I know of him is that he's kind, but a formidable high king in his own right.

Meeting him like this feels clandestine, like he's my paramour, and we're having some kind of sordid affair, only I'm not the one privy to any memory of it. I'm sure that'll all change once I have my memories back, but right now? I'm so nervous I could puke.

A soft knock sounds at the door, and I take a few deep breaths to calm my nerves before opening it. Every time I catch a glimpse of this man, it strikes me how stunning he is. He's like a step out of a fairy tale, with hair so blond it's nearly silver and blue, penetrating eyes, like they can see right into my soul. And maybe he can. He gives me a small, hesitant smile as he steps into the room, and I close the door behind him, sealing us in with a spell.

"Thank you for meeting with me," I start, not really knowing where to begin. "Please, sit wherever you'd like." My heart thrashes around inside me, and other than a brief sweep of his eyes where it thumps against my chest, he doesn't comment on it, and I appreciate it. Probably because I can hear his do the same.

"Of course," he replies easily, crossing the room to take a seat in one of the chairs by the window. He takes in the foliage running rampant from pots and hanging baskets, and I wonder what he's thinking. I don't make it a habit to read minds, and I keep mine locked down tight.

I join him, perching on the edge of my seat and wringing my hands in my lap. "I guess I should start by apologizing. I know I've caused you a lot of pain, and I'm so sorry."

He studies me for a moment, his expression unreadable. "Lana." His voice breaks. "You have nothing to apologize for. I'm the one who failed you. I should have been there for you, and I wasn't. I'm sorry." Grief and shame flashes in his features, and those are emotions I know intimately.

I shake my head. "The way I understood it, you didn't know they'd planned to take me from you. What could you have done?"

He looks away, his jaw clenched. "I should have realized something was off. I should have stopped them."

"Jesus, Finn. You can't blame yourself for that," I say, my voice gentle, though my chest heaves with rising panic. "They tricked all of us. You literally traveled to a whole new realm to get me back."

"That may be so, but I'll spend the rest of eternity making it up to you," he vows.

I reach out and take his hand, giving it a squeeze. "Not necessary. You can make it up to me by giving me back my memories, yeah?"

He jumps from his seat, pulling me to my feet. "Anything you want, just say the word."

My eyebrows pinch together. "That might be a little difficult since I don't remember anything we shared." My next words come out as a whisper. "But I'm ready to remember."

He takes my face in his hands, and I'm shocked at the sudden move. "I'll make sure you never forget me again, my soul. I'll spend forever making sure of it." And then he kisses me like I'm the very breath in his lungs, the beat of his heart, the strength in his will. And maybe I'm all those things, because in this moment, he's stolen my air; my heart tumbles, and my limbs weaken.

The shock of it gives way to magic stirring under my skin. It starts as a gentle prodding, as though asking permission to come out and play. I give it a mental nudge, and the magic unfurls, wrapping us in a cocoon of light. I grunt as it blows past my barriers, surging through each of my limbs. The magic ignites something inside me; a well of power that I didn't know existed. It fills me to bursting, spilling over its threshold, and I cry out as it arcs from my body into Finn's. His eyes widen in shock, and he stumbles back from me.

The magic continues to flow from me; a river of light that refuses to be denied. It pours from me into the room, seeking something—anything to latch onto. And then I see it, a faint tendril of magic reaching out from the other side of the door locked inside me. The magic rushes towards it, and I cry out again as it slams into me. It blows open, and I'm thrown back against the wall. The wind is knocked out of me, and I slide to the ground, gasping for breath.

The room is eerily quiet, and I glance around, trying to get my bearings. Finn pulls himself to his feet near entrance to my room, his hand on the doorframe as he stares at me in disbelief.

"Lana," he whispers, and I see the tears glistening in his eyes. "You did it."

I frown, not understanding what he's talking about. "Did what?"

"Burned through the binds." His voice trembles. "You broke them all by yourself."

I stare at him, still not comprehending. And then it hits me like a ton of bricks. Like a massive horde of keys turning a wall of locks, a vault swinging open, my memories come rushing back. All of them.

I remember everything. The raw beauty, power, and agony of them sends me crashing to my knees. I remember almost dying. Finn, saving me. Denying the connection between us until fate had enough and made refusal impossible. Being ripped from my home, from my family. I remember the brief moment of pain I felt as I lunged at Penn, gouging tears in his skin when he cast the spell to remove my memories.

It was all there, everything that had happened in the past however many moons ago, and it came flooding back in a tidal wave of emotion. I wail; great heaving sobs that shake my entire body. I feel like I'm being torn in two, my chest constricting painfully as though my heart is being squeezed.

Finn is at my side in an instant, gathering me into his arms and cradling me against his chest. "It's okay, soul. I've got you. I'm not going anywhere."

I cling to him like a lifeline, my body heaving with ugly keens as the memories continue to pour in. Every happy memory, every sad memory, every moment of anger, pain, and fear during our short time together. They all come rushing back, and I can't make them stop.

Finn rocks me back and forth, murmuring words of comfort that I can't hear over the din of my own mind. And eventually, the memories start to ebb, flowing back into the recesses of my mind like a tide receding back into the ocean. I'm left trembling and exhausted in Finn's arms, and I rub at the spot in my chest where a tether settles. I can feel it now, a connection to Finn that goes beyond the physical. It lassos us together; less of a rope and more like gossamer, weaving every neuron and particle together, as though we're one entity.

Eventually, I manage to calm myself enough to speak, and I look up at Finn with watery eyes. "I remember everything," I whisper brokenly. "All of it."

He nods, his own eyes shining with unshed tears. "I know, love. I'm so sorry."

Shaking my head, I wrap my hands around his neck and pull him down for a kiss. It's a desperate, needy kiss, full of all the emotions that are running through me. Grief, anger, love, longing. All of it is there in that one kiss, and Finn meets me with equal fervor.

We kiss until we're both breathless, and then we simply rest our foreheads against each other, our bodies pressed close. "What now?" I finally ask, my voice barely more than a whisper.

"We could always kill the kings." He raises a bemused brow, earning a small laugh from me. "But I think we need to have a chat with the others first."

I worry my lip, my expression turning serious. "In the morning, though." Realistically, morning is only a few hours away, and I'll probably have nursed Nova twice by then.

"In the morning," Finn agrees, and he presses a gentle kiss to my forehead before helping me to my feet.

His touch is careful as he leads me back to the bed, and he tucks me in like I'm made of glass. It's sweet and caring, but that's not what I need right now. Yeah, I'm broken, maybe always will be, but I need the hard, stubborn, unbending Finn right now. The one who will be strong enough to keep my head above water, even when I can't.

My mind is wide-open for him, and I see the moment it registers on his face. There's an internal debate in his head, but he sets it aside. He stares at me for a beat, and then he nods once, understanding what I need in a split second. He kicks off his shoes and climbs into bed with me, pulling me into his arms and holding me close. I burrow into him, relishing the feel of his firm body against mine, like slipping on a fitted glove. And then he simply holds me, offering me the silent strength I so desperately need.

We don't speak, we don't need to. This is all that we need, this simple act of being there for each other in this moment. Shutting out the world, making up for lost time. And it's enough.

Eventually, sleep starts to claim me, and I drift off in the safety of Finn's arms, but stir awake to a glow behind my eyelids. I try to ignore it, burrowing deeper into his heat, but it grows brighter and more insistent. A smile cracks my face before I open my eyes, meeting the deep pools of Finn's. "Mornin'," I rasp out, my voice rough from sleep.

He hums, his attention dipping to my mouth, the vivid glow of his skin telling me what's on his mind. "Good morning, my soul."

I'd forgotten about the timber of hearing him speak in the morning until now, all sexy and lazy, as though he knows he's the most beautiful creature to grace this realm and the next. It reminds me of all those mornings I'd spent denying my love and obvious attraction to him when we trekked through Noble Wilds.

I arch up to him, a need to be close bubbling up inside of me. He meets me halfway, his lips crashing down onto mine in a kiss that ignites a fire in my blood. It's less of a flicker of a candle, and more of a strike to an ignition rope soaked in oil that burns low before zipping to a bomb and its inevitable explosion. I moan, melting into him as our mouths move together. We alternate between hot rushes of passion and kissing lazily, taking our time, exploring each other with a tenderness and with an easy affection that comes from finally being whole.

Eventually, we break apart, both of us grinning like idiots. "I missed this," I tell him, because I need him to know. A sharp lump rises in my throat, but I press on. "Without you and the guys, I'd felt so empty inside. I love you so fucking much." I might not have known it only hours ago, but I feel it now, deep in my soul. This is one of the males I'm meant to be with, forever and always.

"I had no doubt I'd be with you again. Whether in this life or the next, I'll always find you. I love you too," he replies easily, his eyes sincere.

His lips find mine again, a question in them that I answer by hooking my leg over his hip and pulling him closer. Sometime in the night, we'd both lost our clothes, the need to feel each other skin-to-skin too great to ignore. My fingers trace the planes of his bare chest, and he shivers in response.

"Are you sure?" he asks, his voice low and husky. "You just had a baby."

"I'm positive," I tell him with absolute certainty. The only wounds that remain are emotional ones.

He settles between my thighs, and I arch up to meet him as he slides inside of me. We both moan in pleasure, our eyes locked on each other as we start to move. Our breaths come in heaving, like billowing sails, the feeling of finally being joined again after far too long sending shockwaves through our bodies.

This is perfect, I think as our bodies come together in a dance that's as old as time. We fit together so perfectly, like we were made for each other. And maybe we were, if that's what happens with soul bonded mates. This rhythm, like the tide, or some deep, cosmic thing I don't yet understand. Maybe this was always meant to be, from the very blink of the universe.

I can feel our bond growing stronger with every thrust, every touch. It's a physical and emotional connection that's unlike anything I've ever experienced. And I know, without a doubt, that this is not the kind of love written about in ancient sonnets; its dimensions too wide, too deep, to ever be condensed into a single tome or even fifty of them. It's not even an epic. No, this is our magnum opus. This is it; our beginning, our middle, our end. A new chapter in our story; one that's full of hope and promise. One that I know will be better than anything that came before it.

I'm not sure what will happen outside these doors; when we must face Luka, his werewolves, my kings, and the realm. How we'll find a balance between where I've planted roots, Earth and Bedlam. But I do know each second for the rest of my life and beyond it, I'm loved beyond measure.

Finn's hands come to my face, cupping my tear-stained cheeks as his deep pools take me in with so much love and adoration. "I'm going to spend the rest of eternity doing whatever I can to make you happy," he vows, his voice full of conviction.

"I believe you," I tell him, because I do. I know that we'll face challenges, but I also know that as long as we're together, we can overcome anything. We're finally where we're supposed to be; in each other's arms, and nothing is going to tear us apart.

He starts to move faster, and I match his pace eagerly, our bodies coming together in perfect harmony. The world falls away until it's just the two of us, lost in each other. Our magic dances; intertwining, pulsating. Relief, passion, and love evident in their movement. It eddies, faster and harder, until we're both crying out in ecstasy. I cling to him tightly as wave after wave of pleasure washes over me, my entire body shaking with the force of it. He follows me soon after, his body going rigid as he spills inside of me. We collapse together, our chests heaving with breathless laughter.

"That was amazing," I whisper, still in awe of what just happened between us.

"It always is," he replies, his eyes twinkling mischievously.

I swat at him playfully before snuggling closer into his side. "Don't get cocky."

"Oh, but I'm so good at that," he coos, his arms tightening around me.

I close my eyes, a content sigh escaping my lips. This is perfect, I think as I drift off to sleep in the arms of my mate.

CHAPTER 56

LANA

The sun still sits high in the sky when we stir. We'd been up on and off for hours, basking in its rays, making love until we were both too exhausted to move. Now we lie in bed, tangled up in each other, both of us pleased and sated.

"I guess we should get up," I say with a heavy sigh.

Finn's eyes drop to my chest, a bemused expression on his face. I look down, groaning at my engorged chest.

"Nova is overdue for a feeding," I tell him, my cheeks flushing with embarrassment.

"I can grab her," he says, his eyes filled with concern. "Do you need anything?"

I shake my head, sitting up and swinging my legs over the edge of the bed. "I've got it."

I tiptoe into the nursery, stepping over Gideon, Oz, and Auguste who've parked themselves at the foot of Nova's crib. My heart melts at the sight of them, fast asleep and looking so peaceful. I know they've been taking shifts watching over her, making sure she's safe.

Vampires don't need sleep, but after the emotional toll of running at full octane for so long, they're probably mentally exhausted. I know

I am. I'm straddled over Gideon's hunched form, reaching into her crib when I hear a deep voice say "hey."

I shriek, causing Gideon to shoot up and nearly topple me over. I catch myself on the edge of the crib, my heart thundering in my chest as his arms come around my legs to steady me.

"Jesus, Lana." Gideon chuckles, his eyes filled with amusement. "You're like a loud, beautiful giant of a ninja."

I shoot him a scowl. "You scared the crap out of me!" I stage whisper to Auguste, who is just sitting in the dark like a psycho killer ready to take me out.

"Sorry," he says, his lips quirking up in a sheepish grin. "I didn't mean to startle you."

"Uh huh," I tell him, reaching over to ruffle his hair fondly. He always wears it so perfect, and I know that as much as he loves the affection, he'll be fixing it as soon as I'm not looking. Though so much of his appearance takes little effort.

I scoop Nova into my arms, holding her close as she starts to root around. I pull down my tank top, baring my breast for her. She latches on with a little huff, her eyes closing in contentment as she eats. I settle into the rocking chair, taking in the finishing touches my parents made on the nursery overnight. With babies being so rare in Bedlam, it wasn't easy to procure items without a little magic. It's why the root of a tree is still attached to each of the legs of the crib, and why there's a soft, mossy rug on the floor. Willow limbs weave in and out of the railing on the crib, creating a natural barrier to keep Nova safe.

I'm so lost in thought; I don't hear Finn come in until he's right next to me. He places a gentle kiss on my temple before taking a seat next to me. Oz settles at my feet, rubbing them, while Gideon and Auguste tinker with some tubing that comes through the wall from outside. It runs along the ceiling, allowing fae flies to light up the room for a natural, ethereal glow.

"What are you guys doing?" I ask, watching as Gideon tries to shove the tubing back into place.

"Trying to figure out how the hell-ooo, uh." He shoots a worried glance at Nova. "How this contraption works," he grumbles.

I stifle a giggle, knowing that he's not really mad. He's just frustrated because he doesn't understand the fae magic that powers it. Not yet anyway. It'll come in time.

Oz grins at me when I groan as he rubs a particularly sore spot in my foot. "Are you sure you're not just milking this for all it's worth?" I ask him, my eyes narrowed in mock suspicion. He's always had a thing for my feet.

He shrugs, his grin widening. "Can you blame me? I finally have a chance to take care of my wife the way I want to, and I'm going to enjoy every second of it."

"I can see that," I say, chuckling as Gideon lets out a string of curses.

Rose barrels into the room, out of breath and looking flustered. "I'm so sorry, I got held up." She comes to a stop next to Gideon, who's still trying to shove the tubing back into place.

Her attention swings to me when she notices Nova isn't in her crib. She puts her hands out in a "gimme, gimme" gesture, and I hand Nova over without protest. Okay, maybe a *little* bit of objection. Gideon finally gives up on the tubing and turns to Rose with a raised eyebrow.

"You held her all day yesterday. When do I get my turn?" he asks, a pouty look on his face.

"I'm sure you'll get your turn," Rose says placatingly. "Maybe when she's my size."

Gideon's eyes narrow in mock irritation before he breaks out into a grin and places a kiss to Rose's head. "Where's your brother?"

"He and Mekhi are helping Grandma and Grandpa draft up the treaty Mom asked them to look into," she says, her eyes lighting up with excitement. "They'll have it for you all to review tonight."

"That's great news," I say, relieved that we're one step closer to having peace between our two peoples. Even if it is just a temporary treaty, it's a start. We have a lot of healing to do on both sides after the war.

"I'm going to go check on them." Rose bounces Nova in her arms as she heads for the door. "I'll see you all later."

"Bye, sweetie," I call out after her. I watch her go and wait several seconds before turning my attention to my men, raising a brow at them. "So, is Mekhi just a friend ... or...?" I let the question hang in the air, hoping they'll fill me in on what's going on between Mekhi and our daughter. I've caught more than enough stolen glances between those two.

"Mekhi is family," Auguste says after a moment, his eyes meeting mine. "Your mates," he tilts his head towards the others, knowing full well he's my mate, too, and continues, "told him in no uncertain terms exactly where he needs to keep his hands. Don't think we need to worry about him any time soon."

"So, what's on the agenda for today?" Finn asks, his hands coming to rest on my shoulders.

"I think it's time we speak to the kings," I whisper. My eyes drift to the window, watching the sky taking on a grayish hue as a storm rolls in off the mountains. "It's time to end this."

* * *

I SIT on the edge of the bed, staring at my reflection in the mirror. My hair is pulled back into a tight bun, and my face is free of makeup. I wear a simple black dress, and after spending months in captivity, my skin has a pale tone, making the outfit look a little macabre.

Auguste comes up behind me, wrapping his arms around my waist. "You look beautiful," he whispers, his lips brushing against my ear.

"I feel like I'm going to my own funeral," I say, my voice trembling as I turn to face him. "How the hell am I going to look them in the eyes and not burst into tears?"

"You're not," he says firmly, his thumbs scoring my cheeks. "You're going to go out there and show them who we are, and that actions have consequences, even for those who claim to love you."

I take a deep breath, trying to steady my nerves. This will not be easy, but it's something I must do. I can't let my mates down, the kings included, or my people.

"Let's go," I say, straightening my shoulders.

Auguste presses a kiss to my temple and takes my hand, leading me out of the room and down the hallway to the nursery. Nova coos softly in Finn's arms, and I can't help but smile at the sight of her. Gideon and Oz fight for her attention with puppets and a book.

"She's so beautiful," I whisper, reaching out to brush my fingers over her downy soft hair and bending over to kiss her little fist.

"Just like her mother," Auguste says, his voice filled with pride.

I tear my eyes away from Nova and look at my mates. "Are you ready?"

They all nod, their expressions solemn. I strap Novaleigh to my chest while Finn affixes my crown to my head before putting his on. This is our first public appearance after the short war, and we want to stand united. We make our way through the castle to the throne room, where Grimm, Penn, and Casimir wait for us in the wings.

Due to the sensitive nature of their crimes, we won't have the public in the throne room with us, and instead, a live, realm-wide broadcast will operate on a two-minute delay. While what they did was terrible, I don't want to put their safety in jeopardy, and the realm needs to understand no crime is without consequence. I'm not sure how my people will react to the news of what happened, and I want to avoid a riot. But first, we'll have a closed conversation with just the family; no guards, no cameras.

We had security bring in more seats for the dais, so no one of us has more authority than the others. I take my seat in the middle, with Finn to my right and Oz to my left. Auguste, Gideon, Rose, and Bennett flank us. On my lap sits Nova, who's already snagged the tiny crown off her head and gums it.

"Bring them in," I say, my voice steady and clear.

The doors to the throne room swing open, and the three kings are brought in by six guards. They're all in shackles, their clothes ragged and dirty, though not for a lack of supplies or showers. Though they helped in my rescue, their guilt rides them hard. I ignore the stab of pain I feel in my chest at the sight of them. It's laced with betrayal, desperation to get my mates out of chains, and a love that hurts.

"Lana." Casimir speaks out of turn, his voice breaking. "I'm so sorry."

"You're sorry?" I echo, giving him a level look. "You stole me from my family, wiped my memories, and made me fall in love with you. You robbed my children of their mother. My mates of their world. And Finn of his right to make me his high queen. All for what? Power?" I shake my head. "I don't understand how you could have done that to me."

"We were desperate," Penn says pleadingly. "You have to understand, we love you. There was no trickery involved when it came to our love, or yours. The feelings you have—" he stumbles over his words. "Had … for us, were real."

"He's right," Grimm speaks up. "I swear to you, I only ever used my incubus magic on you four times; when we first met you, the night you asked me to on the ship, in the throne room when the vampires came, and when you wanted to temporarily forget about killing Gideon. What we have is real, even if we acquired it in the worst possible way. We fucked up."

"I want to believe you," I say, my voice breaking. "But it's hard when I look at you, and all I see are the men I gave my heart to, who didn't realize the value of my gift. Who decided to destroy it, instead."

Finn places a hand on mine, and I meet his gaze. He speaks to me in my mind. *Do you want me to do a truth spell? It takes but a few seconds to implement, and you'll know if what they say is true when their aura turns green.*

Yes.

He cups my cheek, leaning over as he speaks in melodic, archaic fae against my temple. My eyes close as I take in his words, feeling the power of his magic flow through me. It settles in my vision like two glowing orbs, and when I open my eyes again, I see the auras of my three mates. Is this what Finn was talking about seeing all this time?

They shine brightly against the darkness of their clothing, and swirling colors make up their unique magic. But there's something else there; a bright green hue, like fresh cut grass. They're telling the truth. Tears sting my eyes, and I have to blink them away before looking at my mates.

"I believe you," I say, my voice thick. "But that doesn't change what you did. You still kidnapped me, took away my memories, and destroyed my family. There must be reparations. Consequences. Apologies. You may very well spend the rest of eternity making it up to me. To my family."

Their shoulders slump in relief, and I see the hope in their eyes.

"What is your will, my soul?" Finn asks, his hand still on mine.

"I think the first step towards atonements is for you three to tell us what you believe is a suitable consequence. I'll take it into advisement, and we'll go from there," I say. I will also consider the reason for their betrayal, and how they willingly turned themselves back in as soon as I was safe and out of werewolf captivity.

It will not be easy, but I'll have to find a way to forgive them. The blood bond demands it. I swore my fealty to them. They're my mates. And I love them, even if they did break my heart.

Penn's shoulders straighten, and he clears his throat. He's always been the token spokesperson for the trio. "Though we don't deserve your love, we'll earn it if it's the last thing we do. To show our commitment to you, and to your family," he pauses on each one of them, "we're prepared to relinquish our titles as kings, leaving just a high king and queen of Bedlam."

Shock ripples through the dais, and I'm not sure if it's because they didn't expect such a drastic gesture, or because they think it's not enough. My breathing quickens. I know it won't be easy for them, giving up their thrones. Their kingdoms. But it's a start.

"Also," Penn continues, "we think it is fair that you wipe our memories."

"No," I'm quick to say. "I won't do that to you."

"We're willing to go through with it," Grimm pleads, his aura flashing green with a conviction not even I can deny.

"I have two reasons why I won't. The first being, it's a cruel thing to do, and that's not the kind of high queen I want to be. The second is that I want you to spend the rest of eternity knowing how much you betrayed me. At our table. In our bed. Every time you catch my smile directed towards you, or a moment of laughter, you'll know it's because of the pain you caused that I can be strong enough to face the day, despite it all. I want you to remember what you did every time I look at you. What you took away from me. And how despite you ripping it to shreds, I still have a heart to love you."

My voice is cold, but my spirit breaks with every word. These are the men I love. The mates who hold the very core of me. And they broke it. But I'll never stop loving them. They hang their heads, chin to chest, and I see the shame in their auras. It's a start.

After conferring with the family, we agree to stripping the kings of their kingdoms. As a show of good faith, we release the fae army held in the dungeon of Rexuna Castle, and have the former kings give a public address about their crimes and the transition of power.

As my mates, they'll still have input on matters, just as Oz, Gideon, or Auguste would. They just won't hold any titles. And they'll never be able to take my throne, even if they wanted to. It's not ideal, but even doling out this consequence hurts me. I love them. I just hope one day, they'll be able to earn back my trust and prove their love to me, too.

CHAPTER 57

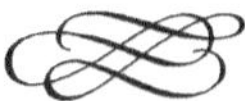

LANA

*N*ovaleigh stirs between us, a whimper coming from her as she stretches her arms over her head. I smile down at her and kiss her forehead. My finger twirls in her dusting of curls, her tresses like silk against my skin.

"Mommy's here," I whisper, glancing on either side of us. "Your daddies, too."

Finn and Gideon are both asleep, their hair mussed and their cheeks still red from the warmth in our bed. Oz runs his hand along my shoulder, and Auguste reads a book, sitting on the far end of the mattress.

"Hey, handsome, what have you got there?" I tilt my head up, trying to see.

He grins, flashing the front cover. "A very worn romance novel you had on your nightstand. Something about a fae and a mortal falling in love."

I snort. "Yeah, I remember that one. It's not as good as the real thing, though." I glance at my fae mates, giving them patty-pats on the head.

He chuckles and sets the book down. "No, it's not."

Finn and Gideon wake at the sound of our voices, and they both smile sleepily at me.

"Morning, beautiful," Gideon croaks, his voice rough from sleep.

"My soul," Finn rasps, leaning over to kiss me. He spent most of the night arguing with Gideon about the best way to ensure fair treatment over who gets to sleep next to me in bed. They took so long; they didn't even get to sleep next to me on account of Oz and Auguste swooping in. Auguste must've relinquished his spot after bringing Nova to me in the middle of the night, though.

"Morning, boys," I coo, earning a scowl from both. I laugh and give Gideon a quick kiss. "And good morning to you too." I crane my neck so I can see Oz behind me.

He leans down to give me a proper morning greeting, his lips sweet and cool on mine.

"Did you sleep well?" I ask when he pulls back.

He rests his chin on my shoulder. "Always with you."

"Good," I say, my eyes drawn to the bundle in my arms. "Because I have a feeling we're going to need all the energy we can get."

Nova's already grown a ton; sitting up, babbling, and getting into everything. She's a handful, but I wouldn't have it any other way. I train my eyes on her, picking out her features. The sweep of her eyebrows, the curve of her chin. All perfect. All ours. I'm so grateful she's here, even if the circumstances aren't ideal.

A melancholy feeling washes over me, and I sit up. "I think it's time," I whisper.

The men swing out of bed, not having to ask what I mean. We change into regal clothing. My dress is a deep forest green befitting of my position as high queen. The bodice is tight, the skirt billowing.

I wear my crown, as does Finn. Oz dons a simple black tunic, and Auguste, button-down shirt and trousers. Gideon forgoes his usual grey sweatpants he's taken to wearing around our private wing of the castle, opting instead for a pair of black jeans and a loose white shirt.

The four of them stand beside me as I take my place on the throne, Nova in my arms. All the court is here, every fae waiting with bated breath to see what I'll do.

I take a deep breath and begin.

"Bring him in."

The clang of the giant metal doors echoes through the room as they swing open. Luka is led in, his wrists shackled and a scowl on his face directed towards the guards handling him. He looks just as handsome as I remember, if not more so. My gaze catalogues his features, noting which ones Nova has inherited. His strong jaw, his tanned skin, and dark hair.

Luka's eyes lock on Finn's as he's led to the center of the room, and I can see the rage burning in their depths, despite the softening of his features when he sees me. His attention flits to Nova for a fraction of a second before he forcibly rips his gaze away, a pain echoing so deep in it, it nearly brings me to my knees.

"Luka." I greet him, my voice cool. "Do you understand why you're here?"

His eyes shine with unshed tears. "I did something unthinkable." His voice breaks on the last word, and he has to clear his throat.

"Many somethings," I add. "You kidnapped me, captured my mate, held us both captive, tortured me, threatened to hurt others, and attempted to overthrow my people." I tick each point off on my fingers. "And you imprinted on me."

He swallows. "I take responsibility for all but the last. There's not a force in this realm or the next that can control who my beast chooses as a mate. That was out of my hands."

"Fair enough." I nod. "But the rest is on you." I lean back in my throne, steepling my fingers. "What do you propose as a solution?"

He looks down at his feet, and the agony in his expression is so visceral, a lump forms in my throat. "I'll leave," he says softly. "You won't ever have to see me again."

The words pinch my heart, thinking of him abandoning Nova, knowing the issues my own abandonment caused me, but I school my features into a mask of neutrality. "And what about Nova?" I ask. "What about our daughter?"

His eyes meet mine, misery etched in their depths. "I'll leave her be," he says after a long moment. "She doesn't deserve a father like me."

"And the pack?"

"I'll step down as king," he says. "Someone else can have the job."

I'm not sure what I expected Luka to say, but it wasn't this. He's basically giving up everything.

"I'm sorry, Luka," I say regretfully. "But I won't be able to accommodate those terms."

"I understand," he says, his voice resigned. I see all the light die in his eyes. "What will you do with me, then? The gallows?" he suggests. "Throw me in a cage of vermini? It's the least I deserve."

Turning towards Finn, I incline my head.

"My mother cursed your line for treachery of the worst kind: an affair of the heart. She was not without sympathy, however," Finn explains.

Rose and Bennett stand, clasping hands. "Our grandmother told us the curse can be broken if a member of your line can find it in their hearts to forgive the one they wronged."

Luka nods, understanding. "And if they can't?" he asks.

"Then the werewolf curse will continue, passed down through the generations," I tell him. "But there is one caveat." I look around at everyone's watchful faces.

"No matter what," I continue. "We'll remove your curse, Luka."

He furrows his brows, stammering, "I don't understand."

"I am a benevolent high queen." My voice steels. "You tried to break me all those months in your captivity, and despite the heinous crimes you committed, I must recognize the lengths you went to for your people. To give them a better life, one not bound by the moon. I also acknowledge our daughter needs her biological father in her life, and it's her decision if she wants to keep you in her life as she ages."

Hope blooms in his eyes, and he starts to open his mouth to speak, but I continue on. "There are conditions I ask in return for this act of mercy. You publicly denounce your pack's war against Bedlam and its people. You will also step down as king, and an interim leader will be chosen by the pack until they decide on a new king or queen. While I remove your curse, you must also be punished for your crimes; you won't become a wolf fae."

Confusion flits across his features. "What does that mean?"

"It means you won't be able to shift into your wolf's form ever again, Luka, because you'll be human. You'll never feel the moon's pull, and you'll be mortal. You'll age and die like a human." I take a deep breath before continuing on. "Should our daughter ever find it in her heart to forgive you, she can choose to turn you with what, no doubt, will be her own formidable power."

He nods his understanding. "I accept your terms," he says after a long moment.

I raise a brow, but don't comment on it. It's not like he had much of a choice. "Very well," I say, rising from my throne, motioning for him to follow me. "Then let's get this over with."

I lead him to the center of the room, where a large moon stone sits. It's unassuming, but it's incredibly powerful. I place my hand on it, and a soft light glows from within.

Luka steps forward and resolve dims his eyes. He takes a deep breath and steps into its shadow. The glow surrounds him, and I watch as his body starts to change. His wolf's form flickers, a whine escaping him as his body convulses in and out of his human form. I see the pain in his features, but he doesn't make another sound. The light fades, and Luka falls to his knees, panting and sweating. He's completely human now, and his face softens, as though he's finally home after years at sea. It hurts to know I caused anyone pain, but it's also necessary. He committed unforgivable crimes, and this is his punishment.

He finally looks up at me, cheeks wet. "I will find a way to make this up to you, Lana." Studying my face for a moment, his attention shifts to Nova, and he adds, "And to our daughter. A part of me was terrified becoming human would remove the imprint, the gravitational pull I feel towards you, but it's still there. I love you just as much as I did the day it snapped into place. But now that I'm human, I'm glad it's still here."

"I know," I whisper. And I do. The imprint is unbreakable, no matter what form he's in. It's also the only reason why I felt comfortable agreeing to his next request. He'd never hurt us again.

"Can I," he hesitates. "Can I hold her?"

I nod, and he scoops Nova from my arms. He holds her close, tears still streaming down his face as he presses a kiss to her forehead.

"What did you name her?" he asks, his voice rough.

"Nova," I reply. "It means 'new star'. Full name Novaleigh Annabelle Drake."

A smile tugs at his lips. "It's perfect. She's … perfect." His lips rest against her temple, a deluge of tears raining down his cheeks and onto hers as he closes his eyes and breaks down.

She babbles, gripping his finger, and in this moment, I know everything will be alright.

CHAPTER 58

LANA

The next morning, Rune, Crucey, and several of the older Tolden join us in the throne room. Luka stands before us, looking like a man on death row awaiting his execution. And for a king who'd been in power so long, it's pretty much the same thing. Teresa leads her pack, standing stoic and strong beside them. Katarina glances at her alpha with a knowing smirk. Teresa's eyes are trained on someone next to me. I follow her gaze, and startle to find it on Bennett. He gives her some love-struck puppy dog eyes, and I have to stifle a groan.

Already? Seriously. I'm not ready for *that* conversation.

I clear my throat to get everyone's attention. "Thank you all for coming on such short notice. As you know, Luka here," I motion to the man in question, "committed some grievous crimes against Tolden and against the fae. He's agreed to accept his punishment."

Rune steps forward. "And what exactly is that?" he asks, eyes narrowed on the former werewolf king. Hatred burns in their depths.

"He'll become human."

A collective gasp goes up around the room, and I see the looks of horror on everyone's faces. For a species who prize their immortality, becoming human is the ultimate penalty. Perhaps even worse than going to Bedlam Penitentiary, where *no one* wants to end up. Maybe even as bad as Aggonid's realm.

"Are you sure that's wise?" Rune asks, turning to me. "He's too dangerous."

"He won't be a threat," I reassure him. "Not to us, ever again."

"How can you be so sure?" he whispers.

"He's imprinted on her," Crucey breathes, eyes wide as she looks from Luka to me. "That's how."

Luka steps forward, eyes on Rune. "I would never hurt Lana, or my daughter. I will find a way to make this up to you, I swear it."

Rune studies him for a long moment before finally nodding. "I can't fault you personally for the crime against the love of my life, only your ancestors. You are, however, responsible for the continued massacre of the Tolden, kidnapping and torturing my friends, and leading a war against our people. Do you understand why Luna cursed your line?"

Luka's brows pinch in sadness. "Because one of my ancestors cheated on his mate."

"That doesn't happen, but it happened to her, and she was *pregnant* with his child. But he kept seeing his mistress, gave her children, and doomed generations. And then she found love and made a life for herself outside of his shadow. But what did the werewolves do? They killed her." Rune's hard glare holds an eternity of heartache. "Generations of misery, because one man couldn't keep it in his pants. You are the product of that man's mistakes, and while I don't fault you for it, I can't let your current crimes go unpunished."

Luka worries his lip. "I understand, and I'm ready to deal with my consequences." His attention turns to Crucey. "What we've done to the Tolden is unthinkable. Destroying your people to save our own. We were wrong, and there's nothing I can do to make it right. But I will spend the rest of my life trying." His eyes land on mine. "I'm not saying this because I want to earn your favor. I'm saying it as a man who feels to the very marrow of his bones the love for his mate, and would do anything to see her happy, even if it's not with me. It's why I don't understand why Luna's mate could do something so heinous as to turn away from the gift of a mating bond. I understand Luna's pain, and why she cursed his people."

Commotion behind Luka draws my attention, and I see the Tolden backing away towards the far wall, their eyes trained to the group of werewolves at the center of the room. Luka's pack has their backs to us, and they're shifting into their wolf forms.

"What's going on?" I ask, confused. The moons aren't full, so this should be impossible.

Luka rushes to me, pulling me back, earning a snarl from my mates. He presses his lips to my ear, primed to speak but gasps instead at the scene unfolding before us.

The pack of werewolves suddenly shifts back into their human forms, and the room erupts into chaos. The Tolden are shouting and running towards the exit, while the werewolves—former werewolves, now wolf fae—are falling to their knees, overcome with emotion.

Luka wraps me in a hug. "It's over," he whispers. "My gods. It's finally over." I'm too stunned to respond, eyes fixed on the sight in front of me.

Bennett leaps off the dais, running towards Teresa, who's being helped to her feet by one of the Tolden. He sweeps her up into his arms, and she throws her arms around his neck, burying her face in his chest.

Finn moves to my side, scaring off Luka before wrapping an arm around my waist. "Are you alright?" he asks, concerned.

I nod, still in shock. "The curse is broken," I whisper.

"Yes," he says. "It appears so."

"What does this mean?" I ask.

"It means," he says, "that the Tolden and the wolf fae are no longer enemies."

The news of the curse breaking spreads like wildfire, and within a week, representatives from both the Tolden and the wolf fae are at our doorstep, ready to start negotiations. It's a long and difficult process, but eventually, an accord is reached. The wolf fae will keep to their own territory, and the Tolden will keep to theirs. There will be no more fighting, no more killing. Crucey will allow the forest to bleed into the Wastelands, giving them common ground once again.

I learn Crucey appears so old because of the magic she expends trying to contain the forest to keep the Tolden safe. In time, she'll grow stronger, and no longer age as she had. Luna was her best friend, and together, they'd maintained their sanctuary for years before Rune came along. He ended up falling in love with Luna shortly before the werewolves killed her. And all those times we'd thought he was off on vacation somewhere, he was really in Castanea, helping maintain the ecosystem for the Tolden.

I sit in on the negotiations, providing whatever help I can, but it's clear that this is a new beginning for both the Tolden and the wolf fae. Maybe it's a new beginning for all of us.

TEN MONTHS LATER

FINN

"You sure about this?" I side-eye Lana while I help her drag our giant bed over to the spot she's marked on the floor.

She pauses, slumping against the wall and carves a hand through her curls. "No," she admits. "But a blood oath is a blood oath, Finn. I love them." Her words twist something in my chest, and I have to look away. She catches on, reaching out to pull me into a hug. "Shoot, I'm sorry."

"I'm not mad that you love them. Although obviously, if you want to get rid of them, I'll help you, but I'm just upset I failed you." I sigh and rest my chin on the top of her head.

"You didn't fail me, Finn." Her words are muffled against my chest, but I feel them, nonetheless. "I love you too, you know."

"I know." I kiss her temple and release her. "So, where do you want this?"

"Here is good." She steps back and looks around the room. "We'll need to clear out some furniture."

"And we're going to knock these down?" I gesture towards the row of doors leading to Grimm, Penn, and Casimir's rooms.

"I want to see the portal when it's open," she says. "Plus, I have a feeling we're going to need all the space we can get."

"For what?"

"I'm not sure yet." She nibbles on her bottom lip, and I can see the wheels turning in her head. "But I'll know when the time comes."

I smirk, knowing full well what she means. We've all felt the desire to give Lana more children, like an ancient drive to ensure the survival of our species.

It's been nearly a year since the kings relinquished their titles, and in that time, we've been using a portal stone to travel back-and-forth between Earth and Bedlam to attend to royal duties with both the fae and vampire courts. When the vampires learned we can turn them into fae, they showed up in droves to get the 'cure'. It's been chaos, and I know Lana is feeling the strain, so I've pitched in as much as I can. We also had to spend several months helping the former werewolves on Earth accustom to being wolf fae. We're sending them to Academia for instruction next month.

So far, each vampire we've turned into fae have become Luna fae, helping repopulate my line. Better yet, news of fae births has been cropping up in Bedlam, which is a good sign that the other fae lines are starting to rebound as well. So much so, the ratio of fae to witches on Academia will swing in favor of the fae for the first time in more than five-hundred years. The twins will attend Bedlam Academy in the fall, with Nova joining the following year with the next crop of students.

Now, more than ever, we need this permanent portal close by. To continue managing both thrones, we've come up with a way to mirror key locations in Convectus Castle with a more modern, vampire-friendly version of it, which Oz and Auguste have built in the Chilean mountains on the Southern Hemisphere of Earth. The old portal in Noble Wilds takes too long to pass through, whereas the portal stone is near-instantaneous, so we've figured out how to replicate its magic for something stronger. The portal stays open in each room, so all it takes is a step through the faint shimmer dividing each side. In the throne rooms, it appears as though the vampire and fae courts are side-by-side. You can hear and see it all. And now, we're building one in our bedrooms, and knocking down the hallways to Grimm,

Casimir, and Penn's rooms, so it's just one giant bedroom with an even bigger bathroom.

A knock sounds at our bedroom door, and I glance towards it. "Expecting company?"

"No," Lana says with a frown. We cross the room, and she opens the door to find Bellamy on the other side, a smirk on his face.

"Bellamy!" Lana shrieks, throwing her arms around his neck.

I chuckle and shake my head as he picks her up and spins her around. "What are you doing here?" I know their history together, and while things are platonic between them now, I don't miss the way his lilac eyes linger on her. Out of any other fae in Bedlam, he's the one I'd have the least issue with being a part of our little family, considering what he tried to do. What he was willing to give up to give Lana the truth.

Who knows what the future holds?

"I was in the area, and I thought I'd drop by and say hi." He sets Lana down and comes into the room when I step aside. "But it looks like I'm interrupting something."

"Not at all," I say. "We were just about to start working on the portal."

"Oh, that's right." He nods his head, and his smile fades a little. "You've been opening these all over the castle."

"We are," Lana says. "But we could use an extra set of hands, if you're interested."

Bellamy hesitates for a fraction of a second before he nods. "I'd love to."

Lana beams at him, and I can see the relief in her eyes. With Bellamy's help, we should be able to get the portal done today. We'd sent the others away so we could have it all as a surprise. The trio of former kings don't know we're expanding the room, either, but it's just one more step towards welcoming them back into the fold.

EPILOGUE

LANA

Finn and I stand sentry in front of the door to our Convectus bedroom, mischievous grins on our faces. Oz, Auguste, Gideon, Grimm, Penn, and Casimir stand in front of us, confusion, and maybe a little fear, clear on their faces.

"What's going on?" Oz asks, his brow furrowed.

"Lana has something she wants to show you," Finn sing-songs, wiggling his eyebrows.

"Oh, really?" Gideon's lips twitch up into a smirk. "And what might that be?"

I step to the side and gesture towards the door. "This."

They all exchange looks before they cautiously make their way into the room, their steps faltering when they see the changes. With the wall gone that was separating the former king's rooms from ours, it's one giant room now. And in the center of it all is the portal, reflecting the Earth side bed right next to the Bedlam side bed shoved together, so it's difficult to tell where one begins and the other ends.

Casimir turns his crestfallen eyes to me. "Lana, I don't understand."

I thought they'd be happy. I take a moment to register why the trio look so devastated. "Oh my gods, you didn't ..." I rush to them, throwing my arms around their necks. "This is for all of us now." I pull back, gesturing to the beds. "Now we'll all fit together."

"All of us?" Penn chokes out, and I nod.

Their shoulders sag in relief, and I see the unshed tears in their eyes. "We're really a family now," Casimir says, his voice rough with emotion.

Plopping myself on the bed, I stretch out. "I've got more news." I grin at their expectant faces and tease it out a little longer. "Well, not really news, but a request." I roll onto my stomach, propping myself up on my elbows. "I was wondering if you guys would want to help me with something."

"Anything," Oz says immediately, and the others nod their heads in agreement.

I beam at them before patting the bed next to me. "Think we can manage to pop another one out in time for the fall semester when Nova heads to Academia?"

Grimm is the first to understand, being of the incubus order and all, and his prowl towards me spurs the others into action. They fall onto the bed with me, a tangle of limbs and laughter, as they all try to vie for my attention. I let them, relishing in the feel of my family around me. Things may not be perfect, but they're damn close. And with my mates by my side, I think we're going to be alright.

ROSE GETS her long-awaited invite to attend a magical university on Academia. But what happens when she ends up at a different academy from those she knows and trusts—in a co-ed dorm room? She's thrust into a world of dark magic, temptation at every turn, and a threat she can't protect herself from because first year students aren't supposed to use their magic. And when she's caught trying, she's made to wear a magic suppression necklace. Can her roommate and his friends protect her? And what if the threat hits a little closer to home? Read Bedlam Academy to find out.

Wondering which supernatural order you'd be in Bedlam? **Take the quiz at kathyhaan.com/quiz** and see if you're a vampire, witch, or shifter. Share your result in our brand new Facebook group, The Bedlam Fae Society.

GUIDE TO BEDLAM & THE CHARACTERS

Please note, these DO contain spoilers. Read with caution.

XOXO

Academia: The small continent where witches and fae attend university to learn magic.

Aedon Shineseer: A lion shifter fae with a gambling addiction.

Aggonid's Realm: Where bad fae go when they die, they'll spend eternity tortured and maimed.

Alphie Bennett: Lana's dad. Life partner of Annabelle Chapman.

Annabelle Chapman: Witch and mother of Lana. Life partner of Alphie Bennett.

Auguste: One of Rose, Bennett, and Novaleigh's dads. Member of the vampire court. Mate to Lana. War hero.

Bedlam Penitentiary: The fae prison located far North of Bedlam. There's no crueler fate.

Bellamy: A soldier at Convectus. He's Pierce and Captain Zara's brother, and is of the dragon order. Deep-set dimples, sun-bronzed skin, blond hair, and lilac eyes. He grew up with Penn on Sundahlia; they're cousins and best friends.

Berserker: A loyal fae order with uncontrollable rage and a predilection for casting curses. Feasting on internal organs helps keep the anger at bay, especially if it's a womb.

Belu: This whale-like creature is a natural predator to basilisks.

Bennett: Twin brother to Rose, has lots of dads, but looks most like Oz. Crushes on Teresa. Luna fae.

Bloodstone: A stone used in blood sacrifice rituals.

Bracky Blooms: Edible yellow blooms found on the Tristique Islands, and if the sap gets on your skin, it'll cause euphoria. It's sweet, like honey or sugarcane. When ingested, its effects are multiplied.

Casimir: Molten silver eyes, wolf order, King of Luporia

Caspari: Violent creatures who eat fae waste. They usually travel in hordes.

Castanea: The underground forest beneath the Wastelands.

Captain Shallowind: Captain of the ship that takes Lana and crew to the islands.

Captain Zara: Older sister of Bellamy and Pierce. Captain of the guard. Mated.

Cerulean Isles: Where the avias nest. Located between Sundahlia and Convectus, and South of the Tristique Islands.

Clara: Chef at Convectus Castle.

Convectus: The main continent where each king convenes for important realm matters.

Crownsees: Giant, tree-like creatures who mean well, but aren't always gentle. They are mostly found in Romarie, the dark fae realm.

Cruah Bush: Provides nuts with healing properties. They don't taste good, though.

The Crucey: Deadliest creature in all the realms, kills indiscriminately, and enjoys every second of it. She rules the wastelands, and no magic can control her. She cares for the Tolden and keeps them safe from the werewolves. Tolden hearts can cure their curse.

Dragonbolt: Built by dragons, it's a small castle of fire and ice on Convectus.

Finn: High King of the fae, and of the Luna order. Lives on Rexuna most of the time. Ashy blond hair, icy blue eyes, he glows blue at times. Lives on a mountain in Noble Wilds during moon season.

Can clean and dry clothes by patting and rubbing vigorously. Smooth, tanned chest, washboard abs. Tattoo just under his belt line that's of four moons, one shooting through the sky.

Gala: A small village on the outskirts of Noble Wilds and Loier Mountain. It has cobbled stones and mostly deserted streets at night. Has a small town hall and a five-bedroom inn with an old-world boutique hotel feel to it where Finn and Lana stay the night. Around the corner is a clothing store.

Gideon: Right hand and best friend to the Vampire King. Lana's second mate. Former vampire, he's now a Luna fae. One of Rose, Bennett, and Novaleigh's many dads. Grew up in the Italian Dolomites, but spent the last two hundred years in Australia. Master koala and crocodile wrangler.

Grimm: A fresh and clean scent like the wind. King of Occasus, he's of the Incubus order. Has dark hair and Tahitian-blue eyes.

Ground Gnomes: Bury your tattered clothes, and the ground gnomes will mend them with their magic. Don't forget to toss in a few coins when they're done, or they'll hunt you down. They don't talk, but they do chitter.

Hannah Mae Yeung: Lana's best friend since childhood. Love interest of Maeve. Owns a flower shop in Shelby, Montana. Has a son, CJ, with autism and sensory processing disorder.

Harpis Siren: The size of a small mountain lion, this beast has sharp fangs, razor-like claws, bioluminescent hair, and a tail. A distant relative to a siren, it's more animal than sentient being.

Ilab: These are bear-like creatures who love witches' blood, and most live in Noble Wilds.

Katarina Donović: Sister to Luka. Werewolf.

Lana Finlandian: Female main character. Queen of Vampires. High Queen of the Fae. Former witch, now a Luna fae. Lover of sleep, cozy things, and snacks. Collects mates like it's a competition. Mom to Rose, Bennett, and Novaleigh.

Loier Mountain: The mountain just before reaching the first town on the edge of Noble Wilds, located on Convectus. Just on the other side of this is the town of Gala.

Luka Donović: King of the Werewolves, father of Novaleigh, and brother to Katarina.

Mara: A servant at Convectus Castle.

Mekhi: A witch born on Earth, who came to Bedlam with his Uncle Blain at eighteen. Has a crush on Rose.

Meloria: Was once the center of Fae trade on Convectus. It's encircled by a waterfall and a mist-filled lake.

Moon Season: Occurs every six months and lasts for thirty days. This is known as the Bedlam Moon. The Luna order is strongest then.

Morte: Leader of the phoenixes in Castanea.

Noble Wilds (on Convectus): The most remote woodlands. There's a portal here, but no one really goes to it. There are lots of wild animals and dangerous fugitives. No witch magic works here and it's warded from sifting in and out. The portal is three hours from the top of the mountain where Finn keeps his camp during moon season. A healing river, the Sanaquam, runs through these woods. It takes four months to walk out of the woods from the portal. High mountain climate.

Novaleigh: Daughter of Lana and Luka. Sister to Rose and Bennett.

Oz Ankida Finlandian: King of Vampires, first mate to Lana. The first vampire ever created. Best friend to Gideon. One of Rose, Bennett, and Novaleigh's dads. War hero. Former witch. Sumerian.

Paduyi Trees: Their fragrance and pollen known to induce giggling and happiness. Mostly a coastal tree.

Parallel Abyss: Some of the most dangerous waters between Convectus and Sundahlia.

Penn: King of Draconus, who can shift into a dragon.

Penn Island: An island located next to Bedlam Penitentiary, where mortals, witches, and other creatures serve time for lesser crimes.

Phelvie: Cat-like creatures who attack those with ill intent. They're sentient-like animals who come from their owners. The only way to create one is for a killing spell to be intercepted by someone else, and the interceptor to sacrifice something great to spare a life.

Pierce: Lana's personal guard. Younger brother of Captain Zara, older brother of Bellamy. Love interest of Sarai.

Prairie Pixie Juice: Liquid courage, a type of drink resembling fae wine. No alcohol, just magic, and it helps you relax. It's sweet like candy.

Relocation Spell: Ingredients are *Heart of a siren, fang of a basilisk, Occasus ruby, Sundahlian sand, bones of a traitor, moon fire ashes, Sea of Triune salt, ground gnome treasure, wood from a shipwreck, a compass, muscle of a berserker, sustai bird excrement, eye of a cyclops, and petal from a moon flower, blood of a mate.*

Rexuna: The continent West of Convectus where Finn is from. It contains Rift Pass.

Rift Pass: Mountainous region where Finn lives most of the time. This is on Rexuna.

Rose: Twin sister to Bennett. Has lots of dads, but just one mom. Crushes on Mekhi, but vows to have multiple mates like Lana.

Ross Van'Astor: Former fiancé of Lana's, treated her like crap, cheated on her. Werewolf.

Romarie: Dark fae realm. Villani goblins live here.

Rune: Trainer with long golden hair, matching eyes, and onyx skin. Gold lines spiderweb his torso like Kintsugi. He owns Titan, and is a fae of shadows and storms.

Sanaquam River: Located in Noble Wilds on Rexuna, this river has healing properties. Careful, Harpis Sirens swim rampant here.

Sarai: Lana's ladies' maid. Fancies Pierce. Can shift into a serpent.

Sea of Triune: A sea on the South side of Rexuna.

Sebastian: Vampire. Boyfriend to Wren.

Serapi City: Where Aedon Shineseer is from on Rexuna.

Sifting: Like teleporting. Not all fae have this ability, and if a powerful enough fae wards a location against sifting, you have to walk. You must be a shifter or royal to sift.

Soapberries: Small, blue berries with cleaning properties. Just squeeze them between your hands to clean skin and hair. Don't eat them.

Sodroot: A root that helps quell nausea when placed between the teeth.

Spearsnakes: Like regular snakes, but have razor sharp tails and live in the water.

Spirit Fish: Large silver fish with wings. No one has ever caught one because they're magic-resistant.

Starseed Apples: A turquoise fruit that's crisp to bite into. The taste is bright and watery like a sweet cucumber.

Sustai Birds: Birds that nest near portals, and leave a slimy excrement.

Terra Order: Can move Earth and grow plants.

Titan: A Phelvie belonging to Rune; formed when struck with a powerful spell, causing a part of Rune to split off from himself, thus forming a Phelvie.

Tolden: Children of the Woods, these creatures are guarded closely by The Crucey. Their hearts cure the werewolf curse.

Tristique Islands: A group of magic-powered islands that float above the sea. It's uninhabited, except when one of the royals uses a house on one of the islands.

Tucker: Luka's second-in-command. Werewolf.

Uncle Blain: Mekhi's evil uncle.

Vermini: Violent, crimson creatures. They'll strip a man to his very bones in seconds.

Villani: Goblins who possess black magic and live on the dark fae realm Romarie.

Wastelands: A dry, desolate place where the Crucey and her Tolden live. It used to be home to a vast forest, but disappeared when the current Luna goddess was cheated on before her murder.

Wren: A member of the vampire court, and was a fight pilot in WWII. He's Sebastian's boyfriend.

Yalsome Root: A root for cramps and numbing injuries.

ACKNOWLEDGMENTS

Wow, what a ride this has been. This may be the conclusion of the Bedlam Moon Trilogy, but it's not the end of Lana and her family's journey. The first spin-off series is Bedlam Academy (Fae Academia Book 1), where Rose ends up in a co-ed dorm without the ability to use her magic while facing threats known and unknown. You'll get cameos with your favorite personalities, and watch side characters turn into main characters with their own stories.

This trilogy was heavy. Heavy to write, heavy to read. I touched on a lot of sensitive topics such as mental health, abuse, abandonment, and trauma. As a domestic violence survivor, I know the weight of living through abuse and forgiving your abuser. It wasn't a decision I took lightly when writing the dynamic between Luka and Lana. Nor was it an easy decision to have Lana come to terms with the kings' betrayal and choose forgiveness despite their unforgivable actions.

I borrowed from my own experience of creating a congruous co-parenting relationship with my ex-husband but recognize the enormous privilege in my circumstance. While Lana and my stories involved abusers who in the end, recognized their destructive behavior and actively made changes to make amends, I know this isn't always the case.

Know that I don't argue for a victim to remain with her abuser. In fact, it's quite the opposite. It's a large part of the advocacy work I do that earned me a Certificate of Special Congressional Recognition from the Senator of Nevada, why I was the 2020 honoree and victress at the Be.A.SHERO Foundation's annual gala, why I appeared in a 12x international award-winning documentary about domestic violence, and why I was awarded SHERO of the Year. Simply put, I'm an activist for this cause (and several others).

If you're in an abusive situation, physical or otherwise, there is help:

If you're based in the US, you can text START to 88788, or call the National Domestic Violence Hotline at 800-799-7233. UK-based readers can call 0808 2000 247.

I have several people to thank:

- **Readers**: Your love of my stories means everything to me. You're why I do what I do. I wrote book three while off-grid in Chile, retracing Lana's footsteps in the Andes. I spent many weeks on developmental edits while off-grid in Kyrgyzstan, tucked into my sleeping bag while hail pummeled my tent, and thunder cracked through the Tian Shen Mountains. As I finish this letter stateside, completely jet lagged and on very little sleep, I'm busy plotting the Fae Academia Series, as well as a series featuring Aggonid and Morte. The first book comes out 12/31/22. You can keep up with my upcoming books and events on my site at kathyhaan.com.
- **My husband**: Thanks for running a tight pirate ship while I chased deadlines, tortured my characters, wept over the pain I inflicted on them, and for helping me keep my wits about me as I figured out how to piece everything back together.
- **My kids**: I know it's not easy when I must hole myself up in my room to get my work off to editing, but I appreciate your support and understanding all the same. You three are my entire world.
- **Brenda**: My soul sister, thank you for being one of my biggest cheerleaders. Your input is invaluable.
- **J**: Your insightful edits, comments, and support gives me life. I know I've said it before, and I'll probably say it again. Thank you.

PROLOGUE TO BEDLAM ACADEMY

ROSE

In the depths of the forest, high atop a sun-drenched mountain, time spins out of control as two hearts collide. Or at least, that's what it feels like as Mekhi and I sit in the warm August sun, desperate to slow it down.

My family took Mekhi in a year ago, and we've since grown closer by the day. But now these little moments together are slipping away, like sands through an hourglass. When our carefree childhood gives way to adulthood, can this—whatever it is between us—survive the transition?

We talk about everything and nothing, always coming back to that single question: what will happen to us once college starts? We don't have an answer, but I feel like something's shifted in our relationship —something neither of us is quite ready to let go of.

The grass tickles my bare feet and I lean back, allowing his arm to slip around my shoulders. Tucked in his embrace, I try to memorize everything: the smell of his scent, the way our hearts seem to sync when near, and the feel of his callouses against my smooth, fae hands. He'd wanted to heal them, along with the scar across his chest, and as a witch, he could. But I like the reminder of our differences; how opposites can come together so perfectly. Like the dimple that only appears on his right cheek, so at odds with the other side, but as a whole, he wouldn't be the same without it.

Having spent the summer exercising with Bennett—my twin brother—and me, Mekhi has grown far from the scrawny street kid we'd met at the market a year ago. He's now a confident, well-built guy. His hazel eyes have a new kind of strength, as though they'd seen more than his years should've allowed. He hasn't forgotten his past, though; he still wears the same puka shell necklace he had when we first met him.

My fingers trail over the strand of coarse shells, and his throat bobs as he swallows. My acute fae hearing picks up an uptick in his heart rate, and I raise my eyes to meet his gaze. Time seems to stand still; all of existence beyond the two of us fades away as he takes my chin in his hand and draws me in until our lips meet.

My eyes close, and I lean into it. The kiss is gentle, sweet, and everything I expected my first to be, though my heart threatens to leap out of my chest. Just a kiss, but it tastes like everything. It's a promise of something more—something that can exist beyond college. We linger, neither one of us wanting to end it, but when the sound of a bird cawing overhead breaks our trance, Mekhi pulls away, a half-smile on his lips as he takes in the blue glow of my skin. My cheeks heat, having been caught. Luna fae only glow when in pain, healing someone, under the moon, or when aroused.

"I can't believe I wasted the entire summer being too chicken to do that." His lopsided grin undoes me. His lips are full and perfect, and I long to trace them with my finger.

"Neither can I, though my dads might've had something to do with it." While they love Mekhi like a son, there's a reason they put him in a room on the opposite end of the house from mine. They're protective of me.

My thumb grazes the stubble on his jaw.

"No regrets, though, yeah?" he asks softly, his voice a rumble in his chest, and his rich tone coaxing me closer, encouraging me to meet his kiss.

I can't help but smile. "No regrets."

He leans in close, his hair falling forward. Soft brown locks frame his handsome face, and his eyes are a deep, warm hazel. Flecks of emerald, gold, and umber glitter in his irises, as though the stars wanted to put on a show, plucked them from the sky, and sealed them in his gaze. "I don't want to let you go," he whispers against my lips.

"So don't."

Mekhi shakes his head, leaning back. "You don't understand. You and I, we can make this work. I don't want to leave without you being mine."

"What are you saying?"

"Be my girlfriend, Rose."

I pull away, my heart pounding and dizzy from the moment. "Mekhi, I—"

"Think about it." He cuts me off, and his expression changes from hope to understanding. He takes my hands in his, squeezing them gently. "I know you need time to explore your options and decide what you want. But you need to know you're the only one I want to be with."

My vocal cords fail to respond, so I nod, my eyes on his. His fingers are tender as they touch my neck and gently sweep the loose strand of hair away from my face, tucking it behind my ear. His touch sends a shiver down my spine, and my heart soars at his words, but a part of me still pictures the miles that will come between us. I reach up to cup his face in my hands, feeling his warmth against my palms as his gaze intensifies. I take a deep breath, then let it out slowly before speaking.

"It's not just the distance I'm worried about. What if they come for you, too, just because you're my boyfriend?" The thought paralyzes me with fear and the only thing grounding me is the sweet scent of his cologne mixed with the earthy smell of the grass beneath me.

"They'd come for me just by my proximity to your family. I'm no more at risk as your boyfriend than I've been sleeping under your family's roof the last year." He cups my face. "You think a little thing like a severed head on castle steps *thousands* of miles away will scare me? They don't even know where we live, Rose."

True. All the letters and boxes come to our family via courier with no return address, all delivered to the main castle on Convectus, where we only stay when entertaining various leaders between the realms. The rest of the time, we're on Rexuna, high in the mountains at our family home, and only our personal guards know about it. With this latest string of threats that vow to kidnap and murder the high prince and princess of the fae—that's Bennett and me—they haven't let us leave the mountain.

It took all summer for Bennett and me to convince our parents to let us go to college to further our craft and make alliances with other families. He and I aren't one to let fear stop us. We both want a real college experience where we don't have to live under the thumb of the crown, and where we can be our own person. They'd only agreed after we made several concessions.

One: no one can know we're really prince and princess. This means we only use the Drake name on official paperwork. Otherwise, our friends will know us as Rose and Bennett Ankida.

Two: we can't attend the same university, so should the threats escalate, they can't get us both at once. One of us will rule Bedlam someday, and spreading the risk is a smart move either way.

Three: we'll let our parents know of anything that might be perceived as a threat as soon as we can.

Four: we won't be reckless with our magic. This one is going to be a little more difficult to navigate because we've both used magic far more powerful than most students will use in their lifetimes. That's what happens when you help your parents fight a war.

Five: we won't lose sight of who matters most. Yes, our realm is important, as are our people in it, but family is everything. We'd raze villages—and have done—to keep each other safe.

"I want to be your girlfriend, but I meant what I said."

"About you wanting to be just like your mom?" His eyes soften.

"Yeah." A smile twitches at the corner of my mouth. "Please don't take this the wrong way."

"You know me better than that."

"I have too much love to give." I wince, trying to phrase this with as much tact as diplomacy as I can. "To only give it to one person."

Back when we thought we'd all be attending the same university, being with him just made sense. We spent just about every waking moment together. He's part of the family, and he knows me—even the ugliest parts I keep hidden from those closest to me. But now that I'll attend Bedlam Academy without him and Bennett? I'm more conflicted than ever.

Surrounded by so much family, I've *never* been alone. The thought of a long-distance relationship, where I must steal time to talk or text, let alone visit, makes me feel like a caged bird—something I vowed never to do. Does this make me selfish and co-dependent? Yeah, it probably does.

"I can't promise you forever, Mekhi, but I can promise you right now." A tingle of magic stirs between us. A fae promise can't be broken.

Unless I want to die, anyway.

"Would you feel any better about us if I agreed to share you?" His lips twitch, as if he's trying to keep a straight face.

My eyes widen. "You'd share me?" The first time I mentioned wanting multiple mates, he'd shut that down quick, and that was before we even talked about dating.

He shrugs his shoulders. "You'll have to get used to the distance between us, but you don't have to be alone. If you make a few friends—"

"Boyfriends."

He sighs. "Boyfriends, then. I can live with that if it makes you happy. We'll make our own rules, just not the usual ones."

"I won't share you. You understand that, right? I'd sooner claw a girl's eyes out." We *did* already establish I'm selfish.

He smirks. "While I'd love to see that, be honest with yourself. You're more likely to lob off her head than claw her eyes out."

"Glad we're in agreement, then." I grin.

His hand slips around my neck and up into my hair. I draw in a breath and tilt my head back, wanting to make sure we understand each other.

"So ... we're official then?"

"Yeah, we're official."

With a final kiss and an embrace, Mekhi sends me off with a silent promise: no matter what the future brings, this summer was our own special kind of magic.

Can Rose and Mekhi's love survive college? What about when she ends up with a male roommate, whose best friends have also taken a liking to her. They're all caught in the crosshairs of a royal vendetta. **Read Bedlam Academy to find out.**

ABOUT KATHY HAAN

A blood descendant of Wild Bill Hickok and a long line of artists and creators, like Jane Austen and Emily Dickinson, **Kathy Haan believes the secret to telling a great story is living one.** The second youngest, in a massive horde of children between her parents, she did her best to gain attention and kept everyone entertained with jokes and wild stories.

She lives a life of adventure with her hunky husband, three children, and Great Pyrenees in the Midwest United States. While this is her debut novel, you might've seen her work in Forbes or Fortune, where she's a regular contributor.

ALSO BY KATHY HAAN

Bedlam Moon Trilogy (Complete)

Lana sets out to find the truth about her past, and when a hot vampire begins to unravel it for her, she's caught up in the web of an evil cult, prophecies, and curses. All while falling for the King of Vampires and his royal court. This is a why choose romance.

Bedlam Moon (Bedlam Moon Trilogy Book 1)

Tales of Bedlam (Bedlam Moon Trilogy Book 2)

Wicked Bedlam (Bedlam Moon Trilogy Book 3)

* * *

Fae Academia Series (Incomplete, 8 planned)

A spin-off of the Bedlam Moon Trilogy, we follow Lana's daughter, Rose, while she attends a magical university. The summer before college is perfect until the family begins to receive threats, and Rose ends up getting into a different college from her twin brother and her boyfriend. A male roommate, his hot friends, and a sexy professor all find themselves eager to win her affection. This is a why choose romance.

Bedlam Academy (Fae Academia, Book 1)

Arcane Scholar (ETA May 2023, Fae Academia Book 2)

* * *

Aggonid's Realm Series (Incomplete)

A Realm of Fire and Ash (ETA March 2023)

When the commander of an elite group of phoenixes ends up dead for real, she tries to convince the fae devil there's been a huge mistake. Can she convince him to let her go before he snags her heart? This is an enemies to lovers why choose romance.

* * *

<u>Fae Gods (Incomplete)</u>

Fae Gods (ETA April 2023)

They watched their charge her entire life, completely invisible to her and only intervening when necessary. When they get fed up with her miserable marriage, Jocelyn's fae god watchers decide to help. After all, no fae of royal lineage deserves to be left to wilt away on Earth. They devise a plan to reveal their true selves to her, calling themselves the Marriage Doctors. But what happens when, during the course of their live-in lessons, the infallible gods fall for their off-limits charge? This is a why choose romance.

* * *

<u>Bedlam Penitentiary (Incomplete)</u>

Bedlam Penitentiary (ETA end of Q3 2023)

At the most ruthless prison in the fae realm, you're either at the top of the magical food chain, or you've got to form alliances with those with the most power. Because at a prison where you must expend your magic or you'll die, it's a no man's land full of dangerous criminals. This is a why choose romance.